W9-BSV-346

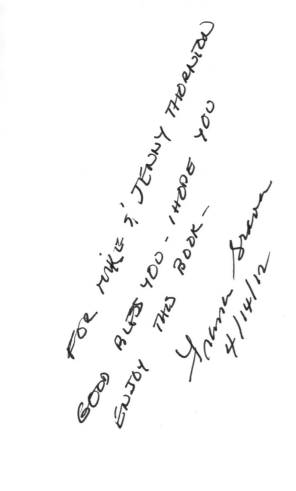

FOR MIKE & JEANY THORNTON
GOOD LUCK YOU - I HOPE YOU
ENJOY THIS BOOK -

Frank Brown
4/14/12

BALANCING
POWER

Francis Graves

A NOVEL

BALANCING POWER

TATE PUBLISHING
AND ENTERPRISES, LLC

Balancing Power
Copyright © 2012 by Francis Graves. All rights reserved.

No part of this publication may be reproduced, stored in a retrieval system or transmitted in any way by any means, electronic, mechanical, photocopy, recording or otherwise without the prior permission of the author except as provided by USA copyright law.

Scripture quotations are taken from the *Holy Bible, King James Version*, Cambridge, 1769. Used by permission. All rights reserved.

This novel is a work of fiction. However, several names, descriptions, entities, and incidents included in the story are based on the lives of real people.

The opinions expressed by the author are not necessarily those of Tate Publishing, LLC.

Published by Tate Publishing & Enterprises, LLC
127 E. Trade Center Terrace | Mustang, Oklahoma 73064 USA
1.888.361.9473 | www.tatepublishing.com

Tate Publishing is committed to excellence in the publishing industry. The company reflects the philosophy established by the founders, based on Psalm 68:11,
"The Lord gave the word and great was the company of those who published it."

Book design copyright © 2012 by Tate Publishing, LLC. All rights reserved.
Cover design by Shawn Collins
Interior design by Christina Hicks

Published in the United States of America

ISBN: 978-1-61777-928-2
1. Fiction / War & Military
2. Fiction / Historical
12.01.24

DEDICATION

In memory of my brother, Selwyn Jackson Graves
1928-2008
A true Latin American hand

ACKNOWLEDGEMENTS

Heartfelt thanks to the people who read the rough drafts of this book. They discovered I was a poor speller, but they encouraged me to proceed anyway: Barb Brown and Jill O'Neil of Bayfield, son-in-law Larry Mix, cousin Marian Banning, nieces Katharine Holiday and Anita Scott, grandson Zachary Graves, and my great friend, Major John Plaster, who provided valuable input. I am especially grateful for the insight provided by my late brother, Selwyn, who shared my interest and love for Latin America. Finally, for the steadfast support of my wife of over fifty-four years, who valiantly coped with culture shock four times as we moved from country to country, and for her patience during the many hours I sat before my word processor working on this book. Also, heartfelt thanks to my editor, Jenn Scott, who gently and tactfully strove to modify my proclivity for verbosity. And, finally, special thanks to Debra Elmore-Nesheim of Apostle Graphics, proofreader extraordinaire.

FOREWORD

Central America has always held a fascination for Frank Graves, the author of this, his first, novel. Graves lived a half decade in Latin America and traveled on business throughout the hemisphere another dozen years. He personally observed the politics, culture, and traditions of that region—including radical revolutions.

In addition to developing empathy for the people, he acquired an understanding and appreciation of the region's realpolitik. He knows of what he writes. In 1986, during the height of fighting in Nicaragua and El Salvador, I accompanied Graves and a congressional delegation to both countries to meet with leading military and diplomatic authorities. In addition to being well-informed, I was impressed by how well he grasped the distinct economies, cultures, and politics of each country.

Equally though, Graves' military experience contributed to shaping this work. A combat veteran of both World War II and Korea, he served nine years active duty, including on the fire-swept beaches of Anzio, Italy. Wounded in France, by the close of WWII he was appointed junior aide to much-acclaimed General George S. Patton, whose strategic views greatly influenced Graves. Thus, this author masterfully explains the interplay between military organization, strategy, and capabilities and—the mark of a true professional—demonstrates that battles and wars are won by superior logistics.

His novel's plot is compelling. It is framed around a coup d'etat in which a commandant of police, in the image of Omar Torrijos in Panama or Hugo Chavez in Venezuela, ousts a democratically elected government in a bloodless revolution and sets about creating a dictatorship by gradually ratcheting down individual and institutional freedoms and replacing them with state controls. All that stands between him and total power is one man, Brigadier General Francisco "Pancho" Portero, a US-educated officer who recognizes the plot underway.

But awareness alone, Portero realizes, stands little chance of blocking the usurper who continues to give lip service to democracy. If he acts too swiftly and forcefully, he could be branded an anti-democratic renegade and incur the distrust of the people and the neighboring countries' governments.

Aptly named *Balancing Power,* the book traces Portero's political and military struggle to counter the moves of the would-be dictator. He has potential clout as he commands the Autonomous Light Infantry Brigade, a regional security force under an OAS-like organization, but he is limited by the fact the unit's charter forbids participation in national political affairs. Further, as a US-educated officer, Portero too easily could be branded a tool of American imperialism. Thus he must walk a tightrope of political and, in the end, military, maneuvering in his effort to save democracy for his country.

This book informs and entertains, but more than anything it provides insight into the real-world balance of politics and power in today's Latin America and the threat imposed by populist strongmen.

—John L Plaster
Major, Special Forces
U.S. Army (retired)

PROLOGUE

The young policeman was bored and drowsy. The night was moonless and dark at 0430, and without road traffic, the quiet was oppressive. He paced back and forth within the confines of the police box, trying to keep alert. This was not the kind of duty he anticipated at the time of his graduation from basic training four months earlier. He expected his new career would be more exciting than the dull routine of his assignment to the Tuxla highway checkpoint detachment.

During his long four months there, there was only one event which was non-routine and memorable. It occurred a month earlier. The detachment was ordered to detain a two-truck convoy from the infantry brigade, which was traveling the national highways without *permisos de transito* documents.

That incident was exciting for the young policeman who was on duty at the time. He witnessed the angry reaction of the sergeant in charge of the convoy, who was abusive and furiously remonstrated with Lieutenant Simoni, the detachment commander, about being illegally detained. The lieutenant did not budge. The frustrated sergeant spent a good hour trying to reach his headquarters by telephone. He must have finally made the connection, because after several hours more, the lieutenant received orders to release the trucks.

He and others in the detachment took satisfaction from the incident. There was little love lost between the National Police and the Autonomous Infantry Brigade, whose members were regarded as arrogant, overpaid, and underworked. The incident confirmed for them that the police did indeed have some power, even over the brigade.

He yawned and stretched, looking forward to being relieved at 0600 and a hot shower and breakfast. Suddenly he came alert. His ear had caught the sound of a truck engine in the distance. He looked up the highway to the north, expecting to see the reflection of headlights, but there was only blackness. He opened the door of the box and listened but heard nothing. Puzzled, he concluded his ears had deceived him, and he returned to his reverie.

He revisited his favorite daydream, a dream he frequently used to entertain himself during idle times since he first decided to become a policeman. He imagined himself courageously facing down a dangerous enemy to rescue the daughter of the Commandant of Police, and thereby winning accolades, fame, and a promotion. He wanted action. His ever-present resolve was to remain alert and ready to act. He was sure the challenge would come when he least expected it, and he was determined to be ready when it did.

He was deep in these thoughts when the door of the police box was violently flung open, and he found himself staring at the muzzle of an M-16 rifle. Behind the weapon was a grim-faced soldier wearing the gray beret of the Lobo Battalion of the Autonomous Light Infantry Brigade.

The insides of the young policeman knotted. His heart pounded. He was afraid. The resolve of a moment before melted, and he raised his hands in submission.

CHAPTER 1

Headquarters
Autonomous Light Infantry Brigade (HJRAF)
Valle Escondido, Republica Naranjeras
America Central
Office of the Commanding General

General George M. Carmody
CINC-HJRAF
Fort Amador, Republic of Panama

General Carmody,

Sir, I have asked LTC, Emelio Sanchez to deliver this letter and the accompanying report to you personally because it is of a most sensitive nature, and I did not want to send it through regular channels.

I find myself in a situation which has the potential to grow out of my control and felt it necessary to alert you early on, because it may develop into something that will affect the operations of the brigade as a unit of the Hemispheric Joint Rapid Action Force.

As you are aware, the coup a year and a half ago replaced the democratically elected government of President Juan Moreno with a junta headed by Colonel Antonio Figueroa. Figueroa's coalition consists of a group of diputados known for their leftward bias, some leaders of major trade sindicatos, and an organized group of militant bureaucrats. It is backed by the National Police Force which, until the coup, was commanded by Figueroa and now by Edson Davidson, who has been promoted to the rank of colonel. (You may remember Davidson, as he served several years as an officer in the brigade until he was discharged for misconduct and insubordination.)

I must report that Figueroa's government has operated reasonably effectively since the coup. But why shouldn't it, since most of the key bureaucrats, and some diputados, have remained in place? The public impression is that nothing much has changed and that is reassuring to many people. Even so, there are many who remain incensed by the *golpe,* despite the fact that, as I am sure you know, there was great dissatisfaction throughout the country with the Moreno government's austerity program. Juan Moreno was well-meaning, but he proved a weak leader who overly trusted his appointees but never really won their allegiance nor the respect of the people. I am sure your intelligence has given you these details, so I will not dwell on them further.

The Figueroa regime would like the people, and the world, to believe nothing has really changed, that it is committed to democratic policies, and that it believes in the Moreno reforms, which it intends to implement but in a more palatable manner. Our information indicates this will be their line. However, my staff and I are convinced their real intentions are quite different. Our belief is, and we have some intelligence to back it, that they have little interest in continuing the democratic system of government Naranjeras has enjoyed for the last six years. We believe it is only a matter of time before they suspend the constitution and rule by decree in the manner of the old *caudillo* governments. We expect that to happen probably within the year, or as soon as they have consolidated power enough to control the people.

Several prominent members of the coalition have been quite open about their belief in centralized power as the most efficient way to govern. There is no doubt the junta's leaders are committed statists, but we believe they will be cautious in pushing their agenda, because many of their second tier people are not ideologues so much as opportunists who see the *golpe* as a means of personal enrichment. They are people who either will have to be converted or culled from the organization as being untrustworthy, and that will take time. The junta's timetable cannot be accurately known, but we believe it will take at least six months to gain the necessary control. When that happens, democracy in Naranjeras will be history.

Now to the meat of the matter. You perhaps have already discerned my problem. Knowing Figueroa as I do, I am sure he will conclude he cannot achieve his purpose that is to completely consolidate power as long as the ALIB remains an autonomous entity subordinate to the HJRAF. Even if we remain apolitical, he will never feel secure until we are under his control. He will always fear any potential we might have to intervene against him.

He knows our capabilities. He knows we are a force of 2,600 well-trained soldiers. He knows his national police force, although almost double our size at 4,000 including auxiliary and reserves, is no match for us should a military confrontation ever occur. We are better trained, better equipped, and far more experienced, and he knows we can be an obstacle standing in his path to power. There is no doubt in my mind that he will seek ways to eliminate us as the potential threat we represent.

Figueroa would like, above all, to control the brigade and make it loyal to him, but he knows that would be difficult and time-consuming. So his second option will be to find ways to neutralize us—to pull our teeth, so to speak. I believe that is what he will try to do, and he will approach the task politically in a way that does not raise any alarm here or with the HJRAF.

How might he do it? I do not know for sure, but if I were in his shoes, I would seek a way to nationalize us, which is to say de-internationalize us. Knowing him, I believe that is what he will try to do. If he is anything, he is a clever politician, and he will try to do it subtly in a manner which will "make sense" at HDO or to our people, in the hope that they will go along with his initiatives.

First, he will give much lip service to the importance of the brigade remaining a part of HJRAF. One reason is that he does not want to lose the subsidy the brigade receives. As small as it is, he will regard it a significant contribution to our GNP, and he will say so.

However while he is talking out of that side of his mouth, he will be working behind the scenes to gain some control of our operations. For example, he might propose that in the name of cost efficiencies, the brigade take on additional domestic assignments which benefit the country but do not interfere with its HJRAF mission—like building bridges or highway repairs—and that such work should be under government control.

If he succeeds in that, he will have his foot in the door and will argue the logic of being able to appoint some officers to the brigade. They, of course, would be men loyal to him. It is easy to understand how a few people like that in key positions could be very disruptive to the unity of our command, which would seriously threaten our ability to fulfill our mission.

Whether or not he succeeds in these efforts, he has another means of neutralizing us. He can threaten our supply lines and also our mobility. He seems to have begun that process. The evidence is that the government has begun harassing our trucks on their supply runs between the Puerto Hondo and our base. A two-truck convoy was detained by the PNN at the Tuxla checkpoint because they did not have permisos de transito. We have been exempt from that requirement since our inception. Two days ago, they impounded four of our vehicles at Puerto Hondo under the same pretext. I am pleased to report that we took action to recover those trucks by show of force, which I am sure did not endear me any further with Figueroa. (The details of that confrontation are contained in the After Action Report attached hereto.)

My problem is that in these circumstances, I am being obliged to counter whatever moves Figueroa makes if I am to keep the brigade ready to fulfill its HJRAF mission. That means I will of necessity be involving myself and the brigade in national politics which is contrary to your clearly stated policy. You have emphasized on numerous occasions the importance of your units maintaining strict neutrality in the arena of local politics. I have always understood the policy and have worked to keep myself, my officers, and men apart from the political scene. However under the present circumstances, I do not believe the brigade can remain an effective part of the rapid action force without defending itself against any action to control or weaken it by this government.

I assure you that I am keenly aware that such involvement is fraught with danger, but I see no other course. In short, I am in a classic catch-22 situation. Either I must disobey your standing orders, or I must allow the brigade to be slowly destroyed by political action. I count on your understanding and ask for your guidance and counsel in this difficult matter.

With warmest personal regards, I remain.

Francisco Portero
General de Brigada
Commanding

Enclosure:
Copy # 2 After Action Report—Puerto Hondo Incident—Secret for HJRAF eyes only

---

HQ 1st ALIBrigade Naranjera
Valle Escondido, R de N
To:CINC HJRAF
From:CG-ALIB
Subject:Report on Incidents of Harassment of ALIB by PNN and   Operation Recovery

The following was compiled by B-3 staff based upon interviews with officer and soldier participants and several civilian eyewitnesses.

It is noted that subject incidences of harassment by the PNN are the first to be recorded since the ALIB was activated, and they seem to coincide with the accession to power by the junta headed by Antonio Figueroa.

Incident No. 1: Occurred on 17 January of this year.

Two vehicles of ALIB's attached Truck Company on a routine daily run to La Capital were impounded at the Tuxla PNN checkpoint for several hours. Sgt. Carranza, NCO in charge, was informed the reason for the detention was the convoy lacked *permisos de transito fiscal.* These permits are required for commercial vehicles and private conveyances over a certain tonnage. They have never been required of ALIB vehicles which have always been waived through. Carranza, who has made the same trip hundreds of times without being detained, showed his official trip, but the PNN officer in charge of the checkpoint refused to honor it explaining his orders had been changed and *permisos de transito* were now being required of ALIB vehicles.

Carranza was able to reach his company commander by telephone to apprise him of the situation. He in turn called brigade headquarters and was able to reach Major Vargas, B-3 Section duty officer, who had served in the PNN Regional Headquarters and kept his contacts there. Vargas was able to reach a friend there who denied knowing anything of an order requiring ALIB vehicles to use permits. The officer promised to intervene and after several hours, Carranza was released and allowed to proceed on his mission.

This matter was considered to be an aberration at the time. The general consensus was that it was a misunderstanding within the PNN Transit Authority and would not be repeated. It was not thought important enough to bring to the attention of the CG.

Incident No 2: Began 10 February and was prolonged through the 13th.

The ALIB Truck Company dispatched three tucks to Puerto Hondo to receive a consignment of prefabricated windows, sashes, doors, and door frames, which had been recently discharged at government dock by a Lykes Line vessel. The cargo was destined for the new family housing project under construction at the brigade base in Valle Escondido. By coincidence, Sgt. Carranza was again NCOIC, and he was accompanied by Lieutenant Flavio Acevedo of our base engineers, who is the officer supervising the construction. Acevedo traveled in a radio-equipped pickup truck.

At 1300, Acevedo reported the convoy had arrived at the government dock and had begun loading the cargo. He also reported that a PNN officer had asked Carranza for his trip ticket and *permisos de transito.* When Carranza failed to produce the *permisos,* the officer ordered them to stop loading and await instructions.

At 1415, Acevedo radioed again to say that men purporting to be representatives of the Construction Workers and the Freight Haulers syndicates had appeared and were questioning the legality of the military hauling freight destined for use by civilians, and also the legality of soldiers constructing housing for civilians. Acevedo explained that such questions should be addressed to the brigade public relations officer and that his assignment was only to receive and deliver the cargo.

At 1530, Acevedo reported with some agitation that they had completed loading the cargo, despite the objections of the PNN officer, and had attempted to depart the port but had been stopped by a platoon of PNN armed with AK-47s. He reported the vehicles, their drivers, and helpers had been moved to an open area near the container dock and were under guard there. He explained that the reason for their detention was their lack of proper paperwork. He also reported that he and Sgt. Carranza's vigorous protests had been ignored. He asked for instructions.

ALIB Action: Upon being informed of the situation, the CG directed Major Vargas to contact PNN Headquarters for an explanation of the detention. After some delay, Vargas was informed that the decision to retain the convoy was taken at high councils of the government and that "regrettably there was nothing that PNN Headquarters could do to change the situation."

The CG then directed Colonel Soto, brigade chief of staff, to have the brigade legal officer draft an official protest citing the violation of the "non-interference clauses of the implementing agreement" between the Hemispheric Council of Participating Nations and Naranjeras. The protest was to be directed to President Figueroa's eyes only, and dispatched by courier and by facsimile transmission. It was also to contain the clause: "Should not this unlawful violation of the aforementioned implementing agreement in the detention of ALIB personnel and vehicles be ended by 1700 hours today, be advised the commanding general of ALIB will be obliged to take action to affect their recovery and, furthermore, to pursue the matter in the courts."

The CG then directed the staff to develop plans for "Operation Recovery." The Lobo Battalion, Major DaSilva, was assigned the mission [with the Oso Battalion, LTC Gutierrz cmdg, on standby reserve at the base]. The Lobo Recon Platoon was to lead, seize and occupy the Tuxla PNN checkpoint at 0330 hours. "B" Company would follow and establish roadblocks around Puerto Hondo and secure the port facilities by 0430. "A" Company would follow and take up blocking positions along Highway 3 between La Capital and Puerto Hondo, its mission to intercept any effort to reinforce PNN units in the port—timeline 0500. "C" Company would then follow its mission to occupy the container dock area and recover the convoy personnel and vehicles. Once that had been affected, the units would then withdraw in reverse order with "C" Company and the interned vehicles leading.

The rules of engagement established for Operation Recovery follow:

1. No ALIB soldier was to fire his weapon unless ordered to by his unit leader.

2. Civilians were not to be threatened, molested, or intimidated in any manner; rather they were to be treated with friendliness and respect in every circumstance. All participating units are to carry a supply of preprinted *claim forms* to be given to any civilian who claims injury or property damage as a result of action by the ALIB.

3. Any PNN personnel encountered were to be immediately disarmed and detained under guard until released by order of the battalion commander at the conclusion of the operation. Use of force in disarming them was authorized only in the event they resisted.

4. All PNN detainees were to be listed by name, rank, serial number, unit, and place of birth. They were to be treated with kindness and respect while in detention.

5. All weapons, ammunition, and tactical field equipment taken from PNN detainees was to be catalogued and transported to the brigade base for delivery to the supply officer at the conclusion of the operation.

Telephone conference with President Figueroa: At 1650 President Figueroa called the CG. He confirmed that the ALIB convoy had been detained pursuant of a decision by the Supreme Council with which he had "regretfully concurred." He took some pains to explain that his government took the action to demonstrate its concern for the economic welfare of the people and that one visible means of doing that was to require the ALIB not to compete with the private sector. A first step was to require compliance with commercial transit regulations.

At that point, the CG reminded Figueroa that no matter how noble his motivation, his action was a clear violation of the treaty and, therefore, the law which established the rights of the ALIB. Figueroa responded that "his people" believed there were some deficiencies in the Treaty agreement, which would have to be corrected by re-negotiation with the Hemispheric Council. He added that he hoped the ALIB would cooperate in this matter in the name of good relations with the government.

The CG responded that there was nothing he valued more than good relations with the government but that he could not and would not cooperate if his cooperation required him to violate a long-established treaty and the laws of Naranjeras—he added that to do so would be to violate his oath of office. Whereupon Figueroa asked what the CG's intentions were.

The CG made it very clear that his intentions were to act, unless Figueroa agreed to order the convoy's immediate release.

Figueroa responded that he wanted to cooperate but would first have to bring the matter back to the Supreme Council, and that he could not do that until the afternoon of the next day, adding that he hoped to avoid a public confrontation with the ALIB—and requested the CG to delay any action until then—and asked if he would comply with that request.

The CG responded that the President would soon know the answer to his question.

ALIB Action & After Action Report: Discussion with the CG and the brigade senior staff officers followed the telephone conversation with Figueroa on the pros and cons of delaying action as had been requested. A consensus was soon reached that to delay would be a public signal that the junta's actions, which clearly were in violation of the law, had some legitimacy. Accordingly the decision was made to proceed with the action as planned and the CG gave the order, at 1745 hours, 12 February.

Lead units of Operation Recovery departed on schedule, which allowed the follow-on units to meet their assigned timelines. Surprise was so complete at the Tuxla checkpoint that the PNN had no time to alert its headquarters of our presence. Lobo Companies reached their objectives with only minor delays, which permitted "C" Company to reach its objective on time. It had no problem disarming the PNN Platoon guarding our vehicles.

Operation Recovery was a complete success. Our personnel, vehicles and cargo were recovered. There were no casualties and no incidents reported. The only shot fired was an accidental discharge of an AK-47 when a soldier from the recon platoon attempted to clear the unfamiliar weapon. All Lobo Battalion units closed at their base by 1300.

Reaction to Operation Recovery: As of this writing, the only reaction has been an outraged statement by the minister of interior, broadcast over several radio stations, in which he accused the ALIB of "outlaw behavior" and then assured the people that the "government had reestablished order and there was no longer cause for concern."

Anticipated Follow-on Reaction: ALIB Intelligence estimates anticipate the junta's counter offensive is likely to be a continuing propaganda campaign designed to portray the ALIB as an organization out of control. That assessment holds that the balance of power is not in the junta's favor and that at this juncture it can do nothing more than wage a public relations campaign against us. However, we believe such a campaign can be effective over time because it has the potential of tarnishing ALIB's favorable image with the people.

Anticipating a possible anti-ALIB propaganda campaign, the CG has ordered a well-advertised press conference be held at Brigade headquarters the morning of 17 February. Invitations to all national and international media outlets, foreign embassies, and to key leaders of the Hemispheric Defense Council and the HJRAF are being delivered by facsimile transmission. The subject will be Operation Recovery. To quote the CG: "This press conference is to be a big deal."

End of Report on harassment of ALIB by PNN and Operation Recovery prepared and submitted 14 February. By order of Commanding General ALIB.

P. Soto
Colonel, C of S
ALIB
Distribution: Standard, Levels 1 & 2
Secret

CHAPTER 2

General George M. Carmody leaned back in his chair then swiveled around to peer out of the window of his Fort Amador office. A huge ungainly Japanese car carrier was making its way up the channel toward the Miraflores Locks. Ordinarily he was fascinated by canal traffic and he enjoyed studying the transiting ships, but today he barely noticed. He was preoccupied by what he had just read. Even before he had finished Portero's report, alarm bells had begun sounding in his head.

He was not a political general. He disliked the term "militician" as much as he disliked those officers whom it identified. He had had a number of opportunities for assignments in Washington but had avoided them as much as he prudently could. He did not want to be identified as a political general, whom he blamed for the public's growing disrespect of the military. Nevertheless, after thirty-three years of successfully climbing the army's competitive ladder, he was sensitive to political situations, particularly those which threatened his ability to carry out his mission. He knew immediately the events in Naranjeras were potentially big trouble for him and his command, and his instinct was to find a way to put a lid on it before it got out of hand.

Damn. I don't need this now, he thought. *Damn that bastard, Figueroa. I never liked the self-absorbed son of a bitch when he commanded the PNN—he'll be worse now. And double damn Juan Moreno. Why didn't he mind the store? These little Central American republics are a pain in the ass. They're too damn volatile. Just when things seem stable and we begin making progress, some power-hungry pissant politico comes along and screws it up!*

Carmody had assumed command at CINC-HJRAF eleven months earlier. It was an assignment he truly wanted and he saw it as his greatest challenge, his last hurrah before retirement. It was really a pioneer posting, a new command with a new mission upon which he could put his stamp. CINC-HJRAF had succeeded CINCSouth, which had been located there in Panama until it was moved to Florida in 1995. With the cessation of the Cold War and the subsequent transfer of the Panama Canal from the United States to Panama in 1999, the Hemispheric Defense Organization had been created by a treaty signed by the United States, Naranjeras, the Central American Republics (except Nicaragua), Colombia, Venezuela, and the Dominican Republic. Brazil and several other South American countries had been debating joining the HDO for over a year but had yet to sign on.

The Department of Defense, compelled to do more with less by Clinton administration cuts in military funding, had sought innovative ways to fulfill its strategic missions in the Western Hemisphere, not the least of which was defense of the canal. It had lobbied for the creation of the HDO as a means of getting the job done on the cheap. Once organized, the HDO set to work developing the Hemispheric Joint Rapid Action Force, with each member nation contributing military units according to its size and the capabilities of its economy.

The secretariat, with the help of military consultants from member countries, had tried to deal with standardizing, organizing, and training HJRAF Units. It became a daunting challenge because political gamesmanship by member nations made progress impossible, and the secretariat finally was forced to admit failure. In desperation it asked the United States to undertake the task as the only member with the experience, respect, and the clout to bring the HDO together. After months of negotiation and congressional debate, the U.S. somewhat reluctantly agreed to take on the mission.

The result was the formation of the new joint command identified as CINC-HJRAF, patterned after the US-regional joint-command structures. It was nominally under the Department of Defense, which was assigned the additional burden of coordinating with the HDO. After months of talks, a political agreement was achieved which was unloved by the State Department, unpopular in the Pentagon, and tepidly welcomed by the Latin American participants who were motivated more by the promise of financial aid to their militaries than anything else. However, once formed, the HJRAF became a reassuring symbol of military cooperation between sovereign nations, and the Pentagon set out to make it work.

The first step was to reactivate the old CINCSouth complex in Fort Amador in Panama and move HJRAF Headquarters there. The move was welcomed by the Panamanian government, which saw economic advantage in having it there. The member nations also approved of the move first because their new joint-command headquarters would be in Latin America—not in the U.S., and second because it was located at a crossroads readily accessible to all.

General Carmody was at home in Panama, as he had served two previous tours there, and he had uncharacteristically lobbied for the CINC-HJRAF job. He welcomed the challenge of building a unified command out of HJRAF's disparate units. It had not been an easy task, but he had made progress and had developed a sense of satisfaction about his accomplishments as well as a growing sense that the concept of a joint international force could be made to work with time.

He had been happy in the assignment and looked forward to completing his tour without major problems. Now it looked like there was a significant problem brewing—a very big problem indeed. He knew it could become a political hot potato, especially in Washington, and dreaded what lay ahead.

"I'll have to earn my pay on this one," he said aloud to himself.

• • •

Of all the units in the Hemispheric Joint Rapid Action Force, he was partial to the Naranjeras Autonomous Light Infantry Brigade, partly because it was a first class, well-trained unit, and also because of his personal friendship with Francisco Portero, its commander. They had first met at the Command and General Staff School at Fort Leavenworth, Kansas, where Carmody, then a colonel, was an instructor and Portero, then a major, was a foreign guest-student. Carmody had immediately recognized the young Naranjero officer as intelligent and dedicated, unlike many of the foreign student officers who had a propensity to play harder than they studied.

Their paths had crossed several times since and they had become friends despite the difference in their ages. Carmody had attended a splendid wedding at Fort Benning when Portero married Elizabeth Anchor Smith, the daughter of Carmody's West Point roommate. But there was more than friendship between them. There was professional respect. Portero admired Carmody as a man and as a soldier and had made the older man his role model. For his part, Carmody thought Portero one of the most promising young officers he knew. He respected Portero's intelligence and professional skills and had watched the younger man climb the promotion ladder with fatherly pride. He very much regretted Portero's steadfast refusal to accept a commission in the United States Army.

So it was with a great deal of interest and concern that he re-read Portero's report. Clearly the situation was dangerous. It not only had the potential for politicizing and neutralizing the ALIB as a unit of the HJRAF, but it also could eventually undermine the Hemispheric Defense Organization itself if it were not properly handled.

"Damn that, Figueroa. I never did trust the man—a thoroughgoing shit disturber. It looks like he is deliberately trying to screw things up. What can I do to head this thing off?"

He rose from his chair and stood before his window thinking.

• • •

Twenty minutes later, Carmody called in Captain Jaime Hanson, his junior aide-de-camp. "Jimmy, we have a little problem in Naranjeras. I want you to go up there and sit in on a press conference Pancho Portero is putting on tomorrow. Your job is to show the flag. All the local media is supposed to be there, along with the reps from HDO member embassies. I want you to be visible. Ostensibly you are there as my observer, just collecting facts. However, let the impression get around that Pancho has my full support. You know some of those media people, I believe. Talk to them off the record but don't, repeat do not, make any official statement. This is a local political flap, so I can't take sides under the treaty. Understood?"

Hanson's blank look made it clear it wasn't. "Here, read Pancho's report and you will."

• • •

In an hour Hanson was back. "Interesting situation, General. I have only one question, sir. How much can I say off the record to my friends in the press, that won't get you in trouble?"

"As little as possible. You're fluent in the language which is full of *doble entiendos*. Get Aesopian. Get the point across that I'm with the ALIB in this without getting me accused of messing in internal politics."

Hanson grinned at his boss. "Looks like a classic no-win situation, but I'll try, General. I have a flight laid on with the air section for thirteen hundred. We should be in Valle Escondido by fourteen thirty."

"Good. Who is taking you up?"

"I believe Captain Lane is the pilot, sir." Hanson said with a straight face.

Carmody smiled. "Your classmate, eh? Well, I agree she is a nice girl. Now get me Pancho on the secure phone. I want to let him know you're coming. Then go get ready for the trip.

"And when you get up there, keep me informed. I don't want any surprises."

• • •

"General Portero is on the scrambler, General."

"Hello Pancho, how are you? And how is Betsy?"

"Fine, General, on both counts, thanks."

"Anything new with your situation there? I've just read your report. I think you did the only thing you could do, but this could really get sticky."

"All is quiet so far, sir. Nothing new yet. It will come though. You can be sure of that."

"How is your press conference shaping up? Is it still on for tomorrow?"

"Yes, sir. At eleven hundred. We know *Diario* and *Vida Nacional* are sending people. Also some TV. The Costa Rican attaché has accepted. So has the army guy from Venezuela. Don't know about the rest yet."

"They'll all be busy getting instructions from home, I imagine. I am sending Jimmie Hanson up to show the flag. I told him I would shoot him if he gets me in trouble. He can't make any official statement but he'll be nosing around among his media friends, doing what he can to support you. His mother was Guatemalan and his Spanish is perfect. By the way, his ETA at your airstrip is fourteen thirty today. Can you put him up for the night?"

"Of course we can, General. And thanks for sending him. At least our people will know we are not being hung out to dry."

"It's the least I can do, Pancho. I wish it were more, but I'll be walking on eggshells until we see how this thing shapes up. Do you see any chance that it will all blow over...just be forgotten and go away?"

"No chance at all, General. Figueroa has been embarrassed, and he cannot let his government look weak. Even if he wanted to give a little, Davidson and some of the others wouldn't let him. We're in the soup, I am afraid. It will take time for them to get their ducks in order, but they will do everything they can to neutralize us. As I said in my letter, I have no choice but to defend the brigade...and that is what I intend to do. If that causes you too big a problem, you should relieve me of command or you could re-deploy us. Get us out of Naranjeras."

"Both possibilities have occurred to me. Neither is a good solution. I'll be talking to the Pentagon later and to the Secretary General at HDO. I'll keep you informed. Meantime, Pancho, don't stir the pot. The press conference is a must. If you don't defend yourself in the media, you will look guilty to the public. But avoid any more confrontations if you can. By the way, what would happen if you agreed to start using those famous *permisos de transito*?"

"The government would declare a victory and then look for a new way to confront us. I think they want to build a legal case against us. Our acceding to their demands would be construed as an admission that we were wrong. But their demands are in clear violation of the treaty and I won't give on this, General, and unless you order me to...and in that case, it would be under a strong protest." Portero's voice had a hard edge.

"I know, Pancho. Don't get excited. I agree with you, but you can bet someone up the ladder is going to come up with that idea. Well, keep me in the picture. I want all the details. And take care of Jimmy. . .oh by the way, his pilot is a female, a very nice girl, a classmate of his at the Point. You'll have to make arrangements for her, too."

"Will do, General. And thanks for your support. I'll keep you informed. My best to you."

• • •

Captain Hanson parked his car at the helicopter pad, grabbed his overnight bag, and walked at a deliberate pace to the concrete surface where a Black Hawk was waiting. He was conscious of its flight-suited crew watching his approach. Captain Christina Lane gave him a welcoming grin and waved. "Hi, Jimmy. Good to see you."

He returned her greeting. "Hi, Chris. Are you driving? You have your license, I presume?"

"Not yet. I'm still practicing. So far they only let me carry expendable cargo."

"Like me, I suppose?"

"Like you," she laughed.

Hanson always liked his academy classmate. He never failed to be surprised at how attractive she was. She was small, five foot two or so, with a trim, athletic body. Her blonde hair was short but still feminine, and it framed her pretty face. Her smiling blue eyes always seemed to reflect a joy and enthusiasm for the world around her. He was glad to see her.

"How the mighty have fallen," he said. "The undisputed racquet ball champion of the academy is now only a lowly aerial bus driver. If they could see you now." He shook his head sadly.

"Well, we can't all be gofers for generals. Someone has to make the army work. And besides, how would you ground-pounders ever get anywhere without us bus drivers?" Her co-pilot, a young warrant officer who looked like he was just out of flight school, and her crew chief, a black sergeant, grinned with her.

She made the introductions and they all climbed aboard. The crew chief rigged a headset for him and showed him how to activate the mike so he could communicate with the crew on the intercom. The doors were closed, and Chris fired up the GE turbo engines. When the pre-takeoff checklist was complete, she added power and looked back at Hanson.

"Are you ready, Jimmy? Then off we go. Next stop: Valle Escondido, in about eighty minutes."

The Black Hawk abruptly lifted into the air.

• • •

The press conference was held in a large tent on the well-manicured lawn outside the brigade headquarters mess hall. The day was sunny and bright, and the sides of the tent were rolled up to allow air to circulate. There were perhaps forty people seated in chairs facing a platform at the end of the tent. About a quarter of them were radio or press reporters. The three largest newspapers were represented, as were stringers from several news services. The remainder was mostly military, including officers and senior NCOs from the brigade and a few military attachés from various embassies. Two television cameras on tripods with their operators were located behind the chairs.

General Portero, flanked by Major DaSilva, Lobo Battalion commander, and Captain Lacerica, brigade public relations officer, spoke from the platform behind a lectern, festooned with the pickup microphones of several tape recorders. He carefully followed his prepared statement, which had been distributed to the audience at the outset. It traced the history of the Hemispheric Rapid Action Force and the Naranjeras contribution to that force, the ALIB. It stressed the specific provisions of the implementing agreement, which prohibited the ALIB from involving itself in national politics and which prohibited the national government from interfering in lawful operations.

Then General Portero explained the reasons he mounted the Puerto Hondo recovery operation, carefully emphasizing the HJRAF had no knowledge of it until it had been completed. He then covered every detail of the operation, from the planning phase through the execution, with painstaking thoroughness. The questions following the formal statement were, as General Portero had expected, less about the recovery operation and more about his reasons for not acceding to the government's demand that the ALIB use permisos de transito.

After a number of questions had been asked and answered, Ramon Sanchez Avila, a senior reporter and columnist of *Vida Nacional,* rose to be recognized. He was one of the most respected journalists in the country, often referred to as the dean of the Naranjeras press corps, and a man known as an unrepentant nationalist, so the assembly grew quiet for him.

He remained silent for a moment, gathering attention. Then in a strong, clear voice he said, "It seems a small thing, General, the matter of *permisos,* certainly not something that would precipitate the kind of confrontation we have seen. After all, the brigade is Naranjero and as such might be expected to comply with Naranjero law." A murmur of agreement rose from the other journalists.

Portero's reply was respectful. "The point, Don Ramon, is that the brigade has always complied with national law and did so in this lamentable instance. It was the government which acted contrary to law by imposing this requirement upon us. We have always operated strictly within the provisions of the treaty agreement and have never once had a problem with either of the previous national administrations."

"Even so, my dear general, the requirement of a simple document like a *permiso de transito* cannot be a great imposition on you. Why have you made such an issue of it?"

"We are not the ones that made the issue. When the Figueroa government detained and impounded our vehicles, which were operating lawfully on official business, it violated the law and in doing so created the issue."

Sanchez Avila was not satisfied. "With respect, General, doesn't the government have the authority over the nation's highways? Hasn't it the responsibility to collect transit taxes? Doesn't it have the authority to enforce compliance of the nation's laws by its own armed forces, even with the ALIB?"

Portero's calm voice concealed his rising impatience. "The answer is yes to all these questions, Don Ramon. However, the government does not have the authority to alter the nation's laws and force us to accept its altered versions of them. And incidentally, do you believe for a moment that the PNN is presenting *permisos* when its vehicles use the highways? I submit to you they are not required to, and neither are we."

He paused, taking time to peer around the room, making eye contact with several of the reporters before turning back to Sanchez Avila.

"Ask yourself, sir, why has the government forced this confrontation with us over so small a thing? It cannot be ineptitude that caused this breach of a long-standing cooperative arrangement between us. And why have they chosen to do it so publicly, without advance notice to us? I submit they wanted confrontation, a public incident, to serve some political purpose?"

"But what purpose, General?"

"I will not speculate as to their purpose. I suggest you ask them."

The exchange ended the questioning. Portero had made his point. He thanked the assembly and invited them to be guests of the brigade at a buffet luncheon to follow.

• • •

General Portero stood with Colonel Soto, his chief of staff, Jaime Hanson, Christina Lane, and Guillermo Lacerica as the journalists and guests entered the mess hall to take their place in the buffet line. He felt good about his performance at the press conference, although he didn't think he had successfully made his point with Sanchez Avila.

"How do you think it went?" he asked his public relations officer.

"Reasonably well, sir. I detected very little hostility toward us, although Sanchez Avila seemed less than satisfied with the exchange between you." Lacerica's reply echoed his own thoughts. "He is an interesting man. He wanted me to make a hostile statement about the government, I think, which I was damned if I would do in front of that crowd. Do you think he is close to Figueroa?"

"No, General, but he tends to be anti-military. Remember he was very opposed to the country joining the Hemispheric Defense Organization and even more opposed to the formation of the ALIB as a part of HJRAF. He probably sees the problems we are having with the government as some sort of vindication of his position."

"Do you know him, Jimmy?" Portero turned to Carmody's aide.

"Only slightly, sir. He interviewed General Carmody once. He wasn't particularly hostile and the article turned out to be pretty fair. But there's no question he is Naranjero all the way. His country right or wrong…perhaps to a fault."

At that point they were joined by Major Antonio DaSilva, who too late realized he was interrupting more than small talk. "Sorry, General," he said, beginning to retreat.

"It's okay, Tony. Join us. Were you looking for me?"

"Actually no, sir. I was looking for Captain Lane."

"Oh, well you have found her," Portero smiled turning to Christina, whose blue eyes smiled back.

"We met before the press conference, sir, and Major DaSilva invited me to have lunch with him, if that's all right with you."

"I am interested in discussing the tactical use of helicopters," DaSilva declared with an impassive face, which dissolved into a smile as everyone laughed.

"Very enterprising, Major. I hope you'll give me a full report of your findings. And perhaps after lunch you can find time away from your duties to give Captain Lane a tour of our base if she is interested."

"I'd be happy to, if she is interested," he said looking at Christina, who he found was smiling as broadly as the others at his growing discomfort. "Please excuse us then, sir…gentlemen." He took Christina's arm lightly and gently guided her toward the buffet table. She smiled up at him, but he marched self-consciously, eyes front and red-faced away from the grinning group.

"Tony's sudden interest in helicopters seems more to do with helicopter pilots than with the machines themselves, wouldn't you agree? But back to Sanchez Avila. He seems a decent man, Lacerica. What do you think?"

"He is, General. He is a journalist of the old school. He guards his reputation for being objective, is overly legalistic some think, but is serious about the ethics of his profession, which few reporters seem to be these days. He can be trusted as much as any of them. More than most, I would say."

"Good. Ask Señor Sanchez Avila if he will join Colonel Soto and me for lunch. I would like you and Captain Hanson to be there as well. Let's try to make him an ally if we can."

· · ·

General Portero, Soto, and Hanson stood to greet the reporter when Captain Lacerica escorted him to the general's table. Introductions were made, and a mess attendant served them from the buffet line.

"I very much appreciate your invitation, General. I was wondering how I might find an opportunity to talk to you further."

"I am very glad you could join us, Don Ramon. I thought you might not be satisfied with our conversation during the press conference and hoped we might exchange some ideas over lunch. I am prepared to give you my view of the government's purposes in engineering the flap over the *permisos,* provided you agree to keep it off the record?"

Sanchez Avila hesitated. "My readers have the right to know what you think about this situation. They should have both sides of the argument, should they not?"

"The problem, Don Ramon, is that what I will say to you might well be construed as political statements, and as you know, I am enjoined by treaty not to involve myself or the brigade in local politics. I cannot be quoted. On the other hand, you are a thoughtful and influential man, whom I believe is motivated by love of country and, as far as I know, you have no political affiliation. You have a reputation as an independent who is not afraid to be objective. You have a national forum which trusts you. You are the kind of newsman I want to have know my positions. You are not, if I am correctly informed, allied with the Figueroa administration." The statement invited confirmation, and Portero awaited the reporter's response.

"You are correct, General. I am not in anyone's pocket, as they say. Forgive me but I should add I will not be in your pocket, either. I can only promise you two things. First, that I will maintain as much objectivity as I can, given my personal leanings and biases, and second, that I will always try to use what influence I may have for the benefit of Naranjeras. If you understand these two points and still want to speak your mind, I will agree not to quote you or attribute any political statement to you. However, knowing how you think will certainly influence the way I write about you. You must understand that."

"I do understand, Don Ramon. Thank you for being candid. The truth is I believe I can trust you and I would rather have you know exactly what I think than to have you publicly speculate about it." The general paused then asked, "Where do we start?"

"Let me start by establishing some facts." He turned to Carmody's aide. "Why are you here, Captain Hanson?"

Hanson took a moment to compose his answer. "I am here as an observer for my boss, General Carmody. He is concerned about the situation in Naranjeras because it involves the ALIB, which is an important unit of the Hemispheric Joint Rapid Action Force, for which he is responsible. I am on a fact-finding mission for him."

"Will General Carmody support the ALIB, should the situation worsen or become a crisis?"

"Like General Portero, General Carmody may not, by treaty, engage in internal political matters of the sponsoring nations. He is a soldier who serves the United States of America and the Hemispheric Defense Organization and is bound by joint policies established by international agreement. He will never act unilaterally if that is your question, sir. On the other hand, it is no secret that the general is supportive of the ALIB within the scope of his military responsibilities. However, he is also keenly aware that the ALIB has been entrusted to the HJRAF by the Republic of Naranjeras and is sensitive of his responsibility to it as the contributing country."

Sanchez Avila smiled broadly. "You should consider a diplomatic career, young man." Everyone laughed, including Hanson. There ensued talk of the weather, the prospects for the ALIB soccer team, and other inconsequential items while the four men ate their lunch.

When his appetite was satisfied, Sanchez Avila turned to Portero. "I must confess I have difficulty sorting out where loyalties really lie among the officers of the ALIB. Here we have a Naranjero unit, which is part of a mixed international force, which is under the command and largely subsidized by the North Americans. Whom do you serve, General?"

"The answer is simple. I am surprised you don't see it. I serve my country, Naranjeras, which has made the decision that her best interests lie in participating in the hemispheric defense effort. If that decision had not been made years ago, I would not be here."

Sanchez Avila responded. "That oversimplifies the situation, doesn't it? It seems to me that Naranjeras does not really control her own brigade. It is bought and paid for by the gringos. It is commanded by the gringos. Its use will be decided by an international group of countries which, in turn, is dominated by the gringos.

"Look, Don Ramon…the mutual defense force was designed to protect the territories of its members. We entered into the pact of our own free will. We weren't coerced into it. We believed a cooperative HJRAF was a relatively cheap and very efficient means of keeping the peace in our region, not to mention a deterrent to aggression from outside the region. The HDO agreed to giving the United States tactical command of the HJRAF for good reasons. They are most experienced in warfare, they have the technology in communications, weapons, and proven training programs. They have no territorial ambitions and never have had. They can be trusted. They were the logical ones to command the HJRAF. I might add that they have a larger investment in the force than any three or four other participating nations combined."

Sabchez Avila was quick to reply. "Why not? They save millions by substituting our troops for theirs. It is cheaper to subsidize our units than field their own. It's no secret they have cut their armed forces to the bone in the last years."

"You ignore the fact, Don Ramon, that they contribute more than half the troops in the HJRAF. And as for their subsidy to usit is not that great. We receive two subsidies only, a weapons and training subsidy designed to put our tactical skills on a par with the rest of the force, and a pay equalization subsidy which augments the Naranjeras pay scale so that our officers and soldiers draw comparable pay with their counterparts in HJRAF. These subsidies on average amount to much less than one third of the Naranjeras budget for the ALIB. We as a nation benefit from the pay equalization subsidy. It is important to our national economy because that is money spent here at home. It is a modest but welcome contribution to our GNP."

Sanchez Avila was an intelligent and educated man. He also was an honest man and suddenly realized he knew less about the ALIB than he should. This young man, General Portero, had given him a new perspective, and he was angry with himself for not having taken the time to research the matter more thoroughly. He realized that his objectivity may have been clouded by his emotional opposition to his country participating in HJRAF. He also was a proud man and found it difficult to admit to his lack of knowledge about the brigade.

"Interesting," he finally said. "This is all a matter of record, I assume."

"I am sure the Ministry of National Defense will be able to confirm everything for you."

"I'll see them next week, thank you. However, I still believe our arrangement with the HDO, and the part we play in HJRAF puts us in a very difficult position. There is a great difference in perspective between a small country like ours and a giant like the United States. We may understand theirs, but can they ever understand ours? It is like a mouse going to bed with an elephant. No matter how tender the elephant may feel toward the mouse, it cannot avoid inadvertently rolling over and crushing it. I really wonder if we can work together as equal partners." Sanchez Avila was adamant.

"Well, it's worked so far, Don Ramon. And I don't think we could have had a more careful and understanding bed partner." Portero smiled. "Our problem is not so much one of difference in size as it is of a difference in purpose, which has only lately manifested itself."

"What do you mean?"

"I mean that the objectives of our government, the government of the United States and the governments of the HDO member nations, have been pretty much in consonance for the last ten or twelve years. With the golpe by the Figueroa people, that may have changed. I wonder if our new government still shares that same objective."

"Why, General?"

"There are several reasons, and remember, Don Ramon, I am speaking off the record. The first reason is that Figueroa is, like you, a nationalist, but unlike you, he has a great antipathy for the North Americans. It is not because they are the elephant… he has a personal animosity toward them. I am not sure why, but I believe it has to do with his political philosophy. Despite his protestations to the contrary, I do not believe he is a democrat. Remember, he studied in Cuba in the seventies and served with the Sandinista armed forces in Nicaragua for a year or so in the eighties."

"But that's all behind him, General. He has publicly disavowed his 'youthful enthusiasms,' as he called them, and has made some very strong pro-democracy and pro-capitalist speeches both before and after the golpe."

"Nevertheless, he seems to be acting more like a statist than a democrat, and the fact remains he did engineer the golpe and in doing so surrounded himself with the most radical leftists in the country, many of whom now hold positions of influence in his government."

"There are some, I admit, but by no means all are leftists. Your counterpart, Edson Davidson, for example. "

"Davidson is no leftist, but he is no democrat either, and he hates the ALIB and me. He will be loyal to Figueroa as long as he is given power. He is a renegade and martinet. He is not a particularly good officer, in my opinion, but ruthless and just the right choice if one intends to use the PNN to stir up trouble."

"You know him?" Sanchez Avila asked, surprised.

"I know him very well. I don't like the man, and I don't trust him."

Portero watched for a reaction from the old reporter. When there was none, he continued. "Another reason I believe Figueroa does not, or will not, share the stated objectives of the HDO is because they interfere with his own objectives for Naranjeras. Figueroa has already shown us his disrespect for the democratic process by the golpe he engineered. If, as I believe he will, he leads the country away from a democratic system and returns us to some version of a caudillo government, he will be out of communion, so to speak, with the democracies of the HDO."

He paused. Then continuesd. "I believe he is more spiritually aligned with Fidel, or Ortega in Nicaragua. The terms of the Hemispheric Defense Treaty, insofar as they require respect for human rights and the democratic process, will be an anathema to his real aims, even though he will give democracy lip service initially. In the end, when he has the power do so, he will withdraw from the HDO and renege on democracy at home. That will not only give him the independence he needs but it will also strategically damage the HDO, thus reducing the threat to his own agenda."

"I must say, General, you do not paint a pleasant picture of the future. In all candor, I think you are wrong. You have misjudged Figueroa and the significance of his coup. I do not believe as you do that the president intends to take the country away from democracy, despite his disregard for what you call the 'democratic process.' Forgive me, but your idea of democracy seems to have been overly influenced by the North Americans. We Latin Americans have had forms of democratic governments throughout our history which, although different from the US model, are democratic in that they clearly reflected the will of the people even when no votes were cast."

The old reporter thought for a moment, then continued. "Figueroa's coup is an excellent case in point. Clearly the Juan

Moreno government had lost the support of the people. If there had been an election at the time, Figueroa would have been the popular choice. Since no election was scheduled for three more years, Figueroa merely accelerated the process by assuming control of the government and thereby fulfilled the desires of the people. The proof of the baking was that the people welcomed the change. And the fact is that the new administration is vowing to carry out the Moreno reforms, but on a more protracted time schedule. There has been no indication that they intend to do anything else."

Sanchez Avila paused. Then he continued in a more conciliatory tone, "I agree the North American tradition of strict observance of the election cycle has served them well. Perhaps it is necessary in such a large country but a less formal system also works, as it has worked for us. I would argue it is, in practice, no less democratic than theirs. I am sorry, General, but I simply cannot agree with your assessment of the situation. I believe your concern is not well-placed."

"That is the kind of thinking that kept Latin America in the political and economic dark ages for the last century or so, Señor Sanchez." There was an edge in Portero's voice, and the reporter and others present did not miss the significance of his substituting the formal form of address for the more reverent "Don" form he had been using.

The general continued. "You are talking about a system that gave the world men like Rojas Pinilla, Perez Jimenez, the Somosas, Rafael Trujillo, Jacobo Arbenz, Omar Torrijos, Daniel Ortega, Manuel Noriega, and others we can scarcely call democrats."

"Some of those you name did good things for their countries…"

"Perhaps, but in balance they are remembered primarily because they forced their power on their people and are indelibly labeled 'dictators.' None of their regimes ended in peaceful successions, Nicaragua being the exception. Their legacy was continuing turmoil, struggle, and violence. Oh, I admit there may have been no way to avoid their kind of governments then, given the evolution of our societies in Latin America, but that time has passed. We now know that true democratic systems work for us, too. There is no going back to *caudillismo* anywhere, least of all here. Figueroa cannot be justified by a theory that he is accelerating the democratic process. I am sorry, sir, but it seems to me such ideas are from a different era."

During the pause, all eyes were on Sanchez Avila. It was clear he had been challenged, and they awaited his response. He sat calmly, thinking less about his response than about this young officer, Francisco Portero, who had proved so able in debate. He was very different than most military men he knew, intellectually broader and more articulate. He was newsworthy, someone to keep an eye on.

"You make your point well, General. I am not sure I can agree, but I want to consider what you have said. Now tell me," he said, looking at Hanson, "does General Carmody share your view in these matters?"

Portero smiled. "You mean, is this all HJRAF doctrine? No. These are my own thoughts. I have never discussed these matters with General Carmody. I doubt he knows my views on politics."

"He'll certainly know now, won't he, young man?" the reporter said, turning to Hanson.

"He will indeed, sir. But I don't think he'll be surprised by General Portero's views."

Sanchez Avila consulted his pocket watch. "Well General, I will be late returning to the capital, so I must leave you." They stood and shook hands. "Thank you for the lunch and for the conversation. I found it interesting and challenging. You have given me much to think about. I hope we will meet another time to continue our talk. And, General, I am mindful of the fact that this has all been off record. Please do not be concerned about that."

"Thank you, Don Ramon. It was a pleasure to have you here, and it is a pleasure to meet the journalist whom has the universal respect of all Naranjeros. Captain Lacerica will escort you to your car."

CHAPTER 3

They sat in a camouflage-painted tracker, looking down on the base from the highland on the western side of Valle Escondido. The broad green valley stretched away to the north on their left and south on their right, but there it turned sharply east three kilometers beyond the base's main gate. A patchwork of small farms spread across the valley and into the highlands on each side to the north and south of the base. A small, slow-flowing river, the Santa Inez, meandered down the valley close to the rising hills opposite, marking the eastern boundary of the brigade's cantonment area. To the south of the base, just outside the main gate, nestled a small, well laid-out village, its neat homes and few public buildings and stores painted in a variety of bright colors.

It seemed a peaceful place despite the faint sound of shouted commands from a recruit platoon engaged in close order drill on the distant parade ground, and the occasional crackle of small arms fire emanating from the rifle range to the left and below where they sat. Beyond the range was the base airstrip, its grass runway extending into the farmland to the north. The Black Hawk squatted patiently on its pad at the near end under the eye of a single sentry, who occasionally circled the bird.

The sky was blue and cloudless from horizon to horizon; the air was cool, crisp and invigorating. They felt the gentle pressure of an easterly breeze on their faces. It was a perfect afternoon, made just for them it seemed.

Captain Christina Lane was enjoying her afternoon thoroughly with Major Tony DaSilva. She was attracted to him and it seemed he to her, also. Their conversation had come easier, as he recovered from the defensive stiffness which had marred their lunch together at the press conference. She sensed the awkward moment with General Portero and the others, when he had come to claim her for lunch, had embarrassed and annoyed him.

It hadn't bothered her in the least, his showing an interest in her. She had been flattered by it. However, she sensed he would have liked to have handled the moment with more aplomb, and she had tried to put him at ease during lunch. She was not experienced in flirtation, but she did what she could to make him refocus on her. She wanted him to understand his interest in her was reciprocal.

She was surprised and excited by the sudden, unexpected new dimension in her life. She had many male colleagues and friends, but none had ever caused the kind of response she felt in meeting Tony DaSilva. As a woman in a man's world, she had deliberately wrapped herself in the protective armor of professionalism to discourage romantic overtures. It had worked well for her, and she was known and respected for her considerable competence by her peers. Those who knew her less well and saw her first as an attractive woman and dared make romantic advances soon learned, to their regret, that she was all business, much to the amusement of those who knew her best.

That hard shell had softened when she met DaSilva. He seemed different and made her feel different. She wanted to feel female with him, and she dropped her protective shield. She was surprised at herself, and grateful and quite amused by the giddiness she felt now with him, a feeling she had not experienced since her teenage years.

DaSilva was having the same sort of feelings about her. He had long held a mental picture of the woman who would be right for him. After thirty-six years as a bachelor, he had begun to doubt she existed. His problem with women had always been his obsession with the military. Women he met were often initially attracted to him, but somehow their interest always seemed to cool as they discovered his single-minded devotion to his profession. He bored them, he knew, and had all but despaired at ever finding the right one. Yet suddenly there she was, unexpected, attractive, and intelligent, and a fellow soldier. The fact that she seemed to respond to him was exciting and encouraging, but it also made him cautious. He did not want to make any mistakes with her.

He remained a little embarrassed by his earlier self-consciousness at lunch. He was afraid he had acted like a lovesick teenager in front of his general and this woman he had sought to impress. He needed to overcome any poor impression he might have made. His embarrassment had begun to fade as he drove her through the base, showing her its key installations. Her interest in the brigade encouraged him, and his natural exuberance, his enthusiasm for the Lobos, the brigade, and for General Portero and his job soon overcame any lingering reticence. As he relaxed, he began to talk volubly about the unit and his life at Valle Escondido.

Chris enjoyed all of it. As a woman she was interested in him, and as a soldier she was interested in the brigade. She did not hide it and soon they were thoroughly absorbed with one another.

At the Lobo Battalion cantonment, he had shown her his headquarters office. There he introduced her to his executive officer, a friendly young major with a big nose named Mix, who joined them for a cup of coffee. They talked about the Lobos for almost an hour.

She learned the battalion was the newest of the brigade's three line units, having been activated only three years before. Despite its inexperience, it had earned a reputation for excellence and professionalism. It had scored very well in recent tests and tactical exercises and, at the moment, unit morale was very high as a consequence of the successful rescue mission in Puerto Hondo.

Christina saw the undisguised pride DaSilva had in his command and she identified with it, remembering the same feelings about her first command as an infantry platoon leader in the First of the Fifteenth Infantry, to which she had been assigned prior to her transfer to army aviation and flight school.

Now looking down at the base, she could see the Lobo Battalion area at the south end of the parade ground. "That's your barrack area there, isn't it?" she said, pointing. "And those other two unit areas must be the Oso and Tigre Battalions, but which is which?"

"The one just by the brigade headquarters building there is the Oso, and the Tigres are there by the river. That unit area this side of the parade ground houses the brigade's Training Battalion."

"Tell me about that."

"It is a conglomerate unit charged with many training responsibilities for the brigade. It contains the brigade band plus four companies. One is a basic training company charged with training recruits for the line units. The second is called the TTC. That stands for Technical Training Company. It runs training courses in various technical specialties, such as radio operation and repair, radio direction finding, GPS skills, computer operation, and things like that. It also trains armorers, cooks, and clerks for the line units. One of its important missions has been to teach basic reading and writing skills to new recruits. It is surprising how many of our recruits are illiterate when they come to us, maybe ten or twelve percent."

Christina was fascinated. "No wonder you have such an easy time recruiting. You really take care of your people and have so much to offer them. I suppose people see you as an opportunity to better themselves."

"That and the fact that we pay well, thanks to the pay equalization subsidy your army gives us. A man can be a soldier with the ALIB and afford to keep a family once he is promoted into the NCO ranks."

He pointed to the village outside the main gate. "That is the town of Valle Escondido. Perhaps eighty percent of its inhabitants are dependents of the military, and many of them have civilian jobs on the base."

"I'm really impressed, Tony. I had no idea the ALIB was such a sophisticated operation. It has all the attributes, and I suppose the problems, of any major base in the States."

"I suppose it does, only on a smaller scale. But our problems are complicated by the fact that we are independent of the so-called defense forces of the country. That means we don't get much direct support from them, so we have to be self-sufficient in administrative, housekeeping, and training matters."

"Speaking of training, you were telling me about the Training Battalion. What do the other training companies do?"

"Yes. I guess I got off the track. Besides the Basic Training unit and the TTC, there is an Opposing Force Company. You call them 'OPFORS' in your army.

"It is the simulated enemy we work against in training exercises. General Portero put that together after he visited your NTC the first time. Its personnel are all experienced men borrowed from the line battalions for a six-month tour. Only the best get this duty. Having served with OPFORS means almost certain promotion when the man returns to his unit."

"And the fourth company?"

"The fourth company is known as the Plaster Company. It is named after Major John Plaster of your army, who is one of the world's leading authorities in marksmanship and sniping. It is responsible for the management of the rifle range and training our recruits in basic marksmanship.

"We Naranjeros are not like you North Americans. We have no hunting tradition, probably because we don't have any animals left to hunt, so we don't grow up with guns as you do. That means we have to spend more time training our men to shoot. That's one of the big jobs for the Plaster Company. But its most important task is training our *tiradores*—our snipers. The tiradores are unique to this brigade and really are its primary weapon. Each line battalion has the equivalent of one full company of these marksmen, who are not only trained shooters but experts in stalking and field craft as well.

"We are a true light infantry unit. That means we are organized to operate entirely without vehicles. This GEO is not part of our TO&E. It is an administrative vehicle we use on base. Each battalion has a few. But our primary method of movement is by foot. We have no equipment we cannot carry on our backs, which makes us eminently air transportable. We are troops for rugged terrain…jungles, mountains…any place where vehicles can't be used. Because we can only operate with what we carry, we are not big on automatic weapons. They burn up too much ammunition. That was the principal motivation for perfecting our tirador tactics.

"Oh, our assault units do carry M16s and light machine guns, but our doctrine stresses the use of aimed fire in preference to automatic fire. We believe we can inflict greater damage on an enemy by careful use of the tiradores and aimed fire by our assault echelons than can units using great volumes of automatic fire. That, at least, is the ALIB doctrine, and besides that, it's a lot cheaper when you are on a limited budget," he added with a grin.

"Makes sense to me. My dad was a career infantry officer, and he always talks about the importance of aimed fire. He claims automatic weapons waste both money and the American talent for accurate shooting. I can hear him now, 'The objective is to kill the bastards, not dirty their underwear.'" She laughed. "He would approve of your tirador doctrine. Tell me more about the ALIB."

"Well, you already know we have three line battalions. They are organized pretty much the same except for the Oso Battalion, which is the oldest. It has four companies versus our three. Its extra company is a tirador company, which they break down into platoons for attachment to their line companies. The Tigre and

Lobo Battalions have a platoon of tiradores organic to each line company so we have identical capabilities as the Osos—perhaps we are slightly less flexible in deploying marksmen, but it saves administrative overhead. The Osos would have probably been reorganized to conform with the other two battalions, except for the fact that Colonel Gutierrez likes it the way it is and the General doesn't want to force a change down his senior commander's throat." Da Silva clearly liked to talk about his Brigade.

"Your general is an interesting man. Tell me about him."

"I think Portero is the greatest soldier I have ever known. As a leader he is demanding and tough, but everyone likes him. He seems to have a genius for organization. He is an expert in infantry tactics, far and away the best in Naranjeras and probably the best in the HJRAF. He is also a patriot. He loves this country and wants to serve it. There are rumors that he has been offered commissions in your army, but he has always turned them down. And you know his wife is North American. Her father was a high-ranking general, I believe. She is a wonderful woman. Everyone respects her. He obviously dotes on her. She is a perfect commanding general's wife—very active with the officer's and NCO's wives. They make a great team."

"Have they children?" she asked.

"None, and it is too bad because she obviously loves them. She does a lot of entertaining of the children of the military families, hiking and picnics, games, that sort of thing. They all think she is great. They call her Doña Betsy."

"I'd like to meet her."

"I'm sure you will if you visit regularly...which I hope you will," DaSilva said quietly.

"We'll see if I can. I'd like to." Chris smiled at him. "But keep going. I want to hear more about your brigade."

"There's not much more to tell you. Each of our line companies is organized with three thirty-man assault platoons plus its tirador component. The Battalion Headquarters Companies each have a hefty reconnaissance platoon in addition to the normal staff support sections and the radio communications section. When we go into the field, we usually have a medical section attached to us from the brigade's Medical Detachment of the Headquarters Company. We might also have one or more sections of Javelin anti-tank missiles and/or Stinger anti-aircraft missiles attached, depending on the situation. These units are supplied by the brigade's Combat Support Company. It has a platoon of Stingers, a platoon of Javelins, a platoon of eighty-one millimeter mortars, and its fourth platoon is an ammunition and security unit. It is oversized with fifty or sixty soldiers. Remember, we must be able to operate without vehicles, so it has a lot of strong backs to carry extra ammunition, primarily for the mortar platoon.

"The trucks you see around the base belong to the 2d Transport Truck Company. It provides logistical support to the base. Technically, it doesn't belong to the ALIB, although the general managed to get them included in the pay equalization package, so they think they are part of us. The same goes for the engineer company, which runs the base. And that is the whole story about the ALIB. We are a formidable force for our little country. There is no other organization here that can challenge us militarily. If it were headed by someone other than Portero, it could also have a significant political influence, but he has always been adamant that we stay out of local and national politics."

"He also seems adamant about not giving into the government on these transit permits. Isn't that political? It also seems a little dangerous."

"He believes it is the government that is playing politics, and I agree with him. It is obvious they are using this flap as a ploy to increase their control over the brigade. They are violating the treaty which established the ALIB as an autonomous unit—it's in our name, for God sakes—of the HJRAF, and Portero is not going to let them get away with it. And yes, it could be dangerous, although the junta doesn't have the military muscle to force us to do anything the general doesn't want to do. I can tell you this. If it ever came to a showdown, the brigade would back the general to a man."

They talked on for an hour, enjoying each other's company and exchanging family histories. He learned that she was born in northern Wisconsin, where her father now lived in retirement. Her mother had died when she was very young and her father had never remarried, so she was brought up as an "army brat" by her father, whom she adored. It had been quite natural for her to seek a military career and when she was offered an appointment to West Point, she jumped at the chance.

She learned that Tony's father was a Brazilian who came to Naranjeras as a merchant seaman. He liked the little country so much, he signed off his ship and stayed. He worked on a cattle ranch north of La Mesona, married the owner's daughter, and eventually took over its management. Tony grew up on the ranch and worked on it as a boy but was always fascinated by the military. He enlisted in the National Police, won an appointment to the officer training academy, and graduated with distinction. When the opportunity came to transfer to the ALIB, he jumped at the chance and found his permanent home.

They became so absorbed with each other's story they lost track of time. When the light began to fade, DaSilva reluctantly suggested they return to the base.

Chris, equally reluctant, agreed. "I suppose we should. It has been a wonderful day. I really enjoyed the tour. Thank you. I am sold on the ALIB and can't wait to tell my dad about it. By the way, has it ever been deployed outside of Naranjeras?"

"Not as a brigade." He started the Geo's engine. "The OSOs were in Somalia for six months as a part of the United Nations force there. They were in the northern part of the country and didn't have much excitement. Except once when the local warlord's thugs tried to raid the food warehouse they were guarding. The tiradores killed them all, and after that, they were left alone. The Tigres had a company in Haiti in '95. All they did was patrol some interior roads and help disarm some armed units. It was largely a political mission. The U.S. wanted to show some other flags. They were mostly bored, I guess. Still it gave them some experience."

He slowly drove down the hill toward the base. "The nearest thing to real combat deployments we've had were our training tours at your National Training Center at Fort Irwin in California, and at the Readiness Training Center in Louisiana at Fort Polk. Simulated engagements at both were very realistic and challenging. All of our battalions have been to Polk, and the Osos have been to the NTC."

"I thought the NTC was strictly for armor and armored cavalry."

"We were there to test what a light infantry unit might do against armor, which turned out to be not much. The opposition soon learned to keep buttoned-up in their vehicles when we were around. Apart from long-range sharpshooting, we were pretty helpless. We did not do well there, but we learned a lot. After the Osos were there, we added the Javelin missile capability, so some good came of it. We did better at Polk, and it was an especially important learning experience for us."

Twilight is short in the tropics, and it was nearly dark as they approached the guest BOQ where Christina was quartered. As they stopped, DaSilva turned to her to ask if she would join him for dinner. "There is a small restaurant in the town called La Cocina. It is nothing fancy, but the beer is cold and they have great sancocho. I'd be honored if you would accompany me, Chris."

It was the first time he had called her by her given name, and it pleased her. "Thanks, Tony, I'd love to. I'll pass on the beer because I am flying tomorrow, but I'm up for a Coke and some good sancocho. What time shall I be ready?"

• • •

The daily papers all gave Portero's press conference front page coverage. The more conservative paper, Vida Nacional's banner was "ALIB Resists Government Demands." The left-leaning pro-Figueroa paper, El Diario, ran a headline which screamed "Portero Defies Government." The third paper, the smaller La Prensa, published in the interior city of La Mesona, whose readers were primarily farmers and ranchers, ran the headline, "Government Meets Its Match."

The articles all focused on General Portero's resistance to the use of permisos de transito . However, each publication treated the story according to its editorial bias. *Vida Nacional* played it straight.

> 17 Feb, Valle Escondido: At a press conference held today at Autonomous Light Infantry Brigade Headquarters, Brigadier General Francisco Portero restated his position in the growing controversy over the recent government decision to require ALIB vehicles to use permisos de transito. The dispute precipitated the recent confrontation between the parties when the general dispatched troops to Puerto Hondo to recover ALIB vehicles, which had been impounded by the PNN for lack of the required documents. The recovery was affected peacefully without violence. Portero called the government action illegal, as it violated the terms of the Hemispheric Defense Organization Treaty signed by Naranjeras when the ALIB was activated as the nation's contribution to the Hemispheric Joint Rapid Action Force, A spokesman for the Ministry of Interior denied any violation of law. He stressed that the use of permisos de transito was an internal matter not covered by the treaty. When pressed, he acknowledged certain clauses of the treaty pertinent to this matter were not entirely clear and therefore subject to interpretation, but he claimed national sovereignty should weigh heavily in any such dispute...

La Prensa, which had been outspoken in its condemnation of the golpe by the Figueroa junta, supported the ALIB in the matter of the transit permits.

> 17 Feb, Valle Escondido: The commander of the ALIB today refused to submit to the government demand that his vehicles use permisos de transito when moving on the nation's highways. He called the demand a violation of the treaty which established the ALIB. General Francisco Portero insisted that compliance with the order would be a violation of the nation's law. As an officer sworn to uphold the law he had no choice but to refuse to comply. He also called attention to the fact that PNN vehicles were not required to use *permissos*.

El Diario took a different approach in its reporting. It attacked Portero and the ALIB.

> 17 Feb, Valle Escondido: In an extraordinary press conference today, General Francisco Portero, the commander of the ALIB, accused the government of violating the nation's law in attempting to enforce transit regulations requiring the use of permisos de transito. The impetuous, USA-trained officer cited certain clauses contained in the Hemispheric Defense Treaty . A government spokesman denied the clauses cited by Portero had any bearing on the government's clear jurisdiction over the nation's highways. Apparently the real purpose of the press conference was to justify last week's raid on Puerto Hondo, when Portero ordered troops into the port-city to remove by force several ALIB vehicles which had been detained for operating illegally. The raid caused considerable consternation among the citizens of the city. Many who know Portero point to the fact that he is one of a group of Naranjeros which holds a strong bias for North America. It is puzzling to many why such a seemingly inconsequential matter as travel permits should have become such a cause

celeb. There are those who believe Portero may have been motivated by political ambition.

• • •

Captain Lacerica, sitting across the desk from his commander, watched Portero's face as he read the news clippings just delivered. The general's expression had not changed until he read the El Diario piece. His face reddened and his jaw tightened. "Who wrote this crap?" he asked, glaring at the offending paper.

"I don't know, sir, but it is the work of the managing editor, I'm sure."

"Who is he?"

"She, sir. The editor is Profesora Hortencia Malapropino. She is an unashamed apologist for President Figueroa."

Portero had to smile despite his anger. "Is that really her name? Well, it fits. Where did she surface from? I've never heard of her."

"I don't know where she has been…outside of the country, I'm sure. She took the job shortly after Figueroa seized power."

Portero was thoughtful. "I guess there is not much we can do to fight innuendo, is there? The problem is I do have a bias toward the United States. I respect the North Americans for what they have accomplished, for their openness in politics, for their professionalism in the military, and more than anything, for their understanding, patience, and interest in Naranjeras. They have been good friends to us. But because I appreciate them does not mean I am in their pocket, as Sanchez Avila would say. I deeply resent…no, I'm goddamn infuriated by the implication that I am less than loyal to my country. Dammit, I am not representing North American interests at the expense of our own and never have! My record ought to be clear on that. What can we do about this garbage?"

"Realistically nothing, sir. It is better to leave it alone. The more we protest, the more credibility we give them. I recommend we ignore El Diario and try to work with the other papers."

"Okay, how do we do that?"

"I'd like to see us arrange an open house for the editorial staffs of *La Prensa* and *Vida Nacional,* and any other unbiased media outlets we can identify. We can show them our base, let them meet our people, put on a parade and maybe some weapons demonstrations. We want them to see we are not anti-government monsters. At the same time, we want them to understand that we are militarily capable…and not pushovers."

"Interesting idea. If we do it, and do it right, we can also show them we are good, loyal Naranjeros. Set up a planning group with the chief of staff. I'll tell him you're on your way. Thanks, Guillermo. I like the way you think. By the way, what about Sanchez Avila's column? Did he write anything about us?"

"Not a word in his column, General, but I have a feeling he had something to do with the *Vida Nacional* story. He might have helped write it."

• • •

Colonel Antonio Figueroa, self-appointed President of the Republic of Naranjeras, stood in front of the massive mahogany desk in the presidential office, looking down at the three men seated before him. A tall, spare man with piercing black eyes which looked at the world through rimless glasses, thinning black hair and a ramrod straight back, he looked every inch a soldier despite the charcoal gray suit he wore.

The seated men were his minister of interior, his foreign minister and his commander of *Policia Nacional Naranjeras* (PNN). The four of them together constituted four-fifths of the junta, which managed the coup which overthrew the Brown government. The missing fifth member was the President of the *Assemblea de Diputados,* and the most experienced politician of the group.

The office intercom on the president's desk announced the arrival of the press secretary, who had been summoned earlier.

"Send him in."

A busy little man entered and greeted each of the seated men with a perfunctory handshake, and turned to Figueroa. "You sent for me, Mister President?"

"Yes. We have been discussing General Portero's press conference and the coverage in yesterday's papers. First, why was I not told he was scheduling a press conference? I knew nothing about it until I saw it on television. Did you know about it?"

"Yes, Mr. President, but only at the very last minute. I alerted your secretary the moment I heard."

"Oh?" The president made a note. "Second...we agree that Hortencia did a good job with her coverage, but maybe she was a little too partisan in her presentation. Tone her down a bit, will you? We want her support, but it should not be so flagrant that everyone will conclude she is anything to us but a newspaper editor. Understand?"

"Perfectly, Mr. President."

"The third point I wish to make concerns the Mesona paper. Their story reads as if they are cheering for Portero. I want you to have a friendly talk with the editor there. Ask him for more even-handedness in his coverage. No threats, mind you, just a plea for fairness. Let him know that his cooperation will be appreciated. You might ask him if he has had any newsprint delivery problems lately. We want him to be happy, don't we? It does still go through Puerto Hondo, doesn't it?"

"It does indeed, sir." The little press secretary hesitated. "Remember, *La Prensa* was quite antagonistic at the time of the golpe, but I am sure that is all behind us now. They are realistic people. There is no reason they won't be fair with us once they realize we can be friendly and supportive."

"Good...Now to the fourth point. I want you to draw up a press release announcing that today I have ordered the PNN to use *Permisos de Transito* whenever its vehicles use the national highways. You will include that I am determined there will be no special exemptions from the law by commercial, military, or public vehicles."

"Except school buses," interjected Interior.

"Except school buses and emergency vehicles, of course," concluded the president.

"We will work on it immediately. Will there be anything else, sir?"

"One last thing. What about Sanchez Avila? There was no mention in his column about Portero's conference. Why not? Was he there?"

"I understand he was there. I am told he asked some very tough questions, which put Portero somewhat on the defensive. He and the general later had lunch together. General Carmody's aide and another officer were also present. My informant could not determine the topic of their discussion, but he reported that at times it appeared to be heated. Perhaps they were having some disagreement." He paused. "I frankly don't think we have to worry about Sanchez Avila. He has always been quite outspoken against the country's participation in the HJRAF."

"Well, good. I hope you are right. That is all for now. Thank you."

When the door closed behind the press secretary, Figueroa took his chair behind the desk. He paused, looking at each of them in turn. "Well, gentlemen, what do you think? How are we doing? Are we on track?"

"So far we're doing fine," said Interior. The others nodded their agreement. "We always believed Pancho Portero would be an obstacle, and so he has proven to be. I frankly did not anticipate he would use force to recover those trucks."

"Nor I," said the President. "We were wrong about that, and I am afraid we could look weak on this one...but perhaps the public will see it as an overreaction by Portero to a minor misunderstanding. We should at least be promoting that thought in the public mind. Are we?"

"We are and, I think, succeeding. Hortencia was a big help in pushing opinion in that direction. She will certainly continue along that line."

The foreign minister was thoughtful. "I am worried about our friend, Portero. He may be more formidable than we assumed. I expected he would negotiate on this matter, but instead he charged in like an angry bull. He certainly caught the public's attention by his raid, and then he set the agenda for public debate with his press conference. It was a clever move. He may be smarter than I assumed."

"Never underestimate Pancho Portero." Edson Davidson, the PNN commander, entered the conversation. "I know him. He is smart and he is tough. We can always count on him doing the unexpected. Let's learn a lesson from this. We are not dealing with a pushover…he is going to be a major obstacle to overcome. We agreed before the golpe that he would have to be neutralized if we were to achieve our objectives. That won't be easy, but we can do it once we set our minds to it. It will take time. At the moment, he is too strong for us. We must start focusing now on whittling away his power advantage. It must be a well-planned step by step process."

"Agreed," said the president. "And the first step must be the *Permisos de Transito*. If we don't win that battle, we lose credibility with the people."

"Well your order requiring the PNN to begin using permisos will pressure him to comply, but it will take more than that," Davidson offered.

"We are doing more, Edson," said the foreign minister. "We're generating some international pressure on him. Our ambassadors are appealing for help from our allies abroad, particularly allies in the United States, in resolving this 'minor domestic misunder-standing' which has unfortunately arisen over the permiso matter.

"They will take pains to reassure the member governments our action does not signal any change in our commitment to the principles of the HDO, that we fully understand the obligations imposed upon us by the treaty, and that we remain steadfastly supportive of the ALIB as an autonomous unit of the HJRAF. Privately and unofficially, of course, they will ascribe the misunderstanding to the inexperience of the new government, and they will urge their support of us in this matter as a gesture of goodwill. I have not the slightest doubt this approach will succeed. The result? I believe it will be that Portero will be ordered to comply."

"Very well. That will solve our domestic public relations problem, but it does not weaken Portero militarily." Colonel Davidson was blunt. "Sooner or later, we have to accomplish that."

Figueroa studied the PNN commander. "I know you well enough, Edson. What's on your mind?"

"I recommend we take steps to exercise greater control over the ALIB's mobility." Davidson waited for the effect of his words. When he saw the questions in their faces, he continued. "You will recall that the 2d Transport Truck Company has been attached to Portero to provide logistical support. It is, in reality, a unit belonging to the Defense Ministry and is not integral to the ALIB. Without it, Portero is on foot. I would like to see us have the option to fix him in place at Valle Escondido if we need to."

"We can't do that! We can't take those trucks away!" The foreign minister showed his alarm. "The HJRAF wouldn't stand for it, nor would the HDO. Besides, it flies in the face of the assurances we are making on being supportive and not interfering in ALIB operations."

"Hold on a minute. Hear me out. I am not proposing we take the Truck Company away from them. It will still be assigned the mission of supporting the brigade. I am simply proposing we move its location out of Valle Escondido to somewhere we can exercise greater control over its operations...should we need to. We can answer any HJRAF concerns simply by claiming we are eliminating inefficiencies and reducing costs. That is reasonable. But between us, we actually will have taken the trucks out of Portero's direct control and put it under ours. That will give us considerable leverage with him."

Figueroa remained silent for several minutes, pondering his police commander's idea. Finally, he agreed the idea had merit. "However, we would have to be extremely careful how we implemented such a step. It would require a great deal of solid justification to the HJRAF. We would have to convince them that we were serious about increasing efficiency in the support operation, and that won't be easy. Pancho will figure it out and squeal like a stuck pig. I can hear him now," he mused. "Let's spend some time thinking how we might implement the idea. But first let's win the battle of the permisos."

Davidson persisted. "I am assuming we will win that battle, Mister President. The foreign minister has just assured us we will. We have to think beyond that. We have to think beyond reducing Portero's mobility, even. If we succeed in that, the ALIB will still be a powerful military force relative to what we have. If we expect to neutralize him, we have to balance the power equation.

"Picture the situation if we don't. Portero is in the interior at Valle Escondido, without transportation, so he has a supply problem. We will control the ports and his major sources of supply. That gives us a critical geographic advantage, but only if we can contain him, which is to say keep him in the field and away from the supply depots. We won't be able to do that with our current forces. I am therefore recommending we commence a buildup of our forces to the level necessary to contain him."

"It will take months, maybe years, and millions of dollars to create a force that can defeat the ALIB. We don't have the time or the resources!" exclaimed Interior.

"That is correct. But, we don't have to be strong enough to defeat him in a pitched battle. We only have to be strong enough to deny him a quick, easy military victory. Remember, he'll be without a re-supply capability and without transportation. In a protracted fight, even at a low intensity level, attrition will eventually defeat him. In that situation, time will be on our side. We only have to be strong enough to insure it is a protracted fight.

Building that kind of strength is one hell of a lot cheaper than a full-blown military force."

Figueroa again nodded his agreement. "Edson is right, gentlemen. We could make it tough for Portero, even without a full-scale buildup. The trade-off, of course, is that the strategy he is proposing, although financially cheaper, will probably be more costly in terms of casualties. It means a series of small fights... blocking actions, raids, ambushes, lots of small unit actions... anything we can do to inflict casualties on Portero. But that means we take casualties as well. We only have to be able to out-last him while denying him the ability re-supply himself. Do you have a plan to build the necessary force level, Edson? And how much will it cost?" The president turned to Davidson and waited.

"Our plan is being finalized now, sir. It will cost some money, but it should be within our means. It entails re-training about half of our police force and converting them into infantry units. We can augment them with new recruits, and possibly foreign volunteers. I suspect there are still Nicaraguans, Salvadorians, and maybe even some Guatemalans who can be motivated to our cause...and plenty of Cubans, of course. We have the contacts in place. Moreover, we will need sources for weapons. I know of several sources which will be sympathetic enough to supply us at a reasonable cost. There is also the possibility of covert foreign financial backing—"

"We know from experience that comes with a heavy price," the president interrupted, wanting to divert the discussion to another subject. "It would be better to do it within our own resources. But you are correct. There are potential backers out there, mostly Middle Eastern countries with an enduring antipathy for the gringos. We have talked to some of them already, and we will be talking again in the near future.

"As for now, I believe we should look seriously at Colonel Davidson's scheme for retraining PNN units. If we can do it quietly, without public announcement or fanfare and at the same time keep it within our financial resources, I for one favor such a step. How soon can we see your plan, Edson?"

CHAPTER 4

February passed into March without further incident. ALIB trucks made their regular supply runs to the capitol and to Puerto Hondo without the disputed documents. At all PNN checkpoints, the agents regularly verified and recorded the fact that they were traveling without the documents, but made no attempt to detain them. Sergeant Emilio Carranza, who frequently lead the convoys, continued to wonder about the procedure which seemed to have become the norm. At first he ascribed it to the fact that after the Puerto Hondo incident, he and his drivers began carrying their weapons and that the larger convoys carried additional armed escorts, all on orders from Brigade. As time passed, however, he concluded the PNN simply was not enforcing the regulation on ALIB vehicles, despite the fact that even PNN vehicles now used permisos when traveling the national highways. That led him to think that General Portero may have won his point in the dispute and that the ALIB was being given an exemption.

Portero, however, was under no such illusion. He was sure the other shoe would drop because of the president's order requiring the PNN to use the documents. However, until something happened, there was nothing to react to. All he could do was try to anticipate and plan for possible contingencies. That brought a shift in the focus of his weekly staff meetings, away from operational and training matters, toward maintaining a continuing estimate of the situation insofar as ALIB relations with the government were concerned.

Privately he was uneasy in this new role, which he saw as being mostly political and therefore outside of his comfort zone. As a military professional, he was attuned to thinking within the parameters of doctrine, strategy, tactics, troop training, and operating procedures, which kept the focus of his endeavors comfortably narrow. However, the uncertainties and unfamiliar terrain of politics were forcing him to think about matters beyond his experience and training. Although he was fascinated by the challenge, he was uncomfortable and unsure about how to approach it. His situation was made worse knowing that he could not seek guidance from General Carmody at HJRAF.

He had discussed his unease only with Betsy. "Maybe I should have gone along with their permit demands. If I had, I might not have been in this mess today. Maybe it would have all gone away."

"Nonsense, Pancho, you know better than that," she had responded, seizing his hand in both of hers as she often did when she wanted his full attention. She turned him to look into his eyes. He had to smile. It was so typical of her.

"Listen to me, Pancho. You did what you had to do. Your instincts are right. For heaven sakes, don't start looking back now. You have to deal with these guys. They are not going to go away. You're the only one in the country they are scared of. You are the only one that can alter the course they seem to be on. And you won't do it by appeasing them. You know I'm right so buck up, Portero."

He laughed. Once again she had restored his confidence, as she so often had when he grew uneasy facing a new challenge. He loved her for it and thought again how lucky he was to have her at his side.

His staff also was uneasy about the new developments, but they never detected uncertainty or any lack of confidence in him.

To them his apparent resolve and sense of direction in the matter was reassuring, and it reinforced their confidence in his leadership.

He had clearly outlined the situation for them in a confidential staff meeting. "For planning purposes, gentlemen, you are to assume first, that the Figueroa government's objectives are not as they publicly claim them to be. Their objective is not to lead the country back into the democratic process with free elections. Assume instead they are statists, not democrats, and their aim is to return the country to a *caudillo* system of government.

"Second, you are to assume the Figueroa junta will see in the ALIB a threat to the successful achievement of their objectives...That they will be seeking ways to neutralize our ability to oppose them...That they will attempt to swing the balance of power from us to them. Finally assume that it is the ALIB's responsibility to prevent them from succeeding in accomplishing those objectives. As of today, gentlemen, I as brigade commander accept that change in our responsibility.

"Accordingly, I want to form a staff study group to track the new situation. Its assignment will be first to develop estimates of possible courses of action available to the junta, which could neutralize the ALIB ability to resist them. Second, it is to develop a set of options for countering each of those courses of action. Any questions about what we are to do? Okay, Colonel Soto will chair the study group, and I want the B2, Colonel Banning, and the B3, Colonel Ochoa, in it for sure."

Colonel Roth, the brigade logistics officer immediately raised his hand. "I would like to be on it as well, General, because an easy way they could limit our operational capabilities would be by disrupting our supply channels."

"An excellent point, well taken. Okay, the B4 is a regular member as well. You will also need a good secretary. It will be a full-time job, so pick a good man who can keep his mouth shut. Maybe a senior sergeant from operations or the B2 section.

"One final point. The true activities of this study group are to be kept top secret. It will look too much like a war-room operation, and people will jump to the wrong conclusion if that perception is allowed to grow. We must not be seen to be plotting against the government. That would be a public relations disaster not only for us but also for the HJRAF. We must find a way to give the operation some plausible cover…To camouflage it so it seems to be something different, something innocent. For example, we might call it the Advanced Tactics Board, or ATB, and make it known that its mission is to study and develop new tactics for employing and supporting platoon and company-sized, independent task forces."

Turning, he nodded to his chief of staff. "Colonel Soto will find a secure home for the ATB, or whatever we decide to call it. If there are no questions, let's get to it."

• • •

Meantime, the brigade's normal training routine continued on schedule. In late March, the Tigre Battalion moved to the ALIB Training Area in the forested mountains thirty kilometers northeast of the City of Mesona. There it would engage in exercises against the OPFORS unit in preparation for its annual Battalion Level Combat Readiness tests.

The absence of Tigres and the OPFORS Company reduced the base population by one third, leaving an activity gap which was partly filled by the arrival of a new group of recruit trainees. As in all armies, the brigade's basic training process was accompanied by an increased noise level: the shouted commands of the drill sergeants conducting close order drill, the marching recruits counting cadence, the rhythmic chants of those leading group calisthenics and manual of arms drills, the sound of road marches leaving and entering the base, and the voices of instructors patiently dispensing their knowledge of weapons, first aid, brigade organization, military customs and traditions, and the scores of other subjects necessary to convert an ordinary man into an infantry soldier.

The Osos and the Lobos continued their small unit training in preparation for their turn in the northern training area. The Plaster Company was occupied cycling the assault companies through practice on the firing range preliminary to weapons qualification tests in the mornings, and honing the sharpshooter skills of the tiradores in the afternoon hours. Consequently, the crackle of small arms fire echoed across the valley and over the base almost constantly during daylight hours.

Christina Lane managed to have herself assigned to the weekly courier flight between the headquarters in Panama and Valle Escondido. The assignment enabled her to be with Tony DaSilva regularly, and their relationship grew to the point when their lives revolved around her trips there. Their friends in the Lobo Battalion and at La Cocina Restaurant shared their joy and marked the passing of their own weeks by the regular appearances of the happy pair. The locals began referring to them as the *noviazgo* and the couple's early self-consciousness gave way to a sense of belonging, of being a part of the little community which cherished and was entertained by their romance. It was like being a part of an oversized family.

• • •

The days passed and as March drew to a close, the late afternoon aguaceros which marked the rainy season in the region began to abate, and with the change came a series of events which ended the brigade commander's uneasy wait.

The first such event was the day-long open house planned for the publisher and editor of the Mesona daily, *La Prensa*, who arrived with their wives and older children, and several reporters and key members of the paper's staff. The editor of *Vida Nacional* sent Ramon Sanches Avila as his representative at the open house.

The visitor day was beautifully planned. They were welcomed by General Portero, who spoke eloquently about the importance of an independent press as being the "eyes, ears and voice of free people and a bulwark against aspiring tyrants." His audience responded with gratifying enthusiasm. They were then briefed on the ALIB, its organization, its distinguished history, and its mission as the Naranjeras contribution to the HJRAF.

There followed a visit to the barracks of "A" Company of the Lobo Battalion, where the visitors were given ample time to meet and converse with the soldiers. An outdoor buffet lunch followed, during which they were entertained by a small ensemble from the brigade band which played favorite Naranjeras folk songs quite adequately, Portero thought.

After lunch they moved to the parade ground, where they watched a full dress parade. The Recruit Company led the brigade, followed by the Oso Battalion in their black berets and the Lobos in their gray. The recruits' lines were a bit tentative and their marching self-conscious and stiff, but the veteran battalions swung by the reviewing stand with an easy stride, having adopted the unaffected marching style of the US Army. Their lines were perfect, and they marched in exact cadence to the band's rendition of the grand old Mexican march, "Zacatecas," a favorite in Naranjeras. The last unit in the parade consisted of six polished vehicles from the 2d Transport Truck Company. Mounted in the trucks were personnel from the Combat Support Company, who sat rigidly at attention and offered the artillery salute by raising folded arms as they passed the reviewing stand. The publisher, his editor and Sanches Avila stood with General Portero to take the salute.

After the parade, the visitors were transported to the firing range, where they were treated to a demonstration of the brigade's weapons by Plaster Company and Combat Support Company personnel. The climax of the afternoon was a camouflage demonstration in which the visitors were invited to identify soldiers concealed in the field before them. They, of course, could spot none of them, and their exclamations of surprise built as one after another of the camouflaged men was ordered to stand, starting with the first one hundred meters out, the next at fifty meters, the next closer, then closer, and closer. When the last man stood up only five meters behind the speaker, the visitors shouted in amazement and erupted in wildly enthusiastic applause. It had been a great demonstration, capping a great afternoon.

When the group had finally been reassembled in the briefing hall, the publisher stood to express the appreciation of the group to General Portero and Captain Lacerica, who had coordinated their visit. His words were warm, sincere, and eloquent. He concluded his remarks, saying, "And now, General Portero, we ask one final favor of you. Please convey to the troops of this splendid brigade our deepest gratitude for the wonderful things they have shown us today. Not only have we seen a fine military organization in which we take great satisfaction, but we have seen also an assembly of young Naranjeros who bring honor to their country through their dedication and excellence. There are none better, and our hearts are exploding with pride in them and in our beloved country, which they so wonderfully represent to the world. If, as you have said this morning, the press is indeed the eyes, ears, and voice of free people, then there is at least this newspaper, which will use that peoples' voice in full support of our glorious Autonomous Light Infantry Brigade. May God bless you all."

"My God, what a moment!" Portero told Betsy later. "I got emotional and couldn't speak, so I gave him a really serious *abrazo*. That was all I could do…I believe we made a friend there."

"Good. What about Sanches Avila?"

"He was polite but not as effusive. He said he was impressed, and I believe he was being sincere. But who knows with him?"

• • •

On the same day in Washington, D.C., a meeting occurred which would profoundly affect the fortunes of General Portero and his brigade. A young secretary left the Naranjeras embassy at lunch hour. She hailed a taxi and directed the driver to take her to an obscure restaurant in Arlington, Virginia.

She took a table in a quiet corner, left a name, not her own, with the hostess, ordered coffee and a sandwich, and waited. In fifteen minutes she was joined by a well-dressed, swarthy man carrying a large briefcase. He took her hand and kissed her cheek. She had never seen him before, but she smiled and welcomed him. To any observer, they were friends or lovers meeting for a quick lunch.

He ordered coffee, and they talked quietly. After about thirty minutes he rose, took her hand and again kissed her, this time on both cheeks, and departed, leaving the briefcase on the chair beside her.

She finished her sandwich, paid her bill, and calmly left carrying the briefcase, which she delivered to the Naranjeras ambassador forty minutes later.

• • •

The young recruit was nervous but determined. "May I speak to you a moment, Sergeant?"

Sergeant Ibarra was a six-year veteran with the brigade and had been the Third Platoon drill sergeant in the Basic Training Company for two of those years. He had trained enough recruits to know that when one of them gathered the courage to ask to speak to him privately, there was usually a good reason, or at least the recruit thought he had a good reason. Unlike some of his colleagues, Ibarra took time for such requests, believing that two-way communication between trainer and trainee helped build mutual respect and made his job easier.

"What is it, Espino?"

"It's about Rubio, Sergeant. The one in my squad?"

"What about him?" Espino asked.

"There is something different about him. I don't know, but he is not like most of the recruits, and I am sure I have seen him before."

"That is possible. So what?"

"Well, Sergeant, he says he is from La Boca, but I think he is from Mesona. I used to see him there when I worked with my uncle. He is a trucker, and I saw Rubio at the PNN checkpoint there. I think he was in the PNN, a corporal or something."

"Are you sure about that?"

"Pretty sure. Except when I asked him about it, he denied it. He said I was confusing him with someone else. He said that he had only been in Mesona once when he was a boy. So I let it drop. But I am sure he's the same guy."

"He is not unusual in appearance. I would say sort of average looking. Are you sure you haven't mixed him up with someone else?"

"Quite sure, Sergeant. It's not only his looks but the way he talks, sort of slow. I remember that, too."

"If you are right, why would he deny it? And why would a corporal in the PNN want to start all over again as a recruit in the brigade? It doesn't make sense to me."

"That is why I thought there was something strange about him."

"Okay, Espino. Let me think about this. Don't say any more about it to anyone. Keep it to yourself, and don't tell anyone you talked to me. By the way, have you told anyone else about this?"

"No, Sergeant, except some of the men were around when I first asked him about it."

"Good. Don't bring it up again…and thanks for letting me know. It may be nothing, but it could be something. You did the right thing."

The next morning, Sergeant Ibarra asked to see his company commander.

• • •

The Advanced Tactics board met following the early April meeting of the brigade staff. It was immediately evident to Portero that these key members of his staff had jumped into the new project with considerable energy and enthusiasm, which pleased him. Colonel Soto controlled the meeting and asked the B4, Colonel Roth, to give his report first.

"I have two items, General. First, a bit of intelligence. The Truck Company has reported that the number of PNN personnel at the Mesona and Tuxla checkpoints has dropped. Both of these posts have had permanent detachments. Mesona usually has fifty or sixty men stationed there because it is a highway patrol base. Now they seem to be down to twenty or less. The same thing at Tuxla. They seem to be down to eight or ten. Normally there were around thirty there."

"How do we know all this? Where did we get the numbers?"

"Our drivers transit these places almost every day. They get to know the PNN people. They talk. The ones still there are grumbling about overwork. They claim the others have gone for special training. No one seems to know where or what the training is."

"What about Vargas's friend at PNN Headquarters? Is he telling us anything?"

"Major Vargas has been trying to reach him. He has not returned his calls so far. We suspect he is among the missing," volunteered Colonel Ochoa, Vargas' boss.

"We're trying to find out more about this, sir," said Colonel Banning, the intelligence officer. "It appears that the population of the PNN Headquarters in the capital is also down, but we cannot be sure."

"We'll keep on this, General," said the chief of staff. "What else do you have for the general, Colonel Roth?"

"Well, it's a recommendation, really. It seems to me that if someone wanted to interfere with our operations, he would try to reduce our mobility. He knows we depend on the Truck

Company for all our supplies and to move troops around. He could really slow us down by cutting off our supply of fuel for the trucks. We normally maintain about two weeks' supply here at the base. It gets replenished by Exxon tankers, which make the trip up from the refinery to service us and the petrol station in Valle Escondido. If someone stopped them from coming, we'd be on foot very soon.

"I'd be a lot more comfortable, General, if we had a larger inventory of fuel on hand. I therefore recommend we increase our on-base fuel supplies to a month or month and a half. At present we don't have the tankage, and it would take too long to install more even if we could get approval to spend the money, which we probably couldn't. However, I know where I can pick up one thousand or more used 200-liter steel drums. It wouldn't take long to clean them up, and we could fill them out of our tanks over a period of months. All the refinery would know is that we were using more fuel than normal, which should make them happy."

"Where would you store them once they were filled? That is one hell of a lot of drums. Don't you need a lot of room?"

"Yes, General, but we can do it. There is plenty of space east of the airstrip. The engineers tell me that they can build four berms large enough to take two-hundred-and-fifty drums each in that area. They would be sufficiently isolated from each other that we wouldn't have a chain reaction if one blew up, and they wouldn't interfere with air operations unless some pilot really misses the strip."

"If one or more of them blew, wouldn't we have a lot of burning petrol flowing down on the base?"

"Yes, sir, that's a problem, but the engineers think they can cut some diversion channels to run it down the valley away from the base where it wouldn't do any harm."

"What do you think of the plan, Soto?"

"Well, General, I think Colonel Roth's plan is a good one. If things happen the way we think they might, we will be very glad we made provision for the extra fuel. If we are wrong, we will have a scarred hillside and a couple of months' worth of extra fuel. Better safe than sorry, I say."

"Okay. Let me think about it. Tomorrow I want to go over the area with you and Roth and the engineer. I'll make a decision then. What's next?"

Soto nodded to Banning.

The B2 said, "Ochoa and I would like to use the brigade Reconnaissance Platoon to reconnoiter the road network around Valle Escondido, say at least fifty kilometers out, with special emphasis on what is between us and the capital by way of El Cacique. We want to use two man teams in civilian clothes driving private vehicles. We'll give them each a GPS unit and a map. Their mission will be to check out which roads are passable for our trucks, with a special look at the capacity of bridges. If there is doubt as to whether they can sustain a loaded vehicle, we want the engineers to take a look. We know the main highways in the country, but we have never really looked at the secondary roads. I guess we never thought we might be operating tactically in Naranjeras. Unfortunately, topographical maps of these areas have never been published, so we must work with road maps which need updating. We can do some of that ourselves. Eventually we can run some unobtrusive, small unit exercises throughout various areas to get our people familiar with the terrain. We think it will require two or three months to complete this reconnaissance properly."

The enormity of what Banning recommended suddenly struck Portero. Here they were, all loyal Naranjeros, contemplating the possibility of combat operations in their own homeland. He paused, thought about it, and then felt compelled to observe, "Isn't it remarkable how merely considering a hypothetical situation can so completely change one's perspectives about what is important? A year ago, it would never have occurred to any of us that we might be considering these kinds of operations. Let us hope that nothing comes of all this."

After a moment, he ended his musing and got back to business. "Well, if nothing else, a detailed reconnaissance will be a good training exercise. But why limit it to the brigade reconnaissance unit? Let's get the battalion Recon Platoons involved, too. And while they are exploring the roads, they can keep an eye out for the missing PNN troops. Let's go with this. Is there anything else, Soto?"

"Yes, General. Colonel Sanchez thinks we've got a spy in the basic training company."

"A spy?"

"Yes, sir. A possible PNN plant."

Colonel Soto recounted the circumstances as described to him by the Training Battalion commander—the recruit Espino telling Sergeant Ibarra his suspicions—Ibarra taking it to his company commander—and up the line to brigade. "The question is what do we do about this Rubio?"

"You say he doesn't know we have spotted him?"

"To the best of our knowledge he does not, sir."

"What sort of man is he?"

"Sanchez says he is a good man. Better educated and more mature than the average recruit. Ibarra and his instructors had him spotted as a candidate for technical training."

"Any recommendations?" Portero asked the group. "It appears we have two options. We confront him and send him back to Davidson with our compliments, or we keep him and treat him as if we did not know who he is, and watch him."

"We have discussed both options. We have mixed feelings, but the consensus is to discharge him. Send him back to Davidson. That would be the simplest and cleanest solution. Banning wants to keep him and watch him on the theory that if there are others, he might lead us to them."

"That's not all, General," Colonel Banning interjected. "We also might be able to use him as a disinformation disseminator. We can play mind games with the PNN through him. I say it is better to keep him as a known quantity here under our thumb than to have them replace him with someone else more difficult to identify. I would rather let them believe they have gotten away with this one than challenge them to do it again, only better."

Portero nodded his agreement. "Spoken like a true intelligence spook. I vote with Banning, and the ayes have it."

• • •

The Tigre Battalion returned from the ALIB Training Area the third week in April, having satisfactorily completed its annual Unit Combat Readiness Test, much to the relief of its commander and his staff. The Oso Battalion was preparing to depart for its own cycle at the training area. The Brigade Recon and Battalion Recon Platoons had begun their quiet reconnaissance of the secondary roads in an extended area surrounding Valle Escondido. Otherwise, except for the mild curiosity aroused by the fact that the Truck Company had been hauling in hundreds of used steel drums, life was normal on the base.

CHAPTER 5

The other shoe dropped for Portero in mid-May. He received an early morning call on the secure telephone from General Carmody, who announced that he would travel up to Valle Escondido to meet with him on several matters of importance. Portero was sure that one subject would be the permiso matter. He had expected it since receiving an unofficial visit from the defense attaché at the United States Embassy three weeks earlier. The young lieutenant colonel, who had gone through ranger training with Tony DaSilva and had taken special interest in the brigade, informed him confidentially of the Figueroa government's vigorous diplomatic campaign aimed at pressuring the HDO to require ALIB compliance with the government's demands.

"We'll be glad to see you, General. When are you coming?"

"Next Thursday, if it is convenient."

"Can you make it Wednesday? We are having a promotion ceremony for Tony DaSilva, the CO of the Lobos. It would add a lot if you were here."

"Okay, I'll try to do it Wednesday. I'd like to be there. I'll be flying up, of course. Jimmy will let you know our ETA. There will just be the two of us plus the flight crew."

"Will Captain Lane be your pilot, by any chance? She and DaSilva have grown pretty close. It would be appropriate if she could be here to see him get his silver leaves."

"It's that serious, is it? Okay, I'll see if she is available."

"Good, General, and thanks. Betsy and I would be delighted if you would stay with us Wednesday night."

"Thanks. I don't want to inconvenience Betsy in any way, but it would be nice to get some home cooking for a change."

"She'll be glad to have you, and so will I. By the way, what are we going to be talking about? I can start thinking about it now."

"There are several subjects which I don't want to mention on the phone." Carmody paused. "One is the question of the famous permisos. Your government has been lobbying pretty hard internationally, and the State Department apparently wants to accommodate them. They have told the Pentagon to go along. That will put pressure on the HDO, and my guess is they will fall into line, too."

"I've been expecting it, sir, ever since Figueroa's grandstand gesture requiring the PNN to use permisos. You give me the order and I'll do it, but it is wrong."

"I know your views, Pancho, and I am sympathetic, but there are some things we have to do, like it or not, when you're in our business. We can discuss it more over a gin and tonic. The other things I want to talk about are more important, anyway."

"Very good, General. I look forward to having you here."

• • •

On Wednesday morning, General Portero, Colonel Soto, and Captain Lacerica waited at the airstrip and watched General Carmody's helicopter fly up the valley and descend toward the airstrip. As the big bird settled on the landing pad, the honor guard of soldiers from the brigade Recon Platoon came to attention behind them. Tony DaSilva, wearing the new silver leaf of a lieutenant colonel, was also there, but he stood apart from the official welcoming committee. He was there to welcome not the general, but the general's pilot.

The moment the big machine touched down, General Carmody and his aide, Captain Jaime Hanson, jumped to the ground, holding their caps and ducking low under the still turning rotor. They walked toward General Portero and his party. The men of the honor guard presented arms. The generals exchanged salutes and shook hands. Portero offered some warm words of welcome, introduced Soto and Lacerica, and invited Carmody to inspect the honor guard.

Christina Lane saw DaSilva waiting and waved, and directed her co-pilot to complete the post-flight checklist. She removed her flight helmet, ran a comb through her hair, jumped from her right seat, and happily hurried to meet him.

DaSilva caught his breath at the sight of her, as he always did, and strode forward to meet her, thinking how beautiful she was. Conscious of the military formalities taking place, he resisted an impulse to embrace her and instead took her two hands in his, and smiling down at her said, "Hola querida. Bienvenido."

Chris caught sight of his new insignia of rank and grinned with pleasure. "Oh Tony, when did that happen?" she asked, grinning.

"I received the promotion order this morning. It will become official at the parade this afternoon, but I wanted to surprise you."

"It's a wonderful surprise. Congratulations!" She threw her arms around his neck and squeezed. "I'm so proud of you!"

When General Carmody had finished his inspection, he looked for his pretty pilot and spotted her standing beside a young officer wearing the gray beret of the Lobo Battalion, and looking very happy. He approached them, returned DaSilva's salute, and addressed Chris. "A nice flight, Captain. Thank you."

"You are welcome, General. It was my pleasure. Sir, may I introduce my friend Major, I mean Colonel, Antonio DaSilva. Tony, General Carmody."

Carmody, smiling broadly, shook his hand. "I am delighted to meet you, Colonel. I have heard about you from General Portero. That was a nice operation you ran in Puerto Hondo. And congratulations on your promotion."

• • •

Portero drove General Carmody to Brigade headquarters in his GEO, displaying the red plate with the four stars of a full general, Carmody's rank. Colonel Soto and Captains Lacerica and Hanson followed in another vehicle. As they left the airstrip, Carmody inquired about the series of excavations they passed along the road.

"Those will be our emergency fuel storage areas, sir. Just in case."

"Just in case what?"

"Just in case our fuel deliveries are interrupted." Portero explained his concerns about losing mobility at the whim of a potentially adversarial government. He looked at Carmody, who sat poker-faced watching the road ahead. "Do you think I am getting paranoid, General?"

"A little, perhaps. I would have been certain of it a few weeks ago but I'm not so sure anymore, for reasons I will explain when we get to the privacy of your office."

Portero led his boss on a quick tour of brigade headquarters and introduced him to the officers and NCOs in each staff section. The two generals then closeted themselves in the brigade commander's office, where a steaming pot of fresh brewed Naranjeras coffee awaited them.

"I am impressed with your staff, Pancho. They exude a sense of confidence, which usually means they know their business."

"They do know their business, General. They are a pretty dedicated bunch, and they believe they are doing something important." Portero glanced at his watch. "We have a couple of hours before lunch. Maybe we should get started, sir."

"Okay, but let me finish what I was going to say. When one has been around as long as I have, he sees many different units. You get to have an instinct about which is a good operation and which has problems, and which ones are bullshitting you. It is strange. I suppose it is a sixth sense which develops with experience, but I know pretty much what I can expect from each unit in HJRAF if we ever get into a fight. General George S. Patton, of World War Two fame, is supposed to have said that a general can always know the character of his divisions by studying the character of his division commanders. I think he was right.

"I see a lot of you reflected in the men I met this morning, your staff, and that young colonel at the airstrip. Your influence is there and it goes down to the lowliest recruit, and that is the way it should be. That is what commanders are paid for, to build and lead capable organizations that can get the job done. I can carry Patton's axiom a step further. Great units have great commanders. And I believe your brigade is a great one."

Portero was pleased and reassured, and also embarrassed by the compliment. He was not accustomed to compliments from his commander and didn't know how to respond. Finally he said, "Thank you for that, General. I appreciate it, doubly so because it comes from you." He paused and added with a smile, "Besides, sir, if General Patton was right, the brigade undoubtedly reflects your character as its commander-in-chief."

"Remember, Pancho, I said I could recognize the bullshitters, too." They both laughed, and Portero poured the coffee.

"Well let's get to work," said Carmody opening a briefcase. "I hand you this order requiring ALIB to cooperate with the government of Naranjeras in the matter of Permisos de Transito. I am sorry, Pancho. I tried to head this off with the chairman himself. At the time we talked, he understood our position and agreed with it. But he must have had a lot of pressure, because he called me last Friday to say that the State Department had persuaded the Secretary of Defense that the USA should cooperate with Figueroa as a gesture of goodwill. Call it realpolitik. Apparently the president himself has personally talked to the secretary general of HDO about their going along, too.

"The chairman might have been tougher, except that he regards this as a relatively minor matter which should not be allowed to sour relations between the HJRAF and Naranjeras. He told me also that your ambassador in Washington has assured State that, with this accommodation, the government will fully honor its treaty obligations not to interfere in ALIB operations."

"A minor matter, eh? Well it sounds like Figueroa has delivered a major ultimatum over this minor matter," Portero commented wryly.

"Read it however you like. That's the way the chairman gave it to me. It might make you feel a little better to know that the secretary general is not at all happy about this. I talked to him on the telephone, and he let me know in the strongest terms that he thought caving on this issue invited future problems. He also said the HDO would reluctantly accept the recommendation and acquiesce. He evidently is no fan of Figueroa. In fact, he sounded a lot like you in that regard." Carmody studied Portero for some reaction. "Are you going to fight me on this, Pancho?"

"No, sir. As I told you on the phone, I've been expecting this. I am disappointed, though. I'll comply with the order but it is a bad decision, one that we will all regret someday."

"Good, and I think you might be right. How do you want to implement this? I can make the announcement or you can. It might be better coming from you."

"We'll do it, sir. I want to think how to handle it. We'll get something out tomorrow, probably. What else do you have on your agenda?"

"First, I want to tell you why I have come to believe you may not be as paranoid about the Figueroa regime as I once thought you were. What I am about to tell you is sensitive stuff. It is EIA, Early Intel Alert, information and as such is intended for CINC-HJRAF intelligence data bank and not normally for dissemination, but I think it comes under the heading of 'need to know' for you. Do you understand me?"

"I do, General. You have my word it stays with me.

"Mind you it is by no means conclusive but there is reason to suspect our friend Figueroa may indeed have an agenda which is quite different from what he publically proclaims. Two things. First, reliable information has it that your friend Davidson has made secret visits to Havana twice during the last month.

"Second. It seems some of our counter intelligence people in Washington have been conducting close surveillance on a Lybian fellow who operates on a Tunisian passport as a journalist accredited to some African news service.

He apparently has been involved in some sinister stuff, because our people have been watching him for some time. In any case, it seems he has had several suspicious meetings with a young woman who, it turns out, is the secretary to your ambassador in Washington. On two occasions he handed her a briefcase which she carried back to the embassy.

"The Libyan is a confirmed bad guy which makes all his contacts suspect. The question is why is the Naranjeras ambassador's secretary making contacts with him? No one knows but it obviousally is business as as opposed to an affair of the heart, and his involvement raises a red flag which generated the EIA."

"Well the Libyans have been involved in this region before," Portero recalled. "They supported the Sandinistas in Nicaragua and have been involved with Fidel. They hate the United States since it trimmed their beard with that airstrike—when was it? In '85 or '86? Sometime in the mid-eighties, anyway. Possibly Ghadafi, despite his capitulation, or maybe some of his people, still harbors a grudge and would like to even the score. If Figueroa harbors the same feelings, as I believe he does, one might reasonably conclude that they are cooperating to do some mischief to the United States."

Carmody nodded in agreement. "If it is that kind of conspiracy and Figueroa is indeed in it, one has to wonder if the HJRAF might not be a target. If the hemispheric alliance could somehow be unraveled, it would be a blow to US prestige all over the world."

"Figueroa is in it. I'll bet on it, General." Portero was vehement. "This strengthens my belief that they want us neutralized, and it explains why they are harassing us. We're in their way. We stand between them and where they want to go. They're looking for ways to pull our teeth." He paused then added bitterly, "And now we are handing them a victory on the permiso question, which they will most certainly crow over publicly. Be damn sure of that."

Carmody nodded his agreement. "It isn't certain Figueroa can build or sustain popular support, though. You seem to have a good share of support of your own. It's going to be a PR battle for a while. He'll be ringing his bell over the permiso thing but he can only ring it for so long, and when he stops, you start ringing yours. You have friends in the press. Use them. We'll help where we can." Carmody was almost as animated as Portero.

"General, you're getting involved at the political level." Portero pointed out with a smile.

"Yes, I guess I am, and it's contrary to HJRAF policy. But if you are right about all this, it becomes a situation where I'm damned if I do and damned if I don't. I'd rather be hung for taking a stand than for doing nothing. I'm going to see the secretary general personally. He is a good man. I think he'll not only understand what is going on here, but he will support us. I am also going to talk to the chairman to be sure he sees the situation as we do. If I can get him to at least focus some of his intelligence assets on this area, we'll be ahead of the game."

Carmody paused. "By God, Pancho, I hope we are right about all this. I am getting as paranoid as I used to think you were."

Portero laughed. "Good, General, may I remind you, just because a man is paranoid, it doesn't necessarily mean that someone isn't out to get him. Anyway, it's really nice to have you on board."

Inwardly, he felt great relief. He had been worried about the possibility of a schism developing between them over the actions he had unilaterally taken. Now that Carmody was seeing things his way, he was less reluctant to tell him about the Advanced Tactics Board and the mission he had assigned to it. He also told him about the mission he had assigned the Recon Platoons, and he told him about the PNN spy planted in the training battalion and what they planned to do with him.

Carmody considered these revelations and thought to himself things were moving too fast. Finally he faced Portero and said with a sigh, "Well, I can't fault you for taking these actions, Pancho. I probably would have done the same thing in your shoes. But for now, let's just keep it all just between us, including your extra fuel supply. I see no use in you making mention of them in your official reports. That would just raise eyebrows and cause questions. However, I would like to be kept informed on all new developments, informally of course, nothing written. Okay?"

• • •

It was not easy to find just the right tone for the press release on his capitulation on the permisos matter. Portero was not a politician, but he knew his message had to be carefully balanced between the requirement for compliance with official policy and an unyielding dedication to principle in order to make the position of the ALIB perfectly clear—especially to the public which had supported its position. It was, he thought, an exercise in the use of Aesopian language in that it had to have a hidden message within the principal message.

He couldn't leave the impression the government had forced him to submit. That would have been construed as an admission that he had been wrong from the beginning, and would have undermined the goodwill of those people who believed he had done the right thing. Also he did not want people to believe he had been ordered to capitulate by General Carmody, because that would have played into the hands of those who sought to paint the ALIB as an organization dominated by foreign interests.

He had to convey an image of the brigade as independent of the government, but nevertheless loyal and dedicated to the welfare of the country. He and Lacerica struggled to find the best approach and finally took the problem to the ATB Group for its ideas. Later he admitted to Betsy that had been a mistake, since there were as many opinions voiced as there were people. The process took longer than he expected, and more patience than he thought he had, to make the staff understand what he wanted and why he wanted it. Finally after wrestling with the matter far too long, a document was produced which satisfied him. It read as follows:

> Headquarters Autonomous Light Infantry Brigade, Valle Escondido: Brigadier General Francisco Portero announced today that all ALIB vehicles would begin the use of transit tax documents in all instances when its vehicles engage in activities which could be handled by commercial transport. He indicated the change in policy had been made after consultation with General George M. Carmody, CINC-HJRAF, who advised that assurances had been given by representatives of the Figueroa administration to the Hemispheric Defense Organization that the principle of non-interference in Brigade activities would be strictly observed.
>
> Portero further indicated that he had not had personal communication with any representative of the government, but the reiteration, made to the HDO, of its commitment to the non-interference clause of the treaty had persuaded him to reverse his earlier decision not to use Permisos de Transito with ALIB vehicles. He also expressed his regret over the disagreement with the government in this matter and his satisfaction in the fact that the matter had finally been resolved. Viva Naranjeras!

• • •

While General Portero and his staff were wrestling with the wording of the press release, First Lieutenant Hank Ruedas, commander of the brigade Recon Platoon, was sitting quietly in the cab of his old pickup truck, parked on a narrow road high on the southern slope of El Cacique, the great volcano of Naranjeras, now extinct. He was in civilian clothes and his face was covered with a three-day stubble of blond whiskers. Next to him in the passenger seat was Sergeant Carlos "El Soldado" Campinas, similarly attired and also in need of a shave. Both men were patiently watching the activity in the shed area of a large citrus finca spread out in the valley below them.

"They are not crating fruit. That's for sure, Lieutenant."

"And they are not farm workers, either. They're military and they are taking instruction of some kind. Each of those groups must be a separate class. It looks like we have found at least some of the missing PNN. I wonder why they are way out here so far from civilization."

"Obviously they don't want to advertise whatever they are doing."

"Well, we'll keep an eye on them for a while. Why don't you relax? I'll take the first shift."

"Okay, sir. I think I'll scout around here to make sure we are alone. If you need me, hang this T-shirt on the antenna." Campinas climbed out of the truck and disappeared in the lush hillside forest behind the vehicle.

Ruedas remained in the cab, periodically checking the men in the camp below. He enjoyed what he was doing. He felt it was the kind of task the Recon Platoon was supposed to do, and he liked that. The fact that this was a real mission and not another exercise added zest. He reveled in his platoon leader assignment and often said he had the best job in the ALIB. As the commander of the brigade Recon Platoon, he had a certain independence not enjoyed by his counterparts in the assault or *tirador* platoons. For one thing, his company commander was usually too busy running the brigade headquarters Company and keeping the brigade staff happy to pay much attention to him. He thought of the B2, Colonel Banning, as being his real boss anyway. He was the man the platoon really worked for.

He saw movement in the camp below and lifted his binoculars. The groups dispersed and shortly reformed into squad-sized units with individual weapons and field packs. He counted twelve such units as they marched into the orchard to the south of shed area. Fifteen minutes later he spotted some of them emerging in extended formation onto a broad open savanna, where they began running squad assault exercises. He could clearly see the instructors gesticulating while the squads ran through their fire and movement drills.

"What have you got, Lieutenant?" Sergeant Campinas had returned.

"I have small unit assault training in that field beyond the orchard to the south. I guess that group instruction in the shed area was the theory and now they are putting it into practice. Those instructors look like they have done this before."

Campinas was studying the area through his own binoculars. "They sure do. Where did they come from? The PNN doesn't have that kind of expertise. And look, can you see their armbands? They look blue, maybe green. They're hard to make out, but all the instructors seem to have them."

Ruedas checked his watch and made an entry in his field notebook. "I'd like to get closer. I'm sure they are PNN, but we should confirm it. I estimate there are more than one hundred men down there, so that would be a company-sized unit. But what is the PNN doing training in infantry tactics? And who is training them? Let's take a look at the map."

They unfolded a road map of the area, oriented it, and working from what they believed was their location, tried to identify the area they were looking at below. It was a most unsatisfactory exercise. Road maps are a far cry from topographic maps which depict terrain features and show contour lines and grid lines, which help a trained observer locate his position. Road maps show only the major features: roads, rivers, towns, and some major land features. The map they were studying left a lot to be desired but it did show El Cacique, which helped them locate the general area they were observing. Having done that, they studied the road network and finally identified a couple of tertiary roads, either of which could be the road they were seeing leading to the finca from the west. The map also showed a small town, identified as La Rioja, located on the main road less than ten kilometers west of where they placed the finca.

"I guess we had better get into La Rioja and nose around. The question is how do we get there from here?" After further study, they determined they would have to backtrack about thirty kilometers to the first road that led down into the valley. It was apparent they would have to travel seventy or eighty kilometers over unimproved roads to reach La Rioja. They estimated the trip would require at least four hours' driving time. As it was late in the day, Ruedas decided to spend the night where they were and start early the next morning.

Campinas fired up their small Primus stove behind the truck and heated a can of black beans and rice, and water for tea. It was a beautiful evening and the light, cooling breeze blowing in their faces discouraged an assault by mosquitoes, which normally should have emerged by that time of the evening.

They relaxed and reminisced, as soldiers do, about units and people they had served with. Ruedas knew Campinas had been a professional boxer but did not know that he had been the WBF Lightweight Campion, a title he successfully defended for several years. He also learned that Campinas had served an enlistment in the US Army, where he became the All Army Lightweight Champion. His success there had led to his professional career, and accounted for his sobriquet, "El Soldado." Ruedas himself had been on the boxing team in college and their common interest helped pass the hours, and it reinforced the bond developing between them.

Campinas learned that Ruedas was Costa Rican by birth but was a naturalized citizen of the United States, where he had lived and been educated. He learned that Ruedas had received an ROTC commission as an infantry officer, had completed the Infantry Basic School at Fort Benning and jump school at Fort Bragg, that he'd been married but lost his wife in a car accident, and finally had escaped his grief by volunteering to serve with the ALIB .

They talked about the brigade, agreeing that it was "the best outfit" either had served with, and about General Portero and duty in the Recon Platoon. "You know, Lieutenant, recon work is about the best duty a man can get in the military. In fact, it would be perfect if we didn't have to pull honor guard detail every time some big shot comes in."

"I thought you liked that duty. You volunteer almost every time we have it. Why, if you don't like it?"

"I don't know, sir. I just think it should be done right and some of the other squad leaders don't care so much. As you always say, the honor guard is the first impression visitors have of the outfit, so we ought to make it a good one."

Campinas's remark pleased Ruedas, who had always admired the little sergeant for his professionalism and leadership qualities. His appreciation had grown as he had come to know him better as his partner on Recon Team One.

They awoke at first light, drank some tea, made a final check of the training camp below to find the men there lining up, mess kits in hand, for their morning meal. They packed up, and just before they departed, Ruedas used his GPS unit to determine their exact location. He entered the latitude and longitude in his field book, and using his field compass, he determined the bearing to the finca training camp, which he also recorded. That done, they turned the truck around and returned in the direction they had come.

The journey to La Rioja took longer than they expected. The road they used into the valley turned out to be no more than a cart path which traversed several small rivers. They forded them cautiously with Campinas walking ahead of the truck, making sure there were no deep holes to fall into. The coordinates of each ford were carefully recorded in Ruedas' field book. A light rain followed them part of the way, turning the road slippery, which slowed their progress further. They breathed a sigh of relief when they finally reached the paved main road and turned south toward La Rioja.

They arrived in the middle of the afternoon, tired, dirty, and hungry. Ruedas filled the tank and checked the oil at the town's only petrol station, which sported a freshly painted Exxon logo. He inquired about places to eat and was told that the cantina by the hotel across the street served the best food. "My wife is the cook there and she knows her business. Just look at me," the station owner said, laughing and hefting his ample belly with both hands.

They took a ground floor room in the somewhat dilapidated two-story hotel, using their correct names but writing *cafetero*, their cover story, in the box marked *ocupacion* on the hotel register. The cantina adjoined the hotel and could be entered through the small lobby. When they found the kitchen did not open until six o'clock, they drank a beer before retreating to their room. They took turns in the in the men's *baño* down the hall, which in addition to a toilet housed a large, not too clean bathtub which happily produced quantities of hot water. They put on clean clothes and while Campinas slept, Ruedas used the pay telephone at the Exxon station to dial the duty desk in the B2 office of the brigade.

His message was short and cryptic. "This is Team One. Current location: La Rioja, Highway Three, south of El Cacique.

Reference the missing peter-nancy-nancy. Located estimated company size unit engaged in small unit training ten to fifteen clicks east. Will confirm. Orders?" The duty sergeant had no orders for Team One, so Ruedas terminated the call and returned to the hotel to rest.

At six thirty they were well into their meal when an unmarked green van stopped in front of the cantina. Four men in green camouflage uniforms without insignia, except for blue arm-bands sewn to their right sleeves, entered through the street door. Ruedas, who was facing the entrance, caught Campinas' eye and pointed with his fork. Campinas turned to inspect the newcomers and returned to his food, signaling his interest with a raised eyebrow.

"*Buen provecho*. Enjoy your meal," the leader of the group said as he passed their table en route to the bar. He was a large, muscular man with graying hair cut short in military style.

"Thank you, sir. *Buenas tardes*," Ruedas responded politely.

The men seated themselves at the bar and ordered beer. Team One quietly studied them as they enjoyed their main course. There was no doubt that they were military men. Their bearing, physical condition, haircuts and self-assurance were unmistakable. The large man was clearly the leader, and the others took seats on either side of him. The man to his right was short and stocky, and unsmiling. He had very large hands, and his sleeves were rolled up to reveal heavily muscled arms. His voice was loud as he ordered from the bartender, and his manner was challenging and arrogant. *There is a first class son of a bitch. A man to be careful with*, Ruedas thought to himself.

The other two men were less threatening. The one to gray hair's left was tall and slender with broad, muscular shoulders. He wore a close-cropped blond beard and glasses, which gave him a professorial look. The fourth man was younger and clearly the junior as he showed considerable deference to the others.

The four had been thirsty and quickly ordered another round. They relaxed as they drank their second beers. At first their conversation was subdued, punctuated by occasional laughter as they exchanged jokes and stories. After several more rounds, their laughter became more raucous and their voices louder. Team One began to hear pieces of their conversation, and they recognized cadences and inflections of speech which definitely were not Naranjero.

When the girl came to remove their dishes, Ruedas quietly asked, "Cubanos?"

She hesitated a moment, looking at him, then answered in almost a whisper, "Yes, sir. They're staying in the hotel."

"How long have they been here?"

"About a month, I think. I'm not sure."

"What are they doing here? Do you know?"

"I don't know, but many say they are working with soldiers in a finca at the foot of the volcano. Can I bring you anything else?" she said in a louder voice.

They ordered flan with candied mangos, and coffee. "Those guys are some of the drill instructors we were watching, Lieutenant. What the hell are Cubans doing here training PNN, or whoever they are?" Campinas spoke in a near whisper, his concern showing in his expression.

Ruedas started to answer but was interrupted when "Gray Hair" stood up and announced that he was going to clean up before eating dinner. He smiled at them as he passed their table, looking from Ruedas to Campinas, then quickly at Campinas again in a classic double take. He paused, backed a step and said, "Don't I know you? You look so familiar. Haven't we met?"

"I don't think so, sir. I am not from this district. In fact, this is the first time I've been here," Campinas replied.

"I'm not from here either, so it must have been somewhere else. I know I know you. Have you been in Nicaragua? Cuba?"

"I have never been either place. I'm sorry. I must look like someone else."

"Perhaps that's it. My name is Molina, Xavier Molina, at your orders."

Campinas stood and took his hand. "Carlos Campinas, at your service. May I introduce my friend, Hank Ruedas."

"A pleasure, Señor Ruedas." They shook hands.

"The pleasure is mine, señor. Will you join us?"

"Thank you. I am on my way to a hot bath. Are you staying in the hotel? Then perhaps I'll see you later. With your permission, then." He bowed slightly and departed.

"He knows you, Carlos." Ruedas said, showing concern when Molina had gone.

"Yes. This used to happen to me all the time. He knows me from boxing. He must be a fight fan."

"What if he remembers? Can he link you with the brigade?"

"I doubt it. No one knows where I am. It's been six years. People forget."

They finished their dessert and lingered over coffee. The three remaining Cubans got louder as they continued to drink. "Tough Guy," the stocky one, kept glancing over at them and finally caught Ruedas' eye. He waved them over. "Join us for a drink, señores. We want to welcome you to La Rioja. We don't see many strangers here in this damned backwater."

Ruedas noticed the bartender's frown of disapproval behind Tough Guy. "Thank you, señor. Perhaps later, when we have finished our coffee."

Tough Guy frowned and started to speak when Molina returned, dressed in khaki slacks and a guayabera. He went directly to Campinas with a big grin on his face. "It finally came to me who you are. Carlos 'El Soldado' Campinas, lightweight champion of the world! I knew I had seen you before. I've watched you fight several times."

He turned to his companions. "Do you know who this is? A real celebrity. El Soldado, one of the greatest lightweights who has ever fought." Then back to Campinas. "Come meet my friends. Join us, Señor Ruedas, please."

They arose and joined the others at the bar. "What will you have friends? Bartender give these gentlemen a drink."

Ruedas ordered a beer. Campinas, an innocent expression on his face, said, "Give me a Cuba Libre anytime."

There was a silence. Gallo glared at Campinas. Molina broke the tension. "Fine. I'll have one too."

"We call those drinks *Capitalistas* in Cuba." There was clear challenge in Gallo's manner. "So you were a fighter. Where did you fight?"

"All over. Mostly in North America. A couple of times in Mexico. Once in Italy."

"He was a great fighter," said Molina. "He was fast and could take a punch. I used to love to watch you. I was on the Cuban team for a while, and we used to study your films. You had a great defense. I was a heavyweight. Pretty good, too, except that I could never get past Stevenson."

"Teofilo Stevenson. I remember him well. He was the best in the world for a while. Wasn't he Olympic champion twice?" Ruedas' enthusiasm for the sport began to show.

"Three times, as I recall."

"You are North Americans?" Gallo made it sound dirty.

"No. I am a Tico, born in Cartago, but I have spent time in the United States," Ruedas declared calmly.

"I am Naranjero, Señor." Campinas said. There was an edge in his voice.

"Why do they call you 'El Soldado'?"

"Because I served in the US Army for a time. That's where I learned to box."

"You must have been sorry about that. Serving in their army, I mean," Gallo probed.

"As a matter of fact, I enjoyed my time in their army. They treated me okay, and I learned a lot. They gave me my opportunity," Campinas responded calmly.

"How a good Latino could do that, I don't understand."

"There are a lot of Latinos in their army. They pay well and they treat you well."

"Putos. Latino maricon putos, who will do anything for money." Gallo's eyes narrowed and his voice hardened.

Both Ruedas and Campinas set their drinks aside and began to stand up. Molina jumped in. "Take it easy, Hernan. These men are my guests. Please show them respect."

"Sorry, Colonel, but I don't like Yankee *putos*."

"Enough, Gallo! Don't say anymore. Do you understand me?" Molina's joviality had disappeared. He was angry, menacing, clearly a man who was capable of backing his authority with physical action. Gallo was silent and seemed to diminish in stature, his belligerency gone. After a moment Molina turned back to Ruedas and Campinas, and he was smiling again.

"Sorry, gentlemen. My friend has had a hard day, and the beer has affected him. Please forgive his rudeness."

"We understand," said Ruedas, who was more interested in learning about these men than brawling with tough guy, Gallo. "But you have piqued my curiosity. What are Cubans doing in Naranjeras, so far from civilization?"

Molina smiled. "First, we're not all Cubans. Simoni here is Naranjero. He is working with us. We are here on a mission for your government. It's all quite legitimate, I assure you. But we have been asked not to talk about it. As you have no doubt surmised, we are military advisers to your army. My belligerent friend here is Major Gallo, and this is Major Serra, and Captain Simoni of your army. Now you know about us. What about you?"

"Well, there is not much to tell about us. We represent a coffee producer. We are on a scouting mission, looking for potential plantation sites. We plan to look at some land east of La Rioja tomorrow. Up toward El Cacique. We are told there is some promising land up there." Ruedas watched for a reaction, but there was nothing beyond a quick exchange of looks between Molina and Serra. *These guys are poker players,* he thought.

"That sounds like interesting work. We ourselves are working east of here. I would like to invite you to accompany us tomorrow, but unfortunately your government has closed the area to unauthorized personnel. It's a pity because it is really beautiful country. May I suggest you check at the local police post before you leave in the morning? They can tell you which areas are restricted and which are open."

"Thank you for the suggestion. We'll do that. And now let us reciprocate. Permit us to buy a round."

The drinks came. They touched glasses except with Gallo, who didn't offer his. Ruedas caught Campinas' eye and turned to Captain Simoni. "Do you belong to that infantry unit?"

"Ah, yes. I am with…" Simoni's voice trailed off. "Ah, which infantry unit are you referring to?"

"The one up east, this side of Mesona somewhere. Is there more than one?"

"Oh, you mean the ALIB at Valle Escondido. No, I'm not with them, but I have worked with them in the past. They are part of our army, but they're attached to the Hemispheric Defense Force. The government doesn't really control them."

Ruedas couldn't resist. "Is it true that they are a great unit?"

"I guess they're pretty good, yes."

"So what unit are you with?"

"Ah, it is a new unit. Still in training, as a matter of fact." Simoni didn't like the direction the conversation was taking. "But I've always been fascinated with the coffee business. How long have you been involved with it?"

"Most of my life, except when I was in the United States. I was born on a coffee finca as a matter of fact, near Cartago, so I guess you can say it's in my blood."

Their conversation drifted to other subjects. After a suitable period, Ruedas and Campinas rose, shook hands all around, and said good night. As they walked into the hotel, they heard Gallo's growl and Molina's angry voice: "Gallo, shut up."

"I don't like that surly son of a bitch," Campinas said as they approached their room.

"Nor do I, Carlos. I thought for a moment we were going to get into it with him. But between his bullshit and your being a famous celebrity, we picked up some information they probably would rather we didn't have. It turned out to be a very worthwhile evening for Team One."

They departed La Rioja early the following morning heading not east, but north toward Valle Escondido and home.

CHAPTER 6

The ATB had a full agenda at its weekly meeting, but the focus of interest was on Recon Team One's report of its discovery in La Rioja. General Portero was pleased with the initiative shown by Lieutenant Ruedas and ordered a letter of commendation be presented to him and included in his personnel file. He would like to have made a public acknowledgment of Team One's aggressive reconnaissance as an example to the other teams but would not for security reasons.

Colonel Banning had forwarded a classified summary of the Ruedas report to the G2 HJRAF, with a specific request for background information on the Cuban officers, Molina, Gallo and Serra, but no information had yet been received.

The name Simoni had a familiar ring, and Colonel Soto remembered that a Lieutenant Simoni had been the officer in charge of the Tuxla police post when the ALIB vehicles had been detained in the first permiso incident. Banning would attempt to ascertain whether or not it was the same man.

A good deal of time was spent speculating on the nature of the training camp Team One had found. Banning summed it all up. "We are estimating that over one thousand PNN are unaccounted for. Ruedas has found a hundred or so apparently undergoing small unit tactical training at that isolated finca. So we have some solid information, but it raises more questions than answers. Is it a company-sized unit in training? If so, why is it so isolated? Is it some sort of special unit? If so, what? Why are Cuban military conducting the training? Is it some sort of special school? Whatever it is, it is important enough to have a colonel and two majors assigned to it."

After some discussion they concluded that the finca camp was not engaged in ordinary infantry training but had a special training mission, which could not be identified based upon the intelligence currently available. They agreed to set a priority on gathering additional information about the operation. A careful discussion ensued as to how. "Send Team One back in," Soto insisted. "They know the setup and have contact with the Cubans. Let them pick up where they left off."

Banning showed real concern for the safety of his Recon team. "I would not hesitate to do that except for the fact that they have identified Campinas and if they dig, they may be able to tie him to the brigade. If they do, we would be putting the team in real danger. If they regard us as the enemy, they will regard Ruedas and Campinas as spies."

Soto countered. "On the other hand, the fact that they know Campinas is a former world champion, may give him some cover. It may never occur to them that he might be with the brigade. They might simply accept him at face value as a cafetero, and let it go at that. As a celebrity, he has some entertainment value for them."

Colonel Ochoa nodded his agreement with Soto's reasoning. "The fact that Campinas is a celebrity might even help gain their confidence. Also, it might not hurt if Campinas and Ruedas, too, for that matter, showed a little sympathy for the government. That could get them even closer."

"That would be a pretty tricky thing to do, don't you think, since both of them have already indicated to the Cubans that they were tolerant and even supportive of the United States? Apparently they almost got into a fight with Gallo over that point. Showing sympathy for the Figueroa regime would hardly be consistent with that." The B2 was adamant.

"Well, how do we get the information we need then?" Ochoa asked. "I agree with Colonel Soto. Team One is our best bet. Besides, we are not at war. Even if they are found out, what could happen to them?"

"They could be killed, for one thing! I agree they probably wouldn't at this point, but I hate putting two good men in danger." Banning looked at Portero for guidance.

"Well, gentlemen, I understand how Colonel Banning feels. I certainly don't want to take chances with any of our people, either. On the other hand, Team One has an in, and it would be logical to use them. I wouldn't hesitate if they had not recognized Campinas. The fact that they did adds a risk factor. I won't order them back down there.

"However, they probably can assess the risk better than we can, having been there." He turned to his intelligence officer. "Why don't you talk to them both and ask them what they think. If they don't want to go back, that's the end of it. If they think it is okay and are willing to take another shot, let them go. But be sure they understand we think there is risk in going back and that there is no pressure on them to volunteer. Understand? It's their best judgment."

The board's attention then turned to the media coverage of the press release on the change of policy on permisos. The three principal newspapers reacted predictably.

La Prensa, as expected, was supportive. Its headline read: "Portero Wins His Point." The front page story focused on the government's agreement not to interfere further with ALIB operations and indicated that Portero's concession on the use of permisos was a generous gesture which demonstrated his goodwill and "his overriding respect for the nation."

Vida Nacional played the story straight, but it also carried Ramon Sanchez Avila's column, "La Opinion Mia," in which he wrote:

> The controversy over the permisos de transito has ended happily, and that is good for the country. It has been a very divisive issue which would have further exacerbated tension between the government and the ALIB, and perhaps even the Hemispheric Defense Organization.
>
> By now, it may be known that I am no fan of international alliances, yet it would not have benefited the image of our nation had this controversy grown. I therefore applaud its resolution. There will be claims of victory by both sides. In reality, neither deserves any accolade, as the matter never should have seen the light of day.
>
> Given the terms of the treaty under which the ALIB was formed, in the opinion of this reporter, the government overstepped in requiring the travel documents of the ALIB. On the other hand, it is also the opinion of this reporter that General Portero seriously exacerbated the situation by his public defiance. It would have been better for all had he chosen quiet negotiations.
>
> That would not have been his way, however. I had the pleasure of dining with the general and found him to be an honest, plain speaking and direct gentleman, who is clearly dedicated to his profession and his country. Although I believe he chose the wrong course, I understand the point he tried to make in resisting the government order. The fact that we hold different perspectives does not lessen the respect I hold for him. It takes all kinds of people to make a nation and though we may disagree on several counts, I believe Francisco Portero is a worthy man and a dedicated Naranjero.

Portero was not displeased with the column. He told the ATB, "He may be not quite a friend, but clearly he is not an enemy, and that's good. Lacerica believes he is sending us a signal that he has come around to our view. I think that may be a stretch, but Don Ramon has not hurt us in this column."

El Diario, typically, took an anti-ALIB view. Its headline declared:

"Portero Capitulates on Permisos." The article went on to extol the government's handling of the crisis through diplomatic channels and declare the people to be the "big winners." The ATB members were inured to the editorial bias of El Diario and reacted dispassionately. However a paragraph buried toward the end of the article caught their full attention. It read:

> General Francisco Portero announced yesterday that ALIB vehicles would begin utilizing Permisos de Transito in compliance with government demands. The announcement came as a surprise, as the impulsive young commander had been adamant in his refusal to use the documents. The concession is seen as a victory for the Figueroa administration, which has been engaged in a bitter dispute over the matter. The minister of the interior, in an exclusive interview with this reporter, declared, "We left General Portero no choice but to comply our order.
>
> It is the opinion of many who follow the affairs of the ALIB that Portero was ordered to comply in this matter by the commander in chief of the HJRAF. The fact that General Carmody made a two-day visit to Valle Escondido just prior to Portero's capitulation gives rise to this speculation. Some feel this is further evidence that control of the ALIB rests more with foreign than national interests.

"How did the paper know General Carmody was here?" Portero wanted to know. "That visit was supposed to be confidential. There was no press release on his visit, and Lacerica has had no verbal contact with the press about it. Did any of you talk to anyone outside of the brigade about Carmody being here?"

All denied they had.

Banning volunteered. "It must have been our friend, Rubio, then. We have been watching him. He has not left the post, except he goes to town every Saturday afternoon. He has a fixed routine, first a haircut and then a beer at La Cocina. He obviously has confederates because he has no way to get information out by himself, insofar as we know."

Banning paused to let his words sink in. "I'll bet on the barber. She is new in town and is quite a dish. She has already lured a number of our soldiers away from their company barbers, and if she is clever, she'll be probing for information out of all of them—not just Rubio. She may be his contact. We are looking for a way to test her. All we need is a traceable story we can drop on her, then see where it surfaces."

• • •

Molly Moran was a happy woman. She was back in harness again, and it felt good. Out of the blue an old friend, a colleague from the eighties, whom she had not seen for twelve years, had invited her to a meeting in the old CISPES office in the Hueman Center on the campus of the University Of Minnesota.

She had accepted without hesitation and was delighted to renew her acquaintance with many people she had worked with during the Central America crisis. In fact, there were so many familiar faces there, she at first assumed that CISPES had been resurrected. The thought thrilled her because it offered her the chance to get back to work on something she could get her teeth into.

She had felt old and useless the last few years, despite the fact she had occupied her time with a number of causes she believed were important: animal rights, nuclear power plants, several environmental crusades, and helping keep Women Against Military Madness alive. These activities gave her something to do but the thrill she had felt working with the Committee in Solidarity with the People of El Salvador was lacking. She had loved that work because it took her to the "front lines," to Nicaragua, El Salvador, and Guatemala. She had loved leading fact-finding tours, organizing protests, and speaking on college campuses, in schools, churches, and women's clubs.

Her disappointment at finding CISPES had not been resurrected was short-lived when it was announced that a new organization was being formed which was to be called Free Latin America from U.S. Hegemony, with the working acronym, FLUSH. She learned that the objective of the new organization was to build grass roots pressure to end US military involvement in Latin America, and that it would adopt the same techniques used by CISPES in the eighties in pursuit of that goal.

It was unexpected and very exciting news for Molly. She now had another mission she could believe in with all her heart. The leaders had asked her to help organize and train volunteers! Once again her life had purpose. She felt like a young girl, despite her seventy-two years. She couldn't wait to get to work.

• • •

The Supreme Council of Naranjeras met formally every two weeks to review progress and problems of the regime. These were normally formal affairs, with each department allotted time to brief the council on its operations. Departmental briefings had become competitive with each seeking to out-perform the others in its presentation, the purpose being to convince the president and his top deputies of the competence of the department leaders. Each briefing was accompanied by briefing books, charts, and graphs designed to impress the audience with the importance of whatever the project being presented was. In isolation it was interesting stuff, but the sheer volume of the material and the speed in which it arrived was overpowering and stultifying. By the end of the day, the council members were tired, having been overdosed with information, which the more conscientious among them would attempt to sort out during the days following the meeting.

Colonel Edson Davidson, commander of the National Police forces and a member of the council, made an effort to attend as many of the departmental briefings as he could, not that he was particularly interested in many of the departments' operations. He attended them to keep up with the ebb and flow of internal politics, carefully marking changes in the political winds. He recognized that he needed allies on the council. He knew most members placed a low priority on military matters and sought to offset that disadvantage by feigning interest in the other departments and supporting a beleaguered colleague when he could, hoping they might reciprocate at times he needed support.

On this day, he was particularly attentive and supportive because he expected criticism when the council retreated into executive session. He had overspent his budget significantly and though he was well prepared with justifications, he was concerned, especially since the minister of finance, who was not a council member, had announced, much to the annoyance of President Figueroa, that government expenditures had not only been exceeding revenues, but were growing at an accelerating rate.

He need not have been concerned, however, because the main topic of discussion during the executive session, though focused on the revenue shortfall, was not how to reduce expenditures but how revenues might be increased.

Mario Fox, President of the National Assembly, the fifth member of the junta which engineered the overthrow of the Juan Moreno government, and the canniest politician and, after the president, the most ardent anti-US member of the group, dominated the session with a proposal guaranteed to redress the revenue shortfall problem.

His proposal centered on the formation of a National Marketing Board which would assume responsibility for exporting the five commodities which accounted for sixty percent of

Naranjera foreign revenues, namely: citrus fruit and juice concentrates, bananas, hides and leather products, prefabricated wood products, and premium coffee beans. The government under the Fox plan would purchase the products at seventy percent of the export market value and resell them at full value. According to his projections, there would remain a ten to fifteen percent profit after handling charges and selling expenses, which would flow into the national treasury.

Interior was immediately skeptical. "The same scheme was tried in El Salvador in the eighties. As I recall, in order to make it work they had to nationalize the banks and impose exchange controls. The net result was that they destroyed one of the best banking systems in Central America and, in the end, the whole scheme failed. There was no incentive. The producers quit producing and the bureaucrats on the Export Board proved they didn't know how to market."

Fox agreed. "That's true, and that was not the only mistake the Salvadorans made. The whole thing coincided with a misguided land reform scheme which, in essence, took the producers out of the picture and gave the responsibility for production to the workers. It was a disaster, and it was stupid. Incidentally, the US government was complicit in developing the plan. It was the Carter administration, as I recall.

"In any case," he continued, "we won't make the same mistakes. No land reform because we need the producers' know-how, and no nationalization of our banks. We won't nationalize the banks because first, we don't know how to run them, and second, to do so would invite severe public criticism, which could bring on a political crisis we could not handle. Instead, we make the banks our allies by inviting their participation. We give them the opportunity to support the operations of the National Marketing Board via short- and long-term loans which we allocate among them according to their resources, and we pay them higher than market interest rates. I have never known a banker to turn his back on an opportunity to make a profit. They may not like us, but they will deal with us if they profit by doing it. Hell, most of them would deal with the devil himself if they could make a profit."

"But how do we insure the producers sell their products to the government board? What's to stop them from running their businesses as usual? Doing their own marketing?" Interior wanted to know.

"We make it profitable to sell to us. We impose an export tax on all targeted goods that are not exported through the Marketing Board. That tax will be high enough to elevate their marketing costs to the point where it will be more profitable to sell to us. The tax will be assessed and collected at the port before the products are loaded. Remember, we have a considerable geographical advantage in enforcing this system because we only have one deep water port and one international airport through which these commodities can be shipped. As long as we physically control Puerto Hondo and the Aeropuerto Internacional, we can control exports.

"There will be a negative reaction initially," Fox continued. "However, I am sure we can persuade a majority in the assembly to go along, mostly on the basis that it will be the least painful way of redressing the imbalance in our national budget.

"Once we have that vote, we can mount a program to convince the public that we are acting in the best interests of the nation. That will leave the ranchers and other producers isolated, and they will have to cooperate with us. If we handle the new system efficiently, they may even come to like it since it will relieve them of the problems and expense of financing and marketing their products. I believe a case can be made that they will realize greater profits selling to us at seventy percent than they have been earning at full price. At any rate, you can be sure that will be the idea we sell to the assembly."

Figueroa looked at each of the council members. "This all sounds good in theory, gentlemen, but we must all clearly understand that its implementation will generate big problems for us, no matter how well we rationalize it domestically and to the world. It will be seen as another step away from democratic capitalism and toward a controlled economy. It is a risk we must be prepared to take, however, because it will solve our deficit problem, at least temporarily. More importantly, it will take us a step closer to achieving the objectives of our *golpe*." He paused. "Mario and his people have done a lot of work on this. What are your thoughts?"

The discussion which followed concerned not so much the substance of the proposal but the political consequences of initiating it. All agreed that establishing the Marketing Board would advance the junta's agenda as well as help solve the deficit problem, but Interior urged caution in taking so radical a departure from the traditions of the country. He feared a popular reaction which could even sweep them from power.

"I would be less worried about this if we were sure we had the means of controlling massive demonstrations by the people. But Pancho Portero and the ALIB are still out there and according to my polling, their popularity is growing. We didn't gain much advantage as a result of our victory on the permiso matter, although we did demonstrate we have some clout with the HDO. But the ALIB is still a force to be reckoned with. We still haven't the power to deal with it, do we?"

"As of now, we do not," agreed the president, "But that situation is changing. We'll have a report from Colonel Davidson in a moment. He is making good progress in his PNN retraining project, and I understand he has other news for us as well. But I want to emphasize that there are other ways, better ways perhaps, of dealing with the ALIB than direct military confrontation. The foreign ministry has been working on one which shows some promise."

He turned to the foreign minister. "Please give us a quick overview of your Washington project, Tercio."

Tercio Ortega liked the limelight, and he made the most of the opportunity. He cleared his throat and looked at each one in turn. "Well, friends, as we all have learned from recent history, often the key to success in dealing with the United States of America —and when we deal with the ALIB, we are dealing indirectly with the United States—is to bring their Congress into the equation. Remember the North American-Vietnamese war. The Vietnamese could not beat the Americans militarily on the field of battle. Yet they won the war. How did they do it?" He paused for effect. "They did it by taking advantage of the popular protests against the war. It became a political matter which they were smart enough to exploit. The US Congress was drawn into the battle, and that brought pressure on the president and his advisors. The rest is history. The North Americans withdrew and gave the victory to the Vietnamese.

"Again, during the period of the conflict in Central America during the eighties, their congress was co-opted by grass roots political pressure. The result? US support in countering revolutionary forces in Nicaragua, El Salvador, and Guatemala was severely limited. Hence, the fighting in those countries was protracted far beyond what it would have been had the US leadership been free to provide full support.

"Also in the Grenada action, as short as it was, the grass roots anti-war forces were able to activate certain members of the US Congress into public criticism of the US Grenada policy.

"As a result of these grass roots pressures, US presidents and other leaders have become very sensitive about over-involvement in foreign military excursions. For example, many believe that had it not been for that sensitivity, President George Bush might well have sent his armies into Baghdad at the conclusion of the Gulf War.

"I take the time to review these facts to provide you with the background for what our president referred to as my "Washington Project." The fact is that in North America there remains a small but dedicated and experienced cadre of people who played a part in catalyzing the grass roots protest movements I have mentioned. They are progressive people who see the weaknesses of the US political system and who have the courage to oppose it when given a cause. That's all they need, a worthy cause, and some financing.

"We have given them both the cause and money, with the help of friends, so our Washington Project is underway as we speak." Again he paused, relishing the drama of the moment. He continued with a lowered voice. "Our message to the North American people is 'Get our soldiers out of Latin America.' It is an appeal designed to motivate those with isolationist tendencies, a segment of their libertarian population, their anti-war activists, and also those who are disaffected from their government, leftists and instinctive rebels, who only need a cause around which they can rally.

"Gentlemen, if we package the message skillfully enough, it will become a movement which will spread to the general population and eventually bring pressure on their Congress. History tells us we can exercise great influence through a motivated, small, disciplined, well-funded minority. It is really a remarkable thing. That is what we are undertaking to do. Are you with me till now?"

They all nodded agreement. Some were smiling. Ortega continued. "Our ultimate objective is to pressure Congress into forcing the government to end its support of the ALIB in Naranjeras, and secondarily, of the other HJRAF units in all the HDO countries. To this end we are creating, with the help of some veteran grass roots peace activists in the United States and the financial support of an ally in North Africa, whom it is better to leave unnamed for the moment, an organization we hope will be the catalyst of a new protest movement. That organization is being called the 'Free Latino America from United States Hegemony' committee. A rather ponderous name, but it lends itself nicely to the acronym, FLUSH. As you perhaps know from watching CNN, the North Americans love acronyms in their political games. This one has an English meaning most appropriate to our cause. Keep watching CNN, my friends. You should be hearing about FLUSH. It will be well-funded, and we hope that through it we can generate a full-blown public debate, both in North America and here at home, on the efficacy of US policy as it pertains to support of the HJRAF. That, gentlemen, is our Washington Project. Any questions, my friends?"

Figueroa wanted the council to understand the full significance of Ortega's undertaking. "The greater success we have with this project, the less likely we will be forced into a major confrontation with the ALIB. Also, and perhaps even more important, the greater our success with this project, the more public attention will be diverted away from our reorganization of the government." They nodded their understanding.

"This is really a new kind of political warfare in which we are engaging. It equalizes the battlefield for the small country contesting with a giant. We paralyze them politically. That is to say that we push them into an absorbing, emotional, domestic debate about their national policies, which denies them a clear cut consensus for action. That result of dividing their political leaders is it paralyzes their ability to act. While they fight among themselves, we are free to pursue our interests, including de-fanging Portero and the ALIB without outside interference."

After a moment he turned to Edson Davidson. "Some kind of confrontation with the ALIB is probably inevitable. When it comes, we must be strong enough to win it. In a previous meeting, we agreed our armed forces must be strong enough to limit Portero's ability to maneuver. We must be able to isolate him and allow attrition to wear him down to a manageable size.

Remember, we don't have to be able to defeat him in an all-out battle early when he is at full strength. We only have to deny him the means of re-supplying himself. We are not yet strong enough to do that, but we are making progress. Colonel Davidson, please bring us up to date on what we are doing to build our military capabilities."

Davidson rose to arrange some covered charts on an easel which stood near the foot of the conference table. "As you already know, we are in the process of retraining about half of the PNN forces as infantry troops. That involves about fifteen hundred people, which will be the core for three battalions. With augmentation by new recruits, we expect this force to almost double. About half of the weapons and ammunition we need are in hand. The balance is expected to arrive during the next two months. We have obtained these supplies at a very favorable price through the good auspices of a North African power which has an interest in inflicting damage on the U.S. We are now in the process of forming these battalions into a brigade which will be named the Second Naranjeras Infantry Brigade. Now it is going to take time to train and organize these units to the point they are capable of taking on Portero's force. I make a special point of this because I know some here will grow impatient. There will be a high cost in building and maintaining these units, but if we commit them before they can do the job, we'll not only lose our investment in them—we will fail in our mission." He looked each member in the eye to make sure they understood.

"In addition to the Second Brigade, we are forming a Cazador Battalion which will be specially trained to track and kill guerrilla-type units. I expect Portero will resort to guerrilla warfare as attrition whittles down the ALIB. This Cazador unit will be small, only about three hundred strong, heavily armed, and designed to operate independently.

"We are also considering forming an international volunteer unit, possibly of battalion size. It seems there are in the world a large number of mercenary soldiers who would like employment and could be recruited to our cause. The problem is most of them demand large salaries which we cannot afford. However some come from less prosperous nations, and we may still be able to put such a unit together. There may be some who may be motivated by an ideological bias which is potentially favorable to us, such as former Sandinistas, FMLN fighters, and Cuban ex-military, who might be in our price range. So we are taking a close look at that possibility."

The president of the assembly was amazed by what he was hearing. "Sorry, Colonel, but I am astounded. How are you training all these people? Where are you training them? I haven't heard a whisper about any of this."

"Oh there have been whispers, Doctor Fox, but generally speaking, we have managed to keep these activities pretty quiet. Most of this activity has taken place on Isla Grande, where we have the largest contingent. We maintain secrecy mainly by restricting the troops and its small local population to the island. We can't do that forever, of course. Only until the troops are ready. We also have a smaller training camp at an isolated finca near La Rioja. That is currently a school for small unit leaders, but we plan to train the Cazador Battalion in the same area. All this is very confidential information, of course. We do not want Portero to learn about these efforts, although he may already know about the La Rioja operation."

Figueroa sat forward. "Really? How could he know?"

"We think he might have sent out some snoopers to find out what we are up to. During my meeting with Colonel Molina last week, he happened to mention he had met Carlos Campinas, the boxer, in La Rioja. He and another fellow were supposed to be scouting for coffee land in the area. His mention of Campinas jogged my memory. I seemed to recall that he at one time was with the ALIB. I have been trying to check, so far with no results. In any case I told Molina about the possibility, in the event they should return to the area."

"Any snoopers around Isla Grande?"

"No, sir. At least not that I have heard about. But our people have been alerted to the possibility. We're keeping an eye out for suspicious people."

When Davidson was satisfied the president had no more questions, he turned back to Fox and continued to answer his questions. "As to how we are training these units, we have some outside help. We do not have a sufficient number of infantry-trained officers in the PNN to get the job done, so we appealed for help through contacts abroad. We are fortunate that the Cubans have responded. They have sent us a forty-five man team of training specialists who have experience in this sort of thing. The head of their team is Colonel Xavier Molina, whom I mentioned. He has the reputation of being among the best in anti-guerrilla warfare. He is an excellent man, and we are discussing the possibility of giving him command of the Second Brigade. Technically, we will have to make him a citizen of Naranjeras to do that, but I assume that can be done."

"Of course it can be done," said the president, "But have you finished with your review of the new units?"

"Not quite." Davidson removed the cover from his chart. "Here you see a summary of the units I have described. This one I have not mentioned." He pointed to representation on the chart of a battalion-sized unit, which was identified with the symbol used for armored infantry units. "When the infantry units I have discussed have completed their training and have been shaken down in the field, we will have a force marginally stronger than the ALIB. If we can field the International Volunteer Battalion or the Second Cazador Battalion or both, we will definitely have the maneuver advantage. In addition, we will still have almost nineteen hundred men in the PNN police units who will be key to our maintaining strategic supply points: Puerto Hondo, the airport, the refinery, our telecommunications stations, and the highway network.

"On paper at least, we should be able to dominate, which is to say, we should be able to contain Pancho Portero in the field. However, I must take into account that his brigade is a well-seasoned organization lead by officers and non-commissioned officers with considerable experience. Though they lack actual combat experience, they have had years of very realistic training, some of it in North America.

"By contrast, our units will be new and green. Our combat leaders will not have anything like the experience of their counterparts in the ALIB. That fact reduces the margin of our advantage. I believe we will retain an advantage, but will it be decisive? That is the question. This unit on the chart is an armored battalion, and I believe it is what we need to insure we have that decisive advantage. It will give me the edge I need to guarantee our victory."

He looked at the president, expecting a comment. Figueroa only nodded and he continued.

"Fifteen 1985 model EE-9 Cascavel armored vehicles manufactured by Engesa in Brazil are available at bargain prices. This model is armed with a 90-mm gun and two machine guns. They are protected by sufficient armor plate to provide excellent protection against infantry weapons. They are operated by a crew of three. They can reach speeds of one hundred kilometers per hour on the highway, and their cross country performance is excellent. They are suited for conditions in this country. These vehicles have been in service in North Africa but have been re-engined and rebuilt by an overhaul team from the manufacturer. They are available to us at a fraction of their current value.

"In my opinion, a company of these vehicles is what we need to give us that decisive edge. With such a unit backed by infantry, we can control the highways or assault almost any defended position, and furthermore, these vehicles are excellent in crowd or riot control situations.

"If we decide to purchase them, I plan to marry them with a company of truck born infantry and a reconnaissance company mounted on four-wheel drive vehicles, and thus form a very mobile, light, armored infantry battalion. Such a unit will give us a quick reaction force which can run circles around Portero."

"What will these vehicles cost us?" asked Interior.

"Thanks to our friends in North Africa, we can buy the fifteen vehicles, sufficient spare parts and tires for three years, ten basic loads of ammunition and a ten man training team for six months for 2.7 million US dollars. That, gentlemen, is a bargain, which we cannot pass by."

Figueroa finally spoke. "That may be a bargain but it is still a lot of money, and you are already over your budget by more than half."

"You are correct, but Mr. President, the hard fact is I cannot give you the kind of military strength you will need for peanuts. These things are expensive if you do them right. We have a choice, sir, between a possible victory or a certain victory. I vote for the latter. We have a great deal at stake in this undertaking. Perhaps even our very lives. Can we afford not to be sure?"

• • •

The following day, Interior asked for a private meeting with Figueroa. "I'll get right to the point, Mr. President. Edson's military buildup concerns me. It is going to be very expensive. It'll only be more so, I'm sure. He is underestimating its cost. That's just the way things are."

"You are probably correct. But what is our alternative?"

"I'm not sure there is one, but have we tried talking to Portero? He must know he is in a corner, and that it is only going to get tighter for him. Have we given him an out? Wouldn't it be better to have him with us than to fight him? It's a long shot, but is there a way?"

"Hmm…let me think about that."

CHAPTER 7

Team One arrived in La Rioja a little after noon. Both Lieutenant Ruedas and Sergeant Campinas were uneasy about returning. They had felt quite secure during their first visit but now the possibility, although remote, that they had been identified as ALIB added an element of risk. Colonel Banning had made it very clear the return trip could be dangerous, and it was their choice whether or not to go back. They had discussed it at length together and agreed they were the logical choice, and decided they would go. They reasoned, given their cover story, it would seem plausible for them to return and they could therefore do it without arousing suspicion as a different team might. They also concluded that even if they had been identified, they were doing nothing illegal, so what could happen other than embarrassing themselves and the brigade? However, they did decide to go armed this time and were carrying their issue M9 Berettas in shoulder holsters under their jackets, just in case.

Their first stop was the hotel, where they re-registered and deposited their overnight bags in their room. After taking a bite to eat, they drove across the street to the Exxon Station to fill the truck's tank while Ruedas telephoned the duty desk of their safe arrival. They then visited the local police post to introduce themselves, using their cafetero cover story, and determined which of the secondary roads were open for public use. After two hours spent identifying the several roads open to them and the one road which was closed to unauthorized people, they had a more accurate idea of the location of the finca training camp they had observed from the slopes of *El Cacique*. They then returned to the hotel to plan a thorough reconnaissance for the following day.

Ruedas went to their room to work on the plan, and Campinas went into the cantina for a cold beer. The bar was deserted except for the bartender, who remembered him and welcomed him with a warm smile. "So you're back, señor. We thought you had gone to look for land elsewhere."

"Well, the company sent us on another small job but we haven't finished here, so we are back. By the way, are those Cubans still around?"

"Oh yes, sir, and they have asked if we had seen you. They seemed disappointed when I told them you had not been here. They asked to be notified if you did return."

"And have you notified them?"

"Yes, sir. When I saw you at the hotel desk earlier."

Campinas arose, intending to alert Ruedas about the Cubans' inquiries, when Major Gallo and Captain Simoni entered from the street. Gallo, without hesitation, walked directly to him. "Ah, so the gringos' *puto* is back. What are you doing here?"

Gallo's rude comment signaled trouble. Campinas felt the adrenalin begin to flow and gathered himself for what might come. He sized up his opponent as he had done hundreds of times in the ring. He knew a sober Gallo would be more dangerous than a drunken one, and he answered carefully. "Hello, Major. Nice to see you, too. We are back to finish the survey we started last trip. They put us on another job for a while, but we're back for a couple of days."

"Where is your home office?"

"In La Capital. Why?"

"Are you sure it's not in Valle Escondido?"

"Very sure. Why do you ask?"

"Because I don't think you are *cafeteros*. I think you are ALIB."
He watched for a reaction from Campinas.

"Why do you think that?" Campinas his body reacting to a
new surge of adrenalin.

"I was told you were by someone who knows."

Campinas's brain was racing, but his voice was calm. "Really,
who might that be?"

"Someone who knows you and the ALIB." Gallo edged men-
acingly closer.

"Well whoever it is, they haven't known me lately. I was with
the ALIB once, a long time ago, but now I am in the coffee business." Campinas was wishing, willing, Ruedas to come.

"Prove it. Show me your identity papers, *puto*,"
Gallo commanded.

Campinas felt hot, quick anger rise inside. He lost his sense
of caution. He told himself not to get reckless, but it was too late.
"Hold it, Gallo," he said softly. "You have no authority to demand
my papers. And don't call me *puto*…you Cuban asshole. Let's see
if you're tough enough to take my papers."

He barely caught the movement, it was so fast. Gallo's left
hand flicked and an ASP, a telescoping steel baton, suddenly
appeared, raised high and descending toward his right shoulder.
"I am tough enough, you Yankee piece of shit!"

Campinas took the first blow on his right forearm and felt
excruciating pain. The second blow struck his right clavicle, and
he felt his shoulder collapse. As he realized the bone was broken,
he struck out with his left arm, catching Gallo high on the temple.

The force of the blow sent the Cuban reeling backward and
Campinas, acting on lessons learned from years in the ring, followed, intent on landing another left before the man could recover.
He never landed the blow. The ASP smashed down again on his
crippled right shoulder with such force that he went to his knees.
He raised his left arm to ward off the blow he knew was coming,
thinking that this was not going to be much of a fight. The blow

came, this time to his head. He saw an explosion of color and his world turned gray. Somewhere in the distance, he heard a voice screaming, "I'm tough enough, tough enough, tough…" And he heard rather than felt Gallo's fists hitting his face and head. He knew the man intended to kill him.

Ruedas had just left their room to join his companion when he heard the commotion in the bar. "Oh my God, Carlos is in trouble." He ran through the lobby and into the cantina to see Campinas on his knees, helpless, his back propped against the bar and Gallo screaming and reigning blows down on him with both fists. He yelled and launched himself at the stocky Cuban, hitting him square in the midsection with his left shoulder. They both flew across the room into a table. Gallo, still yelling, got a knee against his chest and propelled him backward. He felt the air expel from his lungs as his back hit the bar near Campinas. He struggled to one knee and was climbing to his feet when he heard, then saw, Gallo coming at him. He had recovered the baton and it was raised, ready to strike. He raised his arm and took the blow on his left hand and at the same time struck the Cuban with his right fist, a desperation blow in the solar plexus, which folded the man double for a moment. Ruedas had time to get to his feet and take two or three backward steps. He reached inside his jacket for his Beretta. He flicked off the safety and aimed dead center at Gallo's chest. The burly Cuban had straightened up and was charging again, screaming, baton raised.

Hank Ruedas had time only to squeeze the trigger. His bullet caught Gallo high in the chest, stopping him in his tracks. A look of surprise came to his ugly face, he staggered backward, looking down at the wound and then at Ruedas. He turned and stag-gered backward against the bar, dropped the baton, and slowly sat down. "You shot me." His voice was surprisingly strong. "You got me good…I think you killed me."

Ruedas looked at Simoni, who stood transfixed looking at Gallo, then at the bartender who dropped a sawed-off baseball bat he had taken from behind the bar. They quickly raised their hands. The color was draining from Gallo's face, but he was still looking at Ruedas. He beckoned him closer. His voice was now weak and Ruedas had to lean close to hear him gasp. "Too bad...I won't see it...you...ALIB...we're gonna...whip your ...." The last breath of his life left him in a rush of expelled air.

Ruedas knelt by Campinas. "Carlos, can you hear me?"

"Get me out of here, Lieutenant...I want to go home...That Gallo...a real unpleasant son of a bitch." Campinas's voice was thin, reed-like.

"That unpleasant son of a bitch is dead, Carlos."

"Good. D'you kill him? Serves the asshole right. Get me home...please."

Ruedas stood up and pointed his weapon at Simoni. "Is there a doctor in La Rioja?

"No? Okay, help me get him into my truck. You too, bartender." The three of them lifted Campinas and carried him gently to the passenger seat. "Get in the back and lie down," he ordered, and they were quick to comply. He climbed in and started the engine.

Hank Rueda's body was still energized for crisis. His brain was working fast and he was thinking clearly. He noted the small crowd that had gathered outside the hotel and turned the truck south in the direction of La Boca and the capital. He noted the police car coming from the opposite direction toward the hotel. He drove slowly by, looking back as if he was a curious gawker. Several blocks farther near the police post, he turned west and then north two blocks later, bypassing the town. He regained the main road and headed north at high speed, keeping an eye on both the road behind and on the two men in the back. Campinas groaned at every bump, so when he was satisfied that there was no pursuit he slowed to a normal, easier riding speed.

As the adrenaline levels in his body began to subside, Ruedas grew aware of the pain in his left hand. He looked at it and saw it was discolored and swelling. The three middle fingers were twisted unnaturally, and there was blood oozing from between them. He reached under the driver's seat for the old T-shirt he had stuffed there, and caught his breath as an excruciating pain shot through his right side. He had broken ribs once before and recognized that old familiar, impossible pain. He was dizzy, and the road ahead seemed to swim before him. He concentrated on controlling the vehicle. After a moment he recovered and wrapped his hand, checked the road behind again for signs of pursuit, and then gave his attention to Campinas.

The little sergeant was either asleep or unconscious. His body was wedged against the door, supported by his right arm. His head was forward, chin on his chest. Ruedas could see that his eyes were swollen almost shut. There was blood on his face and shirt, which had been flowing liberally from a tear in his scalp. His chest was heaving in labored breaths.

"Carlos, can you hear me?" He thought he heard a low groan in response. "We're on our way home, amigo. We'll be there in a couple of hours, so hang on. We'll get you some help in no time. Okay?"

Another groan.

Ten kilometers north of La Rioja, at the top of a rise, Ruedas pulled to the side of the road and stopped. He pulled the Beretta and climbed painfully out of the truck. Nothing was in sight behind them. He ordered Simoni and the bartender to dismount. "This is where you get off. If you're lucky, you can get a ride back. Otherwise it's a long walk."

They both hesitated. "Thank you, señor, and I'm sorry about your friend. He didn't deserve that beating." The bartender looked him straight in the eye.

"How did it start?"

"That Cuban bastard started pushing him around, and the first thing I knew he was beating him with that club. Your friend tried to fight back, but he didn't have a chance. He would have been killed if you hadn't come."

Simoni agreed. "Gallo went crazy. We were supposed to question you. To find out if you were really ALIB, that's all. Before I knew it, he was all over him with that ASP. I was trying to stop him when you tackled him."

"You were both witnesses, then. Have you a piece of paper? Give me your names and addresses."

Simoni produced a piece of paper and a pencil and wrote down the information. Handing it to Ruedas he said quietly, "I also saw you shoot Gallo. You had no choice. He would have done the same to you as he did to your friend. You had no choice."

Ruedas studied the PNN captain. "The question is will you tell the same story when you get back with your friends. Now get going."

He watched as they headed back toward La Rioja, then reached in to the back of the truck for his sleeping bag. He covered Campinas as best he could with one hand, and they proceeded.

They were near the halfway point when Campinas lifted his head and tried to move. His swollen eyes were open and he was peering at Ruedas. "How are we doing, Lieutenant?" His voice still had the thin, reed-like quality.

"We're getting there, Carlos. How do you feel?"

"I've had better days. I feel numb all over."

They lapsed into silence and Ruedas thought he had gone to sleep when Campinas said, "That Gallo is a mean son of a bitch. He was out to kill me with that club. How did you get him off me?"

"I shot him."

After a long moment, Campinas emitted a weak laugh.

"What's funny, Carlos?

"I was thinking you taught him a big lesson."

"What's that?"

"Never bring a club to a gunfight." He laughed weakly again.

Ruedas smiled at him. He was encouraged that Campinas seemed stronger. "That was the last lesson he'll ever learn, and it came too late to help him. Try and get some sleep. You're going to need your strength."

Three quarters of an hour later, Campinas revived again. "How're we coming, Lieutenant?" There was a note of anxiety in his voice.

Ruedas was shocked to see how pale he had become. His face was ashen, his skin transparent. "It won't be long now, Carlos. How are you doing?"

"Not too good. To tell you the truth, I don't think I'm going to make it."

"Don't talk like that, amigo. You've got to keep fighting. We'll be home soon. You'll be fine."

"Maybe. But there is something wrong inside. I feel funny. I can't see very good, and I am getting cold. Hurry if you can."

Ruedas, with growing alarm, pressed down on the accelerator. Later Campinas spoke again. "Lieutenant...I want you to know I've liked serving with you. You're a pretty good guy...for an officer."

"Thanks, Carlos. The feeling is mutual. I've liked serving with you, too. I only wish we hadn't made this trip."

"Me too....but it's done now....we can't change it."

Later. "Lieutenant...are you a religious man? I mean do you go to church and all?"

"I go to chapel sometimes. I guess I'm religious. I believe in God, if that's what you mean."

"I do, too...but I haven't gone much lately. I used to some, but not lately."

They were quiet for a while as the truck sped on toward home and help. It was growing dark, and Ruedas turned on the headlights. He kept checking his friend who was visibly weakening, and his alarm grew. He prayed the little sergeant would hold on just a little longer.

Campinas seemed to summon new strength. "Lieutenant, please stop the truck...please...now, please."

Ruedas braked to a stop. "What is it, Carlos? What can I do?"

"I've never been baptized…will you do it? Please…My middle name is José."

"Well I've never baptized anyone, but I'll try. In fact, it will be my honor, amigo." Hank Ruedas, commander of the ALIB Recon Platoon, with tears in his eyes moved across the seat and gently slipped his right arm around Campinas' shattered body. He made the sign of the cross with his mangled left hand and said, "In the name of the Father, the Son, and the Holy Spirit, I baptize you, Carlos José Campinas. May God bless you and keep you. Amen." He then leaned down and kissed his battered head.

He was still holding his friend when the dying man whispered, "Thanks, Lieutenant." Then after a pause and with a stronger voice, "Everything is fine now. I see everybody…my mother… I'm fine now."

Ruedas felt Campinas go limp, and he looked through his tears to see the little sergeant smiling. He wept.

In the west, the sun was setting.

• • •

General Portero was furious, livid with rage. He had just come from the infirmary where he had talked to Hank Ruedas and seen Sergeant Campinas' battered remains. He stormed into his office, calling for Colonels Soto and Banning and Captain Lacerica to join him immediately. He was shaking with anger and treated them to a very untypical tirade against the arrogance of a government whose officers would permit such unspeakable brutality. When at last his rage was spent, he became coldly calm and businesslike. He issued each of them precise instructions.

"Soto, I want you to get Ruedas out of here. He has broken ribs and a compound fracture of the fingers of his left hand. He'll need fancier surgery than we can do here. Get a helicopter up from CINC-HJRAF to medevac him. That'll get him out of reach in case those sons a bitches try to find him. He is a genuine first-class hero in my book, and I want him protected. Take the legal officer over there with you and get a detailed sworn statement from him before he goes.

"Lacerica, you get over to the infirmary and take pictures of Sergeant Campinas' body. I hope you have a strong stomach because it is not pretty. I don't know how he lived as long as he did. Get plenty of pictures from every angle, and get a detailed report from the doctors on the damage done to him. When you are done with that, try to get Sanchez Avila on the telephone. Tell him what happened and invite him up here to see Campinas. We need an objective outside witness on this.

"Banning, how many scout teams have you out now?"

"Three, sir."

"Get word to them to be careful. The government might know we're out there. They're not to take chances, and we want them in as soon as they have completed their missions. From now on, all teams you send out are to be armed, and each team is to have a backup, a shadow team, to get them out of trouble in case they get into any. I still want to know where the rest of the missing PNN are. That's your primary mission. Understood?"

"Understood."

"One more thing, Soto. Here are the names of the witnesses to the Campinas' beating. Ruedas took them with him when he got out of town to keep them from calling the police. He got their names and addresses when he dumped them off. That young man has a head on his shoulders. We need more like him. Work with the legal officer. Try and find them and see if we can get statements from them. Hire somebody who knows what he is doing. He doesn't have to know he is working for us. But we want those men's stories if we can get them.

"Any questions? Okay, go to work."

• • •

"It's a deliberate distortion, sir." Guillermo Lacerica had just shown General Portero the article he had clipped from a back page of *El Diario*. "And it is interesting that they buried it inside the paper and didn't mention Gallo by name or that he was Cuban."

The headline was "PNN Officer Murdered," and the copy read:

> La Rioja. A training officer assigned to a PNN unit near the town of La Rioja was shot to death in a hotel bar Wednesday. Two gunmen escaped in an old pickup truck, forcing two hostages to accompany them. Later the hostages managed to escape their captors when the vehicle stopped several kilometers north of La Rioja. Neither the motive for the killing nor the identity of the gunmen has been established. According to one witness, one of the men had been injured when bystanders attacked him, presumably in retaliation for the shooting. The hostages are being questioned by PNN investigators and could not be reached for interview. Their identities have not been released.

"You are sure none of the other papers carried the story?"

"Very sure, General. It makes me believe the story was planted in *El Diario*."

Portero reread the article. He sat for a moment thinking and then looked up at his PR officer. "Yes, and it looks like someone is trying to plant some phony facts…but for what purpose?"

Lacerica shook his head and shrugged. "Whatever it is, it'll be damaging to us. We can count on that."

Portero agreed. "And the problem is we can't react. If we do, we'll be admitting our people were involved. Maybe that is what the bastards are hoping we'll do. If so, they must think we're stupid. In any case, we're not playing their game."

• • •

Ramon Sanchez Avila had the sensitive nose of a seasoned reporter, and he smelled an important story. He also had been puzzled by the *El Diario* article and, like Lacerica, had recognized it as a planted piece. Now sitting in his small, cluttered office in the Vida Nacional building with the clipping on the desk before him, he pondered the situation.

There was a significant discrepancy between the facts as presented in the article and what he had learned during his unexpected visit to the infirmary at Valle Escondido. He was inclined to accept the brigade's version. He had been very disturbed by the shocking condition of the sergeant's body. He had read Ruedas' sworn statement, talked to the doctor and to Lacerica, and found their statements to be credible and consistent.

He did not know why the government—or someone, if not the government, who?—had chosen to plant the distorted version of the incident. But he knew there was a reason, and therein lay his story. Like an old war horse responding to the sound of a bugle, he felt his excitement grow, and he made a decision to pursue it to the end.

His first task would be to confirm what he believed happened in La Rioja. The witnesses to the incident would be keys to his preliminary investigation. He knew who they were from the Ruedas statement, but the *Diario* piece had not named them so he had to be careful not to compromise his source. After giving it some thought, he decided to try the direct approach. He placed a call to the PNN commander.

Colonel Edson Davidson returned his call almost immediately, knowing that he had power and influence. But Davidson was not forthcoming when he asked for the names of the witnesses. "I am sorry, Don Ramon, the matter is still under investigation and the names cannot be released until it has been completed. I will be happy to forward a complete copy of our findings once the process is complete."

"Thank you very much, Colonel. When do you anticipate that might be?"

"It is impossible to say at this point. We haven't as yet apprehended the gunmen. The case will necessarily be open until we have them in custody."

"With respect, Colonel, I am not asking for the names of the gunmen, only the witnesses to the incident. Surely that can't jeopardize the investigation."

"I am sorry, but they cannot be released until the matter has been concluded."

Sanchez Avila had been unable to sway Davidson and concluded his only course would be to go to La Rioja and go through the motions of digging out the witnesses. He decided to drive down the following morning.

• • •

Sergeant Carlos Campinas was buried quietly in the small cemetery by the base chapel on the peaceful banks of the Santa Inez River. At Portero's direction, word had gone out that Campinas and Ruedas had been the victims of an off-duty vehicle accident. The graveside assembly was not small. Except for Lieutenant Ruedas who had been evacuated, the brigade Reconnaissance Platoon was there to a man along with some senior staff members and a few hangers-on. One interested observer noted that among the latter group was Private Rubio of the training company.

• • •

Captain Alfonso Simoni was beginning to understand his situation. At first he had been puzzled by the unexpected orders relieving him of duty as the commanding officer of the Training Detachment in La Rioja and assigning him as administrative officer of the Second Naranjeras Infantry Brigade. He received the orders on one day, and he was in the Isla Grande camp the next. He had never known the PNN to move so quickly. It was clear they wanted him out of La Rioja fast, and it was clear why. They did not want him talking about the Gallo killing.

Two days after the incident, Colonel Molina had called him in for a private talk. He asked him for the details of his escape from Gallo's killers.

"We didn't escape, sir. They let us go."

"Don't be modest, Simoni. Of course you escaped. Why would they let you go? You were witnesses of what happened, weren't you? You saw them murder Major Gallo. You could testify against them. They'd have been crazy to let you go."

"That is not the way it was, Colonel. The big man, Ruedas. killed Gallo in self-defense. He was in the process of beating Campinas to death with that ASP he always carries. Ruedas intervened. He would have done the same thing to Ruedas and had already hit him a couple of times when Ruedas shot him. I'm sorry, Colonel. The man was completely crazy…out of control. I would have done the same thing."

"I have known Gallo for fifteen years and have seen him get like that on occasion. The man could really hate. But he was a colleague and a brave man. We've been through a lot together. I am sure he was just trying to scare Campinas into confessing he was ALIB."

"But Colonel, he never gave Campinas a chance to say anything. No, sir, he was trying to kill him. There is no doubt."

Molina sighed. "Okay, Simoni, you are probably right. It sounds like Gallo. And I know you to be an honest and conscientious officer."

"Thank you, sir."

"Just between us, I grant that Gallo probably lost control. But what purpose would it serve to say that publicly? We have a lot at stake here. Naranjeras has a lot at stake here. I certainly don't want to do anything that might jeopardize what we are trying to do here, do you? After all, the deed is done. We can't do anything about Gallo now, so let's look at the big picture. Wouldn't it be better to use this unfortunate incident in a way that helps our cause, rather than harms it?"

"I suppose so, sir, but I am not sure what you are saying."

"What I am saying, Simoni, is that it would be in the best interests of the country, of you and me, of us all, if the impression were left that Gallo was deliberately killed by ALIB agents. Sometimes we are called upon to do things for the sake of our country which might seem at the time to be, shall we say, a little unorthodox. In this instance, for example, by shading the truth a little we can serve the greater good."

"What good will it serve if I lie about how Gallo was killed, Colonel?"

"Dammit Simoni, don't be naïve! Surely you understand the government is trying to win the support and confidence of the people. We couldn't allow the impression get abroad that one of its officers went crazy and set out to kill a man he was questioning, could we, especially if that man turned out to be with the ALIB? That would just generate sympathy for Francisco Portero and that would not be good for our cause, would it?"

"No. I suppose it wouldn't. But I am not sure that a government which depends on a lie to win support of the people is on very sound footing in the first place. Are you, Colonel?"

"I believe in the government's cause, Simoni, and I am willing to make sacrifices—even very difficult ones like this—to further that cause. Look, man, we're soldiers. We have our duty, and we owe loyalty if we believe in our cause. You do support your government's cause don't you?"

"Yes. I guess I do. But I am not exactly sure what that may be. Are you?"

"Look. There will always be some things we won't completely understand. As soldiers we have to trust our leaders. I trust the president and the men advising him just as I trust you to do the right thing for your country in this case. I hope you in turn trust me in this matter."

"Of course I do, Colonel."

"Good. Then it is settled. Tomorrow the PNN criminal investigators will question you about Gallo's killing. Just tell them how you think it happened and how you managed to escape those men. The bartender will back your story and so will I. Okay, Captain Simoni? You won't regret this. I give you my word."

But the next day, Simoni could not bring himself to give Molina's version of the story. He could only tell the truth. The investigators diligently took their notes and left without comment. That afternoon he received orders transferring him to the Second Infantry Brigade on Isla Grande.

The more he thought about his situation, the more angry he became. The idea that his career had been compromised because he had acted honorably appalled him. He had been proud of his service with the PNN, which he had always respected as an honorable organization, but this incident had raised doubts in his mind.

After two weeks "in exile" on Isla Grande, Simoni's doubts had given way to a feeling he had been betrayed. His anger grew and it focused on Colonel Molina, the author of his betrayal. His resentment became an obsession. How could the service, his service, allow a foreigner to sidetrack the career of a Naranjero regular officer?

When Colonel Molina arrived on Isla Grande with great fanfare to assume command of the Second Brigade, Simoni's life changed forever. The betrayal was complete! He was trapped in a corrupt system. His life and career were in the hands of a man he disliked and now distrusted, and who felt the same about him. He saw no hope. By the end of his second month on Isla Grande, his disaffection was total and he could think of nothing but how he might avenge himself against the organization and the government he had been so content to serve only eight short weeks before.

• • •

The ATB was deep in discussion about the whereabouts of the missing PNN personnel. Colonel Banning was convinced they were on Isla Grande. "If they are in the country, they have to be there. It is the only place we haven't been able to check."

Colonel Soto slapped the table. "Of course! That's where they are. My God, why didn't we think of it before?"

"Sounds right," said Ochoa, the B3. "But we'd better make sure. The question is how do we do it?"

"The easiest way would be from the air. General, do you think you could persuade General Carmody to allow one of his helicopters to wander that far off-course on its way up here?"

"I will call him. A flight will be coming up early next week. Hank Ruedas is out of the hospital and is coming with it. It would help if we could get some photos of what is on the island."

Suddenly the meeting was interrupted by Portero's administrative assistant. After knocking, the aging sergeant entered the room somewhat wide-eyed to announce the president's office was on the telephone asking for the general. Portero immediately excused himself to take the call. "This is General Portero."

"Good afternoon, General," a smooth voice responded. "Hold please for the president."

Portero held for several minutes trying to imagine a reason for the call. The line clicked and the President's voice came to him. "Sorry to keep you waiting, General. Antonio Figueroa here."

"Good afternoon, Mr. President. This is a surprise."

"Yes, I regret we have not seen more of each other. There don't seem to be enough hours in the day to do everything I would like to do. You are well, I trust? All is well with your command?"

"Yes, thank you, sir. How can I be of service?"

"I'll come directly to the point, General. I would like a meeting with you. There are a number of items we should discuss. I would prefer a private meeting. Just the two of us. No staff. No press."

"What sort of items do you have in mind?"

"I would rather not be specific on the telephone. Let's just say I am concerned about the rift that seems to be growing between us, and would like to explore how we might normalize relations. I would also like to personally brief you on the government's plans for the future. Would that be agreeable to you?"

"Most agreeable, Mr. President. When and where would you like to meet?"

"I would like to do it within the next three weeks, if that would be convenient. As to where, I won't ask you to come to the capital, and the council wouldn't approve my coming to you. How about somewhere between? I propose we let our staffs work out the details. They can also work out a joint press release about the meeting. The press will not be invited, but they will have to know that we are meeting. I'll have my chief of staff call yours, if that would be agreeable."

"That would be fine, Mr. President. And may I suggest that they also work up an agenda for our discussion so that I might be better prepared."

"I really hoped we might have an open, freewheeling, and confidential discussion on a number of topics. But we can work up some agenda items which will focus on the general areas for discussion, if that would be all right."

"That would be fine."

"Very good, General. I look forward to seeing you again. I hope we can find ways to work together. It's important to the country. Good-bye."

The line disconnected before Portero could reply. *I wonder what you have up your sleeve, Figueroa, you slippery son of a bitch. I am going to have to be very careful with you,* he thought as he hung up.

CHAPTER 8

Ramon Sanchez Avila returned to his office after five mostly frustrating days in La Rioja. It had been a tiring trip. He hadn't planned to be gone so long, but it took that much time to dig out the information he sought. At first he was met with a stone wall of silence. No one would talk to him about the Gallo killing. The local PNN agents admitted they were under orders not to talk to reporters pending the outcome of the ongoing investigation. Hotel personnel wouldn't talk either. They knew nothing, claiming they had not been present. Even the petrol station operator was silent despite the fact that his business was just opposite the hotel and he probably witnessed much of what took place.

By the afternoon of the second day, he had learned nothing. But as his frustration grew, so did his determination. He knew the locals had more information about the incident than they were admitting, and he was sure they were not talking because they had been told not to. In desperation, he asked the hotel manager if he might see the hotel register for the month, but she refused, saying her records had been seized by the PNN investigators.

"Surely, señora, you must remember who has stayed in your hotel lately. It isn't very large, and you're not exactly on the mainstream of tourism. I doubt you have been overwhelmed with guests."

"You are correct, señor, but we have been told not to talk about the incident to anyone."

"Who told you not to talk about it?"

"The PNN investigators."

"But I am not asking you anything about the incident, señora. I'm simply asking you who has been staying in your hotel. Surely it's okay to give me that much. I promise you I will not reveal you as my source."

"I'm sorry. I cannot."

"Look. As you know, I am a reporter. A great many people read my paper. If I put in a good word about your hotel and cantina, it will help your business. It's like free advertising."

"I know, señor, but I cannot do it."

The next day, however, she quietly passed him a sheet of paper containing sixteen names and dates. The list included the names Xavier Molina, Hernan Gallo, Roberto Serra, Alfonso Simoni, all listed as PNN officers, and farther down, Hank Ruedas and Carlos Campinas, listed as cafeteros. He finally had documentary corroboration of the names he had from the confidential ALIB report.

Armed with those names, he spent two additional days asking people about the key figures in the incident. Knowing he had names, the people of La Rioja were more forthcoming. Most readily identified Gallo as the man who was killed and a few even volunteered he was not liked. Several identified Campinas and Ruedas as the killers and hostage takers. The petrol station owner reluctantly confirmed Simoni and the bartender had been the hostages.

No one knew the whereabouts of any of the men. Molina, Serra, and Simoni had left the area immediately after the incident, but nobody knew where they had gone. The bartender had remained in town for a while but had eventually been taken away by some PNN officials and had not returned. They knew nothing about Campinas or Ruedas except that one of them had been injured during the incident. Apparently, no one except the bartender and Simoni had seen what had happened inside the cantina, not even hotel employees who had been pursuing their duties elsewhere.

After many inquiries, Sanchez Avila managed to locate a girl-friend of the bartender, but she had no idea of his whereabouts. She was very worried about him and willing to talk. In response to his questions, she revealed that her friend had insisted Gallo had started the trouble, and not vice versa, as the story circulated by the local PNN had it. She also volunteered that Ruedas had allowed her friend and Simoni to go free several kilometers north of town. They had walked most of the distance back.

On the basis of the information he had uncovered, the old reporter concluded that Ruedas' sworn statement was an accurate account of the incident. To be absolutely certain he would have to talk to Simoni and the bartender, but how could he find them? After some thought, he decided to take the direct approach. He placed a call to Colonel Davidson but was told that the PNN commander was traveling and would not return until the following week.

• • •

At the same time Sanchez Avila was pondering how he might find the people on his list, General Carmody, in his HJRAF headquarters in Panama, was considering some of the same names with more than passing interest. On the desk before him lay copies of the dossiers of the three Cuban officers which had been requested by Colonel Banning of the ALIB.

The men had interesting backgrounds. Xavier Molina, a colonel of Infantry, was born in 1945 in Santiago, Cuba. He graduated from the Military Academy in 1964. He served as a company commander in Angola, where he was decorated for gallantry. Later as a major, he attended an advanced course in special operations in the Soviet Union. He spent three years as a military advisor to the Ortega regime in Nicaragua during the early eighties. He was reputed to be a specialist in anti-guerrilla warfare.

There was considerably less information on Gallo. Apparently there were two *Hernan Gallos* identified. One was a military doctor. The other had been a specialist and trainer in small unit infantry tactics and an instructor in hand-to-hand combat. That Gallo had served in Nicaragua in the eighties.

Roberto Serra, Major of Infantry, was born in Havana in 1955. He graduated from the Cuban Military Academy in 1973. He studied civil engineering at the university. He had been taken prisoner by US forces in Grenada but was released and repatriated. He was thought to be an expert in demolition and explosives. It was believed, but not confirmed, he had spent a number of months on a training mission in Libya and Syria.

The fact that these men were now in Naranjeras working in an official capacity for the Figueroa regime only confirmed in Carmody's mind that Pancho Portero's suspicions were well founded. He no longer had any personal doubts about the aims of the new government, but he thought it might be difficult to convince Washington to see it that way. On the other hand, he was confident that the HDO Secretary General would understand immediately.

Carmody was awaiting Portero's arrival. He had asked the ALIB commander to come down to discuss strategies for dealing with the situation. Carmody recognized there would be political risk, but he was fully prepared to provide limited covert support to the ALIB. He believed the brigade was the only agency inside the country with the power to frustrate Figueroa's plans and therefore was the best hope for keeping the country a democracy.

Carmody was prepared to let Portero take the lead role in the effort. He trusted his young commander's judgment and motivation, and knew he was a pro-democracy patriot who knew the people of Naranjeras well. In his mind there was no better choice to lead the opposition to Figueroa. He was ready to put the HJRAF in a quiet, low profile, supporting role. There would be limits to what he might do without completely violating the obligations of the HJRAF Implementing Agreement, but he would go as far as the law and good sense allowed, and perhaps a bit further. He was not sure exactly what help Portero needed or how the HJRAF might play a part. That would be the subject for his discussions with Portero.

Carmody heard the helicopter letting down as it passed over the headquarters building. A short time later, his secretary showed General Portero into the office. Carmody rose to greet his younger colleague. They settled into comfortable chairs in a conference alcove of the office. He offered Portero a fine Dominican cigar and lit one himself. Carmody, a widower, always inquired about Elizabeth Portero, whom he regarded much as he would a daughter-in-law. The pleasantries over, Carmody asked about recent developments.

Portero told him about Figueroa's request for a meeting. "He wants it to be a private meeting just between the two of us. He gave me no idea of his agenda except to say he wants to resolve our differences. I have no idea what that means. He has something up his sleeve, but I can't guess what it is. I'll keep you informed, of course."

"Yes, by all means. Anything new on the location of the PNN units?"

"No, sir. We are pretty sure they are on Isla Grande. I need confirmation, however, because if they are not there, they are out of the country somewhere, and that would add a whole new dimension to our problem. Can we get that over flight?"

"Yes. We're laying it on, but Pancho, we're taking a big risk doing it. We absolutely cannot afford to get caught. You sure you want to take the chance?"

"I am, General. I must know what I am going to be dealing with."

"Very well. We'll let you know when we figure out how we're going to do it. Probably by helicopter. They'll never give us a U-2 for that, and I wouldn't ask for it anyway. Anything new on the Campinas killing?"

"No, sir."

"You've seen the files on those Cubans, of course?"

Portero nodded.

"They are the final nails in Figueroa's coffin as far as I am concerned, Pancho. This information confirms what you've been saying. He is a bad one, and I am now even more convinced he means to end democracy in your country. That's bad enough, but what is worse from my point of view is that all this is going to badly disrupt the HDO. We have to find a way to stop him. The question is what can we do?"

"'We,' sir?"

"Yes, we. I am going to recommend to the Secretary General that we give you as much low profile support as we can. I believe he will agree to it. I expect to have more resistance from Washington than from him. Not the Pentagon so much, but from State and maybe some congressional circles. That's the reason whatever we do for you has to be low profile. We have to underplay it all the way."

Portero had been sure Carmody would be ready to help and was grateful for it, but he also recognized it would be politically dangerous for his friend and mentor, and for the HJRAF, if it became known. He also believed it would be the wrong thing for Naranjeras. He chose his words carefully.

"Thank you for the thought, General. I have been doing a hell of a lot of thinking about this lately and have come to the conclusion that you and the HJRAF, and the HDO, can help best by staying out of it." He paused to allow Carmody to think about what he was saying. "From the perspective of the people of Naranjeras, this trouble boils down to an internal dispute. It would be best if Naranjeros resolve it themselves internally. You and I and the Secretary General see this as an international problem because it threatens regional security. However, most

Naranjeros will see it as their problem and typically will believe it should be solved locally. It is a matter of national pride. They will react negatively to outside help…for either side. They will soon discover Figueroa needs outside help, and I am betting that will work to our benefit as the situation develops.

"If the HJRAF intervenes on behalf of the ALIB, it will be universally seen as foreign interference in domestic affairs, and a lack of confidence in the country. I submit that no matter how low the profile, how quiet, how covert the support you might give us, it can't be hidden for long. Sooner or later it will be discovered, and there will be hell to pay when it is. Imagine what the Figueroa people would do with that. The headlines would be screaming, 'Yankee Interference Not Only in Naranjeras But All Over the World'—that hue and cry would be used by Figueroa to justify outside help for his cause.

"In another time, when the United States commanded greater respect in the world, you might have gotten away with some covert support of us, but not now. We both know that your last administration managed to squander a lot of goodwill by its inept, naïve foreign policy. You used to be respected even by your enemies, but today you are regarded as a paper tiger in many circles, a rich paper tiger, good for financial aid but without any teeth. Your former president talked tough but never backed up his talk. Your new administration appears to be stronger, but it will have to prove itself if it is to regain that lost prestige."

Carmody was visibly uncomfortable. "I would not permit any-one else to talk to me about my country that way, even if I agreed with the sentiment. However, I know that you love the United States as much as any man and you are not intending to deni-grate it. Just between us, I know we have lost some respect in the world, unfortunately, and we didn't have to. Had we had a few even semi-competent statesmen in charge these last eight years, it wouldn't have happened. Instead we had a group of arrogant, self-serving amateurs without experience or qualifications, other than they were exceptionally gifted in political manipulation. They entered office uninformed about the world and unprepared for the responsibility, without a plan or even a coherent philosophy, and without skills except in bombast and empty rhetoric. Their knowledge of the way things work internationally was so severely limited, they allowed themselves to believe they could jawbone the world into accepting their leadership by flaunting the might of the United States. They pursued a kind of hit-or-miss foreign policy, mostly for the benefit of the US electorate. When they occasionally succeeded, they trumpeted their success via the willing but ignorant media. They ignored their failures, often passing them off as a United Nations problem. We remember Bosnia where they had some success, but who today remembers the flops in Somalia, Haiti, North Korea, or even Iraq after Desert Storm? Well that kind of 'foreign policy for domestic consumption' failed. It might have fooled some people at home for a while, but it lost a great deal of the world's respect for us. In the end, their naiveté resulted in their being manipulated by people a lot smarter than they were. It was the pros against the amateurs, and we lost.

"Now, thank God and the wisdom of the American voter, the situation has changed. We have good people in this new administration, and I believe we will recover the respect we have squandered, but it will take time. And Pancho—you never heard me say any of this!

"However, your point is well made. Neither the HJRAF, the HDO, nor the United States can afford to be seen as influencing Naranjeras politics through the ALIB. I see it could be a political disaster for you and for us, too. Still you are going to need some help, so my question is how can we help without being perceived as helping?"

Portero laughed. "Well, General, there will be no action for several months. It will take at least six months or more before Figueroa has the strength to take us on. Until then, our relationship with the HJRAF should be business as usual. When the trouble starts, I think you should denounce us and publicly cut off our support. That's the only way you can hope to keep the HJRAF from becoming a target itself. There will be plenty of anti-Yankee politicians looking for an excuse to bring you down. The survival of the HJRAF is important to the region and to the world. If it costs the loss of the ALIB and Naranjeras, so be it. In the long run, it would be worth it if the HJRAF survives as a stabilizing influence.

"The flip side of the coin is you also have to resist being sucked in on the other side. It goes without saying we can't have you actively engaged against us. I believe our chances of defeating Figueroa are good, provided he gets no outside help from our friends. To put it plainly, I'm asking you to watch our backs at the same time you are denouncing us."

Carmody drew on his cigar, thinking. "I must say, Pancho, you are proposing a strange and interesting relationship. You want me to oppose you publicly while I protect you privately. It's an intriguing idea, to say the least. It will take a lot of doing, but maybe it can be pulled off. I wonder if there is an ethical question in it somewhere? I want to think about that."

"Okay, General, but meantime there are some things we will need after hostilities commence which you might consider giving us now, before you cut us off."

"Oh, what might those be?"

Portero asked for a substantial increase in his ammunition inventory and in his medical supplies, and he coolly asked for an integral air section. "We will need two or three, preferably three, helicopters, aircrews, fuel supplies, and the maintenance personnel to keep them flying. They will be essential for scouting, re-supplying, medevac, and troop transport-type missions."

• • •

In early May, Hank Ruedas, his left hand still in a cast, returned to Valle Escondido on the weekly liaison flight from Panama. Christina Lane, his pilot, wondered about the larger than unusual number of soldiers she could see waiting by the helo pad. As she drew closer, they formed into the ranks of an honor guard.

"It looks like you have a reception committee, Lieutenant," she called to Ruedas over the intercom. As the big machine headed into the wind for its touchdown, the honor guard, standing stiffly at attention, came into Ruedas' view.

The trip from Panama to Valle Escondido had become routine for Christina. She had flown it almost weekly for the last three months. It had become "her run," and she treasured it because it made it possible to be with her fiancé regularly. She had come to regard the brigade and Valle Escondido as her primary home, and she always felt the excitement of anticipation when she approached the beautiful valley. It was not only that she would be with Tony DaSilva but she also had come to know the people and the place, and she felt comfortable there.

This trip had not been routine, however. First, the aircraft was carrying almost a ton of extra fuel aboard in four well-sealed fifty-five gallon drums. She would need to use most of it to top off her fuel tanks in the event it was decided she would deviate from her normal route to over fly Isla Grande on the return trip. She had been alerted to the possibility and given a confidential briefing by her company commander and told that the final decision would be made at the ALIB.

Second, she was nervous about making that detour because the route would take her into restricted airspace. Her commanding officer had assured her that General Carmody was aware of the restriction but had authorized the flight, provided General Portero continued to think it was necessary.

She had been emphatically warned "not to get caught," however, and that added to her nervousness. That meant to her that she could not simply blunder off her flight plan to pass over the island and then apologize to the Naranjeras flight controllers later for her navigation error. It meant she would have to do it surreptitiously, which would involve a complicated flight plan. She would first have to disappear from air traffic control's radar screen, which would require some considerable deception. Then she would have to fly beneath their radar coverage and run to the island at sea level, make her pass, and get out fast before anyone could identify her. She had brought along five gallons of white water-soluble paint, which she intended to use to disguise her army green bird should she have to make the trip.

The thing worrying her most was that Isla Grande lived up to its name. It was indeed a big island, and if she didn't find what they were looking for on the first pass, she would have to make a second or third pass, which would seriously reduce the element of surprise and increase the chances of being identified. Also, she didn't really know how the people on the ground might react, but the probability was that it would be unfavorably given the fact she would be an illegal intruder. They might even try to shoot her down, a prospect she did not look forward to in the least.

As the big machine's engines were winding down, Hank Ruedas followed the crew chief out of the aircraft. He had seen from the air that his entire platoon formed the honor guard. He saluted Colonel Banning and his company commander who headed the reception committee. Banning welcomed him home on behalf of General Portero and the brigade. It was a surprise to Ruedas, who had not expected any such ceremony. He was suddenly overcome with emotion and unable to speak but managed another smart salute and shook their hands gratefully.

"Welcome home, Lieutenant," said his platoon sergeant, saluting when he stood before the honor guard. "The men wanted me to call your attention to our new guidon." The guidon bearer presented so Ruedas could see the words "Campinas Platoon" superimposed in red over the blue field with its white crossed rifles.

"The men voted to do this, sir. I thought it was a great idea. Hope you agree."

Ruedas managed to thank the men of the platoon for their welcome and to congratulate them on their new guidon. "Carlos would approve," he concluded.

When the little ceremony was completed, Colonel Banning invited Captain Lane and her copilot to meet in his office that afternoon to plan the reconnaissance mission.

• • •

The helicopter without markings flew toward the sunrise. It stayed low, and as the day brightened, it dropped even lower into the shadows, threading its way east through the valleys, avoiding population centers. It approached the Exxon Refinery's deserted airstrip, hovered for a moment close to the ground, then simulated a takeoff, climbing to two thousand feet on a southeast heading. Over Puerto Hondo it turned to follow the coastline south.

Its pilot, Captain Christina Lane, alerted her crew over the intercom. "Air traffic control should have us by now if they're awake. If they call, Jeff will answer using the phony tail number. Remember, we are a PetroCarib Exploration ship. We hope they don't know all of PetroCarib's choppers are working down in Costa Rica. Jeff, you answer in Spanish then switch, and speak in some kind of an accent and don't use good radio procedure. We don't want to sound like we're the US Army. If they want us to squawk, we won't but tell them we will."

They passed to the east of the capital and were forty-three kilometers northeast of La Boca and beginning to believe the air traffic control radar was down or the controllers were indeed asleep when the call came.

"Unidentified aircraft on heading one two six zero to La Boca, this is Naranjeras departure control. Over."

"Let him call again, Jeff."

After the third call, the co-pilot keyed his mike. "Buenos dias, señores departure control. Are you calling me? This is PetroCarib helicopter nueve siete cero…er, nine, ah, seven, ah, zero."

"Nine seven zero, departure control. Have you filed a flight plan? We have no record. Over."

"No flight plan. We are VFR to an area fifteen kilometers east of La Boca. Cambio."

"This is departure control. Please squawk 3230. Over."

"Hokay, Squawking 3230. Cambio."

"Nine seven zero, departure control. I'm not getting your signal. Check your transponder. Be advised you are approaching restricted airspace. What is the purpose of your flight? Over."

"This is nine seven zero. We is working for Ministeria Interior. They authorize flight. Transponder checks hokay. Cambio, er, over."

"Nine seven zero, departure control. Standby."

"Hokay, señores. Nine seven zero standing by."

The copilot grinned at Christina. She grinned back and gave him a thumbs-up signal. After twelve minutes, the controller called again. "Nine seven zero, departure control. We have no record of your flight. Who at Interior authorized your operation? Over."

"Say aga—er, repeat please. Over."

"Who at the Ministry of Interior authorized your operation? This is departure control. Over."

"Please hold. I must look at my dispatch orders…Control, this is PetroCarib. My dispatch is signed by Ingenero Grajales, or is it Morales. I don't read his signature very good. Over."

The aircraft was now fifteen kilometers northeast of La Boca and beginning a slow descent. The controller's impatience began to show in his voice. "Nine seven zero, this is departure control. You are entering restricted airspace, repeat, you are entering restricted airspace. You are directed to return to Capital

International to straighten out your flight plan. Do you acknowl-edge? Over."

"Control, this is nine seven zero. Understand. Return to International. Will do, but first must pick up ministry passengers north of La Boca. Hokay? Over."

"Negative, nine seven zero. Return to Capital International immediately. Acknowledge. Over."

Jeff waited a full thirty seconds. "Departure control, this is PetroCarib. Do you read?"

"Nine seven zero, I read you loud and clear. Do you read me? Over."

"Departure control, departure control, PetroCarib. Hello, hello. Do you hear me? Cambio."

Jeff laughed into the intercom. "I guess we are out of range, Skipper. They don't seem to hear us," he said as the sound of the controller's voice came clearly over the radio, repeating his call to nine seven zero.

By then they were on the deck, twenty feet over the turquoise Caribbean heading directly toward Isla Grande, a long blue mass which rose from the sea ahead.

After eight minutes, Christina keyed her mike. "Dry mouth time, guys. Got your cameras ready? Jeff, you have the left side and Sergeant Boyd, you've got the right. I only want to make one pass, so be alert and get those pictures. Everybody ready? Here we go."

The big bird swept in over the shoreline near the center of the island, climbed over a forested ridge, and dropped into a large central valley directly over a group of buildings and tents arranged in the unmistakable pattern of a military base.

"Bingo," yelled Christina. "Are you getting pictures? Good. I am going to make one wide sweep of the area to the left starting now. Keep snapping and try to get a feel for how many troops are down there. When we're done, I am going back out the way we came. Once our feet are wet, I'll get on the deck and swing around the east end of the island and we'll head for home."

CHAPTER 9

General Francisco Portero's shiny black staff car, preceded and followed by GEO Trackers, each mounting a machine gun, arrived at the Tuxla School precisely at ten o'clock. The president's party had not arrived, but the TV cameras and the press crammed the space across the road from the entrance of the two-story building.

Portero dismounted from his vehicle and climbed the steps to wait at the door for the president. He was an imposing figure, resplendent in his best field uniform and crimson beret, polished parachutist badge, and with a large silver star superimposed on a crimson sleeve attached to each shoulder epaulet of his starched blouse. He was conscious of the cameras and made an effort to stand straight and appear unperturbed.

Actually, he was nervous. He was aware that he was out of his element. This was a political game he was playing, and he was uncomfortable in it. He was not sure he could carry it off. He had spent two days trying to prepare for the meeting, but not knowing what the president wanted to discuss made it difficult. The agenda outline he had requested never came, so he was going in cold with only his own speculations as the basis for his mental rehearsals.

The one message he was determined to deliver to Figueroa was the condition that any truce between them must be a commitment to hold free elections within six months from that date. Other than that, he was prepared to play it by ear.

Figueroa was late, purposely so, Portero thought, *to signal his importance.* Portero recognized posturing for the cameras and the press was part of the political game, and he knew the president was an expert at it. He thought he was not but was nevertheless determined not to be outdone. When the president's limousine finally arrived twelve minutes later, he did not descend to meet it but waited at the school entrance, compelling Figueroa to climb the steps to greet him. He saluted, not waiting to have it returned, and shook hands, smiling as he did. He maneuvered so that he was facing the battery of cameras while the president's back was to them. He then gestured for the president to precede him into the building. Before he followed, he paused to look around as if to assure all was in order.

He smiled to himself, quite satisfied with his performance. He hoped it would seem to any viewer that the president had come to call upon him. Colonel Soto standing below smiled benignly while the president's press aide standing nearby seethed.

Figueroa was aware he had been upstaged by Portero and was inwardly annoyed, but he struggled to remain affable. "You missed your calling, General. You should have been a politician or an actor," he said, smiling.

"I don't understand, sir," replied Portero innocently.

The hell you don't, thought the president, still smiling. "Never mind. It was not important."

The school was a large concrete-block building constructed around a large inner courtyard, now empty. The classrooms were placed along the outside of each floor. A wide balcony ran around the second floor on the courtyard side and formed a covered walkway for the first floor rooms below. There was a reception area, administrative office, and a teachers' lounge to the right of the school's entrance.

The two men entered the lounge where two large armchairs had been arranged facing each other across a large, low coffee table of polished wood, which Portero assumed had been brought in for the occasion. A tray with a pitcher of ice water and two glasses was on the table, and a pad of writing paper and some sharpened pencils were neatly arranged before each chair. Portero deferred to the president in selecting a seat and sat opposite him. He waited for Figueroa to begin.

"Thank you for agreeing to meet me. I have been looking forward to this for some time, and I wanted to do it on neutral ground, without aides or interruptions or recorders. We have much to discuss informally and off the record. Here, as you requested, is a brief outline of the topics I would like to cover with you."

Portero read the single sheet of paper the president had passed over to him. It contained only four items in bold type.

1. Relations with ALIB

2. General Objectives of the Government

3. Plans for the Ministry of Defense

4. Exchange of Ideas

He looked at the president and nodded.
"Do you have comments or additions?"
"No, sir."
"Then I have a question for you. What can I do to improve relations between us?"
"Are you speaking about relations between your government and the ALIB, or between you and me, sir?"
"Both, I suppose. They are really the same thing, aren't they?"
"Well, Mr. President, relations between the government and the ALIB have always been excellent until your administration came into power. With previous administrations, I have had regular periodic meetings with the minister of national defense. Whatever problems might have arisen were straightened out in such meetings. I have yet to have any such meeting with anyone

in your government. In fact, I don't believe you even have a minister of defense yet. Do you?"

"Not yet. That's a matter for discussion with you today."

"It is important to have these periodic meetings. Regular dialogue is the only way we can get to know each other. Beyond that, if relations between us have soured, they have done so as the result of certain initiatives taken by your government, and not by our side."

"You refer to the *permisos de transito* quarrel."

"That and the slanted stories in *El Diario,* your pet newspaper." He could not resist the adding the final barb.

Figueroa smiled. "You seem to have a pet newspaper, too, in *La Prensa.*"

"*La Prensa* has been supportive of us, but they are independent of us. They are anything but our captive propaganda organ."

"Nor is *El Diario* ours."

"Come, Mr. President, I'm not naïve. *El Diario* helped put you in office. The moment you had wrested power from the Moreno government, Profesora Hortencia Malapropino arrived out of nowhere to become managing editor, and immediately the paper's theme became 'the government can do no wrong.' She attacks anyone who questions the administration or anyone whom she believes might be in opposition to you. And she is not above distorting the facts in doing it. You cannot believe that I, or anyone else in the country, haven't made the connection between your regime and the profesora or her paper."

"The truth is that any government needs a friend in the press. Hortencia happens to be ours. She has been very supportive of what we are trying to do, for which I am very grateful. You cannot fault me for that, surely."

"What I fault you for is that you allow her to put out misleading and false stories about me and the brigade, which are clearly designed to discredit us in the eyes of the people."

"Come, General, I have denied she is our 'pet,' as you claim. You surely don't expect me to control what the press writes, do you? We don't have censorship in Naranjeras. Besides, I am not sure those *El Diario* articles were that far off the mark. Many people believe you may be overly influenced by the North Americans."

"That's bullshit and you know it," Portero said calmly, looking into the eyes of the president. "I am serving my country, Naranjeras, in accordance with a legal international treaty, negotiated and signed by a freely elected government. I work for Naranjeras, not the United States, and I damn well resent insinuations to the contrary from a man who heads a government not freely elected."

Figueroa was taken aback by the vehemence of Portero's words. He remained silent for a moment, gathering his thoughts.

"General Portero, I did not mean to imply that you were less than loyal to Naranjeras. If you took my remarks that way, I apologize. I only tried to say that some people believe your association with the HJRAF may have influenced your perspective, away from how we think, to a more North American viewpoint. It was an innocent remark, but it does reflect the differences between us. I assure you I did not come here to fight with you. Quite the contrary. I came because I want to clear away some of those differences. I would like nothing better than to make a friend and ally out of you. Can't we explore some ways that might happen?"

"We can explore ways that might happen, if you wish. However, I should warn you that before I could be a friend or ally of your government, you are going to have to make some alterations in the course you seem to be taking. One important change would be your setting a date for free presidential elections."

"That is reasonable. As a matter of fact, I have said from the beginning that elections would one day be restored, and I mean it. Before that can happen, however, this government must first establish a track record so the people can understand where we are trying to take the country. Once they have that understanding, they will support us. I have no doubt about that."

"Perhaps you should start by telling me where you are trying to take us."

"My vision, and the vision of the Supreme Council, is of an independent country that is responsive to the needs of the people, a country which provides for the general welfare of its citizens. But not in the sense that socialist governments try to do it. On the contrary, we believe state socialism has proven a failure. It has had many opportunities to prove itself in various venues, but it never has succeeded.

"On the other hand," he continued, "we have seen that certain forms of capitalism have clearly succeeded in terms of creating economic growth and strength. We believe, however, that uncontrolled and unregulated capitalism has some very serious weaknesses which can be, and must be, avoided if the society is to benefit all its people. Clearly the United States has provided the world with its best capitalist model, although it too has problems and, may I point out, it imposes some rather severe controls through the regulation of its business communities.

"If we were a large country with vast resources and a huge population, we might adopt the North American model for our own. But we are not. We are small with less than seven million people and relatively limited resources, and we haven't the capital base to make the US model work here, unless of course we were to be somehow integrated into its larger economy. I am not willing to do that. That would mean surrendering our sovereignty. That kind of integration would mean we become just another market, another labor source, another raw material supplier for them. It would mean we become another branch USA. We would eventually lose our national identity and our independence. We would become just another vassal state without the capability of surviving outside their hegemony. In effect, we become a latter-day colony."

"Excuse me, Mr. President, but why is that so bad if our people also remain free and can live better lives? You make interdependence sound like a tragedy. The world is fast becoming an integrated economy. There is no such thing as an independent national economy anymore, is there? They only exist in the most backward and primitive countries. We happen to be in the western hemisphere, and that puts us within the US sphere of influence. If we were located in Europe, we would be involved in that common market. If we were in the Far East, we would be influenced by Japan and China. I don't see what is so bad about being part of the American sphere."

"What is bad is Yankee economic hegemony comes with cultural oppression as a byproduct. Their influence dominates and suppresses national identity. Look at Puerto Rico, as an example. Since it became a commonwealth, it has lost its uniqueness as a Latin American nation. It has been absorbed by the giant in the north and, in a sense, has lost its influence in our region. That does not happen in Europe or the Far East. Those nations retain their own unique identities."

Portero's response was immediate. "We certainly see the same situation in very different ways. You talk about the United States as if it were a cultural monolith. It is not. Its people live in as many different cultural traditions as there are nations in the world. To be sure, they also have a common culture, too, which is the lingua franca of their combined society. Because they write their laws in English does not mean that those of Hispanic origin do not speak Spanish nor cherish their own cultural heritage. Same goes for the Chinese, the Greeks, or the Swedes."

Portero was warming to his task. "You cite Puerto Rico as proof of your point. You say Puerto Rico has lost its influence. I fervently disagree. Because it became a commonwealth, which is almost a state, it has not only grown into an important economic force but has also gained influence and political clout it never had as a protectorate. When it becomes a state, as it certainly will someday, it will have two United States senators in Washington and, what, four or five congressmen? Each of the three or four million Puerto Ricans will have exactly the same political influence as a New Yorker, a Texan, or a Californian. They would never have that kind of power if they had remained an independent country. Look what Puerto Rico was under Spain—a poverty stricken colony without hope or influence. Furthermore today as a part of the United States, their perspective, their unique Latin American perspective, is being merged into mainstream USA and will influence not only domestic policy but US foreign policy as well. I think we Latin Americans now enjoy a new and growing understanding from the US government precisely because of Puerto Rico's unique relationship with that great power. We now have people in high office we can talk to, people who understand us, people with whom we can dialogue. How much greater will that kind of access be when it becomes a state? I might add I hope something comes of the statehood movement in Panama for the same reason. That would also improve our access."

Figueroa was learning. Their verbal sparring had shown him that Portero was more than a good soldier. He was a broadly educated, intelligent man. The revelation added to his conviction that the general would be a powerful ally if he could be persuaded in that direction. By the same token, he also recognized Portero also could be a most formidable opponent. *If I cannot make a friend of him, I will have to eliminate him. That would be a regrettable waste,* he thought.

Portero was also having his own private thoughts. Figueroa seemed to be more forthcoming and reasonable, and less devious, than he had expected. Their conversation thus far had built his self-confidence. He was beginning to believe he could hold his own with the president, and he was enjoying the challenge.

When the president spoke again, he wanted his words to reflect the candor he felt about their relationship. "It is clear, General Portero, that we hold opposite opinions of the role the

North Americans play in Latin American affairs. You seem to believe their interest in us is benign and a force for progress. I, on the other hand, am convinced their motives are self-serving, that their only interest in Latin America is purely exploitive, that we should serve only to build their economy at the expense of our own. Therefore, I believe that close involvement with them is inimical to our national interests."

Figueroa paused, smiled, and continued in a more jovial tone. "I think we both can admit, General, that our personal views on these matters have probably been reinforced, perhaps even exaggerated, by our political agendas. I freely admit mine are to a degree and I believe yours must be, too."

"Pardon me, Mr. President, but I do not have a political agenda."

"Ah, but you do, my friend. Perhaps not in the sense that you aspire to public office, but you are known as one who subscribes to the North American notion of democracy, and you often say so publicly. That is political, and since you are a respected national figure, your words carry weight. But as I was about to say, with respect to our differing views on US involvement in our region, a position somewhere between the poles we represent might well be philosophically and politically tenable for both of us. What is your opinion? Please be candid. Frankly, I feel there is room for compromise on my side."

Portero wondered where the man was going. He remained silent, waiting for more.

"I suppose, General, that I am enough of a political pragmatist to realize that there are many roads to Rome. If I want to go there, it doesn't matter, within reason, which road I take. In this case, Rome is our vision of democracy in Naranjeras, a democracy in the sense of free elections, a free economy within certain fairly liberal parameters overseen by the government and free from economic domination by foreign powers. How does that vision look to you?"

"Not perfect but a damn sight better than a return to caudillismo."

"Then how about helping me get the country there?"

"How might I do that?"

Figueroa paused and smiled. "By joining my administration. As you earlier pointed out, we need a defense minister. I would like you to take that job."

Portero was more than surprised. He was shocked, flabbergasted. Figueroa had blindsided him. In his wildest speculations, he had never thought of such a possibility. He was stunned, unable to collect his thoughts for a moment, and he showed it.

The president smiled and said, "Take a moment. Think about it."

Portero's mind began to work again. "That's not much of a job, Mr. President. The defense minister has no portfolio since he has no troops to speak of. A truck company and some engineers."

"On the contrary. He has an important portfolio. He is our liaison with the HDO relative to HJRAF affairs. That responsibility would carry even greater significance if you had the post. The alliance certainly has immense respect for you. You could be tremendously influential in their councils, and your presence in the job would be of immense significance to our own people. So I believe it is an important job in its traditional configuration.

"But it is going to be even more important. As you already know, we are in process of strengthening our armed forces. We are re-training a number of PNN and are forming an additional infantry brigade which will be similar in organization to the ALIB. We are also forming other smaller units. The bottom line is I need someone with your experience to manage the buildup."

"And what is the purpose of this buildup, Mr. President? I do not see a need for additional military strength. How can the country afford more military?"

"We can afford it. New initiatives are in place which will cover the added costs and more, and I must add, without imposing a burden on our citizens. You will learn more about that in the near future when a general announcement is made, probably next month. As to the reason for the new units, we believe they will help insure our independence from possible encroachment by the USA. Don't be shocked, General. We don't think the North Americans intend to invade us, nor do we plan to wage war against them."

He paused, watching Portero's reaction. "Candidly, we believe they have too much power inside our country already. Their tactical control of the HJRAF and therefore the ALIB gives them that power. Our purpose in creating these new units is to balance that power with an offsetting force of national troops. When we do that, we also minimize any influence they might wish to exercise on our domestic politics. It is as simple as that. I am being as forthright about this as I possibly can be."

Portero protested. "You know perfectly well, Mr. President, the ALIB has never tried to influence domestic politics, nor does it pursue any political agenda for the United States or the HDO. You know that! We are a unit of the joint regional defense effort. Nothing more. And that will not change as long as I have voice in the matter."

Figueroa nodded. "Up to now that has certainly been the case. But the potential is there. Who knows what the new US administration may do? Who knows how another man in your post may act? Recent tensions over the permisos de transito matter have demonstrated conflicts can arise which, if carried to the extreme, could endanger our national system. No, my dear general, the potential exists, and it is only wise to anticipate it and to offset it as best we can, don't you agree?"

"Frankly, sir, I do not agree. I understand your words, but I think your rationale is so very thin that it is completely without substance. Historically, there has never been an incident that remotely suggested the ALIB or the HJRAF had any interest in our domestic politics. As near as I can tell, we have always been a source of pride for our people and a symbol of national strength, certainly not a threat. If there is any concern now, it is because you have raised it through some singularly inept moves by your administration."

"I won't argue the point, General, nor will I deny that we have made a few mistakes. We are, after all, learning. However, the concerns have been raised, and the fact is they are now there. It is incumbent on me to allay them if I can. What better way to allay those concerns than for us to join forces? Your joining the government would send a powerful message not only to Naranjeros but to our allies as well. Whatever concerns there might be would immediately disappear. It would unite us as a nation, and our people could be confident about the future."

He did not show it, but Portero continued to be in a state of disbelief over Figueroa's astonishing proposition. His mind raced. There was much to consider. *Could the man's motives actually be sincere? Or is he trying sucker me into some compromise?* He believed it was the latter, but was nevertheless intrigued and amazed at the audacity of the proposal.

"I must confess, Mr. President, that I am astounded by your proposal. It is the last thing I could have imagined we would be discussing. Frankly, I am quite intrigued. Let's explore the possibility more. How would it work? How much authority would I have as Defense Minister? Who would I be responsible to? Would I be able to make my own decisions or would I have to get everything rubber stamped by the Supreme Council? There are plenty of questions."

"As Minister of Defense, you would be reporting directly to me. I alone would have veto power over your authority. The Supreme Council is not expert in military affairs. Colonel Davidson has experience, but nothing to equal yours. I am sure he would defer to you. Besides, I would recommend him as your replacement at ALIB."

"General Carmody would never accept him for that job."

"He would if you recommended him."

"I am not so sure about that. After all, he is a member of your council. That makes him political. Besides, the ALIB staff would never work for Davidson. They know him."

"Davidson would resign from the council. He is not one of its philosophical leaders, in any case. That would leave a vacancy which would be yours to fill if you were interested. As for the ALIB staff, I expect Davidson would prefer to build his own, and that you would want to move your people into the defense ministry, where their experience is needed."

"Perhaps I have a suspicious nature, Mr. President, but what guarantee do I have that I won't be fired after all these changes have been affected?"

"If my word is not enough, there are certain other guarantees I can give you. I will be willing to draw up a contract with you which not only describes your authority but also restrains frivolous intervention by the government. The contract will be made public, even published in the newspapers.

"But perhaps the more important guarantee I can give you would be the public announcement I would make on your promotion. At that time I will outline your brief and my commitment to you, and acknowledge that you have influenced my thinking, not only about military matters, but about the role of a democratic government as well. The announcement would be made in a manner that commits me to you, as much as it commits you to me. It would be like a marriage vow made before all the world, difficult to break, and committing us to a course for the future which invites universal approval. I could not arbitrarily fire you after making such commitments, could I? If I did, I would lose all credibility with the people. However, the more important aspect of all this is our joining forces would relieve the internal tensions in our country as well as any concerns the HDO and the North Americans may have. Can we agree that is a desirable objective?"

Figueroa watched Portero's reactions. He thought the young general seemed intrigued by his proposition. He understood that it was not self-glorification that would motivate Portero so much as what he could accomplish for the country with the power and influence the post would give him. He also was a realist. He recognized that Portero did not completely trust him or the Supreme Council, and he knew he had to deal with that before any agreement could be achieved.

"There will be a number of perks for you if you decide to accept this responsibility. Of course you will have the salary of Minister of National Defense, which is somewhat higher than your present one, and you will also have the privileges and allowances due a cabinet minister. All of this can start today if you say the word."

"This is not a decision that one makes lightly, as I am sure you understand, Mr. President. Your offer interests me, I'll admit. If you are sincere about your commitment to a truly democratic government, I would like to help. As a matter of fact, I frankly doubt you can do it without me, given the makeup of the Supreme Council.

"Furthermore, Mr. President, I am surprised and, I might add, a little troubled by the fact that you have shown me a different Antonio Figueroa than the one I have known. No offense is intended but which is the real you? We have never been close so I ask myself, why this sudden overture? On the surface, it appears you are seeking to neutralize me as a potential adversary for some reason. Yet you are willing to put power in my hands which, practically speaking, guarantees the character of your regime will change. I have a great deal to think about. This kind of decision needs time. How long do I have to give you my answer?"

"Look, General Portero. I need you. The country needs you. In a way, the HDO needs you in the defense job. Your presence in my government would be significant. It would be reassuring to everyone. I have said I want you there and am willing to say it publicly. I would like your answer soon, now if possible. There is nothing more I can say. Perhaps words alone can't do it, but there is something I can do to prove my sincerity."

He reached into his briefcase and took out an envelope, which he handed to Portero. The general opened it and pulled out a cashier's check payable to him in the amount of one million dollars. He looked at Figueroa with amazement.

"Will that demonstrate my sincerity? Join the administration and that check is yours. Another one just like it will be paid to you at the end of your first year with us. You will receive checks for two million dollars at the end of each subsequent year for as long as we retain power. That, I hope, will show you how much we need you. That is not tax payer money, incidentally. It comes from a private donor who agrees that we need you in government. Please consider this offer."

Figueroa rose and excused himself to seek the bathroom, leaving the astonished general alone with his thoughts. Portero knew a bribe when he saw one, but this was spectacular. He was flattered more than anything, and he begrudgingly admired the audacity of the offer. He was very much aware that the sums offered were more than he could expect to earn in a lifetime as a soldier, and for a fleeting moment wondered what he might do with such a windfall. But in his heart, he knew what his answer to Figueroa's proposition would be. He calmly took time to plan his response. He was smiling when Figueroa returned.

The president saw the smile and returned it, hoping it was a sign he had succeeded. "What do you think, Pancho? May I call you that?"

"Certainly, Antonio, please do." Portero's smile broadened. "If we are going to be colleagues, let's do it as friends."

Figueroa's smile became a grin. "Then you have decided to join us? Excellent!"

"I have, sir." Portero's answer was measured and calm, concealing the excitement he felt. "I am impressed by your sincerity and your avowed commitment to a democratic government. And

I am overwhelmed by the financial offer which, in a way, demonstrates the importance you place on my joining you. It is most flattering really, and I want you to know I appreciate it. Yes, I will join your government, but under conditions somewhat different than those you offer. I do not need the money. You can save that for a better use."

"Oh, what are your conditions then?" Figueroa's smile faded and there was a note of caution in his question.

"My conditions are that you walk out with me now to meet with the press representatives waiting outside, and commit to a general election to be held no later than July fifteenth of next year. If you do that, I will announce at the same time that I have agreed to accept your kind offer to join the government."

Figueroa's smile disappeared. His face paled and hardened with anger. His eyes narrowed and his head shook and his voice was cold. "You know I cannot do that now… The timing is wrong. Arrangements must be made. It is out of the question."

"You are a clever man, Figueroa. You can do it now, and I'm ready to go out there with you. I was beginning to believe you were sincerely committed to democracy. This is your chance to show the world. My offer stands. It is now or not at all."

"Who in hell do you think you are to put that kind of pressure on me? I don't accept ultimatums from anybody…especially from people who don't have…" He didn't finish the sentence.

Portero coolly watched the man's fury take control of him. "What will it be, Figueroa? Are we going out there or not?"

"Go to hell, Portero!" The president trembled with rage uncontrollably. "You will learn it is better to have me as a friend than an enemy. You have just lost your chance for friendship. I am going to destroy you."

Portero sensed he was living an historic moment, a turning point for his country. He thought it was a time for him to make some memorable comment. His mind raced, he searched for the words, but all he could muster was "Kiss my ass, Figueroa."

• • •

Portero was quiet on the return trip to Valle Escondido. Colonel Soto, accompanying him in the staff car, was very anxious to learn what had transpired in the meeting with the president. He made several attempts to open a conversation, but the general remained preoccupied and, except for a perfunctory grunt or two, was unresponsive.

Portero had mixed feelings about the meeting. He was reliving it, trying to critique his own performance. He knew he had crossed the point of no return with the president, which would eventually lead to hostilities between the brigade and the government. In that sense, the situation was worse than when he went into the meeting. A part of him regretted what had happened. He knew the road ahead would be a rough one for the brigade and for the country. He knew his relationship with the HJRAF, with the people of Naranjeras, and with his beloved ALIB had changed forever, and he wished he could go back to what was.

But another part of him was excited. He had defied the president, a man who would not tolerate defiance and who, he sensed, would stop at nothing to redress the insult. In his heart he was glad to have drawn the line with Figueroa, and he looked forward to the challenges with something akin to pleasure. He felt exhilaration and a new confidence despite his trepidation. He wondered where it would end.

He knew he had time. The balance of power favored the brigade for the moment. Figueroa could not move until the new PNN units came on line. Then the balance would shift away from the ALIB, and that was when the hostilities would begin. His days would now be occupied getting his units ready to win whatever battles lay ahead.

Still he worried that he had precipitated the breach by his aggressiveness with the president. Had he gone too far? Could this crisis have been avoided if he had played it a little smarter? Well he had gone into the meeting determined to make his point about elections and he had done that, but where was he now? Had he jeopardized what he had tried to do? Had he put the ALIB at an unacceptable risk? What about Carmody, the HDO, and all that had been built? He thought it likely he had upset the equilibrium that it had taken so long to build. From then on, it would be a struggle to maintain the balance of power in favor of the ALIB. But could he have done it differently? He didn't know, but the die was cast. "*La suerte esta echada*," he remembered his grandfather's saying.

"What happened, General?" Colonel Soto could stand it no longer. It was more a demand than a question, and it brought Portero back to reality.

"I'm sorry, Soto. I was just thinking what I might have done differently." He turned to his chief of staff, smiling. "What happened? Well, in a nut shell, the son of a bitch offered me the job of Minister of Defense."

Soto's head snapped around, and his mouth dropped open in surprise. "My God! What did you say?"

"I accepted."

"You what?"

Portero's smile became a grin. "I accepted. I accepted on the condition that he go out and tell the press people waiting there that he would call elections next year. He refused, of course, and became quite angry. That pretty much ended our meeting."

"You were in there over two hours. What was going on?"

Portero recapped the meeting for his chief of staff in as much detail as he could, emphasizing what the president had told him about the formation of new military units. He withheld nothing excepting the bribe offer, which he found embarrassing. He would tell no one about that except Betsy.

When he had finished the story of the meeting, he said, "One thing is certain, Soto, there is trouble ahead for the brigade. We have to prepare for a fight."

• • •

President Figueroa was still angry when he arrived at the presidential palace in the capital. He was angry with himself more than with Portero. He had made two mistakes. First he had underestimated his opponent. He had gone into their meeting believing he might persuade the ALIB commander to join the government. He hadn't imagined any sensible person could have refused his offer, but Portero had.

His second mistake angered him the most. He should not have so abruptly refused Portero's demand to set elections. Although he could not have made any announcement to the press there and then, he might have bought some time by holding out some hope that he would do it later. He thought he might have tried, no, he knew he should have tried to negotiate the date for elections. He might have been able to string Portero along even until the new military units were ready. But he had allowed Portero to rattle him to the point he lost control of the meeting, and that rankled.

"Well, it is done. *La suerte esta echada*. I can't change what has happened so we must move on from here." He summoned the minister of the interior. He summarized the meeting for him, ending with Portero's refusal of his offer.

"I am surprised. The man must be an idiot," said Interior.

"He is no idiot," the president said vehemently. "He is a very intelligent and clever man. In a way, I admire him. But he is a danger to us. He will be our opposition, perhaps our only effective opposition. He will be a dangerous opponent. We have no choice. He must disappear. Cut off the head and you kill the snake. Without Portero, the ALIB is nothing. I will discuss the problem with Davidson. Tomorrow."

CHAPTER 10

Two weeks after Portero's meeting with the president in Tuxla, a series of events began to occur which were disruptive to ALIB. The first was an *El Diario* front page article which expanded coverage of the Gallo killing.

The headline read, "New Evidence Links ALIB Agents to Killing." The column one story, datelined "La Capital," was succinct.

> The Ministry of Justice announced today its investigation of the murder of a PNN training officer in La Rioja has revealed the killers were agents of the ALIB. A warrant has been issued for the arrest of two soldiers currently serving with that unit in Valle Escondido. The victim, Major Hernan Gallo, was stationed at a PNN training base near La Rioja.
>
> Colonel Xavier Molina, commanding officer of the base, in an exclusive interview with *El Diario*, reported he had received information that the two men who had been seeking information about the PNN unit training near La Rioja might have been agents for the ALIB, and he had ordered Gallo to question them. According to Molina, eyewitnesses told investigators the tragedy occurred when Gallo attempted to question the men in a hotel bar regarding their possible affiliation with the US-controlled ALIB. The men reacted violently and assaulted Gallo. A fight ensued which ended in the fatal shooting of Major

Gallo. The men then fled in a small truck, taking with them an employee of the hotel and another PNN officer as hostages, both of whom subsequently managed to escape their captors.

A warrant has been issued for the apprehension of the killers, who have been identified as Carlos Campinas and Enrique Ruedas, officers said to be currently serving with the ALIB. A spokesman for the brigade admitted the men were members of the unit but denied the allegation they were on a spy mission. He disputed the facts presented by the Ministry of Justice and promised a thorough investigation of the matter by ALIB investigators, stressing the fact that the implementing protocol authorizing the creation of the ALIB gave it jurisdiction in criminal matters involving its personnel.

As soon as the article appeared, Lacerica, at the direction of Portero, placed a telephone call to Ramon Sanchez Avila at *Vida Nacional*. The old reporter angrily denounced the distortions contained in the *El Diario* article in unequivocal terms. He agreed to refute them in a future column but wanted to delay, pending the outcome of his appeal to Colonel Davidson to interview the witnesses. "I am not very hopeful it will come to pass. He has not been at all cooperative, but as long as there is a chance, why jeopardize any opportunity we may have of talking to these men? I have put some pressure on him, but so far all he has offered are copies of the investigators' reports. They will be useless. I expect they will only confirm the allegations contained in the article."

Lacerica agreed, and they promised to stay in close communication on the matter.

• • •

The second event took place that same evening. A ministry of justice officer served a warrant on the ALIB brigade duty officer, which demanded Ruedas and Campinas be immediately taken into custody and transported to federal court authorities in La Capital.

General Portero, after consultation with his legal officer, directed a letter to the minister of justice, in which he advised of Campinas's death from injuries sustained at the hands of Gallo, and confirmed Ruedas' arrest as demanded.

In a subsequent paragraph, he referred the minister to the *Crimes and Military Justice Section* of the Treaty, which provided that responsibility for prosecution of criminal offenses "perpetrated within a military context by its personnel" belonged to he ALIB. He further advised the minister that he was prepared to convene a courts-martial immediately upon the availability of the witnesses to the incident.

Portero then called Hank Ruedas to his office and, in the presence of the legal officer, placed him under arrest and confined him to the base, and directed him to continue his normal duties pending the findings of the investigation. He then quietly ordered a twenty-four hour guard for Ruedas against the possibility that government agents might try to seize him surreptitiously.

• • •

Three days after the *El Diario* article appeared, a third disruption took place which confirmed Portero's belief that Figueroa was building a campaign designed to weaken the ALIB.

The commanding officer of the 2d Transportation Truck Company signed for the sealed envelope delivered directly to him by a courier from the ministry of defense. His curiosity was immediately aroused. It was unusual for the ministry to communicate with him directly. His orders normally came through the brigade, so it was with some anxiety that he opened the communication.

The packet contained orders signed by Colonel Edson Davidson, acting Minister of Defense, directing the redeployment of his unit from the ALIB Base in Valle Escondido to the PNN Headquarters compound in the capital. His unit's mission would continue to be the support of the ALIB but from the new base. He was to leave one of his four truck platoons at Valle Escondido while the remaining three were to close on the new location no later than three weeks hence.

The orders contained extensive administrative detail relative to the new cantonment area, the transportation and housing of dependent families, and the disposition of spare parts and expendable supplies. He was not immediately interested in such detail and did not read further. He sat in stunned disbelief as the full implications of the orders struck him.

He would have to leave Valle Escondido. It had been his station for over five years, ever since he was first assigned to the Company. His family was settled there. His children had spent most of their young lives there. It had become their home, and they were happy there. He knew his wife would not take the prospect of change well. He dreaded giving her the news.

He also liked the area, and he liked his duty with the brigade. He identified with the ALIB, and he regarded his mission there as uniquely important. He had come to especially cherish his relationships with brigade personnel, particularly with Colonel Roth, from whom he took direction. Therefore it was with a sinking heart that he contemplated the disruption these orders would cause in his comfortable world.

He wondered if Colonel Roth was aware of these orders. He picked up the telephone to call the B4 office.

• • •

The Truck Company redeployment order did not surprise General Portero. He expected something to happen relative to his transportation since the possibility had been an item for discussion at the ATB meeting. However, he had not anticipated such a short timeline. Also the manner in which the orders arrived angered him. Military courtesy should have dictated he be consulted or at least be given a forewarning before such change was ordered.

His anger subsided, though, as he realized there was not likely to be any further courtesies from Figueroa following their bitter exchange in Tuxla.

It was clear the battle had now been joined. The *El Diario* article, the Ruedas arrest warrant, and now the redeployment order were the government's opening shots, and he knew more would follow. He also knew he had to somehow respond, start firing shots of his own, or stand in danger of losing by default any chance of prevailing in this new, and still political, contest.

A quick reassessment of the situation confirmed the military balance of power clearly favored the ALIB at the moment, and would still continue to do so for the next few months. It would not change until the government's new combat units were fully trained and back on the mainland. For the present, Figueroa's only leverage against him would be in the political and legal arenas. That meant any "return fire" from Portero would necessarily have to be in the same arenas. Clearly any kind of preemptive military strike against Figueroa was not an option, because it would not be condoned or even understood in either the domestic or the international communities. Neither the United States nor the hemispheric powers were yet seeing Figueroa for what he was, so any early action would only brand the ALIB as an out of control rogue organization and could accomplish nothing except earn him general condemnation. It would isolate him at a time when he needed to win political allies and public support.

In any case, the brigade was not ready to take any early action. For one thing, the additional supplies Carmody had quietly agreed to provide had not yet arrived, nor had the requested helicopters. More importantly, he felt the brigade was not psychologically ready to take the field against the government.

He knew it was adequately trained and had the skills necessary for the task, but he was not sure his officers and soldiers were mentally prepared to act against their countrymen. He didn't believe they fully understood the true nature of the growing conflict nor the possibility the ALIB might have to act on its own, without the justifying authority of the HJRAF. He believed their loyalty to him was firm and deep, but would it remain so if he asked them to take actions which some might construe as being outside the law?

The thought worried him and led him to musing about his own motivations. Was he doing the right thing in opposing Figueroa? Had he the right or the responsibility? The idea of taking up arms against Naranjeros was most disturbing to him. It was an emotional and personal conflict deep within him, which he needed to resolve before he could ask the brigade to do it. It would be so much easier to stand aside and let the situation take its course without his intervention, but he knew he would never be able to live with himself if, because of his inaction, Figueroa succeeded in his purposes. Yet the annoying doubts persisted. None of his training had prepared him to face this kind of dilemma, and there was no one he could consult or confide in except Betsy.

Then he remembered reading somewhere a quote from the American General Patton: "Never take counsel of your fears. The time to consider the consequences is before you make your decision. When you have all the facts and have made your decision, turn off all fears and proceed without further hesitation." It was sound advice, and he took comfort from it. He snapped back to reality and re-examined his position.

First, he had complete confidence in his assessment of the situation. After all, he had had it from Figueroa's own lips, real democracy would end in Naranjeras if the man remained unopposed. Second, the ALIB was the only entity in the country which could successfully oppose him. Only the brigade had power to frustrate Figueroa's plans. Only the brigade could keep the country in the democratic camp, and, to him, that was a cause worth any risk. Finally, he was certain his purposes were honorable and right. He had no private ax to grind. Personal ambition was not part of his motive for opposing the president. These thoughts helped restore his confidence.

His mind returned to the practical matters at hand, and he once again became the single minded, highly focused brigade commander of his public image. His first task would be to prepare his officers and men, mentally, to meet the challenge ahead. They had to know exactly what he was planning, and he had to elicit their agreement; because without their support, there could be no hope for success. He would start with a briefing of his key staff members and commanders on the situation and on his plans. Their reaction would help him assess their willingness to follow him. He thought some might hesitate to take up arms against their countrymen. Any who expressed doubt would be offered the opportunity to opt out. He would have to be well-prepared for the meeting, and he resolved to begin immediately.

His second immediate task was to find a way to keep his trucks. The Truck Company was essential to the ALIB. Under the circumstances, allowing its redeployment was unthinkable, as it would mean surrendering his only means of supplying and transporting his units. On the other hand, he could not simply refuse to obey the Defense Ministry's order. The time was not right. And he grudgingly believed the order was technically legal, however suspect its motivation, so an outright refusal now could not be defended at HJRAF and could become an embarrassment to General Carmody.

Beyond all else was the practical matter of organizing the brigade for the coming struggle, which would take time. He needed at least two months more to be ready. He pondered how he might delay releasing his trucks while leaving the impression he intended to comply with the redeployment order. He searched for a plausible argument which would be convincing to the Defense Ministry, but none immediately came to mind. Finally he decided to give the problem to the ATB, which was scheduled to meet early the following week.

. . .

"Colonel Molina tells me you are an explosives expert." Colonel Davidson, the deputy minister of defense, was sitting with the Cuban, Major Serra, in a parked staff car on a dark road outside of La Rioja.

"I have some experience, yes, sir."

"Are you aware of the job we have to do?"

"Colonel Molina outlined it to me."

"Can it be done?"

"Building the package is the easy part. That will be no problem. The difficult part will be getting it into the car undetected."

"Leave that with me. I have the means to do it. When can I have the package?"

"In ten days, I think. It will take some time to find the electronics. You want to detonate by radio, I understand. Is that correct? Once I have the equipment, I'll need a week or so to test the system and build the package."

"Very well. It'll take time to set the operation up, anyway. Please proceed. Molina will let you know when we are ready for the package. Any questions?"

"No, sir. Everything seems clear enough."

"Thank you, Major."

Serra opened the car door and stepped into the darkness. "Good night, sir."

"Good night, Major." Davidson started the car and drove a kilometer before he flicked on the headlights.

. . .

"We have a solution to the truck problem, General," Colonel Soto announced as the ATB meeting convened. He, Ochoa, and Roth had worked during the weekend to have a recommendation ready for Portero.

"You know, General, there may be more to this redeployment order than just a try at limiting our mobility. We believe they might really need those vehicles. When they bring those units Chris Lane found on Isla Grande back to the mainland, they will need more transport than they now have, so by taking our trucks they kill two birds with a single shot. They put us on foot, and they enhance their own mobility."

Portero nodded his agreement. "That gives us a double reason to keep our trucks. Let me hear your recommendation."

Soto outlined the plan. "We inform the Defense Ministry that we will comply with the order but that we will be unable to meet the October first target date. We tell them we have been ordered by HJRAF to conduct brigade-sized maneuvers during October and November, and must have the truck company for that exercise. We are betting they will be reluctant to interfere with training. Our problem is we have no such orders. Can you persuade General Carmody to go along with us and cut some?"

"Perhaps. I'll call him this morning."

The chief of staff continued. "Now you have directed that we find a way to prove our good intentions. To that end, we propose we send them one truck platoon on October first, with the promise of the other two they have asked for in December after the maneuvers. That should mollify them through the interim and it leaves us with eighteen trucks, including the platoon they intend we should keep. That is enough to move one battalion, complete with its equipment. At the same time, by sending them only one platoon in October, we are only marginally enhancing their mobility."

Portero was pleased with the recommendation. He congratulated them on their creativity and suggested the six trucks to be sent in October include whatever problem vehicles the Company might have. He directed they be freshly painted and made to look like new before the transfer. "This also offers an opportunity to get rid of problem personnel. If the Truck Company has any, let's send them on with the trucks."

It was agreed Colonel Roth would work with the Truck Company commander on readying the platoon and, with the appropriate authorities at the Ministry of Defense, on the details of the transfer.

Colonel Banning, next on the ATB agenda, gave a brief intelligence report. There was nothing new on the Isla Grande garrison; however his recon teams reported increased activity at the La Rioja camp. They were now estimating a battalion-size unit in training there. He concluded with a report from a contact at the Capital International Airport of the arrival of several groups of men from the Middle East. Some of them were confirmed to be traveling on Libyan passports. Each group of five or six had arrived on different international airline flights originating in Europe and was met by representatives of the Defense Ministry. However, the contact insisted the new arrivals did not appear to be military men.

Colonel Ochoa then reported on the status of training of each battalion and provided schedules for October.

Colonel Roth followed to give his report. When he had finished, all turned to Portero.

"Gentlemen. I am going to change the subject. I want to talk to you about the situation we are facing. There is not the slightest doubt in my mind that Figueroa's ultimate aim is to neutralize the ALIB. He knows we are a threat to his agenda. We stand in his way, and he is determined to put us out of business. And he seems to have a plan for doing it. His offer to me at Tuxla, the recent *El Diario* article, the arrest warrant for Hank Ruedas, and the truck redeployment order are not just coincidences of timing. They are almost certainly a part of a plan designed to harass us, embroil us in losing political skirmishes, and besmirch our image with the people. His goal is to weaken us as the opposition.

"You can bet more of the same kind of stuff will be coming. If he is able to successfully attack us politically, if he can discredit us in the eyes of Naranjeros and with the HDO, he can avoid a costly fight in the field.

"I believe we must respond in kind—at the political level. We simply cannot allow him to build up too much momentum. However, in responding, we must be very careful not to cause embarrassment to the country or to the HJRAF. So how we do it is very important. As a rule of thumb, our responses must be primarily directed at defending the rights of the brigade. The country has seen us do that before and will understand our motives. Our responses must also always be the truth. We have our supporters within the country and we must keep providing them with the information they need to speak on our behalf. Captain Lacerica has the responsibility for providing that, and it is a big job. Incidentally, he has sufficient time in grade and will be promoted to Major next month. Soto is in the process of beefing up his staff so that he can handle the increased load.

"I intend to be personally engaged in an intensified public relations effort in Mesona. Lacerica will be involved in this one too as a coordinator, but I plan to take the lead. Our top priority will be to build upon the goodwill there and in the north which is already building. As this conflict intensifies, we are going to need political allies. The Mesonenses and the ranchers in the north have always been somewhat disapproving of the government, but they have become especially antagonistic to this Figueroa crowd. That makes them natural allies, and I want to build on that.

"A political alliance with the people of Mesona suggests a military strategy for us. By a fortunate accident of geography, Mesona and the north will be of strategic importance to us should we ever have to fight the Figueroa forces. Valle Escondido lies between the capital and Mesona, which means we are in a position to deny the northern area to Figueroa if and when the time comes. Mesona, with its intervening pass through the mountain, is obviously defensible and therefore important strategically.

"I want the ATB to place a priority on developing a 'northern strategy' which assumes Figueroa will try to dislodge us if we hold the region. I believe he will be forced to it since the northern area accounts for almost half of the country's export revenues. He will not want to surrender control of that to us, as it would weaken him economically and politically. He will have no choice but to force us out of there. To do that he will have to extend his supply lines, which will be vulnerable to interdictory raids by our forces. He will be obliged to secure his rear, which will weaken the main effort force he will bring against us. That will level the playing field somewhat, and if we can avoid getting tied down in a direct engagement and can stay mobile, we can pick and choose where we fight him. However, to succeed in any such hit-and-run strategy, we must have the support of the local civilian population. That is why we must place such a high priority on building our relations with the Mesonenses. We cannot make a northern strategy work without them. Any questions?"

Portero waited, but there were no questions. He continued. "If it comes to a fight, we'll need to win it early. We won't have much re-supply or replacement capability, which means we would lose a protracted engagement. We have to hit him with continuous short, sharp blows when and where he least expects it. We will have to always do it with sufficient force to inflict heavy casualties on his forces at minimum cost to us. That must be our standard tactical doctrine. The key to success will be surprise, and that means we must retain the initiative. We must keep them reacting to our moves and not give them time to plan their own.

"We are infantry, but we must act like cavalry. Our biggest problem will be fatigue. If we exhaust our troops we lose, so we must plan to keep them fresh by rotating our units into secure rest areas during the hit-and-run phase, another reason for having support of the civilian population.

"I see the northern strategy as Phase One. We will use it to wear the Figueroa forces down to the point we can defeat them in the final battle.

"Phase Two will be for control of Puerto Hondo and the International Airport. Victory will go to the side that can seize and hold those strategic objectives. That last battle will be an all-out effort for us. It will take everything we have left to win it. We will have to husband our strength, our supplies, and our will to win it. If we fail there, we lose everything."

Again Portero waited for comments or questions. None came so he continued. "What I have just outlined amounts to my 'Commander's Intent' as to how we will conduct this fight should the situation deteriorate into a shooting war. I will have my Intent in written form for you tomorrow. Your job now is to develop war plans for carrying out that general strategy." He paused then added. "One more thing, gentlemen. In planning, you are to assume the ALIB will be operating alone, without support from HJRAF."

"No support from HIRAF?" It was half-statement and half-question from Colonel Ochoa, the B3.

"Plan on none. The most help we can expect from HJRAF is that it won't intervene on Figueroa's behalf, at least initially. However, practically speaking, the longer the conflict, the greater the international political pressure will be on the HDO to stop it. That's another reason we must make it a short, fast operation.

"This will be a lonely battle, gentlemen. We'll be on our own. If we win, we will have preserved our democracy. If we lose... well, you know the answer."

"We'll go to work, General." The chief of staff hesitated, then added, "And may I say I like your style, sir."

Portero smiled and responded slowly. "I hope so, because I am compelled to also tell you...I am not unmindful of the seriousness of the task I have asked you to take on. I have asked you to prepare to fight our fellow Naranjeros, to fight a war for which we probably all will be condemned and vilified. It will cause considerable hardship in our country. There will be casualties. If we lose, we might all be shot, or at least tried by courts-martial. If we are victorious, we will have saved the country, but we probably won't get much thanks for it. Remember Pinochet? Despite all that, I believe it is the right course. Preserving democracy in Naranjeras is the right thing to do, and for me, it is worth the risk.

"However, I must add that I am fully aware that what I propose is beyond any understanding of what our responsibilities were to be when we accepted our commissions with the ALIB. I therefore assert to you now that I do not believe I have the authority or the right to compel you to participate in this adventure."

He looked closely at each man, trying to sense reactions. "You have the right to say no. If you have any doubt or are uncomfortable following the course I have outlined, you should withdraw. I give you my word, you may step aside without prejudice. I know each of you well. You are honorable and courageous men, and I am grateful for the magnificent contributions you have made in building this organization. I will respect you no less should you decide not to participate in this undertaking. Please let me have your thoughts."

Soto turned to face the group, waiting for someone to start. The faces around the table were sober. Ochoa was the first to speak. "General, we have devoted much of our lives to building this brigade. It has become something important in the country. I have always believed it was committed to the service of the citizens of Naranjeras. Now is the time to fulfill that commitment. Speaking for myself, it would be unthinkable not to act on their behalf in this crisis. It would be traitorous not to defend our constitution, and therefore it would be an act of cowardice not to resist Figueroa and his gang of thugs."

Everyone nodded his agreement. Soto looked at each man, silently inviting additional comment. When none was offered, he turned to Portero and said, "Well General, I think we are in unanimous agreement with Ochoa. From my own perspective, it would be a terrible waste, and a crime, if we were to step aside and let these bastards have their way. I would much rather have the brigade go down fighting. At least then we would be fulfilling our responsibility. Even if it may be technically outside the legal provisions of the treaty, it is still within the spirit of why the ALIB was created. All our efforts will not have been wasted even if in the end we should lose."

Colonel Banning cleared his throat. "Do you remember how Naranjeras used to be when it was governed by *caudillos?* We were a divided society. On one side were the rich and the privileged, who depended almost completely on the government to grow their riches and expand their privileges. In return they gave the government dutiful support. On the other side were the poor and underprivileged. The docile poor were ignored. The not so docile poor and dissidents were suppressed, usually by economic means, but sometimes by violence. That is how it has always been with authoritarian governments, and that is how it was in Naranjeras. Remember?

"But in the past number of years, under democratic regimes, we have begun to free ourselves of that no-win, no-hope kind of existence. We have only to remember how things used to be and then look to see how different they are today to appreciate the change. Small businesses have sprung up everywhere, wages have risen as has the standard of living, not only for the privileged and middle class but for the poor as well. Schools have improved. Illiteracy is dropping. The number of skill jobs are growing and being filled. Our people have hope…more than hope, they have confidence in the future. Admittedly we still have a way to go, but the changes so far have been profound, and there will be more to come if we can keep our freedom.

"Naranjeros have learned a great deal about making democracy work, and we'll learn more given the opportunity. It is certainly our right to try, and I believe it is a right given to us by

Almighty God. If that is true then no man, not Figueroa, not the devil himself, has the authority or the power to take it from us, nor have we the authority to surrender it. I for one am not willing to surrender my democratic rights, nor yours, nor any of our countrymen's. I add my vote to Ochoa's. I am with you, General."

Once again Soto waited. His colleagues were nodding and smiling, signaling their agreement with Banning. He turned to Portero. "We are all with you, General. And may I add, so will be every officer and soldier in the brigade. I guarantee it. We await your orders."

Portero felt a load lifted from his shoulders. His concerns had flown, and he had to stifle a surge of emotion. "Thank you all. With men like you, we cannot lose. Now let's get to work. I want to meet with the battalion commanders, their execs, and their sergeant majors. They should know the situation just as I have given it to you. And those who are uncomfortable with the course I intend to take should also have the option to opt out. Colonel Soto, please set up a meeting for next week."

• • •

The aging general cargo freighter of Greek registry eased her rusty side against the government wharf in Puerto Hondo at midnight. A group of swarthy men dressed alike in khaki work clothes waited dockside to take charge of the cargo under the watchful eyes of two platoons of PNN troops, who had sealed off the area to any curious passerby.

The ship's crew had already rigged out the vessel's heavy cargo booms and uncovered the cargo hatches. One by one the large, grim shapes of olive green Cascavel armored cars began to emerge from the ship's hold. By dawn, fifteen of them had been transferred onto the dock and rolled into an adjacent warehouse.

The big vehicles were followed by thirty-three forty foot containers. Some of them marked, "Danger-Explosives," were loaded on flatbed trucks and transported away from the port area under PNN escort. The remaining containers disappeared into the warehouse with the Cascavels, and the dark men in khaki with them.

At sunrise, with the aid of two harbor tugs, the ship moved to a dock in the commercial area of the port. Nothing at the government wharf remained to show that it had unloaded there. It was deserted except for the PNN sentries guarding the entrances to the government warehouse area.

• • •

The morning following the ATB meeting, Soto and Banning came to Portero's office. Banning was eager to make a recommendation. "I've been thinking about this truck transfer, General. This gives us an opportunity to send our own agent with the trucks. Someone knowledgeable, who knows what he is about, and who can communicate what he sees to us. It could pay big dividends, having a friend in their camp. Those trucks are going to be where the action is. They'll be involved in troop movements, supply deliveries, and a lot of other activities we will want to know about. It will be important to have someone with them who can keep us apprised of what they are doing."

"It would have to be someone beyond suspicion, someone they will trust. Do you have anyone in mind?"

"No, sir, but I will work on it."

They discussed how such a thing could be handled, and the meeting concluded when Portero authorized Banning to proceed with "Operation Hawkeye."

CHAPTER 11

In mid-October, the government initiated its planned export controls and announced the formation of a National Marketing Board. The National Assembly, dominated by its president, Mario Fox, had managed to pass the enabling legislation earlier in the month, despite strong resistance from northwestern diputados whose constituents were the principal producers of the affected commodities.

Reaction to the announcement was strong and swift in coming. As expected it was centered in the northwestern districts, but the Supreme Council was surprised by its vehemence. After considerable discussion and consultation with its political advisors, it postponed the program's implementation date from January to March, and recognizing the need for "educating the public," it announced a series of town hall meetings to be held around the country. It also doubled the media buy for its carefully crafted campaign, designed to "sell" the concept to the people.

The editors of *El Diario* swung into action with their support. Column after column, interview upon interview, the op-ed and "Letters to the Editor" pages all sang praises on the concept of a National Marketing Board.

Vida Nacional was less sanguine about it. Typically it reflected the questions and concerns of the man in the street. It reported a general consensus for caution in implementing the proposed program. Many believed it represented a too radical departure from traditional practices. In his column, *La Opinion Mia,* Ramon Sanchez Avila weighed in with a reminder that the export sector of the national economy had always been strong, and it was the leading producer of foreign exchange and therefore ought not to be tampered with.

La Prensa, published in Mesona, the business center of the northwest, condemned the move as anti-producer and anti-free enterprise. It unequivocally opposed the initiative and warned it was a first step toward centralizing control of the economy. It published a series of articles on the disastrous effect of a similar scheme, which had been tried in El Salvador in the early eighties. It also ran a series of interviews with nationally known opinion leaders, soliciting their views on the marketing board proposal. General Portero, through his spokesman, Major Lacerica, declined to be interviewed, declaring it was a political, not military, matter.

La Prensa's strong stand stimulated demand for the paper, enabling the publisher to increase his print runs and expand distribution. The paper's circulation jumped progressively for several consecutive weeks. Then suddenly, there were problems with the newsprint supply imported through Puerto Hondo. The problems miraculously disappeared, however, when the shortages forced its publisher to cut back circulation to normal levels.

• • •

Despite his refusal to be interviewed, Francisco Portero did not conceal his strong opposition to the Marketing Board plan. He discussed the matter at length with the publisher and editor of *La Prensa* in an "off the record" private meeting. At their urging, he agreed to doing "not for publication" private meetings with the leaders of the influential Cattlemen's Association and the Tanners Board. Word spread of his interest in the problems of the district and he found himself in demand as a speaker, always with no press present, at business and fraternal organization functions, and at a few churches. Each speaking engagement seemed to generate additional invitations until he found himself making one, sometimes two, trips to Mesona each week. Each trip required the better part of a day placing a heavy demand on his time but building good relations in the north was an important part of his Northern Strategy. The more he spoke, the better known he became and his popularity grew, and with it support for the ALIB.

His frequent trips did not go unnoticed in La Capital, however, and Figueroa managed to have observers at many of his speaking engagements to record not only what Portero was saying, but also who was listening to him.

• • •

Molly Moran returned to her little home after another satisfying tour of duty at the FLUSH Office, only three miles away on University Avenue, just off the Minnesota campus. It had been a beautiful fall day in Minneapolis. The air was crisp and clean, the trees were well into their bright fall colors, and she had seen her first flight of Canadian geese honking their way to somewhere South. Yuri, her old cat, greeted her, rubbing insistently against her leg to remind her it was past his feeding time.

Molly was consumed in a feeling of well-being. Life was so good now that she again had a purpose. Her duties with FLUSH had been expanded, confirming how much her work was appreciated. In addition to training new volunteers, she now helped plan and direct local demonstrations. The week before, she had organized the Saturday rally on the steps of O'Shaunessy Auditorium. It had been a great success with plenty of TV coverage and an animated crowd. She guessed there had been three hundred fifty demonstrators there, but the *Tribune's* estimate was "over eight hundred."

Bless them, she thought. *They are exaggerating our turnouts, just as they used to do for CISPES. It's so encouraging to know the editorial staff is still with us.*

The sound bites from her speech to the crowd had been repeated frequently on the weekend TV newscasts, always against a background shot showing her FLUSH demonstrators enthusiastically waving their placards and plumber's friends. The good coverage had given her new clout in the movement, and it certainly had raised her visibility with the press and with the police, which was wonderful.

She would try to get herself arrested the following Tuesday. They had planned a sit-in at the office of Minnesota's junior senator in the downtown federal building. Unlike the senior senator, he was a conservative and not likely to be sympathetic with the FLUSH cause. She hoped they would be able to generate some sort of incident for the television cameras. Tuesdays were normally slow news days so, with any luck, she should make the national evening news. That would be marvelous! She felt the old remembered exhilaration and sense of power, like a general in command of a great battle must feel. It was heady stuff, and it took her back to the eighties. She laughed and stroked old Yuri.

FLUSH had made wonderful progress in a short time. The old CISPES hands knew how to make it work, and there didn't seem to be any shortage of money. To be sure, most of the people with whom she was working were new and younger, but she saw in them the same clear-eyed dedication, the same courage, the same zeal and willingness to sacrifice for the cause. And what better cause than to expose the corruption and brutality of that horrible military machine in the Pentagon!

Molly had never doubted the righteousness of this new crusade. Had there been any doubts at all, they would have been dispelled by the marvelous speaker she had heard at a suburban church the week before. It had been a woman. Hortencia somebody-or-other, who was the editor of the leading Naranjeras newspaper.

She had told them things, shocking things which one could never read in most American newspapers, about terrorist acts carried out by thugs from a US sponsored military unit stationed in that country. Most people would never believe Washington could condone the kind of violence and murder which had taken place. She however, was not surprised. She could believe anything of the government having seen first hand the atrocities committed by those secret US surrogates in El Salvador and Guatemala in the eighties. In any case the events in Naranjeras were confirmed in a *New York Times* story which reported on the murder of that policeman by those US sponsored gangsters.

Molly was thrilled at the prospect of visiting Naranjeras. That Hortencia what's-her-name had invited a group of FLUSH volunteers to visit the country on a fact finding tour. Molly had been first in line to sign up. The thought of returning to Central America and the Caribbean gave her great joy. She had never been to Naranjeras which, she heard was a beautiful little country, and she had always wanted to see it. Now she would have her chance, and the best part was, she would be able to campaign there. She once again would be helping make history. Life was so good.

• • •

Captain Simoni, the administrative officer of the Second Infantry Brigade in training on Isla Grande, was unusually busy with record keeping. The last training stage was nearing completion and his small section was working overtime posting qualification certificates in individual personnel files, and in recording a rush of NCO promotions.

Except for the temporary excitement engendered by an unusual over flight by a mysterious helicopter, his life there had been uneventful and routine.

Simoni found his work tedious and dull but at least, during the day, it kept his mind off his personal problems. Nights were different however. He had difficulty sleeping because his thoughts returned to the great injustice done to him by the Cuban, Molina, who now was his commanding officer. Any hope for redress through PNN channels was clearly gone. His resentment, his frustration and sense of violation, had grown and festered until it had become an obsession. He desperately needed release and he was now convinced release would only come when he had avenged himself. The idea possessed him and he spent his waking hours plotting his revenge.

The first step had to be revealing the truth about the Gallo shooting. He had read the articles in *El Diario* and knew they were planted lies. But how could he expose them? No one was allowed off the island. He had no access to a cell telephone and mail to the mainland was censored, especially his. He was quite certain Molina was having him watched. It was too dangerous to attempt smuggling any communication off the island with the La Boca ferry-boat crews. And if he could find a way to communicate with the outside world, whom should he contact? The press? Certainly nobody at *El Diario* could be trusted since that paper had obviously become the voice of the Government. Perhaps *Vida Nacional*. He hadn't seen it since his exile but he had read it faithfully on the mainland. He particularly liked Sanchez Avila's column and sometimes thought he might be the one to contact but where might he stand today? Would he even be interested, or would he think him just a disgruntled officer with a personal grievance? Could he trust anyone? Would anyone listen to him anyway? He didn't know.

He only knew the day would come when he would reveal the truth. It might not be until he was back on the mainland but it would come, and he was living for that day.

• • •

Life had changed for the soldiers and civilians alike at Valle Escondido. The February raid on Puerto Hondo had begun the process. The stockpiling of fuel supplies, the death of Sergeant Campinas, rumors of a meeting between the general and the president, and now the whispers about the brigade losing its truck company all added grist to the rumor mill. Soldiers have an uncanny sensitivity to events which may affect them and because these events, seemingly unrelated, were outside the normal, they fired the imagination of the group mind. Rumors grew and were distorted, precipitating more questions and more rumors, and a general uneasiness and tensions increased.

When word filtered down of Portero's unusual meeting with the battalion commanders and the sergeant majors. The grapevine had it that the government wanted to replace Portero and the senior officers, and the brigade was preparing to resist any such move, a stance which met general approval among the rank and file who held their general in high esteem. Although there had been no change in the normal brigade routine, the troops sensed something building, and a new sense of urgency took hold throughout the command.

Private Rubio, a trained observer, duly noted the changes, and he carefully passed on all the rumors in his secret weekly reports. He wished he had more substantive intelligence for his superiors but it had been difficult to gather while he was assigned, out of the mainstream, to the recruit training company. However, he had recently been promoted to corporal and assigned to the ALIB personnel section in the brigade headquarters. He couldn't believe his good luck! He was now at the heart of things and would have greater access to hard information. His handlers would be pleased with him.

In late October, three noteworthy events took place, which Rubio dutifully reported. One definitely fit the hard intelligence category. It was the conversion of the Brigade Training Battalion into a line unit. He was able to supply considerable detail. He accurately reported that the OPFORS Company, the Plaster Company, and elements of the Technical Training Company, augmented by advanced cycle recruits from the Basic Training Company, had been reorganized into a headquarters company, a reconnaissance platoon, and three line companies. The Band and Basic Training Company had been detached and assigned to the brigade headquarters. The Basic Training Company had been augmented by personnel from the Technical Training Company, and was continuing to train early cycle recruits. Rubio was able to report the new unit had been designated, "Toro Battalion," and Lieutenant Colonel Emilio Sanchez had been assigned as its commanding officer.

The second event he reported was the marriage of the American helicopter pilot, Captain Christina Lane and Lieutenant Colonel Antonio DaSilva, commanding officer of the Lobo Battalion. A dinner and dance reception celebrating the event had been organized at the Base Officers' Club by Major Mix, the Lobo executive officer. All battalion officers and senior non-commissioned officers and their wives had been invited. General and Mrs. Portero and the brigade staff had also attended. Also present were a number of civilians from town, mostly habitués of La Cocina, who became friends of the happy couple over the months of their courtship. He could personally attest it had been a great celebration, having volunteered as a waiter to help serve the large number of guests. He was under no illusion the affair qualified as hard intelligence, but his orders were to report all unusual happenings, and this was certainly unusual.

The third event Rubio included in his report was not hard intelligence, either. He debated reporting it at all but did so as another unusual event because it had generated so much interest on the base. It was a fight in the post-motor pool between two non-commissioned officers. The combatants had been longtime friends, both senior sergeants assigned to the Truck Company, Emilio Carranza, a platoon sergeant, and Natan Blas, the maintenance sergeant. It had been a sustained brawl which had ended only when the Truck Company commander intervened.

According to reports, the captain received some blows from the enraged Carranza while trying to break up the fight. Rubio also reported the incident had resulted in disciplinary action. Carranza had been charged with striking an officer and reduced in rank from Senior Sergeant to Sergeant.

• • •

For several days following his meeting with the battalion commanders, executive officers, and sergeant majors, Portero lived in a state of near euphoria. The unit leaders had backed him to a man, and his fear that some might balk at the prospect of taking up arms against their countrymen had proved groundless. Most saw the situation as he did, and considered it their duty to defend the nation's constitution. A few more were motivated only by their desire to defend the brigade against a takeover by Figueroa. Whatever their motivation, they had given him their unanimous and enthusiastic support, and he was profoundly grateful for it.

However as preparations for the coming conflict progressed, the general began to experience a new uneasiness, the way he always did when forced to deal with a problem outside his comfort zone. The feeling first came upon him when he made the decision to approve the ATB's recommendation to convert the Training Battalion into a line unit. He was concerned by the fact the change was made without the knowledge or approval of General Carmody, the HJRAF commander. What concerned him most, it violated the trust that existed between him and Carmody. He felt discomfited by the realization that he was beginning to isolate himself from his friend and mentor.

When the staff presented him with a series of options for preemptive moves against the government, the uneasy feeling grew. They were reasonable options designed to avert bloodshed and to pressure Figueroa into capitulating on the National Marketing Board scheme and on his refusal to call early elections. But still they would require he move against the government he had sworn to defend, and in doing so shatter any hope he might have for explaining his opposition to Figueroa in terms of the Implementing Treaty.

The favored option called for simultaneous occupation of Puerto Hondo and La Boca by units of the ALIB, with the objective of forcing concessions from Figueroa by interrupting the flow of commerce in the first instance, and by preventing the units training on the Isla Grande from returning to the mainland in the second. Portero had seriously considered the strategy but in the end rejected it on the basis that it would almost certainly invite early intervention by the HDO. His unease intensified into an anxiety which preoccupied him during waking hours and kept him sleepless at night.

For the first time in his life, Portero began to feel isolated and insecure. Throughout his career, he had been a part of a larger whole. Even as the commander of the ALIB, he was subject to direction from the HJRAF, which had always given him a sense of belonging. Now, however, he was beginning to cut himself off from the larger organization and the guidance from a senior headquarters. He was indeed moving outside of his comfort zone, and it frightened him. His confidence was slipping and he began to question his ability to undertake the task before him.

• • •

For as long as he could remember, Francisco Portero had wanted to be a soldier. His happiest memories as a child on his father's ranch near Ensenada were of playing war games with his brother and the children of his father's vaqueros. As he grew older he discovered books, especially novels, which he devoured at the rate of two or three a week. When he was not engaged with his ranch chores or his school homework, he read. Books transported him away to great adventures in foreign lands. They fired his imagination and gave him a sense of the world beyond Naranjeras. His early favorites were tales of courage and heroism, wherein the protagonist overcame great odds to affect astonishing rescues or win great victories.

His literary world broadened as he began to read English, and by the time he was twelve, he was exploring the Wild West, great sea battles as depicted by Cecil Scott Forester's *Horatio Hornblower* series, the American Civil War, Napoleon's campaigns, and the Boer War. Later he discovered and devoured Patrick O'Brian's historical novels of the British navy in the eighteenth century.

While his brother loved the ranch, he longed to see the outside world, and his parents, although well to do by Naranjeras standards, sacrificed to send him to high school in the United States. He spent four glorious years at Culver Military Academy in Indiana, reveling in the discipline, military traditions, and absorbing the training. He graduated as Cadet Adjutant, an honor student, with varsity letters in wrestling and baseball, and with a distinguished record on the academy's debating and chess teams.

He returned to Naranjeras and enrolled in the National University, intending to study law. He soon missed the discipline of the military and joined the PNN Reserve, where he served part-time as a student officer candidate. His military school experience proved to be a great advantage, and he was commissioned a reserve lieutenant in the PNN before he completed his second year at the university. He tired of the law and, with the help of friends in the Ministry of Defense, was awarded a scholarship to Virginia Military Institute in Lexington, Virginia. He graduated from VMI in three years with honors in history.

Once again he returned home to serve on active duty as a basic training officer with the PNN. He was shortly promoted to Captain and reassigned to the operations staff. One of his duties there was as liaison officer with the US Army Allied Exchange Officer Training Section in the Pentagon. He took full advantage of the position to obtain several choice school assignments for himself, including the Infantry Officer Basic Course at Fort

Benning, Georgia, followed by jump school at Fort Bragg, North Carolina. Two years later he graduated, third in his class, from the Advance Infantry Officer Course at Benning.

He wangled a one-year assignment as an exchange officer with a battalion of the Third Infantry Division, where he served first as platoon leader and later as company executive officer, wearing the rank of First Lieutenant. In those capacities, he gained hands-on experience in small unit leadership and he did well, so well, in fact, that he was offered a commission in the US Army and a fast track to US citizenship. After considerable soul-searching, he declined the offer. He cherished his service with the American army, but he loved his own country and wanted above all to serve it.

Shortly after his return to Naranjeras, he was promoted to the rank of Major and assigned the task of organizing and training Naranjeras's first modern infantry unit. It started as a company but in two years grew to become the Oso Battalion. A very limited budget forced him to compromise on weaponry and led him to develop the concept of sharp shooters, tiradores, as the unit's primary tactical weapon.

His success in developing the Oso Battalion led to his assignment as a student at the Command and General Staff School at Fort Leavenworth, Kansas, where he typically distinguished himself academically. It was there he first met General Carmody and became reacquainted with Elizabeth Anchor Smith, a lovely "army brat" he had met earlier when he stationed at Fort Benning. They fell in love and three months after his graduation were married in the Fort Benning Post Chapel.

When Naranjeras joined the Hemispheric Defense Organization and formed the ALIB, Portero was the best qualified officer to command it. He was promoted to Lieutenant Colonel and given full authority to build the brigade. He moved his Oso Battalion to a small police post at Valle Escondido and built the organization and constructed its base simultaneously.

In another year, he was a full colonel and had earned an excellent reputation in Naranjeras and United States military circles. When he was promoted to Brigadier General, the ALIB had two battalions, the Osos and the Tigres, and a training battalion, and planning was underway for a third battalion which would fill out the brigade organization plan.

Portero had always been happy in his career. He found the work satisfying and was comfortable living within the disciplines of military life. There was a kind of certainty to it which fit his personality. He found freedom within the martial order. He knew he was a good officer and he enjoyed the respect of his colleagues, but he sometimes thought success had come too easily. He never took personal credit for his accomplishments. His was a gift, he believed, for which he was profoundly grateful, but he took no false pride in it. He believed his career had been preparation for the real test he would one day have to face. On occasion when in a rare reflective mood, he wondered if he would be up to the challenge when it came.

Well it appeared the challenge was now facing him, but it was a far cry from anything he had envisioned. It was not the military problem he expected. He had prepared himself to deal with military matters, but the challenge he now faced was political— involving both national and international politics. It was beyond his experience and expertise, and certainly outside his comfort zone. It loomed before him like a massive forbidding mountain, which he was not sure he could climb. He had spoken to his subordinates about the consequences of failure in the enterprise facing them, but it suddenly occurred to him his own personal inadequacies might be the cause of that failure. They trusted him, but was he deserving of their trust? He was not sure, and not being sure weighed upon his mind, and his anxiety grew.

• • •

Betsy Smith de Portero loved her husband deeply. Over the years of their marriage, she learned to recognize when something was troubling him. She usually had some inkling as to the cause, but this time she didn't. As the daughter of a general, she understood the kind of pressures a man in her husband's position had to face, and she believed it her responsibility to understand and help and support him as she could. As a child of the military, she had known many officers, the good ones and the not so good ones, and she had learned to recognize the difference. From their first meeting, she recognized Portero as a good one with potential, but after several years of marriage she had become convinced he was among the great ones. She was quietly proud of his accomplishments and grateful for the blessing of being able to share his career as wife, counselor, and dedicated cheerleader.

She loved her husband and respected and admired him for his intellect, his honesty, his dedication and professionalism, and for his modesty and quiet good humor. She also recognized in him an occasional tendency to doubt himself—to discount his own abilities. She found it an endearing but sometimes an exasperating trait. Occasionally she wondered if the fact they had no children might have contributed to his occasional dark mood. She didn't know what had precipitated his present preoccupation, but she believed it her duty as wife and teammate to find out. She had to help if she could.

Betsy wasn't sure how to approach the matter with him. He wasn't volunteering anything as he sometimes did when worried. He was unusually quiet and withdrawn. His responses to her conversational overtures were perfunctory and vague. It worried her and hurt her feelings because when they were home alone together, they usually sustained a stream of affectionate, happy back-and-forth banter. Often they read together, played cribbage or chess, or listened to music from her sizable collection of compact discs. But now his mind was elsewhere and try as she might, she hadn't been able to draw him out. She decided she had to take control of the situation, plan her strategy, and patiently await her opportunity to implement it. She wasn't a general's daughter for nothing.

The moment came in an evening when he seemed more relaxed. She had prepared his favorite dinner of chicken breasts baked in sour cream, which he ate with gusto, and even commented on her cooking skills. They were preparing for bed. She had donned her most alluring nightgown. It was her favorite, not only because it was exceptionally lovely, but also Portero had given it to her for Christmas. He liked to call it "her seduction suit." She applied a dab of cologne behind her ears and between her breasts, and gave her long dark hair an extra brushing. When Portero saw her, his face brightened. His comment was "Wow."

"So there is someone in there after all." She laughed at him.

"What do you mean?"

"I mean I might as well have been a piece of furniture around here for the last week for all the notice you have taken of me."

"I'm sorry, Sweetheart. I guess I have been neglecting you…I suppose I've had a lot on my mind." Then he gave his imitation of an evil leer and rose to approach her. He took her hands. "But seeing you in your present state of dishabille brings me back to the real world…And gives me certain other ideas."

"Oh, what kind of ideas?" She giggled.

"Well, conjugal kind of ideas."

"Oh really? That is very flattering, but what makes you think I share those kinds of ideas?"

"Because you are wearing your seduction suit for one thing… And because you can't resist me, for another."

She giggled again and stood on her toes to kiss him. "You damn generals think you know everything, don't you?" She extricated her hands from his and grabbed an old terry cloth robe. "First, my dear general, we are going to talk."

"That's blackmail," he protested. "What are we going to talk about?" They sat facing each other on the bed.

"I want to know what is bothering you."

He denied there was anything in particular, but she continued to gently press for an answer. Finally, he took her hands in his again, looked her in the eye for a long moment, hesitated, then said, "The truth is, Betsy, I am afraid I have bitten off more than I can chew. I am not sure I am capable of doing what I have set out to do with this Figueroa thing."

"What do you mean?"

"I'm not sure I am the man to lead this thing."

She was incredulous. "Who else is there, for God's sake? The brigade is behind you one hundred percent…So is most of the country…and Figueroa is not that formidable. I've heard you say many times he is more politician than soldier."

"It's not just Figueroa I'm worried about. If it were only him and his forces, the damn thing would be a lot simpler, although I hate the idea of having to fight my own countrymen. It is outside intervention that really concerns me. It's the HJRAF. Figueroa is trying to make me the villain in the international community. He has already started and he has made some headway, and I can't see how to stop him in that venue. He is trying to make me look like a renegade, a loose cannon revolutionary. If he succeeds, the HDO may well intervene before we can get anything done. We can't fight the world, and I certainly don't want to put my officers and our good men into a fight they cannot win…which will certainly bring dishonor to all of us if we lose."

"But I thought you had talked to George Carmody about staying out of it…to give you some time…?"

"I did and he will try, but if the HDO orders him to intervene, he will have no choice."

"Okay. I see the problem." Betsy sat silently in thought for a long moment. Then asked, "Do your commanders and staff understand the risk?"

"Partially, I think. Not fully. To tell you the truth, most of them believe I can do anything…That I have the situation in hand…which I don't. But I can't tell them I don't. I can't tell them I have doubts about the outcome. I can't tell them I have doubts about my ability to carry it off…And I am now wondering if I have the right to ask them to take on a fight I have doubts about winning."

His wife remained silent, thinking. When she finally spoke, her thoughts came in a torrent of words. "Okay, Pancho, let's review the situation. Figueroa is a bastard. He'll destroy the country if he has his way. Right?" Portero nodded. "You and the ALIB are one thing, the only thing, in the country that can stop him. Right?"

"I guess so. Right."

"So…Your cause is worthy…And the brigade is with you. Right? So are a lot of people in the country…maybe all the people in the north…They want to be rescued…and they are looking to you to do it…Right? So you've got a just cause…You've got public support…And you've got the power to get the job done…So what is the problem? The problem is you are afraid of a possibility that outside intervention may come in and reverse the balance of power and cause you to lose?"

"Exactly."

"Sometimes you make me mad, Portero." She was clearly annoyed. "I've never known you to be timid!"

"Dammit, Betsy, I'm not—"

"Well you're sure giving a good imitation of it if you're not! You're sitting there telling me that you must have all the cards stacked in your favor or you won't play? That is not you! My God, Pancho, if everyone in history had refused to stand up for a worthy cause because the cards were against them, where would the world be? North America would still be a British colony. Europe would today be a part of the Thousand Year Reich…and for that matter, the Israelites would still be slaves in Egypt."

She paused for a breath. She continued in a quieter tone. "There is no one but you….here and now…who can defend Naranjeras. Who can lead the brigade? If you don't do it, who will? There is no one else but you, Pancho. Don't you see that? And even if you should lose…wouldn't it be better to have at least tried to save the country then to have sat by and done nothing because the odds weren't quite as favorable as you wanted them to be? My God, sweetheart, is that how you want to be remembered in history?"

"Of course not, Betsy." Portero was irritated by her tirade. "You don't understand, dammit. If the HDO intervenes, it will all be over before we can get Figueroa out. It will all have been for nothing."

"How do you know that? You really don't know, do you? If George Washington had felt that way at Valley Forge, what? Or if Moses had listened to his doubts…?"

"I'm not Moses…And besides, he had God on his side."

"So did Washington…and so did Patton…and so will you. Oh, Pancho, you must never doubt that. Remember the opening line of my favorite hymn? 'Be still my soul, the Lord is on thy side'? Your cause is just, and He will be there at your side."

"I guess I do know that. I guess I forgot it for a moment…also, I guess I have taken too much counsel of my fears, which Patton warned against. You are right, Betsy. You are right once again."

He sat quietly for several minutes. The concerns which had weighed so heavily on his mind suddenly seemed less important. He felt a great relief and turned to his wife who watched, wondering at the change in his facial expression.

"The demon has gone." He smiled at her. "Thanks for keeping me straight. You always are there when I need you. You are wonderful…What would I do without you? I couldn't make it without you…I love you and I need you." He had tears in his eyes when he kissed her. So did she.

They held their embrace until their emotions quieted. Finally, when he recovered his composure, he said with his typical grin, "It was sure a good move capturing you."

"It was the other way around, señor. I captured you, and it was a great move."

"Well, however it happened, it was the best thing that ever happened to me. I need you around. Don't ever go away."

"Don't worry, I'm not going anywhere." She stood and removed her old robe, smiling at him, her face glowing. She was delectably beautiful standing there, her silken nightgown clinging to her.

"Take that off, too."

"No, sir. That's your job."

• • •

Portero returned to his work with renewed confidence. Betsy's tender counsel had had a profound effect on him. It had transformed his perspective on the situation. He still did not like the odds for success in opposing Figueroa, especially if the HJRAF should intervene, but he now realized he indeed was the only national leader with any chance to succeed against the dictator, and that it was his obligation, his duty, to lead the opposition, win or lose. Having accepted the fact there was no other option, he could now focus all his energy on the task ahead.

The ATB staff never knew of his uncertainty. He had never let them see it, knowing the deleterious effect it would have on their morale and ability to carry out their duties. Instead he had tried to exude a confidence he had not felt and loaded them with tasks and planning assignments which kept them focused and working long hours. Its attention was primarily focused on strengthening the alliance with the people of Mesona and the north and training their newly activated Toro Battalian.

The Toros had come together smoothly, well ahead of schedule, a testimony to the experienced NCOs the battalion had inherited from the OPFOR, the TTC, and Plaster Companies.

It had sailed through its small unit training and was two thirds of the way through its company level and communications training phase. A couple of weeks of battalion level exercises would bring the unit to a reasonable state of readiness. The public relations project with the Mesonenses was also developing nicely. Portero's close relationships with the publisher of *La Prensa* and the presidents of the Cattlemen's Association and the Tanner's Board had led to a close friendship with the venerable old gentleman who was mayor of La Meona. He had been a career teacher and was a poet of some renown, popular with his people—he had held the office for over a decade. He had a wonderful sense of humor and reminded Portero of his father. Their growing friendship greatly strengthened the general's public relation effort. He had been so taken with the old gentleman that he had sent the brigade band to help celebrate the city Founder's Day centennial. The band had been so well-received that it had returned to present two additional Saturday evening concerts from the bandbox in the Mesona Central plaza.

The most important product of the PR effort had been the signing of several stand-by "emergency contracts," negotiated by Colonel Roth, for goods and services the ALIB might require in the event some unmentioned catastrophe cut it off from its warehouse at the government dock in Puerto Hondo. More recently, Roth had been exploring the possibility of chartering one of the Cattlemen's Association's two helicopters for the use of the Commanding General and his staff.

While the ATB wrestled with these challenges, it also applied itself to the problem of fleshing out the implementation of Portero's Northern Strategy. To that end, it had developed a series of scenarios based upon probable government actions against them and on plans for countering them. It was a fascinating process for Portero and the staff, a war game which forced them to focus on how best to employ the assets and capabilities of the brigade under each scenario. The ATB was driven by pressure to complete the process, be ready before the government had developed its capability to move against them.

Banning's intelligence estimate gave them only six weeks to complete their preparation. That deadline forced the Staff and the Headquarters Company personnel into an emergency mode, which required considerable overtime effort and a twenty-four hour per day operation. A parallel effort occurred at the battalion level, which focused on physical training and accelerating unfinished small unit training cycles. All this stimulated new excitement throughout the brigade, which quickly transformed into a renewed sense of purpose among its soldiers. A fact that Corporal Rubio did not overlook.

12

CHAPTER

The report from his agents in Valle Escondido would have caused Colonel Davidson, Deputy Defense Minister, considerable concern had he not known that the ALIB problem would soon change. He had given the order to proceed with the special operation. The package had been delivered and his action team was ready and waiting only for the opportunity to implement the plan. A few days more and Figueroa will have become less agitated, and Pancho Portero would no longer be a concern.

In a way, he would miss the man. He did not like him, there had been bad blood between them since the time of his discharge from the ALIB, but he respected him as a capable adversary. In his heart, he would have preferred humiliating the ALIB commander on the field of battle, but this course was much less risky. There was simply too much at stake to take the chance.

There could be no doubt Portero was preparing the ALIB for military action. The stockpiling of fuel, the increased schedule of field exercises, the overt courting of the people in Mesona, and now the creation of a fourth line battalion were sufficient proof for Davidson. The lingering question in his mind was where the HJRAF stood in all this. He had counted on Portero remaining under the control of the HDO and therefore expected him to take no action without its blessing, but the sudden activation of the Toros startled him into questioning that assumption. The treaty required consultation and approval by the government of the participating nations relative to "any change in mission, organization, command structure or troop strength" affecting the ALIB. The fact no such contact had been made seemed to indicate that Portero was acting unilaterally without the knowledge of the HJRAF. Either that or the HJRAF was party to the ALIB buildup. He did not believe it was the latter. Figueroa would have known and would have certainly said something to him about it.

Well, soon it wouldn't matter. Whichever the circumstance, the ALIB would be out of the picture. "Strike the head and kill the whole snake," so instructed a bit of Naranjeras folk wisdom remembered from childhood. With Portero gone, the ALIB would be perhaps not dead, but so wounded and demoralized that it would take months to recover its effectiveness.

The specter of preemptive strike by the ALIB against the government had haunted Davidson in recent weeks. His anxiety stemmed from the fact that he would be unable to oppose any such move for at least two months. The second brigade on Isla Grande would not complete its shakedown exercises and field tests for another forty-five days, and then it would require at least another ten days to move it back to the mainland. The Cazador Battalion at La Rioja could be ready in a month. He was very pleased with the way that unit was coming together.

The armored battalion was also shaping up well, but it would not be ready for at least another thirty days. The Cascavel crews had been trained and were showing considerable skill in gunnery and in maneuvering their vehicles, and he believed he could employ them now if he had to. The reconnaissance company had been equipped with its Trackers and Ford Rangers and was showing great promise. In fact, it was almost ready to go. The problem was the battalion's infantry company, also in training at La Rioja, needed two more weeks there before it could begin to exercise with the Cascavels. He guessed that process would take at least two weeks more, even if he hurried it.

The bottom line for Davidson was he would not be ready to oppose Portero for two more months, and the thought that he and his colleagues could lose everything by default weighed heavily upon his mind and had prompted him to advance the timing of the special Portero operation by ten days. As the date grew closer, he allowed himself to relax a bit. He took comfort in the knowledge that once the blow had been struck, he would have all the time he needed.

• • •

The platoon of trucks, which had been readied for redeployment to the PNN main base in La Capital, departed Valle Escondido not quite three weeks after the October first target date. The six big trucks were mostly older or problem vehicles culled from the Truck Company's four platoons. However, fresh paint, new bumper markings, and newly painted tarpaulins made them look as if they had just come off the production line. They were carrying the dependents of the platoon personnel, their baggage and household goods, and had just enough fuel in their tanks to take them to their destination.

A number of off-duty Truck Company personnel and their families were on hand to wave good-bye to their friends. Some of the children were in tears at being separated from their playmates.

Sergeant Emilio Carranza, NCO in charge of the platoon, sat in the passenger seat of the lead vehicle and did his best to look pleased to be leaving. He managed a few derisive waves and mock salutes to former friends and acquaintances as the little convoy departed the base. He was, however, experiencing very mixed emotions. He was excited by the special mission assigned to him by Colonel Banning, but he deeply regretted leaving the ALIB under the cloud of recriminations which had been heaped upon him since his fight with Nino Blas ten days before. He had succeeded in becoming the company pariah.

He still wore the marks of combat. His blackened right eye was now turning green and yellow. The bridge of his nose was still taped, and there was a more substantial bandage high on his forehead, where six stitches had recently been removed. His right hand was still splinted to immobilize the broken middle fingers. The soreness of his body had faded, but it still showed bruises where Blas' big fists had pounded him.

It was not his physical ills that bothered Carranza, however. It was the condemnation and humiliation he had suffered as a result of the fight. His friends all thought he had lost his senses and treated him with a cautious diffidence, as if they no longer knew him and expected him to go berserk again. He had been particularly concerned by Nino Blas's continued anger with him. The two had been the closest of friends, and that relationship had ended. Carranza desperately wanted Blas to understand why he had goaded him into the fight. He had even urged Colonel Banning to advise Blas of the plan, but the intelligence officer had convinced him the fewer people who knew, the more secure he would be in his new mission.

Despite its downside, Carranza found the game he had begun to play interesting, not exactly fun, but exciting and demanding. He had now to be always in complete control of himself, careful not to inadvertently say or do something that might arouse a suspicion that he was playing a part. This was particularly difficult when he was in the company of those who had been friends and, for that reason, he actually looked forward to the opportunity of getting away from Valle Escondido to somewhere he was less well-known. He was not used to playing the villain, and it was particularly galling to pretend a rage against the ALIB, which he so loved and respected.

He thought he had passed an important test of his acting skills with the village barber. At Banning's suggestion, he had gone to her for a haircut the week before. He had tried to maintain a dower expression as he entered *Peluqueria Angelita.* The shop was empty except for its proprietress, Angelita herself. She concealed the fact that she recognized Carranza immediately, although he had not been a regular customer. She had relayed the details of the fight and Carranza's demotion to her PNN handler.

"My God, what happened to you, Sergeant? You look like you've been through a meat grinder." The tone of her voice showed concern.

"A fight, but I don't want to talk about it."

"Right. We won't talk about it and I won't ask you about the other guy. How do you want your hair cut?"

She worked in silence for several minutes. Then suddenly she exclaimed, "It just came to me who you are. You're the famous Sergeant Carranza, aren't you?"

"I don't know about the famous part—infamous, maybe—but I am Carranza,"

"Everyone seems to be talking about you. People are saying you got screwed…I mean with your demotion and all."

Carranza grunted. "Me included," he said with a tired vehemence.

"What happened? They say you hit an officer."

"I guess I did, but I didn't mean to. Someone jumped me and I let him have it before I realized who it was. I was pretty damn mad and I guess out of control."

"Couldn't you explain how it happened? They certainly should understand you didn't do it intentionally."

"I tried but they wouldn't listen—the bastards. I've been stationed here a lot of years and I have a clean record. They wouldn't even listen to my side. It really pisses me off."

"I don't blame you. You have a right to be mad. It must be tough working for an outfit that treats you that way."

"Not for long. I'm getting out of here. The bastards made a mistake. They've assigned me to the platoon they are transferring to La Capital. At least I won't have to work with this chicken shit brigade anymore."

"Congratulations."

"No, they're just using this as an excuse to get me out of here. They don't want me around anymore. That's okay with me. I don't want to be here, either." Carranza hoped he was not over-doing it, but he couldn't help adding, "Every dog has his day, and I'll get mine. They'll be sorry. I'm going to show the bastards."

Sitting in his truck, Carranza smiled to himself, remembering the conversation with Angelita. He hoped he had been convinc-ing. If she had believed him, he expected to be contacted by the PNN intelligence people shortly after his arrival in La Capital. That would be his next big acting challenge. Banning had told him to expect the sincerity of his disaffection from the ALIB would be tested, and if they knew what they were doing, it would be a challenge for him not to fall into any trap they might set. Their approach would be to solicit as much information about ALIB operations as he knew, which they would test against con-firmed information they may have in hand.

"Tell them what you know. Do not embellish and do not try to mislead or misrepresent anything which you know to be true. Making that mistake would prove to them that you are not what you are supposed to be, and they will never trust you. Above all, your version of the fight must be consistent in every detail, because they will know everything about that." Banning's often repeated instructions were clear in his mind.

Once he had gained their trust, he would be free to begin his assignment, which Banning had code-named "Hawkeye." His communication plan was simplicity itself. He would use pub-lic telephones to relay information to brigade contacts outside of Valle Escondido area. He was to avoid using his cell phone, except in the event he had been discovered and was avoid-ing capture.

His secondary communications channel would be the truck company's tactical radio. All his transmissions would be moni-tored by ALIB listening stations when he was within range. The ALIB would hear any radio communication he might have within his platoon or with other PNN radios on that same frequency, so they would know where he was and hopefully what he was doing. If he had a specific message he wished to pass on, he would alert the listening station by simply mentioning the time early in his transmission. That would be their signal to activate a voice recorder. His job would then be to disguise the message he wanted to relay in a manner which would not arouse the suspicion of any PNN radio operator who happened to be listening. That would be the tricky part, but he had been coached in several simple techniques he was prepared to utilize.

Carranza gave a final wave to the sentry at the main gate as his little convoy departed the base. Although he was saddened at leaving the place that he had come to regard as home, he was excited and looking forward to the challenges that lay ahead. He felt he had been well-coached and was confident he could carry out the assignment. Perhaps someday Nino Blas and his other friends would understand the role he was now playing. The thought of a future reunion with them, with the truth known, was comforting.

• • •

The ATB was well into a Saturday meeting when it was interrupted by an urgent message from the Headquarters Company commander, reporting that the commander of the guard was holding five tourist buses, a television broadcast van, and some PNN vehicles at the main gate. The guard had been turned out to prevent the convoy entering the post. A foreign woman seemed to be the spokesman for the group, and she was backed by a number of people carrying placards. She was at the moment remonstrating with the commander of the guard over being prevented from entering the base, and demanding to speak with the Commanding General. He added that TV cameras were documenting it all.

Portero immediately ordered the Lobo Battalion, the designated emergency standby unit for the week, be alerted. It was to immediately post extra security around the brigade headquarters, the fuel dump, and the communications center. He directed Colonel Soto to proceed to the main gate with a handheld radio, and determine who these people were and what they wanted. Major Lacerica was to accompany him to deal with the TV crew and any other press representatives who might have come along. He directed Colonel Banning to contact CINC-HJRAF on the scrambler to report the situation.

At the main gate, Soto found the forty-man Post Guard, with arms at the ready, confronting a crowd of perhaps one-hundred-and-fifty civilians, men and women, Naranjeros and foreigners, all of whom were chanting something unintelligible in Spanish. Many were waving toilet plungers and there were a number of placards and signs, all of which seemed to contain the word "FLUSH" in some context. Their leader seemed to be a thin, gray-haired woman, ludicrously dressed in a Mexican costume including a serape and a large charro hat perched on the back of her head. Its chin strap was tight and had etched red welts on her wrinkled neck. He couldn't help smiling. Her prominent nose and piercing eyes brought to mind the image of an imperious turkey hen leading her brood. She was armed with a handheld bullhorn, with which she led the chanting. Her amplified voice was high-pitched and thin, adding to the turkey image.

Colonel Soto, still grinning, approached the woman and, after a moment, succeeded in getting her attention. The chanting faded as the demonstrators saw her turn to him. He introduced himself in English and asked who she might be.

"I am Molly Moran, and I am spokesperson for this delegation from FLUSH. We demand to see General Portra." Her answer was loud, meant to carry for the TV camera, and her tone was imperious.

"For your information, Miss Moran, the general's name is Portero." He spelled it for her. "Now, may I ask, what is FLUSH?"

The notion that this officer might not know about FLUSH seemed to surprise her. "FLUSH? Why, sir, FLUSH is the international grass roots movement opposed to American hegemony in Latin America. Surely you know of us."

"I am sorry, madam. I have not heard of your group until now. How can I help you?"

"Take us to your commander. We have come to speak with him."

"May I tell the general what it is about?"

"You may say we have come to demand the surrender of the murderers, Campinas and Ruedas, to the police officers accompanying us." She indicated the group of eight PNN personnel standing aside from the demonstrators. With the exception of their leader, a self-assured young captain, they were all armed with AK-47s.

A few drops of rain fell, leading the shower which could be seen sweeping over the hill to the west.

"I will inform General Portero of your request, madam, and I will get back to you. I'll ask you to wait here. You may wish to wait in your buses, however. It appears we are in for an *aguacero* shortly. You don't want to get wet."

Soto was joined by Lacerica and they returned to Brigade Headquarters, where Portero, the key staff officers, and Colonel DaSilva of the Lobos were waiting. He explained what he had learned from the woman concerning FLUSH, and the demands of the group.

"There appears to be twenty or thirty North Americans in the group. They are carrying most of the signs. The rest appear to be Naranjeros, mostly young people, maybe university students. They seem to be enjoying themselves, as if they were on a picnic outing."

Lacerica had checked with the media people accompanying the group. "There is one TV crew from Naranjeras and another from Minneapolis. The only press people are from *El Diario,* which makes me believe this is being staged by the Figueroa people."

"This is just a publicity stunt, General. Don't see them. Send them back to the capital." Colonel Ochoa was adamant. Some of the others nodded their agreement.

Portero considered the recommendation. "It is a publicity stunt, and a pretty well organized one at that. They've brought their own TV and press to make sure they get coverage. They win, no matter what happens. If I see them, they will claim a victory, showing they have power to which we yielded. If I don't see them, they will claim a victory, claiming we were afraid to talk to them. Let's think about this. Perhaps we can somehow turn this to our advantage.

"Meantime get them out of the rain. Soto, invite them into the mess hall. They can dry off and can demonstrate for their cameras all they want to in there. Once they're in, DaSilva, put a guard around them and don't let them out. Get plenty of coffee to them and have the cooks make sandwiches. Treat them with respect, especially the Naranjeros. We want them to take away good memories of our hospitality.

"I'll see the woman later in the conference room. She can bring some of her people, and be sure several Naranjeros are there, too. Lacerica, invite the TV people to set up there, especially the American crew. Be sure none of them have any hidden weapons. Any questions?"

"What about the PNN people?" Soto asked.

"Invite them to stay in the mess hall. But disarm them. But I'll want the officer in charge in the conference room with the woman. Okay? Get going."

Soto, Lacerica and DaSilva departed to carry out their orders. Colonel Ochoa, Banning, Roth, and Major Vargas remained. Portero could see that Ochoa and his deputy, Vargas, were in agreement. He smiled at his operations officer. "Trust me, Octavio. We can win this one." Then to Banning: "Peter, have Ruedas stand by and wait in my office."

. . .

Major Lacerica seated the FLUSH delegation at the conference table. The general would sit at the end, facing the camera. Molly Moran was seated to the right of the general's chair. Next to her were three of her fellows from the United States, one of whom had been introduced as a staffer from the office of Minnesota's senior senator. On the general's left, he placed the four Naranjero delegates and the PNN captain. The TV cameras, including an ALIB video-cam-recorder normally used in troop training, were set up and ready in the back of the room, and the reporter from *El Diario* was given a seat next to the North Americans. Lacerica and the brigade legal officer seated themselves with Colonel Banning, next to the five Naranjeros.

The delegates had taken their seats, and the cameras were panning for background shots when General Portero and Colonel Soto entered. The ALIB officers stood and the others followed, all but Molly Moran and the North American delegates. Introductions were made by Lacerica. Portero walked around the room smiling and shaking everyone's hand, including the camera operators, before taking his seat at the head of the table. He wore a freshly starched uniform, and the delegates and cameras saw a tall, pleasant looking, self-assured young officer who, with the camera light on him, clearly dominated the room.

Once all were seated, he welcomed them and, turning to the woman on his right, he smiled and addressed her. "Miss Moran, I understand you are the spokesman here. Your visit has been quite a surprise to us. Had we expected you, we would have given you a better reception. Have you been treated well?"

"We are not here on a social visit, sir. We are here on a most serious business matter."

"And what might that be, Miss Moran?

"We are told you are harboring criminals who are wanted for the murder of a police officer. We are here to demand you surrender them immediately to this young officer in order that they can be brought to justice." She spoke in loud, measured tones, turning slightly toward the camera.

Portero looked at each delegate in turn. The North Americans defiantly returned his gaze but the Naranjeros, for the most part, seemed ill at ease and would not meet his eye. He matched her tone. "First, please tell me by what authority you make this demand?"

Molly did not hesitate in her answer. "We have the moral authority of people everywhere who love justice. We are an official delegation of FLUSH, which is an international grass roots movement which opposes American military involvement in this country and in Latin America. We are here to call attention to the fact that this US-sponsored regiment is defying the law and the government of Naranjeras."

"Oh? What law are we defying?"

"You have refused to hand over these murderers, Campinas and Ruedas."

"What makes you think they are murderers?"

"Come now, General, don't play games with us. We are well aware of the incident in El Rio. Did you think it would not be in the news in the U.S.? Well you should be aware the *New York Times* published a detailed story about the murder of that officer. There have also been several speakers from here talking about the crime, including the editor of your leading newspaper. Furthermore, we were given a detailed briefing about the incident here by representatives of the press and your government. We are well-acquainted with the facts, I assure you."

"I think you are not, madam. From what you have said thus far, you clearly do not have the facts. First, let me point out the Autonomous Light Infantry Brigade is not a US regiment. It is a Naranjero brigade. Second, the incident to which you seem to be alluding occurred in La Rioja, not in El Rio. I know of no place called El Rio in this country. Third, Sergeant Campinas, whom you have twice called a murderer, is dead, himself a murder victim. He died of injuries received in the beating he suffered at the hand of Major Gallo in La Rioja. And fourth, I have read all of the articles published about the incident, and none of them reflect the facts as they occurred. You, madam, have been misled."

Molly Moran was flustered. She stared at Portero for a moment, then engaged in a whispered conference with her companions. Turning back to the general, she asked, "How do we know Campinas is dead? How do we know you are not just saying that to put us off track?"

"I have a copy of the death certificate here. Incidentally, the Department of Justice also has a copy. I have here photographs of his body taken in our infirmary the same day of the incident." He passed her a portfolio of photographs. "I also have the sworn statement of the doctor who examined him, which detail his injuries and the cause of death."

It was obvious the news of Campinas' death was a surprise to them. Portero noted the woman looked angrily at one of the Naranjero delegates, who shrugged and spread his hands, indicating he had not known. He guessed the man was from the government. The PNN Captain also seemed surprised, and he took time to review a document from the briefcase he carried.

"What about the other man? Ruedas? Is he dead, too?" It was more a challenge than a question. It came from the Naranjero delegate, the government man.

"No, but he might have been if he hadn't defended himself. Gallo attacked him when he intervened to help Campinas. The man broke three of his ribs and fractured his left hand. Lieutenant Ruedas finally had to shoot him in self-defense." The camera continued to roll.

Molly Moran was visibly agitated. The confrontation was not going the way she had envisioned. She was losing the initiative. She looked to her companions for help. The government man finally said, "That story does not square with the testimony of two eyewitnesses. We have a copy of the transcript."

Portero quickly examined the document. "This appears to be an investigator's report which alleges to be a transcript of the witnesses testimony. I note that it is signed only by the investigator. I see no signature by the witnesses named—er…Alfonso Simoni, nor by Hipolito Gomez. What you have here is hardly evidence. It would not be admissible in any court as such. No, ladies and gentlemen, I am afraid you have been misled in this matter."

Molly had regained some presence of mind. "Even if the evidence we've seen is incomplete, that is not necessarily all there is. After all, your government has issued arrest warrants for these men—or at least for Ruedas. Why won't you surrender them—or him? Let him face a trial, where all the evidence will be considered. If he is innocent, so be it. If he is guilty, justice will be done. In either case, you have no right to use your status as a US military unit to obstruct the laws of this country."

She glanced quickly at the camera to make sure they were rolling. The other delegates all nodded their approval, and a "hear, hear" was voiced by someone.

"We demand you surrender Ruedas now. The world is watching and waiting to see if justice will be done." She looked into the camera as if she were inviting the agreement of the viewer.

General Portero sat quietly until Molly and her delegation returned their attention to him. "Miss Moran, you have stated that you have been briefed by government representatives. Obviously it was not a thorough briefing because, for example, you were not informed of Sergeant Campinas' death. Nor were you informed that jurisdiction in cases such as this lie with the ALIB. By law we have the responsibility to try by courts-martial military personnel accused of such crimes. As it happens,

Lieutenant Ruedas is currently under arrest and is awaiting trial. The government is aware of this and should so have informed you. Had they done so, it would have been less embarrassing for you and your delegation."

"Then why haven't you tried him? Why are you dragging your feet?"

"Miss Moran, you have stated that you and your delegation are interested in seeing justice done. So am I, and I assure you so is every officer and soldier of this brigade. However in order to find justice, we first must come to trial. We have not convened the court because we have no evidence a crime has been committed. We have only allegations of a crime as set forth in this government report." He waived the paper which had been handed him by the government delegate.

"In this country, as in yours, an accused is presumed innocent until he is proven guilty by legal process. To date we have no evidence against Lieutenant Ruedas. We have asked the government to produce the witnesses named in its investigation. So far they have not been made them available. The moment they are, we will proceed to trial. We are ready and waiting."

Once again Molly had a whispered conference with her colleagues from North America. The meeting was clearly not proceeding according to plan. After some minutes, they called the government man to join them, and they whispered some more. Portero sat quietly back in his chair, waiting. Finally they seemed to reach a consensus and resumed their seats.

Molly began, "We might have expected this kind of response from you. It is clear you are trying to obscure the basic facts with legal technicalities and put us off the scent. We will not be fooled or sidetracked by your tactics. The fact is that a horrible crime has been committed and nothing has been done to bring the criminal to justice. You are not cooperating with your own government in this matter, and we understand that is all too typical of this unit. I am informed it is normal for you act with arrogance and non-cooperation in your dealings with your own government, and it is clear that pattern is continuing here in this case."

As she spoke, her voice grew louder and shriller. She was finding it difficult to play to the cameras from her position in the room and address Portero at the same time. She would say a few words, pause, and then favor the cameras with a lingering look. At which time the news cameras would dutifully zoom in on her, as noted by Portero. He also saw the reporter from *El Diario* writing furiously in his notebook as her harangue unfolded.

She continued, "My point is, General, none of this non-cooperation, none of this arrogant behavior, would be happening if this unit were controlled by your own government. Only the fact that you are sponsored and controlled by the United States Army makes your…ah, defiance, we'll call it…ah, possible. Our delegation is very much aware…"

Portero could stand no more. He interrupted her in midsentence and stood. The cameras quickly swung to him. He was angry but controlled himself and managed a calm voice. "Because the world is watching us through the medium of television, I am compelled to again set the record straight on a number of points. First, in regard to the status of the Autonomous Light Infantry Brigade." He looked directly into the camera from the Naranjeras TV station.

"This woman has made several casual declarations that we are a US Army unit, that we are controlled, or that we are sponsored by, the United States. She is wrong on all counts and I believe she knows it, but it serves her purpose to leave the implication that we are somehow under the direction of the North Americans. I declare to her and to all who may be watching what every Naranjero already knows, that the Autonomous Light Infantry Brigade is a unit of the Naranjeras army, organized pursuant to the provisions of the Hemispheric Defense Organization Treaty. It operates as a unit of the Hemispheric Joint Rapid Action Force, which is the military arm of the HDO, designed for the defense of our region. The only connection it has with the United States, other than the HDO connection, is that from time to time it has engaged in training exercises in North America, no different than any other HJRAF unit. It is neither sponsored nor is it controlled by the United States."

He paused to look at the delegation, inviting comment. When none was offered, he returned to the camera and continued. "Now Miss Moran has accused us of being arrogant and uncooperative. As to arrogance... what could possibly be more arrogant than this unofficial delegation of North Americans coming to our country and lecturing us on our own law and on how we should conduct our affairs?" Turning to Molly Moran: "Who invited you? I didn't, but because you were here I agreed to meet with you as a matter of courtesy. I am sorry you have refused to accept the established facts about the Ruedas case. I had hoped you would...Now let me say to you and to all who see this...I do not regret meeting with you because you have shown yourselves to be what you are, a group of political activists who are less interested in truth and justice than you are in pushing your own political agenda, which clearly seems to be to embarrass your own government, and your own country. You are clearly trying to use the ALIB as an excuse. You are trying to make us the medium for staging your show before these TV cameras, your purpose being to push your cynical agenda. It is quite clear your aim is to distort the truth and build distrust of the HDO and the HJRAF, and tangentially your own US Army.

"I believe everyone present here knows the actual truth of this situation, and I believe those who may watch these proceedings on TV will know it, provided of course reality is not edited out of the end product." He paused and waited. "Are there any questions?"

Portero's statement had been quietly delivered. No one had a question. Molly Moran fidgeted. She knew she had been bested before the cameras, and she was angry. She now knew her briefing on the incident in El Rio, or whatever that damn place was called, had not been complete and had left her unprepared to face Portero. She felt betrayed by her briefer, the very people she came here to help. That thought added to her anger. But she realized that was not the time for recriminations. That could come later. What she had to do now was salvage something out of the situation which would benefit the greater cause. She desperately cast about for a way to continue the dialogue. The cameras were still rolling. She rose, determined to face the standing Portero.

"Just a minute, General, I have not finished with you." Her tone was imperious.

Portero looked down at the stubborn little woman. She obviously was a leftist gadfly and professional rabble-rouser, and she was adept at playing to her audience, which clearly was the North American media audience. Successful reasoning with her was clearly out of the question. He did not like her but he was amused by her spunk, and he had enjoyed sparring with her.

He smiled at her. "I am sorry, Miss Moran, but I have finished with you. Thank you for coming. Major Lacerica will show you to your buses. You should be able to make it back to the capital before dark if you leave now."

He bowed to her and left the room, ignoring her sputtering protest. His staff followed. As they met at the door, Banning winked at the legal officer who wore a half grin. They could hear the woman's shrill voice addressing the government man as they departed.

• • •

"Who the hell do these people think they are, General?" The legal officer asked .

"They are clearly working their own agenda. They don't really care about Ruedas or justice or, for that matter, the ALIB, except as a convenient target for their phony propaganda campaign. They are not interested in the truth. Their interest is in distorting the truth in a way which serves their cause. My guess is their cause is the undermining of United States prestige in Latin America and at home. They believe they can do that by building a link between the US and the ALIB, and then discrediting us and the HJRAF in the public's mind by making us look like something we are not. They seek to influence public opinion enough to pressure their Congress into debating US policy in Latin America."

"Can they do that?"

Banning nodded and said, "Maybe they can. Remember, they had considerable success with the same tactic in eighties. They were able to pressure their Congress into withholding support of the Contras in Nicaragua, in defiance of their president's stated policy. Remember the Iran-Contra scandal? They did it before, and they no doubt believe they can do it again."

"Are the North Americans that stupid?"

Portero responded with some vehemence, "They are not stupid. They are naïve, perhaps, about us. The great majority up there know very little about Latin America. And they probably don't really care—they are so busy living their lives, earning a living, and running their businesses. They just do not focus on us. However, they have a strong sense of right and wrong, and when they believe there is injustice, they react. They are pretty trusting people. If they read or hear something which sounds credible, they are inclined to accept it as the truth. That makes them vulnerable to clever propagandists who wish to influence the public mind. Their source of news is the press and television, so if an organization like our friends with FLUSH can plant stories which seem credible but which distort the facts to some degree, the people, not knowing the complete story, are inclined to accept what is presented, especially if it is not publicly refuted.

"That is what they are trying to do here. They are trying to make a conection between us and the US Army and at the same time paint us as a rogue organization full of lawless thugs. If they succeed in that, they have not only discredited us, the HJRAF, and the HDO, but they have also built public distrust in their own army and in their nation's foreign policy. That puts pressure on their Congress to react."

Major Lacerica had been following Portero's comments closely, nodding his agreement. "If their purpose is as we think it is, it is a safe bet they will not acknowledge the facts the general gave them regarding the legal jurisdiction of the ALIB and the status of Lieutenant Ruedas, much less about the games the government is playing in this case. If this visit from FLUSH is meant to mislead and confuse the public about the facts, it may succeed if we don't get the full story to the people. My recommendation is that we send a press release to all media outlets in the country covering our visit from FLUSH. The document should include the details of the government's refusal to provide the names of its alleged witnesses to the La Rioja incident and citing that as the only reason we have not proceeded with the courts-martial."

"Good thinking, Major. Is there any reason we should not name those witnesses since the government is being so coy about it? And while we are at it, why should we limit the release to Naranjeras? Send it to US and HDO media as well. And what about copies of our audio-visual recording of the meeting? Can we do that?"

"It will be a big job. But we can do it."

"Good. Do it. And be sure that lady writer at the *Wall Street Journal* gets a copy of everything."

Portero turned to his intelligence officer. "Banning, be sure Ruedas knows what we are doing. The spotlight will be on him, and we want him to play the part. We also want to be damn sure he is protected. If they could somehow eliminate him, our court-martial ploy dies, so make sure his security detail stays focused. They must be made thoroughly aware of what's at stake. Any question, anyone?"

CHAPTER 13

The ATB reconvened Sunday afternoon to complete the agenda interrupted by the FLUSH people. The first order of business was a critique of the handling of the incident. There was agreement that it had been handled well and that la Señora Moran and her followers had been effectively check-mated, as any honest witness of the proceedings would conclude. However, the question of how it all might look after editing and published in the US media remained.

Lacerica had begun to put together a full transcript of the FLUSH meeting with the recommendation that it be disseminated together with copies of the ALIB videotaping to all Naranjeras newspapers, radio and television broadcasters, and to all of the various international wire services, news bureaus, and stringers maintaining offices in the country. It would be an expensive project, but the ATB agreed it would be worth doing. Portero directed that the same package be delivered to General Carmody in Panama. "And don't forget that copy for that *Wall Street Journal* woman."

Lacerica also reviewed his plans for widely publicizing the arrest and pending court-martial of Lieutenant Ruedas, emphasizing the brigade's continuing insistance the government produce their witnesses.

The next order of business was a discussion about base security prompted by the B3, Colonel Ochoa. "Those buses arrived without any warning. What if they had been carrying armed troops instead of those ridiculous FLUSH people? They could have been on the base raising all manner of hell before we even knew they were there. We cannot afford to be surprised. Given the state of relations with the Figueroa bunch, we ought to assume they are capable of making hit-and-run raids against us, even though they have no capability to fight us yet. I am recommending we prepare to defend ourselves against that kind of raid."

There was general agreement and the decision was taken to construct fortified roadblocks one kilometer beyond the main and back gates to the base. In addition, it was decided to establish a series of listening posts on the ridges east and west of the base. The roadblocks and listening posts were to be manned twenty-four hours a day and connected by field telephones and radios with the base defense communications center, which would be established in Colonel Sanchez's Toro Battalion Headquarters. A combat ready "reaction platoon" from the alert company was to be on twenty-four hour standby to support the outposts.

There followed an intelligence update from Colonel Banning. He reported his reconnaissance patrols still had found no indication of any preparation to return the troops on Isla Grande to the mainland. However, his observers had reported a marked buildup in the numbers of PNN troops at the La Rioja training camp. They were now estimating the new population at three to four hundred men.

Banning then reported that the public reaction against the Export Board ruling had not subsided, except perhaps in the capital area. He thought that if anything, it had intensified elsewhere, and particularly the La Mesona region, where *La Prensa* editorials continued to condemn the scheme.

Colonel Roth, the supply and logistics officer, then announced that he had successfully completed negotiations with the owners of an abandoned ranch building complex east of La Mesona for use as a secondary supply base. It lay some ten kilometers from the city on open ground, abutting the forested hill country the brigade used as its field training exercise area. The buildings were very old but of stone construction and very rugged, and they were surrounded by a high stone wall, which gave them the aspect of an old fort. With some roof repairs, there was ample storage for food, weaponry, ammunition, and other supplies. There also were sufficient facilities to house at least a company of troops and warehouse personnel. There were two wells in the complex that would yield adequate supplies of good water. One hundred and twenty meters down the slope from the ranch complex was an abandoned abattoir shed with high doors at each end which, he said, despite a lingering odor, would serve well as a maintenance facility for the truck company. Revetments for the storage of fuel areas could easily be constructed.

"Gentlemen, this will make an ideal logistics base from which to support our northern strategy. There is an excellent road leading to it and plenty of room for a helicopter pad. If I have approval to lease this property, I would like to get it ready for occupancy. I estimate it will take about three weeks to complete the work, providing I have sufficient manpower."

"What will you need to get the place in shape?" asked Colonel Soto, the chief of staff.

"Let me have one company and as many of the base engineer detachment as you can spare, with their bulldozer and backhoe, and a platoon from the Truck Company, and we'll get it done."

Portero turned to Ochoa. "I believe you indicated the Osos would be the Mesona-area battalion in our northern strategy plans, correct? Okay, so ask Gutierrez to assign a good hardworking company to Roth for this project." He turned back to Roth. "When do you want them, Guillermo?"

"As soon as possible."

• • •

At the time Portero was meeting with his ATB group in Valle Escondido, the HJRAF commander, General George Carmody, was in his office at Fort Amador, Republic of Panama, contemplating the imminent arrival of the Secretary General of the HDO.

The Secretary General had faxed him a list of items for discussion which he had just read. Most of the items were routine, but there was one that caught his attention. The item read: "Query from Ortega, Min/Foreign/Aff, Rep of Naranjeras, re ALIB activation of new battalion."

What the hell is Pancho doing now? He had had no report from the ALIB commander on any such new unit activation, which he certainly would have if it had happened, so he doubted the report was true. He guessed the Figueroa regime had picked up some bad information, but he decided he had better check the matter to make sure before the Secretary arrived. He picked up his telephone and directed the duty officer to get General Portero on the secure telephone.

• • •

The ATB meeting was just breaking up when the Duty NCO announced General Carmody was on the secure telephone for General Portero. Portero took the call in his office.

"Hello, Pancho. I'm glad I caught you. How are things going up there?"

"Okay, General, but I can say things are heating up. Yesterday we had a visit from some left-wing demonstrators from the States. They came onto our base with a bunch of TV people and tried to make us look like bad guys over the trouble in La Rioja."

"Yes, I just read the report Banning sent down. It sounds like you handled them all right…but we probably haven't heard the last of them yet. What else?"

"You already know the bastards are trying to take my Truck Company away. So far we have them stalled on that one. Let's see. What else? With regard to their plan to introduce an Export Board...the country is pretty much up in arms about that, especially in the north. Also, I don't think I told you I had a meeting with Figueroa a couple of months ago, my God the time is passing fast. He offered me a job. His purpose was clearly to get me out of the picture. He would not accept my terms, so I told him where he could go. We did not part friends. Now they are putting more and more pressure on us. The vise gets a little tighter every day. No armed confrontations yet, but they'll come. Our estimates are that they will be ready to take us on in a month or two when they bring their new brigade back from Isla Grande. We're getting ready."

"That bad, is it? My advice to you is don't rush it. Let them start it. That way they become the aggressor and you the defender. But the reason for my call is I have the Secretary General arriving this evening. He has a long list of subjects to discuss tomorrow, one of which is an inquiry from your government about you activating a fourth battalion. Anything to that?"

Portero paused before answering. "I haven't activated a fourth battalion, General. I have the same number of units as always. But...I am converting Emilio Sanchez's training unit into a line battalion. We're designating it 'Toro Battalion,' and its mission is the security of the Valle Escondido base. It is pretty much the same outfit, except it has an added mission. As a training unit, it did have security duties, except it will have more firepower now and greater mobility...and we are going to need both, I'm afraid."

"Dammit, Pancho. You should have let me know you were doing that! I could have run interference for you. Now, no matter how we rationalize it, they'll spin it as a back-door violation of the spirit of the treaty."

"I expect they will, General. But it is no more a violation than what they have been doing to us. I didn't let you know because I didn't want to put myself in a position of having to disobey your orders…I was afraid you might have told me not to do it."

"Maybe I would have and maybe not. It's done now, and I'll try to support you in it. But dammit, Pancho, I have asked you to keep me informed, and I am damned sorry you didn't in this case. I'll have some explaining to do to the Secretary, and I'll need your help. So I want you down here bright and early tomorrow to help me brief him on the situation up there. He's a good guy and he likes you and he doesn't trust Figueroa, so I think he'll be somewhat sympathetic, although he'll be pissed if he thinks you violated the treaty. By the way, bring Banning and Lacerica with you. My intelligence people will want to debrief all of you on those FLUSH clowns."

"General, I have a very important trip to La Mesona laid on for tomorrow. It is a traditional fiesta day up there, and Betsy and I are guests of honor. It has been planned for weeks. Can I come down Tuesday?"

"No, Pancho. The Secretary is leaving tomorrow for Washington, and it is very important he hears about the Naranjeras situation from you. I need you tomorrow. Have Soto represent you. Give Betsy my love and tell her I'm sorry."

"Okay, sir, if it is that important. She'll be disappointed but she'll forgive you…but probably not me. What time will your chopper be here?"

• • •

At ten thirty Monday morning, General Portero and Betsy arrived in front of Brigade Headquarters. Colonel Soto, splendid in his dress uniform, was there waiting by the general's staff car and its two Tracker escort vehicles, ready to depart for La Mesona.

Portero was genuinely sorry he could not make the trip. He had grown close to the people of La Mesona and felt he was letting them down. Betsy had understood and promised to carry his apologies and explain that he had been called to Panama. *She is a precious jewel,* he thought as he looked at her smiling at everyone. She was dressed in a most becoming suit, and she looked happy and beautiful. He admired her so, and suddenly felt the surge of joy which she always evoked in him whenever he paused long enough to put his mind on her.

She had brought along an empty suitcase and announced to all that she was going shopping after the festivities and intended to fill it. The smiling driver took the case from her and placed it in the trunk of the sedan. Portero saw that several attaché cases and the PowerPoint projection equipment had already been loaded.

Portero shook Colonel Soto's hand. "Thanks for standing in for me on such short notice, Pedro. Give everyone my apologies and try to keep Betsy from making me a pauper."

He kissed his wife. "*Hasta mañana, querida.* Have fun and don't spend too much. See you tomorrow."

The little convoy departed, waved at by a small band of smiling well-wishers, including Colonel Banning and Major Lacerica, and several enlisted men who presumably had helped load gear and given the sedan a final polish with the rags some of them still carried. Portero saw that Rubio was among them, wearing new corporal stripes, but looking unhappy. *I wonder what's wrong with our PNN friend?*

Portero checked his watch. It was time for him to get to the airstrip. He picked up his overnight bag and, followed by Banning and Lacerica, climbed into a waiting Tracker.

• • •

Betsy and Colonel Soto had been on the road three quarters of an hour. Their little convoy had reached the national highway which connected the capital with La Mesona, and was climbing the grade leading to the pass over the low mountain range which separated the great central valley from the Mesona region . It was a beautiful day. The sun was warm, and the air was dry and clear.

The leading escort vehicle was one hundred meters ahead, and the trailing one was immediately behind them.

The highway traffic was light. They passed several trucks and a bus making their way cautiously down the grade in low gear. Their drivers honked and waved their greetings at the sedan, assuming the popular ALIB commander was aboard. Most passenger cars sped by too fast to realize the significance of the military vehicles, although some slowed and one, a small white sedan, almost stopped as they passed, its two passengers peering into the staff car.

• • •

"That's him. Right on schedule. Get ready," said the driver of the white car.

"I'm not sure. The general's star was covered. Maybe Portero is not in the car," said the man in the passenger seat.

"It's him, I tell you. I saw him sitting on the right side. I saw his wife clearly. She wouldn't be there without him, would she? Arm your transmitter."

• • •

Betsy was cheerful and talkative. She was excited about the visit to La Mesona and glorying in the clear air and the mountain scenery. She had paused in her conversation to wave at the passengers of a white car which had slowed as they passed, then resumed what she was saying. She always enjoyed talking to the chief of staff. He was intelligent and often witty, and they had one thing in common, her husband. They both loved him in their different ways and liked to compare notes about him. Soto had observed that he had thought the general had seemed preoccupied lately, that he obviously had much on his mind with the growing tension between the brigade and the government, which was understandable. He hesitated then added the general had seemed a little less sure of how to handle the situation than was normal.

Betsy understood. She knew what had bothered her husband lately, but she was quick to reassure her companion. "Don't worry about him, Pedro. He'll work it out. Pancho has enormous strength of spirit. I don't think he yet knows exactly how to handle it, but he'll find the way, and when he does it will be—"

She never finished the sentence. In an instant, Betsy Portero, Colonel Pedro Soto, the young sergeant and the driver, and the crew in the trailing escort vehicle ceased to exist.

The explosion was powerful. Its shockwaves reverberated through the hills, echoing and rolling back upon themselves again and again, diminishing, and finally fading into silence. The sedan had disappeared, disintegrated. The trailing Tracker was smashed into an unrecognizable heap of twisted metal.

The leading vehicle was far enough ahead to escape damage, but the force of the blast slewed it so violently around that it came to rest across the highway, heading slightly downhill. Its crew sat silently, staring back in stunned disbelief at the wreckage. Slowly and painfully, they began to comprehend the significance of the column of dirty black smoke rising from the highway behind them.

• • •

A pale, grim-faced Portero stepped out of the helicopter. Colonels Ochoa and Roth and his four battalion commanders, Lieutenant Colonels Juan Gutierrez of the Osos, Carlos Johnson of the Tigres, Antonio DaSilva of the Lobos, and Emilio Sanchez of the Toros, were there to meet him. He showed the strain of the agonizing ninety-minute flight from Panama, during which he struggled to face the reality of Betsy's death. Colonel Banning had remained in Panama but Major Lacerica had returned with his general, wanting to help but not knowing how.

A sober-faced General Carmody and the Secretary General had been awaiting his arrival at the CINC-HJRAF Headquarters helipad. They informed him of the tragedy in Naranjeras. It was a dreadful moment for the two men, having to break the awful news to a smiling Portero as he stepped from the aircraft. He received it in stunned silence. "A bomb in the car, you say? Oh my God...My poor little Betsy...it's my fault...I've got to get back there."

Carmody had anticipated Portero's wish and had Chris Lane's helicopter standing by. He walked the younger man to the waiting bird, watching the agony and rage play across his face. He sought some way to reach out to him but only managed to choke out a few words. "You know how much I loved Betsy, Pancho...I hope you get the sonsabitches that did this."

"It was Figueroa. He meant it for me. And I will get him," Portero had declared in a low, hard voice, staring ahead. Then he turned to his friend and added in a softer tone, "You know, General, if you hadn't ordered me down here, I'd have been with her...I wish to God I had been."

General Portero held himself in firm control, stiff and erect, as he faced his senior officers. Inside he felt numb, insensible, still unable to fully comprehend the significance of the horrible event. He wanted to escape, to be someplace where he could hide, but he knew these men were his friends, and he was compelled to acknowledge their presence. He slowly approached them and shook each hand and thanked each man for being there.

Before he entered his waiting Tracker, he paused to face the group. "Thank you all...very much...for coming out this evening. It means a great deal to me....more than I can tell you...well... thank you."

Then, turning to Ochoa: "Ride with me will you, Colonel?"

Once in the car, Portero asked, "Do we know what happened?"

"Only what the escort people reported, sir. It was a powerful bomb in the sedan...They never knew anything, General."

"I suppose that's something…"

"Yes, sir. I suppose it is."

"My God, Octavio…I never expected anything like this…those bastards…those rotten, evil, murderous sonsabitches. I can't believe it."

Ochoa felt his general's anguish but could think of nothing to say. He waited while his friend struggled for control. After a very long moment, Portero asked, "Do we know how they did it?"

"Not really, sir. We believe Rubio was part of it, but we don't know for sure. He's being questioned. He seems very shaken up and frightened. He swears he only helped load baggage."

"Okay, keep on him. I want to know who ordered this done." Portero paused and looked at Ochoa. "I'd like you to assume Soto's duties. You're senior and have the credentials for the job. Will you do it?"

"Of course, General, if you want me."

"Good. That means we'll have to replace you in operations. Got any ideas?"

"I haven't thought about it, sir."

"Well I have. Juan Gutierrez is senior battalion commander. He is smart and has the experience, and he is a fine tactician. What do you think?"

"He is a good choice. He is a bit stubborn, but I like working with him."

"Good, then that is done."

"There is only one problem. Gutierrez has no exec. Diaz is being evacuated. They think it was a heart attack."

"When did that happen?"

"Last night, sir. He's going out on your chopper now."

"I am sorry to hear that…Okay, then we'll need a battalion commander for the Osos. Who is ready?"

"Vargas or Mix. They're the senior majors and are both excellent men. Mix has had more troop experience."

"Gutierrez will need Vargas to show him the ropes up here. It had better be Mix…Will you see to the orders? And inform the staff. Incidentally, Banning will stay in Panama for a couple of days. He should be back Wednesday. Thanks, Octavio…I want to go home now."

"Is there anything I can do for you, General?"

"Thanks, my friend. I wish there were…Just give me a couple of days."

• • •

Portero's self-control failed as he entered the little home he and Betsy had shared. He was suddenly overwhelmed by a sense of loss. Her essence was there in every room, in every corner. He felt her everywhere. Yet she was not there. The house was silent. No sound of her sweet voice singing or from the CDs playing the music she so loved. There were no sounds from the kitchen. There was only silence.

He could not accept the fact that she was gone. She couldn't be. She was such a part of him. Life without her was inconceivable. He wanted only to escape the awful reality. It all was a dream, a terrible nightmare, from which he must soon awake. But he knew he would find no relief when tomorrow came, or ever. He knew it clearly, yet he had to somehow escape the unbearable agony engulfing him, if only for a moment. Tomorrow he would try to deal with it, but now he couldn't. He didn't have the strength. He was not a drinking man, but he went to the kitchen cupboard and poured a half tumbler of scotch.

The next morning, he came slowly awake. He found himself still seated in his living room chair, the empty glass at his feet. Before he came to full consciousness, he felt the terrible sense of loss. He felt empty. The house felt empty. He remembered sensing her presence last night. Something of her had been there with him. Now even that was gone. He was alone.

Remembering the events of yesterday, outrage welled up in him. He leapt to his feet with an angry cry. He looked around at all their familiar things. They seemed alien to him. The room seemed small and confining. He needed air. He quickly changed into a sweatsuit and left the house. It was five o'clock in the morning, and dawn was just breaking in the east.

The soldiers of the brigade were accustomed to their general's early morning runs . However, those who saw him that morning were surprised to see him so early the day following his wife's death. They might have marveled at his toughness and determination had they thought about it. But Portero was not running to show he was tough. He was running to escape reality. He was running to exorcise his rage. He was running to exhaust himself, to punish his body. He was running to avoid thinking of Betsy and the men who murdered her. He ran farther and longer than usual, and by the time he returned to his house, it was fully daylight and he was exhausted. He rested, ate something, showered, and shaved.

He was struggling with a letter to Betsy's parents when Colonel Ochoa knocked on his door with a briefcase full of papers. "Orders to be signed, sir. How are you, General?"

"I'm okay, I guess. I had kind of a bad night but took a long run this morning. I think I'm feeling better…What's your news?"

"Rubio is sticking to his story. He insists he only helped the driver load luggage into the car. But we have a couple of witnesses who saw him carry a large briefcase into the headquarters and then to the car. He still denies doing anything wrong, but he is getting tired and may be weakening. They are continuing the interrogation.

"Gutierrez has accepted the operations assignment and seems pleased about it. He approved of Mix as his replacement. He has worked with him and likes him. Mix is very pleased and excited about taking command of the Osos…but, of course, DaSilva is not happy about losing his exec.

"The entire staff sends their best. They're concerned about you, General."

"Thanks. Tell them I'm getting along."

Ochoa finally exhausted his list of discussion items, many of them contrived to keep the general occupied with business and off his loss. They drank coffee together and he departed, assuring his commander that everything was under control. He promised to keep his suffering friend informed and hesitatingly offered again to remain if the general needed someone to talk to.

"Thank you, Octavio. You're a good friend, but I need to be by myself."

That afternoon, Portero's sergeant/administrative assistant arrived with a briefcase full of telephone and e-mail messages, and faxes from people all over the country expressing sympathy and support. He was particularly touched by a handwritten note from Ramon Sanchez Avila, in which he wrote, "Mrs. Portero is now where there is only happiness and fulfillment, and perfect love. We, who are left behind here in a lesser place, will remember and miss her always, but we must also always be happy for her, there." The note ended offering "my full support" and was signed, "Steadfastly, your friend."

A fax from the publisher of *La Prensa* decried the brutality of a government that would resort to bombing its political opponents. He declared it an act of cowardice and announced his paper would publish a series of editorials condemning the government and supporting the ALIB. He added that he expected his actions would invite retaliation, for which they were preparing.

The most touching messages were from strangers, people he had never met, who had admired him and Betsy and wanted to tell him so. Most also expressed their outrage.

Portero managed to contain his grief during most of the afternoon by occupying his mind with official matters, but in the evening, as the shadows lengthened, he was forced again to face the fact that Betsy was gone. If she could not be there in body, he wanted her to be there in spirit, and he tried to recapture the feeling of her presence he had experienced the previous evening. He roamed slowly through their home, room by room, touching the things she treasured. He went to her closet to inhale the sweet scent of her on her clothing. He carried her robe into the living room and sat with it, feeling the material, smelling it, and holding it against his cheek as he listened to her music. She was North American, but she loved the traditional music of Latin America: *Guaranias* from Paraguay, *Chamames* from Argentina, *Huapangos* from Mexico, *Cumbias* from Colombia, and *Sones Naranjeras*. She loved them all.

He found himself replaying her particular favorites: "Recuerdos de Ipacarai," "Si Quedara Sin Ti," "Ojos Españoles," and "Alborada," the old Mexican serenade which always brought tears to her eyes. He reveled in the music, thinking of Betsy, remembering how she smiled when she listened to it and how she sang along, mimicking the singers.

Suddenly he was weeping, emitting loud, grating sobs which he could not control, try as he might. Finally he was drained emotionally and physically exhausted, and he sank into a deep, quiet sleep.

Sometime during the night, he heard her calling him. "Pancho… Pancho…my dearest…" He stirred, but her gentle hand restrained him. "Shh, don't wake up, my love."

He sensed her keeling before him.

"Betsy, are you here?" he heard himself say.

"Don't worry about me, Pancho. I'm fine. Pedro and the others—we're all fine—so you mustn't worry about us. Do you understand?"

"I'm trying…but it's hard, sweetheart."

"I know, but remember, I'm with you, and I'll always be. I love you and I'll stay close, always." Her sweet, gentle voice continued. "Now, Pancho, the important thing is you. The brigade needs you. The country needs you. The people need you. It's time to end grieving and think of them. You can save them. You can stop those evil men, not for revenge, not for me, but for your country. You are a good man, a God-fearing man, and a great soldier. You have been preparing for this all your life. Fulfill your destiny. Do you understand me, Pancho?"

"Yes. I hear your words."

"Believe them, my love, and act. Have confidence in yourself and in your people. You will find the right way. You are going to win...And remember, I love you and will always."

Suddenly she was gone. He wanted to protest and call her back, but he couldn't speak. He groaned, then fell back into a deep, peaceful sleep.

He awoke refreshed in the morning. Betsy's words, sharp and clear, remained in his mind. Was it a dream? Could a dream be so clear, so real? Eventually he rose from the chair and, looking around the familiar room, he immediately felt her presence. Dream or not, he knew she was there with him. Suddenly he felt renewed, with a keen sense of purpose. He had work to do.

He shaved and bathed and put on a fresh uniform. He was hungry and made himself a big breakfast.

14 CHAPTER

The national newspapers remained in character in their treatment of the assassination of Elizabeth Portero and Colonel Soto. Major Lacerica had the clippings ready for the general when he returned to his office three days after the death of his wife. The *El Diario* headline read, "Wife of Controversial General Killed." The article was short and was no more than a recitation of the bare facts:

> The wife of General Francisco Portero, Colonel Pedro Soto, and six soldiers of the ALIB were killed Monday by an explosion. Apparently an explosive device had been placed in a vehicle which was transporting them to La Mesona by persons unknown. There has been speculation that the perpetrator may have been a disaffected soldier of the Brigade who held a grudge against General Portero or Colonel Soto. According to an ALIB spokesman the general had been scheduled to make the trip but had been called to Panama at the last minute.

The editor of *El Diario* placed a bold-faced box insert following the bombing story:

> President Antonio Figueroa announced today that he had sent a personal letter of condolence to General Portero on the loss of his wife. He condemned the crime as brutal and cowardly and untypical of Naranjeras. He offered the assistance of the government in apprehending the perpetrators.

La Vida Nacional's front page article contained the same facts but showed considerably more outrage about the incident. It also dedicated a paragraph to the political tensions that existed between Portero and the Figueroa administration, reciting the history and origins of their differences. It boldly, for that paper, concluded:

> These tensions have sparked some speculation that the government itself may have been indirectly responsible for the bombing of the vehicle. It is no secret that General Portero's political philosophy is somewhat aligned with the anti-Figueroa faction in the country, and that the ALIB has the potential for becoming the "muscle" behind a counter-golpe, should one come. There is speculation that some unscrupulous supporters of the current administration might believe they can win favor to themselves by eliminating Portero as a symbol of the opposition.

La Prensa typically pulled no punches. Its headline screamed, "Assassination Attempt Kills General's Wife and Officer." The article which followed recited the facts dispassionately, and offered heartfelt sympathy to General Portero, Mrs. Soto and the families of the soldiers who died "by the outrageous criminal act". It then went on to suggest the possibility that the Figueroa Government was complicit in the perpetration of the atrocity. The editorial contained the following:

> There is much speculation as to who is responsible for this act. We believe each citizen, in his heart, knows the perpetrator but most are reluctant to speak it openly. This newspaper believes recent actions by the government against the ALIB lend credence to rumors that the perpetrator may have been acting with the full knowledge of some government official.

When Portero finished reading the clippings, he called Lacerica into his office. "That is pretty strong stuff from *La Prensa.* I worry about our friends there. Don't they realize they are inviting retaliation? Figueroa cannot tolerate that kind of defiance. They're forcing him to take action against them, and what he'll do is shut the paper down, and that would not be in our interests. We need them publishing. Call the publisher, and ask him to tone down his rhetoric before it is too late. Make him understand why it's important."

• • •

On the fifth day of his interrogation, Corporal Rubio broke and gave his interrogators the information they sought. He had been steadfast in denying he was a PNN agent and that he had any involvement in the bombing, other than admitting he had helped load baggage into the general's sedan that day.

However, the interrogation had been well-planned by Colonel Banning, assisted by the legal officer. The interrogators had been carefully selected and briefed in their roles. Banning had devised a "good cop-bad cop" interrogation plan. Two sergeants from the brigade intelligence section had been chosen for the "bad cop" role, and Sergeant Ibarra, who had been Rubio's drill sergeant in basic training, was to be the "good cop."

Rubio had been held incommunicado in an isolated, windowless cell in the base stockade. It was equipped only with a hard bunk and portable toilet. He was allowed only six hours' sleep each night. He was provided a bowl of black beans and rice, water, and a lump of sugar twice each day. At five o'clock each morning, he was taken from his cell into a sparsely furnished interrogation room, also windowless, where he was subjected to three interrogation sessions, each lasting three to four hours. Between interrogations he was left alone in the interrogation room, manacled and seated on a hard, wooden chair. On the first day of formal interrogation, Colonel Banning, accompanied by the interrogators and the legal officer, had spent an hour reading and explaining to Rubio relevant portions from the *Manual of Military*

Justice and Courts-Martial, used by both the ALIB and the PNN. He emphasized the sections entitled "Deliberate Homicide," "Providing Aid or Comfort to an Enemy," and "Conspiracy Against Lawful Authority." He pointed out the penalty for these offenses were specified in the manual as "dishonorable discharge, imprisonment, or such other penalty appropriate to the crime as the court determines." He took care to explain that the "other appropriate penalty" clause possibly could include execution by firing squad.

Banning's purpose was to discover how the bomb was planted and, if possible, who ordered it done. He calculated the first step had to be inducing Rubio to confess he was a PNN agent, and he set that as the first objective in the interrogation plan. Consequently, the interrogators' initial focus was that objective. They kept reminding Rubio that they knew he was an agent and could present all the proof necessary to convict him in a trial... stressing that he had violated the "Providing Aid or Comfort to an Enemy."

Each time he denied the charge, they subjected him to a series of rapid fire, seemingly random questions, insisting on instant answers from him: When were you born? Where were you born? Who was your father? Where is your mother? What is wrong with your sister...or is it your brother? Why did you join the PNN? How long were you stationed at the La Mesona PNN post? Are you homosexual? Why did you lie to people about being from La Boca? When were you promoted to Corporal by the PNN? Why do you have a northern accent? Why are you spying on the ALIB? Where did you learn to type? What school did you attend? When did you join the PNN? Why do you hate the ALIB? Who trained you to be a spy? When are you going to stop lying to us? Why don't you believe we can prove you are a PNN agent? Who is Angelita?

These sets of questions were asked repeatedly in every session. His answers were noted and as time passed and he lost energy, they began to show inconsistencies. That triggered a whole new set of questions: Why did you tell us so-and-so yesterday? What is wrong with your memory? Why are you trying to deceive us? Are you afraid of telling us the truth? Who trained you to be deceptive? Do you enjoy being a spy? When will you tell us the truth?

By the third day, Rubio's only wish was to be left alone. He needed rest. His resolve was weakening, and he was losing confidence in his ability to continue resisting. His mental state was apparent to his inquisitors, and they agreed the time had come to spring the trap they had been building.

They were well into the second hour of the third session. Sergeant Ibarra was present, and the two intelligence sergeants were grinding out their questions. Rubio's answers were coming more slowly. When he began to give "I don't know" answers, they added pressure.

"What do you mean, you don't know? You knew yesterday. You knew this morning. What the do you mean you don't know?" They were shouting and standing over him threateningly.

Rubio collapsed, sobbing, and he repeated, "I don't know. I don't know...Leave me alone. Please leave me alone...I don't know...I can't answer any more."

They bent low and shouted in his face, "We won't leave you alone...You will answer or else we are—"

At that point, Ibarra stepped in. "Leave the poor bastard alone, for God's sake! Can't you see he's had it? You're not getting anywhere. Get out of here and give him a rest. Let me talk to him."

They arose and left the room without protest. Ibarra sat quietly beside Rubio while the man struggled for self-control.

Ten minutes later, when he was somewhat calm, Ibarra put his hand on Rubio's shoulder and spoke in a kindly voice, "Look, *Hijo*, these guys know you are an agent. Why don't you admit it and get it over with? What they really want is to pin the bombing on you, and they will certainly do it if you don't defend yourself. You can only defend yourself by telling them what really happened…I like you. You were a good recruit. My advice is to admit your connection to the PNN and put yourself in a position to defend yourself against the assassination charge. Think it over."

Rubio agreed to admit he was a PNN agent. Colonel Banning was called, and he arrived with a stenographer. When all had assembled, he quietly admitted he was a sergeant in the PNN and had been ordered to enlist in the ALIB to be in a position to pass information about the brigade.

"That is the truth, Colonel. But…I know nothing about that bomb. The only thing I did was help load the baggage."

"Okay, Rubio, we'll get to that later. Now I want to know all about your espionage operation. Who recruited you and who ordered you here?"

"One day my detachment commander…when I was at the La Mesona Post, spoke to several of us. They were looking for someone to volunteer for a confidential mission. They promised extra pay and a promotion to the man selected. I was bored and thought it sounded exciting, so I volunteered along with three others. Eventually I was chosen. They sent me to the capital for three weeks' training. I was introduced to a man who was to be my commander. His name is Antonio. I think he is a civilian, but I'm not sure. He communicates by telephone and e-mail, sometimes by written note through the barber shop, mostly to set up information drops."

There followed detailed questioning about contacts, methods of communication, codes, the kind of information Antonio was asking for. Rubio was forthcoming. He didn't know as much as they had hoped, but he gave them what he could. The process was thorough and lasted through the fourth day of interrogation.

On the fifth day, only Colonel Banning, Sergeant Ibarra, and the stenographer were waiting in the interrogation room when

Rubio was brought in. His manacles were removed, and he was invited to sit down.

"Corporal Rubio, or should I call you 'Sergeant'?" Banning began. "Yesterday you gave us a great deal of information, which we are in the process of verifying. So far it all checks out. If it continues to check out well, I can tell you your cooperation will have helped your case quite a bit. You were wise to cooperate. I hope you will continue to help us.

"Now I want to know about the bomb. How did you get it? Who gave it to you? What were your instructions? Please tell us."

Rubio paled visibly and leaned back in his chair. "I've already told you. I know nothing about the bomb. I only loaded baggage. That is what I know."

"Yes, that's what you told us, but we don't believe you. You have admitted to being a PNN agent. It is almost certain that the bomb was the work of the PNN. You have admitted helping load baggage into the sedan—something you have never been known to do before, and now you want us to believe that you knew nothing about the bomb. Come on, Rubio. Do you think we're stupid?" Banning's tone was hardening.

"I don't think you are stupid, sir. But I have told you I knew nothing about a bomb."

Banning arose and waved to the stenographer. "Okay, Rubio. Let's play it your way." He turned to Ibarra. "You stay with him, Sergeant. Put the manacles on him. I'll send my interrogators back in."

When they had gone, Ibarra picked up the manacles and approached Rubio. "Well the fat is in the fire now, *Hijo*. You've done it to yourself. Put out your hands."

"Wait a minute, Sergeant. Keep those bastards away from me. Before you said if I admitted to being an agent, I would be able to defend myself...How can I?"

"By telling the truth."

"I have told the truth. I really knew nothing about a bomb. I was told it was a sensitive recording machine. I really believed it was some kind of a tape recorder, Ibarra. If I thought it was a bomb, I wouldn't have put it the car...I respect Portero, and I wouldn't be a part in killing him. Now that's the whole truth."

• • •

The memorial service for Betsy Portero, Colonel Soto, and the six soldiers was held the following Sunday. The site was moved from the town's little Catholic church, which doubled as the brigade's chapel, to the parade ground because of the large numbers expected. In addition to the townspeople of Valle Escondido and a huge turnout of soldiers from the brigade, there was a sizable delegation from La Mesona, including the bishop, the mayor, the publisher and editor of *La Prensa*, the presidents of the Cattlemen's Association and the Tanners, and other regional dignitaries. There also was a smaller delegation from the capital, which included Ramon Sanchez Avila and other representatives of the press, including a television reporter and camera crew.

A canopied platform and alter had been erected. A public address system had been installed, and seating for the brigade band and about one hundred dignitaries had been provided.

The band played familiar hymns as the crowd assembled, and by the time the service began, there were more than fourteen hundred people in attendance.

The Bishop of La Mesona gave the invocation, and the local priest conducted the service. Eulogies were given by Colonel Ochoa, the Mayor of La Mesona, the President of the Cattlemen's Association, and the most moving of all, by Lieutenant Colonel Carlos Johnson, commander of the Tigre Battalion, and a long-time friend of the Porteros.

Charlie "Gin Pot" Johnson was universally admired by the soldiers of the ALIB. He was the only senior officer who had begun his career with the brigade as an enlisted man. He was a large, powerfully built black man, born in Panama of Jamaican ancestry. His father had been a senior sergeant in Panama's *Guardia Nacional,* but fled to Naranjeras after publicly accusing a senior officer of corruption. He enlisted and served in the PNN. When the ALIB was organized, he urged Carlos, then in his late teens, to enlist for it. There young Charlie found a home. He was intelligent, good natured, and a conscientious student, and he proved to be a natural leader. Less than eight months after completing recruit training, he was promoted to corporal and one year later became the youngest sergeant in the brigade.

He quickly caught Portero's attention and was sponsored for the PNN Officer Training Academy. There he compiled a distinguished record as an officer candidate, graduating first in his class. He was commissioned a Junior Lieutenant and opting to return to the ALIB, became the youngest officer in the brigade. He rose steadily through the officer ranks and finally achieved command of the Tigres.

Aside from his color and size, his most distinguishing characteristic was his almost perpetual broad smile. He, like his father, was an Evangelical Christian, and he lived and practiced his faith with apologies to no one. He had become the unofficial chaplain for the Protestants in the brigade, a duty he cherished.

He wore the unlikely sobriquet, "Gin Pot," like a badge of honor. The troops of his first command, a rifle platoon, had given him the name because of his constant railings against the cheap cantinas and bars, which always seemed to appear outside military bases. He called them "gin pots" and regarded them as the "tools of Satan, designed to lure fine young soldiers into habits of sin and inebriation."

Colonel Johnson's eulogy was most moving for Portero. Betsy had been close to Jovita, Johnson's Naranjera wife, and their eight well-scrubbed, well-mannered children. So for him, it was painfully emotional when Johnson spoke warmly and eloquently of their friendship with Betsy and "the joy she had brought into the lives of ALIB families."

Johnson concluded his remarks, saying, "We have lost cherished friends and brave comrades by a cowardly act. It is human to want revenge, to seek to balance the account, to do to them what they have done to us. But think...the voice we hear urging such a course is not the voice of God. It is the voice of His enemy. It is the voice of Satan. We should not...we must not...we will not...heed that voice, because vengeance is not our responsibility. That is God's domain...and we can be sure the evil men who perpetrated this act will one day reap the bitter harvest they have sown. We must wait patiently, knowing...vengeance will come to them in God's own good time.

"I personally hope, and I pray, and I believe, that we of this good brigade may someday be God's instrument in that mission, but it is not for me, or for any of us, to choose. Until the time comes when we know if we are to play a part, we can only remember our fallen comrades and cherish their memory. They will remain dear to us forever...and they will someday be avenged, but in God's good time, not ours."

As he made the final statement, he turned to look at his brigade commander. Portero caught the look and smiled, thinking, *I've got your message, Carlos. I hope I can live up to it, but this has become personal for me. Today I pray I have a part to play in God's plan for vengeance...and I hope it is soon.*

• • •

It had been five weeks since Sergeant Emilio Carranza led his truck platoon out of the ALIB base at Valle Escondido and to its new station at the PNN Main Base east of the capital. They had been attached to the First Transport Company and put to work immediately, often putting in over ten hours a day on the road.

Carranza was physically tired, but he was more relaxed about the double life he was leading. When he had first arrived, his new company commander did not conceal his suspicions about him. He had been repeatedly quizzed about the circumstances of his departure from the ALIB, and it became clear that his new superiors had been well briefed about him. They questioned him in great detail about his fight with Blas, and with his old company commander. They probed as to how he felt about his reduction in grade and the ALIB. Their questions confirmed his belief that the PNN did indeed have a spy at Valle Escondido; they knew too much about him. He now understood why, and was grateful Colonel Banning had insisted his mission be kept a tightly held secret.

It was also perfectly clear to him that his new commander continued to be suspicious of him, not only because of the continuing questioning, but also because he obviously avoided sending the platoon into sensitive areas. Accordingly, Carranza took pains to demonstrate his bitterness toward the brigade and his satisfaction with his new assignment. He thought he may have succeeded, because after several weeks, they had begun to accept him for what he represented himself to be and their vigilance seemed to have relaxed. The questioning ended, and they began giving him new assignments which took him into the sensitive areas. Carranza remained on his guard, however. His superiors had assigned an Assistant Platoon Sergeant to him, whom he suspected was there to keep an eye on him.

The platoon had made five trips to the training camp near La Rioja, delivering comestible supplies, and new field uniforms and personal equipment, and some small arms ammunition. Carranza, always alert for information, had learned that the unit in training there was designated a Cazador Battalion, that it was organized to operate against guerilla forces. The word was it was an all-volunteer unit commanded by a Cuban major named Serra, and it contained a number of foreigners: Cubans, Nicaraguans, and Salvadorans. He had also learned that there had been tensions between some of the foreigners and the Naranjeros, which had resulted in some fights. Carranza had eagerly passed this information on to the ALIB through his communication channels. The platoon had also loaded one thousand six hundred heavy metal containers in Puerto Hondo, which were marked "auto parts—handle with extreme care" in English, but also carried labels written in a strange alphabet which he thought might be Arabic. Carranza surmised they were ammunition cases of some kind. The load was delivered to a warehouse just inside the entrance of a large, forested PNN training area. Security around the area was unusually tight, which aroused Carranza's curiosity. On the pretext of finding a latrine, he had walked behind the warehouse and found a long, open-sided shed. At one end, soldiers were working on a large armored vehicle with a turret, which mounted a large caliber gun equipped with a muzzle brake. It looked like a tank, but it had six large rubber-tired wheels. He approached the men and asked directions to a latrine. A corporal pointed behind the shed. He thanked the man, turned to leave, then hesitated and said pointing at the vehicle, "That's a big damn machine. What the hell is it, some kind of a tank?"

"That, my friend, is an EE-9 Cascavel recon vehicle. They're built in Brazil," the corporal told him with pride.

"It sure is big," Carranza said as he headed through the shed to the latrine. On his return, he stopped to chat with the corporal. "How does that thing drive? I'm with the Truck Company. Is it like a truck?"

"Better than a truck…it's easier on the road. It's pretty easy cross-country, too. Would you believe the thing weighs thirteen tons and it will travel one hundred kilometers per hour."

"You're joking. Really? I'd sure like to drive one of those."

"Well we are still looking for people, I think. You can talk to our first sergeant, he'll know. We are just a new outfit, an Armored Car Company, part of the First Armored Battalion. We have fifteen of these machines. That's a lot of firepower. That is a ninety millimeter gun, and they also carry a couple of machine guns."

"Where can I find your First Sergeant? Do you think there are still openings?"

"I think so, but he'll know for sure. He'll be back in a couple of hours."

"Damn. I'll be back on the road by that time. Maybe I can see him on the next trip."

"We're supposed to be here for a couple of weeks more, finishing our driver and gunnery training, so you can probably see him any time you get back. But do it soon, because we seem to be filling up fast."

A Tracker driven by a very large black officer stopped in front of the Cascavel. Carranza stared at the man. His first thought was that it was Colonel Gin Pot Johnson, but the man was wearing a PNN uniform with a major's insignia on his collar. He and the corporal both saluted as the officer approached.

"Do you have a problem, Corporal?" he said, pointing to the vehicle.

"Fuel pump, Major. We just replaced it. She is about ready, sir."

"Good." The officer turned to Carranza. "Who are you, Sergeant?"

"Carranza, sir. I'm with the First Truck Company. My platoon is unloading at the warehouse."

"What are you doing here?"

"Just coming from the latrine, Major. Stopped to ask about this tank."

"Impressive, isn't it? Okay, you had better get back to your outfit." Turning to the corporal, he said, "Get her closed up and join your platoon on the training course."

He climbed into his Tracker and departed.

"Who was that?"

"That is Major Johnson, our battalion commander. He's a good officer and a tough son of a bitch. But the men like him. He is willing to get his hands dirty."

Carranza returned to his platoon, which was still unloading. He was excited and was mentally cataloging the bonanza of information he had been handed in an idle ten-minute conversation. It was important stuff, and he was planning how he would deliver it to his ALIB contact.

• • •

A very angry President Figueroa called his minister of interior, his PNN commander, and his press secretary into his office. He held a sheaf of newspaper clippings in his right fist and waved it in their faces. "What the hell are we doing about those *La Prensa* assholes? Have you read the crap they're putting out? They are openly defying us. I thought they were supposed to be under control."

"They were until the bomb, Mr. President," said Press Secretary.

Colonel Davidson winced. He had had a very unpleasant private conversation with Figueroa the previous Tuesday when it was learned Pancho Portero was not in the car. He and his staff had been called incompetent bunglers, among other unflattering names, and he had been forced to defend his plan. How could anyone have anticipated that Portero would be called to Panama at the last minute? If that had not happened, the problem would have been solved!

"Bomb or not, we can't let those bastards openly challenge us. This is sedition! If we don't act, we'll look weak...and we'll lose our support. I want them closed down. Arrest the publisher and his senior editor. Get them down here and try them for sedition...and throw away the goddamn key. If we don't send a message now, we'll have to face more and more this kind of defiance."

"But Mr. President, won't that stir up the Mesonenses even more? Are you sure you want to...?"

"Don't argue, Davidson. Damit. Do your job. Obey my orders."

CHAPTER 15

On Friday evening of the week following the memorial service, Portero took an urgent call from his friend, the extremely agitated mayor of La Mesona. "They have arrested the publisher, his editor, and the print shop manager, and they have locked the doors of *La Prensa*. They have guards around the building."

"Who has?"

"The National Police."

"I'm not surprised. Something like this had to happen. Figueroa can't allow *La Prensa* to continue editorializing as they have been lately. Has there been any explanation?"

"The local police commander has informed me by telephone that our people have been accused of sedition and are to be tried in La Capital. They are to be taken there immediately. Can you help us, General?" The Mayor seemed frantic.

"Of course—we'll do what we can, Mr. Mayor. I am no lawyer, but 'conspiring to commit sedition' sounds like a manufactured charge to me. I thought sedition applied to people advocating the overthrow of the government. As far as I know, *La Prensa* has never done that. Their recent editorials have all but accused the government of murdering our people, but I don't think it ever came near suggesting the overthrow of the government."

The Mayor agreed. "That is correct. They have been careful about that. The government is acting illegally and they are violating the constitutional right of the press to operate without censorship."

Portero took a moment to think. "I agree. Do you know if they have left La Mesona with the *La Prensa* people yet?"

"Not yet. But four vans full of well-armed PNN arrived from the south, so I assume they're waiting to transport them. At the moment, they have them under custody at their base. They probably don't want to move them through the crowd. There is a very large group of protesters around their base. I called the local radio station and it has been broadcasting the news of the arrests. Our people are very angry about this, and a great many have rallied to demonstrate around the police post."

"Good. I'm not sure what I can do yet. I'll need little time to organize something. Try to buy me some time. Can you have the radio station encourage more people to join the demonstrators? Can you go out there yourself and lead them? Try to keep the protest going as long as you can. I am hoping they will be reluctant to move those men while the crowd is there. If they try, see what you can do to block them…and please keep me informed. Can you do that, Mr. Mayor?"

"We'll do our best, General. You can count on us, and thank you."

• • •

Portero felt excitement as he reviewed his options for dealing with the new situation in La Mesona. He knew he had to act. Allowing the government to close down *La Prensa* was unthinkable. That newspaper was the glue that united the northern region, and it had now become the national voice and symbol of the anti-Figueroa opposition. Furthermore, it had courageously supported him and the ALIB since the trouble with Figueroa began. Holding the northern region together was essential to his Northern Strategy. He sensed this crisis might be the trigger for open hostilities with Figueroa. He welcomed it because he now could act on the side of the people. He was now in the position of upholding the law in the face of the government's violation of it.

He called Colonel Ochoa, his new chief of staff, and asked him to assemble the battalion commanders and brigade staff immediately. An hour later he briefed his key officers on the situation. "I expect they will leave their base as soon as the demonstration dies down. I will ask the mayor to pull his people out of there by midnight. If the convoy leaves at one or two, it should reach Colina between two thirty and three thirty. That gives us time to prepare an intercept.

"Colina is the ideal place for an intercept. The highway narrows down as it passes through the town. There are a couple of sharp turns where the buildings are close to the curb. Should be a good place for an ambush. Once they are stopped, there is no place for them to go. We want enough force there to do it right. Which battalion is on standby alert?"

"We are, General," said DaSilva, the Lobo Battalion commander.

"Okay, Tony, you have the assignment. There isn't much time, so get moving. Gutierrez will help you put a plan together. Do it right…and let's have no shooting, if possible. I don't want anyone hurt, especially our newspaper friends."

LTC DaSilva left to alert his troops.

Portero turned to the others. "Remember this date, gentlemen, because it will mark the beginning of hostilities. Our campaign against Figueroa starts now. Tonight we initiate Northern Strategy. Ochoa, please issue the necessary movement orders. You all know your missions. Use the weekend to prepare and to move into your assignments Monday.

Portero turned to the Oso Battalion commander. "But your work starts tonight, Major Mix. Have you communications with your company at the Mesona supply base?"

"Yes, General."

"Alert them to be ready to move on the Mesona PNN compound. I want it occupied at first light tomorrow morning. If you surprise them, there shouldn't be much resistance. Remember, they are at reduced strength…thirty or forty at the most… their guard may be down once the convoy leaves with the newspaper people. You should be able to surprise them. Disarm them and hold them in their lockup…and keep me informed. Any questions?"

"None, sir. May I be excused?"

"Get going."

• • •

Bravo Company of the Lobos quietly moved into ambush position in the center of Colina, the town's business district. It was after midnight, there was no moon, and the streets were deserted. The only light came from an occasional dim streetlight strung over intersections. They made their preparations to intercept the PNN convoy just after it made a sharp left turn in the narrow street which doubled as the Nacional Highway. The trucks which transported the company to Colina were concealed well back on side streets.

LTC DaSilva and the B3, LTC Gutierrez, had hurriedly developed a plan for the ambush itself, and they deployed the battalion's recon platoon in concealed position on the highway one kilometer north of the town. From there it could observe both the highway and a secondary street leading to the east side of Colina. The platoon's mission was to advise DaSilva and his Bravo Company commander of the approach of the convoy by radio.

At 0420, the recon platoon leader reported headlights of four vehicles approaching. The little convoy, which they could now see consisted of four large Suburbans with PNN markings, stopped one hundred meters past the platoon's position. An officer dismounted from the second vehicle and conferred briefly with the man in the passenger seat of the lead vehicle. The lead vehicle then proceeded down the main road into Colina. The officer spoke to each of the remaining three vehicles, and some of their occupants dismounted to smoke or to relieve themselves at roadside.

The recon platoon leader reported these events, speaking into his radio as quietly as he could, his back to the PNN people so his voice would not be carried in the cool night air. "It appears they are sending a vehicle ahead to scout the route. Recommend you let it pass through your ambush unmolested, sir, if you can."

DaSilva agreed. The company commander passed the word to his platoon commanders to keep hidden and let the first vehicle pass. He directed the platoon be deployed along the southern perimeter of Colina to intercept and seize the vehicle in the event it should turn back into the town.

The vehicle passed the ambush site, unaware of the Lobos hidden in the dark shadows of the side streets, and proceeded. Twenty minutes later, the Recon Platoon leader reported the remaining three vehicles had started their engines and were proceeding into Colina by the main road.

DaSilva and his men could see the headlights approaching and quietly took their positions. As the little convoy made the left-hand turn, it was suddenly confronted with two ALIB trucks blocking the roadway. As the PNN vehicles braked to a stop, a third truck pulled out of an alley behind them to block a retreat. Before the PNN personnel in the vehicles could react, they were surrounded by Lobo soldiers with weapons raised. The doors of the vehicles were yanked open, their occupants were pulled violently out, disarmed, and slammed against the building walls, where their wrists were bound behind them with plastic ties.

The PNN's three prisoners, the *La Prensa* executives who sat handcuffed in the second van, were gently helped out of the vehicle and shortly released with a key found on the person of the PNN lieutenant in charge. They were as stunned by the sudden events as were their captors, but as they began to comprehend they had been rescued, they grew animated and, grinning, asked for the leader of their rescuers. Tony DaSilva soon joined them, introduced himself, and relayed special greetings from General Francisco Portero. He offered them coffee from a thermos his driver carried. It was lukewarm, but they savored it with considerable relish.

The entire operation was over in less than fifteen minutes. It was done quietly and efficiently. No shots were fired and almost no voices were raised. Aside from PNN pride, there had been no injuries. The fourth vehicle, which had been allowed to pass through the ambush, having lost radio contact with its convoy commander, turned back and reentered Colina, where it was promptly seized and its occupants taken prisoner.

In all, nineteen PNN men had been made prisoners. They were promptly loaded on an ALIB truck, which immediately departed for Valle Escondido. It was soon followed by Bravo Company, its convoy of four trucks augmented by the four PNN Suburbans. The happy and laughing *La Prensa* men rode in comfort with DaSilva in the lead Suburban. They were excited and already planning the front page story of their rescue.

• • •

The Mesona PNN compound, located one kilometer north of the city in the center of a large hay field, consisted of three low barrack buildings, a mess hall and recreation facility, a headquarters/communications building containing a lockup for holding criminals, and a garage and maintenance building. The compound was neatly surrounded by a rectangular, waist-high brick wall. There were small, covered sentry posts at each corner and at the main gate. In the open spaces between the wall and the buildings were immaculately groomed lawns and a number of citrus fruit trees and patches of vegetable gardens, attesting to how the police agents used their time when not occupied with official duties.

Charlie Company of the Osos deployed undetected one hundred meters short of the south-eastern perimeter of the compound, two platoons abreast with the third in reserve fifty meters to the left rear. It was dawn. The eastern sky was beginning to lighten when the Company commander blew one long, shrill whistle blast to initiate the attack. With a great yell, the men charged into the compound to surround the barrack buildings, catching most of the PNN personnel asleep in their beds. The reserve platoon leader waited five minutes, then having determined the assault had gone without resistance, raced ahead of his platoon, leading his men toward his secondary objective, the base headquarters building.

The PNN sentry at the main gate, recovering from the shock of the surprise attack, reacted to the men running toward his position, raised his AK-47 and fired blindly in their direction. It was his last act in life. He was immediately cut down by a fusillade of return fire from the lead elements of the charging platoon, but not before one of his bullets had found its mark. The young platoon leader lay dead and still bleeding from a bullet wound in the head.

The thirty-four surviving PNN were rounded up and jammed into the lockup in the headquarters building. The six men guarding the *La Prensa* complex were later added to their number. The compound was methodically swept for holdouts and loose weapons. A perimeter defense was established against the possibility of counter-strike. When he was sure all was in hand, the Company commander reported his mission accomplished by telephone to the Oso Battalion commander awaiting word in Valle Escondido. "I regret to report also that Lieutenant Evan Gutierrez was killed in action. He was our only casualty. One PNN was also killed."

The ATB conference room had now become the war room. A composite map of the Naranjeras, overlaid with a sheet of clear acetate, was mounted on the wall opposite the room's bank of windows. A sergeant from operations, with blue grease-pencil in hand, was delineating the territory now controlled by the ALIB. The solid blue line encompassed the northern third of Naranjeras from the eastern border, running southwest and swinging west at the town of La Campana, passing just south of Valle Escondido, then swinging northwest to the Pacific coast to include the little fishing port of Ensenada. It was a graphic representation of Portero's carefully planned "Northern Strategy."

Symbols on the map indicated the progress of the Oso Battalion's movement onto the Mesona plateau. The Oso Alpha and Bravo Companies, and one platoon of its tirador company had closed on their new base of operations, the former Mesona PNN compound. Charlie Company had returned to its Abattoir Base, where it would soon be joined by the Battalion Headquarters Company and two platoons of the Tiradors.

The map showed the dispositions of the other three battalions. The Tigres were deployed along the Nacional Highway from La Campana north. Its Alpha and Charlie Companies had established a roadblock and were digging in at La Campana. Gin Pot Johnson had located his Headquarters just north of the town in a large farm complex shaded by a stand of eucalyptus. His reserve, Charlie Company, was also deployed one hundred meters north. The battalion's recon platoon had been dispatched to Colina, twelve kilometers to the north. Its mission: to establish a checkpoint at the junction of the Nacional Highway and the northern road to Valle Escondido.

The Campana roadblock had been established to control traffic between the capital and the Mesona region. Its orders were to allow only bona fide civilian traffic to pass in either direction. Southbound government vehicles were to be inspected and allowed to pass after any weapons, radios, or cell phones they might be carrying were confiscated. Northbound government vehicles were to be stopped and turned around unless they had a pass signed by the Commanding General of the ALIB.

The map showed the Toro Battalion deployed around the ALIB Base at Valle Escondido. Its mission was to defend the base against raids or an attack from the Figueroa forces. Emilio Sanchez was occupied overseeing the fortification and camouflaging of his roadblocks and listening posts, digging in the wire connecting his sound-powered telephones, preparing fields of fire for his Tiradors and booby traps on certain approach trails in the hills south of the base. He also had devoted time to pre-planning defensive concentrations of fire for the brigade mortar platoon, which had been attached to him.

The map placed the Lobo Battalion at the Valle Escondido base and designated it as Brigade Reserve. The ATB staff more often referred to the Lobos as the "maneuver battalion."

• • •

The publisher and his key men accompanied one of the Oso contingents to La Mesona. The three were delivered to the *La Prensa* office and printing plant complex, where they were greeted by the mayor and a group of cheering employees and well-wishers. The PNN guards had been replaced by several city constables who had unlocked and inspected the buildings and reported no damage. The publisher recounted the story of their rescue with unstinting praise for General Portero and the men of the ALIB. He had harsh words for Figueroa and "his traitorous thugs" and promised a special addition of the paper the following day, declaring the government to be in flagrant violation of the nation's constitution.

• • •

Portero had been saddened by the loss of young Evan Gutierrez. He knew the young man as a promising officer, and the nephew, and almost like a son, to Juan Gutierrez, the new brigade opera-

tions officer. Gutierrez had taken the loss hard. Portero understood his feelings only too well, but was not sure if his attempts
to console the man had had any positive effect.

The general now sat in the war room, reflecting on the fact
that all was progressing according to plan. His battalions were
getting in place. Ninety percent of his reserve fuel, enough for
forty-five days of conservative operations, would be in storage
at the abattoir in the north by the end of the week. His reserve
stores of rice, beans, and canned beef would follow the week after.
The engineers were renovating buildings in the abattoir compound to house the band, the brigade personnel section, and the
Basic Training Company with its fifty half-trained recruits. All
was indeed going according to plan.

He turned his mind to the challenges ahead. He had been
considerably troubled by recently received intelligence relative to
the PNN acquisition of fifteen Cascavels. These would be the
most formidable weapons they would have to face, and he had
asked the ATB to develop anti-Cascavel tactics. Their first recommendation, which was to assign a couple of Javelin anti-tank
missile sections to the Tigres at La Campana, had been implemented. He had confidence in his Javelin platoon, which had
consistently scored high in training exercises. His only concern
was that that he had only eighteen Javelins available in inventory.

"So what is new about that? We only have about six or seven
basic loads of ammunition, anyway. This damned fight must be
won fast…within sixty days…or we lose."

He returned to his office to call General Carmody.

• • •

Carmody was eager to take Portero's call. They had not talked
since the black day two weeks before, when he had to inform
his friend of Betsy's death. He had kept close tabs on Portero's
passage through the mourning process and the interrogation
of the PNN agent through his staff, which was in communi-

cation with counterparts in the ALIB. He had also read with great interest the various newspaper accounts of the assassination and of the memorial service at Valle Escondido. Both he and the Secretary General believed the bombing had been the work of the Figueroa administration.

But he had not known of the events of the last three days, the arrest of the newspaper people, their rescue, the seizure of the Mesona PNN post, nor of the La Campana roadblock until Portero's call.

After briefing Carmody on these events, Portero quietly added, "I am faxing you a copy of my own resignation from the ALIB, along with the resignations of all my senior officers, General. I hope you will understand I have no choice. We are going to be in a nasty fight with Figueroa, and I can no longer pretend that I can serve the interests of the HJRAF and the interests of my country at the same time. There is an insoluble conflict of interest here.

"I want you to know none of this alters my respect for you personally. And also…I fully understand that what I am doing may well be interpreted as disloyalty…to you and to the HDO… and it will certainly be embarrassing to you both. For that I am very, very sorry. But, General, I have no choice. These thugs are destroying our country, and we are the only means of stopping them. I have no regrets about what we are doing…except that it will reflect badly on you. I can't help that…but I don't want to lose our friendship."

Carmody was closer to Portero than any of his HJRAF commanders. He was his protégé, almost like a son in whom he had taken great pride. He heard the anguish in Portero's voice but he understood that the younger general's decision was firm, that he had passed the point of no return, and that there was now nothing he could do to reverse the situation.

"Okay, Pancho. I will accept your resignation officially when I receive it. Between us, I will tell you that I understand the reasons

for your decision and am personally sympathetic to your cause…
and our friendship is not in jeopardy. However, officially, I cannot
condone what you are doing nor can the HDO, although I have
reason to believe the Secretary General may feel as I do. Officially,
I would order you to stand down from this course…but you have
taken yourself from under my orders. It now becomes a political
matter between your government and the HDO and the United
States to unravel.

"I might add parenthetically that it will take months, perhaps
years, for the diplomats to find a solution, and whatever solution
they might eventually agree to will probably not be helpful to
the cause of democracy in Naranjeras. However, if this situation
can be brought quickly to some conclusion, the diplomats will be
presented with a fait accompli which they could not, would not,
ignore. Do you take my meaning?"

"Yes, sir. I think we have sixty days."

"Do it in less if you can, Pancho…and good luck! I cannot
help you…but I would like your permission to send up some
observers…non-combatants, of course. I think I will be able to
justify it on the basis of evaluating the training we have given
you…and to monitor the conduct of your troops for violation of
human rights and all that sort of thing. That should be something both the liberals and the conservative in the US Congress
would approve, given all the fuss about FLUSH. I'll let you know
if I get the approval."

"We would welcome observers, provided they only observe
and don't get in our way. We have nothing to hide. Let me know."

• • •

President Figueroa called an emergency meeting of the Supreme
Council. He waited until his four colleagues had taken their cus-
tomary seats around the highly polished mahogany table before
he entered the small, secure, executive session conference room
adjacent to his office. He was in a foul mood and he spoke in the

tight, controlled voice he used when agitated. "Events are not going as we planned, gentlemen, and I want to know why, and what we are doing about it."

They looked at him with stony faces, knowing he expected no reply.

"First, your export control scheme, Mario, seems to be blowing up in our face. Second, our supposed propaganda coup with those pathetic FLUSH people has pretty well backfired. Then there is the matter of *La Prensa*. What the hell happened with that?" He glared at Marco Menendez, Minister of Interior, and Colonel Davidson, his PNN commander.

"We arrest those damned people and shut them down one day. Portero takes them from us the next day and now they are back in business. Can't we do anything right? And now the son of a bitch has set up a roadblock, and we can't even get to La Mesona. People are laughing at us. Have you read the papers this morning? Sanchez Avila says, 'The Figueroa administration has shown signs of weakness, which portends loss of the people's respect if it cannot demonstrate it is in control.' My God!"

He looked each of his colleagues in the eye, one by one. "Sanchez Avila is right. We must demonstrate we are in control…If we don't, everything we have worked for will come to nothing. We will lose and if we lose, we lose more than power. We could even lose our very lives.

"I'm not ready to let that happen." He turned to face his PNN commander. "Davidson, I want that goddamn roadblock destroyed, and I want that goddamn newspaper shut down…and I don't care what you have to do to get it done. Do you understand me?"

"Clearly, Mr. President. I'll be ready to move in three weeks, when—"

"We haven't got three weeks! My God, man, don't you understand what is happening out there? We are losing the support of some of our friends, even. We don't have time. We have to show we're in charge…now, or it is over!"

Davidson showed his irritation. "Look, I am not a miracle worker. I need the Second Brigade back from Isla Grande, and I need the Armored Battalion and the Casadors ready. They're almost there…but it will take time to get the brigade off the island. I can give you what you want but, dammit, I need the tools to do it!"

"What will it take to knock out that roadblock?"

"If we don't have to go on to La Mesona, we can do it with elements of the Armored Battalion, with some support from the Casadors. We should hit it with overwhelming force so it depends upon how strong the ALIB force there is. If it is a platoon, it'll be easy. If it is a company, no problem. If it is a battalion, we should be able to do it with the firepower of the Cascavels. But I'll need more power than that to go all the way north."

"All right, make it a two-phase operation. The roadblock first. Get your troops off the island and then we go to La Mesona. How soon can you start on phase one?"

"In three days, sir."

"Okay. Go. But be sure you get the job done. Get that roadblock out of there fast and take and hold La Campana. We'll need it as a staging area when we go north. Who'll lead that taskforce?"

"Major Marco Johnson…the Panamanian…He knows his business, and he is tough and aggressive."

"Johnson…Isn't his brother with the ALIB?"

"Yes. They call him 'Gin Pot Johnson.' He commands their Tigre Battalion. But we don't have to worry about that. They don't get along. Marco thinks his older brother is a nut. He'll do the job. Don't be concerned about their family ties."

CHAPTER 16

The village of La Campana is situated atop a low east-west escarpment, which changes to rolling hills in the west and ends in a steep banked ravine cut by a small river, dry except during rainy season, in the east. The eastern limit of the village abuts the ravine. The willow-lined riverbed emerges from the ravine and runs in a southerly direction for two or three kilometers before it swings to the east, where it bypasses a rocky knoll, which is the highest ground southeast of the village. The Nacional Highway, which connects Puerto Hondo and La Capital with La Mesona in the north, runs parallel to the riverbed until a point about two-hundred-and-fifty meters south of La Campana. There it departs the river to climb into the town by means of a massive landfill causeway. At the point it enters the village, the roadway is ten meters above grade. There is a stout metal crash fence on either side, which extends the length of the causeway.

Originally an agricultural center, La Campana's small population's principal business had evolved into servicing the heavy vehicular traffic which flows between Puerto Hondo, the capital, and La Mesona. There are two service stations, including a multi-pump Exxon plaza, a combination repair garage and auto parts store, several restaurants, a general store, and a number of roadside kiosks which hawk fresh fruit, beer and soft drinks, and empanadas to passing travelers. The dominant landmark in the center of the town is the old church of Santa Cecilia with its tower and loud, clear bell which echoes throughout the valley Saturdays and Sundays, and gives the town its name. An east-west road from Valle Escondido intersects the Highway Nacional north of town.

La Campana is ideally suited for a military defense against any force approaching from the south, which is why Portero and the ALIB staff had chosen it as the site for the roadblock. The terrain to the south forms a natural funnel bounded by the precipitous bank of the river in the east and the hills to the west, which emerge from the escarpment just to the west of town and run off in a southwesterly direction for five hundred meters before swinging again to the west. A fan-shaped field, green in the spring but dry stubble in the summer, lies west of the highway. It slopes up to the hills in the west and narrows toward the town. The topography makes La Campana a natural chokepoint into which any military force approaching from the south would be forced to compress itself into what would become a relatively compact killing zone.

The roadblock installed by the ALIB is in the center of the village. It is a series of breast-high sandbag barriers with lift gates, well-defiladed and out of sight of anyone approaching on the highway from the south until he enters La Campana at the top of the causeway.

• • •

PNN Major Marco Johnson, commander of the First Naranjeras Armored Battalion, sat cross-legged on the rocky knoll near where the highway crossed a low ridge two-and-a-half kilometers south of La Campana. Three kilometers behind him, the taskforce hastily organized by Colonel Davidson to eliminate the ALIB roadblock was parked at roadside, awaiting his orders. It consisted of the Recon Company, a platoon of five Cascavel armored cars, the Armored Battalion's Infantry Company, and a reserve, a company of the Casador Battalion mounted on trucks.

At his side lying prone was his Recon Company commander, studying the approaches to La Campana through a spotter scope mounted on a low tripod. "I can see no activity in or around the village, Major. If they're there, they are certainly lying low."

"They are there all right, Captain. We know that from our intelligence reports. Besides, if they weren't, there would be traffic coming south out of the town. The question is how strong are they?"

Johnson had seen several estimates from witnesses who had come south through the roadblock within the last week, which indicated the ALIB strength in La Campana was probably a company-size unit. He put little faith in those reports, however, because the sources were mostly civilian employees of the government who knew little of the military. He was sure Portero would certainly have more than a company supporting the road-block…unless the ALIB commander was convinced PNN forces would not move against him until the Second Brigade was back on the mainland. He considered that a possibility…but he was wise enough not to gamble on the accuracy of that assumption.

Better to be safe than sorry, he thought. *I am going to assume he has at least a couple of companies there, and I'm going to do some probing to make sure. Davidson will be impatient with the delay, but that's tough. I'm going to do this right.*

"Captain, I want to make sure we know what we are up against before we move on La Campana. I am concerned about that high ground which extends south from La Campana to the left there, do you see the fence line below the crest there, west of the high-way? An enemy force up there would threaten our left flank if we assault the town along the highway. I want you to find out what is up there. If they're occupying that ground, we'll know soon enough. You may need some firepower, so send a full platoon. If they are not up there, I want you to occupy and hold that high ground until you are relieved by the infantry company. Once relieved, move on toward La Campana until you make contact.

It'll take a couple of hours for your people to get on the hill, so you'd better get them started. Any questions?"

"None, sir."

"When your troops get to the high ground, we will make a feint toward La Campana along the highway. Use another of your platoons, reinforced with a section of Cascavels, for that. That should divert attention from your operations to the west. If the hill is clear, your platoon on the highway will advance into the town. I will follow with my command group and the remaining Cascavels, and the Casador Company and your third platoon, which I will hold in reserve.

"On the other hand, if the hill is occupied, we won't go up the highway. We'll take the high ground and go into the town from there. You and your radio operator stay with me until we see how the situation develops. I hope we can finish all this before dark. Questions?"

"In the event that high ground is occupied, I will need more than my platoon to take it. Can I commit my third platoon there?"

"No. If it is occupied, they will certainly have enough force to defend it, and it is a made-to-order defensive position. We'll need more force than two recon platoons to take that hill. No, if it is occupied, have your people stop and wait. I'll send in the infantry company with some Cascavels to provide heavy duty supporting fire. As soon as they get on the hill, pull your people back to join the reserve platoon. Understood?"

"Yes, sir. Hopefully, with a little luck we won't have to use the Infantry Company".

• • •

Lieutenant Colonel Carlos "Gin Pot" Johnson, sitting in the Tigre Battalion command post which he had established in a tractor shed of a farm just north of La Campana, studied the tactical maps of the area. He knew from telephoned reports received from the brigade Reconnaissance Platoon, which was in concealed position overlooking the highway seven kilometers to the south, that a battalion-size PNN taskforce was approaching La Campana. He knew that it included five Cascavel armored vehicles, which caused him concern.

He suspected, but was not sure, his brother Marcos might be commanding the taskforce, because earlier intelligence reports had established the fact that he had been assigned as the PNN Armored Battalion commander. That possibility also greatly concerned him. He had never been close to Marcos, who was younger and had proclaimed himself an atheist at an early age and had finally succeeded in alienating himself from the Johnson family as a teenager. Still, he was his brother, and he loved him as such, although he did not like him much. Now he had mixed emotions at the prospect of the possibility of facing him in combat. On the one hand, he was pleased by the prospect of a contest between them, which he was confident he would win, but on the other, he disliked the idea of having to raise his hand against a son of his mother.

Gin Pot had deployed his companies in what infantry commanders call a "deliberate defense." Bravo Company was his anchor, deployed in positions along the southern limits of the town with one platoon west of the highway and another to the east. The company's third platoon had been operating the roadblock and would now become the company's reserve force. There had been ample time to dig in and camouflage, and Bravo's positions were virtually undetectable from the south.

The Bravo Company commander had deployed a Tirador Squad on the hill southwest of his position, its mission to protect his right flank.

All three platoons of Alpha Company were dug in on Bravo's left flank, along the high ground on the east bank of the river, where it had an unobstructed field of fire of the highway approaching the town. The Battalion Reconnaissance Platoon, reinforced by two tirador teams from Alpha Company, had taken up blocking positions across the dry riverbed one hundred meters to the southwest of Alfa with the mission of preventing a flanking attack from the south.

Gin Pot had located his Charley Company near his battalion headquarters as his maneuver force. He fully expected to use it. Its commander and platoon leaders had carefully reconnoitered the terrain to the east and to the west of La Campana, and had developed contingency plans for moving in either direction. Johnson's battle tactic was to draw any force sent against him into a close-range ambush, pin it down, and destroy it piecemeal with his maneuver force. He would follow the classic Patton edict often quoted by General Portero, "Hold 'em by their noses and kick 'em in their asses."

• • •

Sergeant Ramiro Sandoval's tirador squad watched the men and vehicles approaching his position on the hill. They came cautiously across the stubble field, spread well out and alert, their assault rifles pointed forward toward the high ground three hundred fifty meters ahead. He counted twelve of them in the lead, but they were followed by four vehicles, each carrying a pedestal-mounted machine gun manned and pointing up the hill. Sandoval could see the gunner in the middle truck studying their position through binoculars. His spotter, Corporal Jose Villalobos, lying prone beside him, studied the approaching men and each of the vehicles through the team's spotter scope.

Sandoval was leader of the first squad of the Tirador Platoon of the Tigre Battalion's Bravo Company. He and Villalobos were sniper Team Alpha. Their firing position, called a "hide," was at the base of an old stock fence which angled around the hill diagonally away from the village of La Campana four hundred meters to their left. The Porrowood fence posts had been set when they were still green and had taken root to form a living fence. Their leafy branches provided perfect concealment for the camouflaged sharpshooters lying behind.

From their hide, they had a clear view to the southeast of the valley below and of the highway into La Campana. At its closest point, the highway was one hundred and sixty meters from their hide. Sniper Team Bravo was in its own hide along the same fence line twenty-five meters on Alpha's left. Team Charley was fifteen meters beyond Bravo in a stand of papaya trees. It had a clear field of fire over the depression paralleling the highway, which was screened from Alpha and Bravo.

"The sixth man from the left looks like an officer. He is carrying a handheld radio," Villalobos reported. "The two vehicles in the middle look like some sort of four-wheel drive pickups with open cabs. They have fifty caliber machine guns mounted on pedestals in the truck bed. The outside vehicles are GEO Trackers with light machine guns. There are three men in each vehicle except in one pickup, which has a fourth man sitting next to the driver."

"He's probably the commander of the operation. It's some sort of reconnaissance patrol, and it looks like they want to come up here."

Sandoval activated a switch which powered the voice-activated microphone attached to the headset of the radio transceiver on his belt. He called his company commander. "Tiger Bravo One, this is Rifle Team Alpha. Over."

"This is Tiger Bravo One. Go ahead, Alpha."

"This is Alpha. We have a PNN recon patrol of about twenty-five men and four vehicles mounting machine guns approaching our position from the south. It looks like they want to be where we are. They are now about four hundred meters south of us. I am going to need more firepower at my position. I am moving Bravo and Charley up here by me. Over."

"This is Tiger Bravo One. Standby Alpha…This is Tiger Bravo One, Alpha okay to reposition Bravo and Charley. I am sending the second squad up to you. Their ETA should be about forty minutes from now. You are free to engage your target when it is in range. Repeat, engage when in range. Over."

"This is Alpha. Roger. Estimate I can engage in twenty or thirty minutes. Out...Bravo and Charley, did you copy my exchange with Tiger Bravo One?"

"Charley copies and we are on our way."

"Bravo copies and we'll be with you in five."

"This is Alpha. Roger. Take your time and stay low. Don't let them spot you moving. We are going to give these *pendejos* a warm reception."

• • •

General Portero arrived at the Tigre Battalion command post just as its commander received the information about the patrol moving toward the Bravo Tirador squad's position. Gin Pot turned to Portero. "These guys are smarter than I gave them credit for, General. I was hoping they would come charging up the hill at us. But they're apparently not going to do that. It looks like they want to secure the hill to the west first. They have what I take to be a platoon from their recon company, dismounted scouts backed up by some heavy weapon vehicles, heading up the hill. Bravo Company has a squad of Tiradores up there now, and he is sending another one up. They should be able to stop this bunch but if the PNN send in a larger force, we can't hold with just two Tirador squads. I have alerted Charley Company to prepare to move out there."

"What about the rest of the taskforce? Have you seen anything of those Cascavels yet?"

"No, sir. We know there are five of them somewhere down the road. We'll see them as soon as they find out we are on that hill, you can bet." Johnson hesitated and looked at Portero. "Did you know my brother, Marcos, may be commanding this taskforce?"

"I thought he might. Banning has confirmed he is commanding their armored battalion. Looks like most of it is coming at us now…so he probably is. How do you feel about facing your brother?"

"I am sorry about it but if that's the way things are, that's the way they have to be. I'll just have to whip him. I always could when we were kids, so why should I stop now?"

"Yea, but it is a tough situation to be in," Portero reflected. "And it gives us a foretaste of what we are facing. Naranjero against Naranjero. Brother against brother. It's a tough thing we have to do."

"Yes it is, Pancho, but we have no choice. We can't let that servant of Satan, Figueroa, take over the country. I have no doubts. What we are doing is right."

"Nor do I, Gin Pot…so give 'em hell. Do you need any more help from me? You have a section of mortars, and I'm sending up a Javelin Team just in case they come on with those armored cars. It should be here within the hour. We don't have a big inventory of the missiles, so don't waste them. Also, DaSilva's battalion is saddled up and on ten-minute alert should we need them. He can close here with his lead company on trucks in one hour after the order to move. Just say the word."

"Will do, General. But I think I'm alright with what I've got. If the situation changes, I'll holler."

• • •

Sergeant Sandoval and Corporal Villalobos watched the enemy recon platoon as it made its careful way toward their position. It was now within two hundred meters of them. Team Bravo had hastily set up its hide along the same fence line twenty meters to their right and lower. Team Charley was preparing its position some fifteen meters beyond and above Bravo in the edge of the thick brush which covered the hill above the road.

Sandoval spoke into his microphone and ordered his team leaders to switch to the frequency used by his squad for intercom purposes. "Teams Bravo and Charley, this is Alpha. Do you read?"

"Bravo reads."

"Charley, loud and clear."

"Okay, here it is. We'll let these bastards get as close as we can. Primary targets are officers and sergeants, and the machine gunners and drivers in the vehicles. Bravo, your first target is the man number six from left of the dismounted people. I believe he is an officer. After he is gone, take all targets of opportunity among the dismounted people. Engage at my shot. Acknowledge."

"Engage on your shot. Target is number six of walkers."

"Correct. Charley, you take the vehicles on the right, gunners and drivers, then targets of opportunity. Engage on my shot. Acknowledge."

"Wilco, engage on your shot, the right two vehicles."

"Okay. Alpha will take the left two vehicles. I intend to wait until they are within one hundred meters. Wait for my shot. The second squad should be closing with us soon. I intend to deploy them along the fence line to my left when they get here. Remember, they're ours, so don't shoot them."

When all teams acknowledged his last transmission, Sandoval settled down to the business at hand with growing excitement. He checked his rifle, a British bolt-action Accuracy International with a fiberglass thumbhole stock. He had great confidence in the weapon which had become as much a part of him as his arms. It was ready. He confirmed the settings on his Leupold Rifle Scope. They were correct. He checked Villalobos. The spotter was already tracking the second vehicle. He watched the officer seated to the drivers right through his scope. They waited.

It was a beautiful, cloudless day, clear and cool. Behind him a bird sang and was answered somewhere to his right. The buzz of bees exploring the few blooms along the fence was loud in his ears. The clean summer smell of a dry hayfield came to him. All seemed peaceful except for the sound of engines of the approaching vehicles, and an occasional shouted comment from the line of men leading them. He waited, reluctant to disturb the peace.

The dismounted men were now close, sixty meters to their direct front. The vehicles were thirty meters behind them. It was time. He moved his weapon slightly until he steadied on the driver, then shifted to the left to center the crosshairs on the officer's chest. He flipped off the safety. "Alpha is ready." He breathed into his mic.

The replies came instantly. "Bravo ready."

"Charley is ready."

"Okay, everybody. On my shot."

He drew in his breath and held it. He squeezed off his shot. He saw the officer lurch to the left against the driver. He worked his bolt, and three-and-a-half seconds later, he was centered on the machine gunner who was swinging his weapon. He fired and the man fell backward. He swung on to the driver who leaped from the vehicle and flattened himself on the ground. The GEO on the left had stopped and began to back up. Its machine gun was firing, spraying the hill without effect. He sighted on the driver, fired and missed. He reloaded and made himself take time. His second shot found its mark. The vehicle swerved to its right and continued backing, the driver slumped forward. Sandoval saw the gunner trying to reach around the driver to the steering wheel.

He took stock of the situation. The other teams were still firing. All the dismounted PNN were on the ground, but he could not tell which were casualties and which were trying to make smaller targets of themselves. The third vehicle was stopped and deserted. The machine gun on the last GEO suddenly ceased firing, and he saw the gunner slump over. All was quiet.

"Good shooting," said Villalobos quietly. "Four shots, three kills."

"Yea. Damn, I missed that driver the first time. I got excited… too much in a hurry, dammit! What are those PNN bastards doing?"

"Nothing that I can see. Most of them are lying low. Not even returning fire."

"Bravo and Charley, concentrate on the vehicles. Put 'em out of action…engines and tires."

The firing resumed a series of deliberate shots. Sandoval could hear the occasional metallic *tink* as a round pierced the body of the vehicle. He and Villalobos were watching the line of men lying on the ground for movement. A head lifted. He swung his rifle, sighted, and fired. "Bingo," said his spotter.

The explosion was close. Twenty meters to their left and just short of the fence line. The concussion jolted them. "What the hell was that?"

"There, down on the highway," Villalobos said quietly.

Sandoval looked. Two Cascavel armored cars had appeared. They were five hundred meters away, but he could see their guns pointed up the hill at them. *Kkurraaasch-harumpf.* The second Cascavel fired as he watched, he saw the muzzle flash, then, the round exploded just behind them, and he could hear the hot metal fragments cutting through the brush on the hill.

Kkurraaasch--kkurraaasch-hurumpf--hurumpf.

Both fired within a split section of each other. The first round exploded just in front of the Alpha team. The second to their left. They were enshrouded in a cloud of dust and smoke. Sandoval's ears rang. He was coughing, trying to catch his breath. He looked at Villalobos. He saw that the spotter scope was mangled and twisted. Then he saw his spotter facedown and lying very still. He knew he was dead. "Aw, Pepe! Aw, Pepe. Aw, mi buen amigito." He lowered his own face into the dirt in shock.

"Alpha…Alpha, this is Bravo…are you okay?" The words came faintly to Sandoval through his headset.

"This is Alpha. I'm okay, but Villalobos is dead. How are you?"

"We're okay and so is Charley. What do you want us to do?

Kkurraaasch-hurumpf. The Cascavels fired five more rounds. All landed well to the left of Sandoval, well away from his squad's position. "Looks like they spotted the second squad coming up… Bravo and Charley, keep an eye on those sonsabitches in front of us; if they move shoot them. Nobody gets away. Understood?"

• • •

The Bravo Company commander heard the tank fire before he saw the Cascavels almost a kilometer south of him. At the same time, his spotters in La Campana reported what appeared to be an infantry company unloading from trucks along the highway well beyond the armored cars. He picked up his radio. "Rifle Team Alpha, this is Tiger Bravo One. Over."

Sergeant Sandoval switched to the company command channel on his radio. "This is Alpha. Over."

"This is Tiger Bravo One…Looks like those tanks are shooting at you. What is your situation? Over."

"This is Alpha. We have one casualty, dead from tank fire. We have that PNN patrol pinned down fifty meters to our front. I believe all four of their vehicles have been knocked out. We are still operational, but it is getting pretty hot up here. Over."

"This is Tiger Bravo One. Has the second squad reached your position?"

"This is Alpha. Negative. I believe those tanks are shooting at them now. We have no contact with them…Hold it. Stand by, Bravo One." Sandoval heard a voice behind him. He turned to see the assistant squad leader of the second Tirador squad, Corporal Mejia, crawling toward him. The man was blood-splattered and breathing hard.

"Are you hurt, Mejia?"

"No, Sergeant. This is Garcia's blood, mostly. He is dead and so is our Bravo Team. Two of our radios were destroyed. The other isn't working. Is that Villalobos? What's wrong with him?"

"He is dead. Hold on while I report…Bravo One, this is Alpha. Second squad just closed with us. They've taken casualties. Three dead. No radios. Two rifle teams still operating. I'll put 'em to work here. Any orders for me?"

"Tiger Bravo One…hold your position…repeat, hold your position. Have the second squad dig in with you. Can you see some activity behind those tanks? Looks like a company-size infantry unit may be coming your way. Can you see them?"

"Stand by." Sandoval lifted his binoculars and looked south beyond the Cascavels. "There, see the bastards," he said to Mejia.

"Bravo One, this is Alpha. I confirm, an infantry company now leaving the highway and forming into assault formation in the field to my south. I can see three more Cascavels with them. If they are after us, we're going need some help. Over."

"Roger, Alpha. Help is on the way. I'll call you back with info ASAP. Meantime, dig in. Tiger Bravo One. Out."

• • •

Help was on the way. Gin Pot Johnson had called in his Charley Company commander, briefed him on the situation, and gave him orders moving his unit into position to attack the left flank of the PNN Company as it approached the ridge the tiradors occupied. Charley was already moving. It was to pass to the west of the ridge, circle back, and engage the approaching enemy from the high ground southwest of Team Alpha's position. It had over three kilometers to cover, so it was moving fast in order to be in position at the appointed time, about one hour hence.

Johnson also ordered the section of 81mm Mortars, which he had originally deployed some twelve hundred meters north of La Campana to support the immediate front of the defense, be moved forward into a new position in the town. The move made it possible for the mortars to engage targets over five thousand meters south of the town.

"If it is Marco out there, I am surprised he hasn't sent those Cascavels up against us by now. He is being uncharacteristically cautious. It makes me wonder if he is running their show. If he did send them up, we would be hard-pressed to stop them until they got into town…then they would be sitting ducks." Johnson spoke idly to General Portero, who had sat quietly by while the battalion commander had developed his plan and delivered his orders.

"He knows that…and I'm sure he doesn't want to risk losing any of his Cascavels. He can get better use out of them by keeping them out of harm's way and employing them in a direct-fire support role as he is doing." As he spoke, they heard a new volley from the armored cars directed at the Tirador's position. "In any case, if he should change his mind, your Javelin Team will be here shortly. How will you deploy them?"

"Initially we'll put them with Bravo Company's first platoon, with their machine gun…bore sighted down the causeway…just in case."

• • •

Major Marco Johnson had entertained the idea of sending his Cascavels up into La Campana. He didn't believe the opposition had the means to stop them on the approach. Small arms fire alone wouldn't do it, but they would become vulnerable once they were into the village, where they could be attacked with satchel charges and grenades. They were too valuable to risk in that way.

From his vehicle parked on a slight rise, he watched the Cascavels one hundred meters in front of him continue their periodic harassing fire on the ridge with their 90mm guns. He could see their commanders standing in the open hatches of their turrets, studying the effect of their rounds through binoculars. But he kept a closer eye on La Campana, trying to discern where the ALIB positions might be. He had seen nothing. No movement. No dust. No reflections, and he wondered if they were really there. He'd look pretty silly if they were not…but he knew they were there. They had to be.

Parked next to him was his Recon Company commander, who was in radio contact with a sergeant squad leader of his platoon pinned down on the approach to the ridge, despite the support of the Cascavels. The man was clearly demoralized and had reported both the platoon commander and platoon sergeant had been killed and all their vehicles out of action. He estimated five others killed and four badly wounded. He insisted they had been unable to move because every time they made an attempt, they received deadly accurate rifle fire from unseen sharpshooters on the higher ground to their immediate front. The sergeant estimated they were facing at least a platoon-size force, and begged for continued gunfire on the ridge.

From his position, Major Johnson was also able to see his infantry company forming into an extended formation in the stubble field to his left rear. The Cascavel Platoon commander had determined the dry ground would support his fourteen-ton vehicles and was prepared to advance on the hill with the infantry. He placed two Cascavels ahead with the leading elements of the dismounted men, and his own vehicle behind with the infantry company commander, with whom he could communicate through a sound-powered telephone mounted on the rear of his vehicle. From that position, he could direct the supporting fire of his three Cascavels.

Johnson signaled the combined arms team to advance and watched as they began to move. He estimated that in forty minutes they would be in a position to relieve what was left of his beleaguered reconnaissance platoon. He turned to his Recon Company commander and ordered him to deploy his third platoon as a defensive screen along his right flank facing the creek bed, and to begin his diversionary advance on La Campana along the highway, with his second platoon supported by the Cascavel section firing on the ridge. The diversion was to coincide with the assault group's attack on the ridge.

Then, he ordered the commander of his reserve unit, the Casador Company, to advance along the highway to a position two hundred fifty meters behind his location on the rocky knoll and await his orders.

"Okay, I am now committed. There is no turning back. Brother Carlos, if it's you up there, here I come."

17 CHAPTER

War planning is an imprecise art. It is based upon a series of assumptions which, in turn, are based upon gathered intelligence which itself is seldom complete and sometimes inaccurate. War planning assumptions focus on the enemy: his intentions, his strengths and capabilities, his experience, the quality of his leadership, and his logistical capability. It also takes into account those same factors as they pertain to the planner's own forces, as well as many other neutral factors which might affect operations, ranging from weather, terrain, availability of roads to the cost of the operations, the degree of popular support, and to the effects of the war on the viability of the state when it ends.

The commander must plan on two levels. War planning is concerned primarily with strategy development, while battle planning is concerned primarily with tactics. Unanticipated changes in the situation, upon which plans at either level are based, must be matched by changes in plans. Plans can never be "set in concrete." The commander must always be flexible, ready to react to situational changes and adjust to them.

A miscalculation, a mistake by a commander on one side or the other, can sometimes dramatically alter the strategic or, more likely the tactical, plan. A competent commander will be constantly on alert for any opportunity his enemy's mistake might offer—as in a game of chess.

As he watched the action at La Campana unfold, General Francisco Portero recognized the possibility that Davidson, the PNN commander, may have made major miscalculations. First, it appeared he had miscalculated the strength of the ALIB forces defending the roadblock and had sent an inadequate force to neutralize it. Second, the force committed clearly represented a significant portion of the total PNN forces known to be on the mainland. If Portero's perceptions were correct, Davidson had made a serious strategic blunder which the ALIB could now exploit.

Portero took time to mentally review the situation. He knew the danger of acting on impulse. The more he examined it, the more certain he became that Davidson had indeed blundered, and in doing so had opened the door for the ALIB to take swift action with minimal risk—actions which could end the war quickly and thereby preempt the buildup of international political pressures against him. General Carmody's advice to him was very much on his mind: "If you must move, bring the situation to a quick conclusion so the diplomats will be faced with a fait accompli, which they cannot ignore."

Portero made his decision.

He called Colonel Ochoa, his chief of staff. After updating him on the situation at La Campana, he declared, "Octavio, I am considering a major change in plans. I believe Davidson has made a serious mistake in not sending a larger force against us here. We have the strength in Gin Pot's reinforced Oso Battalion to defeat this taskforce they have committed against us, and by taking decisive action, we can shorten this damn war. In fact, if we act now, with a little luck, we can win it in a matter of weeks. I want to abandon our Northern Strategy and replace it with a new one, a blitzkrieg operation which isolates La Capital from the rest the country. We have the forces to do it with the addition of Sanchez's Toros. The key is to get it done before Davidson can get his new brigade back on the mainland. We'll be taking some risk, but I believe it is a better option than hoping to win a long, protracted war which, by the way, might bring the HJRAF into it.

"The first step…and this is absolutely essential! We must significantly weaken the PNN force. That means we must totally defeat their taskforce here. We must kill or capture every one of them. Gin Pot will do his part. His battalion will do most of the damage, but I don't want even one PNN to escape to return to Davidson. We have got to prevent the possibility of them withdrawing from this fight with any unit left intact.

"Alert the Lobo Battalion for immediate movement. Have them prepare for an extended combat deployment. DaSilva's mission will be to block all possible retreat routes south of La Campana. No one gets by him…especially those armored cars or any other vehicles. Do you understand, Octavio?"

"Yes, sir. Loud and clear. No one escapes. It looks to me like Tuxla is the place. Tony can take over the Police Post there and set up blocking positions all across the valley."

"Whatever you and DaSilva decide. But get it done…And remember those Cascavels. It would be a plus if we could capture any intact…but he is not to allow any of them to get by him. You'd better give him a section of Javelins, just in case."

"Will do, General."

"How soon do you think he can get started?"

"Well, we have a platoon plus of trucks available now. We can have the Lobo lead company on the road in an hour, I would guess. The follow-up companies can start off on foot, and the trucks can come back and shuttle them on as soon as they drop the lead company. I'll have DaSilva start his Recon Platoon off immediately to make sure there are no ambushes waiting down the road. Anything else, General?"

"That's it for now. It's in your hands, Octavio. I'll keep in touch. Otherwise, how are things going there?"

"Well, sir, you will be pleased to hear that two Black Hawks arrived from HJRAF this morning. They are both equipped with machine gun side mounts. Chris DaSilva is the lead pilot. Captain Hanson is the officer in charge, and he has ten Spanish-speaking green berets with him. They are here strictly as observers. Hanson's orders are to report directly to General Carmody and to keep him informed on everything we are doing. Hanson wants to meet with you as soon as possible."

"Well I'll be damned." Portero was surprised. "Carmody told me he was sending observers but I was not sure he would, considering what is happening here. Send Hanson up here. We'll give him something to observe."

• • •

An excited Portero returned to the Tigre Battalion Command Post. Gin Pot and his staff were tracking the progress of the PNN units being deployed in the stubble field west of the highway. A number of observers were feeding in regular reports over the battalion's tactical radio net. They were also tracking the progress of Tigre Charlie Company, which was moving rapidly through the high ground to the west to a position from which it could stage a flanking attack against the PNN unit.

"This is going to be close," Gin Pot said to no one in particular. "Those Bravo Tirador squads have got to give Charlie Company time to get into position. They have got to hold their position at all costs. Make that clear to Bravo One." The latter order was to his operations sergeant operating the radio.

"Who is leading those squads? Do we know?" Portero asked.

"I believe it is Ramiro Sandoval. A buck sergeant. Been a Tirador a long time. A quiet, soft spoken guy. Fairly young. As I recall, he is one of our best marksmen. Good leader. Dependable."

• • •

Sergeant Sandoval, while continuing to direct the fire of his marksmen against the survivors of the recon platoon they had pinned down below their position, kept a worried eye on the PNN company now fully deployed on the stubble field. He counted ninety-five men. They had deployed with two platoons forward with the third platoon behind, probably being held as their maneuvering force. He put his head against the scarred ground to think. There are too many of them, he thought. What the hell do I do if they come up at us?

He suddenly found his body shaking. The shelling they had taken from the 90mm Cascavel guns had been a surprise. A violence he had never experienced. It was intimidating to the point that he only wanted to be away from it. For a moment while it was going on, he had even thought of ordering a withdrawal.

"What are we going to do, Sergeant?" Corporal Mejia's voice was anxious.

"We are going to hold this goddamn hill, Mejia. That's what we are going to do. And we are going to hold it until help arrives…Or until we are dead." The last was under his breath.

As he spoke, he heard shots from his Charley and Baker teams. He was satisfied his Alpha team were alert and tending to business. He reached for his spotter scope and then remembered it had been destroyed when Villalobos had been killed, so using his binoculars, he studied the PNN troops forming in the distance. He estimated they would have to climb fifteen hundred meters of open field before they would be in optimum range of his shooters.

"Oh shit." The expletive came as he watched three Cascavel armored cars pull off the highway and fall in behind the infantry unit.

"Tiger Bravo One, Tiger Bravo One, this is team Alpha. Over."

"Alpha, this is Bravo One. Over," came the immediate reply.

"We've got a new situation up here, sir. Be advised three of those tanks have joined that PNN unit on the field below us. Two of them are passing through the lead platoons. The third one is back with the third platoon…and now the whole bunch is advancing. They're headed this way."

"Stand by, Alpha."

Sandoval waited, his mind racing. "I hope the captain has some ideas, because I'm fresh out. There are eight of us here and over a hundred of them down there plus those tanks." He spoke quietly to Mejia.

"Team Alpha, this is Bravo One. We are aware of your situation. You are to hold your position and engage that bunch as soon they get in effective range. Slow them down. Help is on the way. Tiger Charlie is moving behind you now and will make a flanking attack from your right front. They expect to be in position in forty minutes. Don't mistake them for the PNN. Charlie has a Javelin team with them to take care of those tanks. Also, Alpha…we will engage that PNN unit with eighty-one millimeter mortars before they can get close to you. Stay on this channel and be prepared to adjust our fire. You can see them better from your position than we can. Don't worry, Alpha…between us, we can stop those bastards, at least until Charlie is ready to jump off. Over."

Sandoval acknowledged. He felt considerably reassured and no longer isolated. He had confidence in his Company commander and knew he would be supported. He relaxed a little and formulated his plan for engaging the approaching PNN. He reviewed it in detail with Mejia, who would have to carry it out should something happen to him.

Finally he keyed his mike and called his rifle teams. "Okay, listen up. You all see our new target down there. It's that infantry company hiding behind those tanks heading up here. They want to get where we are. Will let them come on up. At one hundred fifty meters, we'll engage. At that range, we won't miss. There's only about a hundred of them. Don't let their numbers scare you. We are going to have some help. Bravo One advises they will begin hitting them with mortars in a few minutes. That will slow them down but it also means those tank crews will probably button up, and we won't have a shot at them. If they should get brave and don't button up, make them your primary targets. Otherwise, the infantry officers and noncoms are primary.

"One more thing. Charlie Company is on its way up here. They will make a flanking attack on those bastards from our right. When they do, we'll cease fire and let them handle the situation. It should be an hour or so before they are in position. It is up to us to hold until they arrive. Questions?"

His rifle teams acknowledged the information but had no questions.

"Okay, here is how we will engage. We will set up a crossfire. My teams Baker and Charley on the right of our position will engage their platoon to the left as we see them. Second squad's team Charley, and my team will engage the platoon to the right. That will give us a chance of hitting those guys hiding behind the tanks. They are probably the company command group. As soon as the shit hits the fan, those tanks will begin shooting our way but they don't know exactly where we are, so they won't be zeroed in. Everybody dig in to protect yourself from shell fragments as best you can but don't let them see you doing it, or they'll be shooting us before we can shoot back. Any questions? Report."

Each team leader repeated his orders in turn. Sandoval could hear the tension they were feeling in their voices. When the last one had reported, he keyed his mike once again. "Okay muchachos, we have trained for this moment. I actually feel sorry for those poor bastards down there. We're going to give them a lesson in marksmanship they will never forget. Engage on my shot. Repeat, engage on my shot."

Then they waited in silence, watching the enemy's slow advance toward their position, and listening to the sound of the Cacavel engines, the buzz of grasshoppers, the songs of birds, and the grass rustling in the breeze , and to the beating of their own hearts.

• • •

Captain Dilberto Quiroz at forty-five was a veteran of other battles. As a young lieutenant, he had distinguished himself in a losing cause when the Yankees invaded Granada. Later he had been an advisor to General Noriega when they invaded Panama. He and five other Cubans narrowly escaped capture there by slipping out to sea in a commandeered shrimp boat in the dark of night.

Now he was a volunteer in Naranjeras, commanding the infantry company of the country's new armored battalion. He had served with Colonel Molina on several assignments in the past, and they had developed a mutual respect and friendship. He had been delighted when Molina invited him to his special operations contingent in Naranjeras. At the time, he had been bored with his training assignment in Cuba and jumped at the chance of seeing some action again.

But now he was not sure volunteering for this assignment had been a good decision. He had believed it would be an easy campaign against the local rebels here. Too late, he learned that the rebels were in fact a US-trained, reinforced brigade with considerable experience. His enthusiasm for the assignment was dampened even further upon discovering that that brigade had the support of a significant part of the country's population.

But here now, he was entering battle against that very unit. At the moment, his thoughts about Molina were less than kindly. However, he did respect his battalion commander, Major Johnson and, like any good soldier, was determined to do his duty.

His orders were to occupy the high ground west of the village of La Campana with the support of three Cascavels. He was uneasy because his unit had had only a minimum of training working with the armored cars. He also was unhappy because he was being ordered to take his unit across more than twelve hundred meters of open terrain, where it would be exposed without cover of any sort for an extended period of time. He counted on the assurances from Major Johnson that the ALIB had no artillery, only a few mortars which had a limited supply of ammunition and therefore would be a minimal threat. He had been advised that the ALIB did have excellent snipers, but they should be easily neutralized by the Cascavels.

Quiroz knew the rebels occupied the high ground, which was his objective, and that they had sufficient firepower to pin down the recon platoon which had preceded him. He hoped the information that there was at most only a platoon up there was accurate. If so, he believed he had the force to complete his mission. To be sure, the snipers were of some concern, but the Cascavels could handle them. His confidence was tempered, somewhat, by the fact that his company was untested. It had trained well and had coalesced into a solid unit but most of the men had never been under fire, so it was difficult to predict how they would act if this engagement proved to be more than a skirmish. Oh well, he would soon find out.

He positioned himself with his small command group just ahead of his reserve platoon and beside the Cascavel platoon leader's vehicle. There he and that young officer could communicate over the noise of the engine and of battle by means of the sound-powered telephone mounted on rear of the tank. When he was satisfied all elements were ready, he ordered the advance.

After fifteen minutes, the lead elements of his taskforce had traversed three hundred meters. There had been no resistance, and Quiroz began to breathe easier. His leading platoons were moving together and maintaining their extended formation. It occurred to him that the rebels may have withdrawn in the face of such a force.

They advanced another fifty meters when the crack of an exploding mortar shell reverberated around the valley. It struck just behind the leading elements of his right flank platoon. He saw two of his men go down, struck by shell fragments. The remainder of the platoon hesitated and, seemingly in response to someone's shouted order, they all hit the ground. He reacted swiftly. He keyed his mike and ordered all units to stand up and move forward at a run. His platoons responded reluctantly, but he finally got them moving again.

Then came a barrage of shells raining down and striking in the midst of both leading platoons. Again the men went to the ground, and the advance stalled. The Cascavel crews pulled in their heads and closed their hatches and stopped with their escorting infantry.

Quiroz knew that if he didn't get his units moving forward, they would continue to be vulnerable to the ALIB mortars. He ordered the Cascavel commander to fire at the fence line along the high ground ahead, and at the church tower in the village. He then ordered his infantry units to move forward by squad rushes the moment the tanks began their covering fire.

• • •

"Bravo One, this is Alpha team. You're right on target for their leading platoons. Repeat fire for effect."

"Roger. Repeat fire for effect…Stand by…On the way, Alpha. Three volleys. Over."

Sandoval could hear the distant *tuunk, tuunk, tuunk* of the mortars firing. The mortar shells whispered down and exploded slightly to the rear of the leading platoons which had begun to move forward again. He noticed that now there were gaps in their formation.

"This is Alpha. Right two five, add two five. Repeat fire for effect. I'm shifting to their command group around the third tank."

"Bravo One. On the way. Three volleys. Over."

Sandoval counted nine *tuunks* in rapid succession, and waited. The shells rained down in a pattern which bracketed the Cascavel. He heard the *kraack-kraack-kraack-kraack* of their explosions, and waited for the smoke and dust to clear. Using his binoculars he studied the target and noted that one of the rounds had struck within inches of the tank, and its left front tire was now in shreds. He keyed his mike to report when…*Kkuraasch-kkuraaasch-kkuraaasch-hurrumpf-harrumph.* His position was enveloped in choking dust and smoke.

The rounds from the Cascavel's big guns had struck to the left and to the right of where Sandoval lay. He felt a blow to his right leg. He looked at Mejia and saw he was okay. He was coughing and spitting dust but appeared unhurt. Then he called his fire teams. Baker and Charley reported all okay, but the Second Squad's Charley team did not respond.

Three more rounds hit, but this time well behind their positions. The dust and smoke drifted away, and Sandoval saw the Cascavel on his left was firing at something to his right. He assumed it was some target in the village.

"Alpha Team, Alpha Team, this is Tiger Bravo One . Do you read? Over."

"Bravo One, this is Alpha. Loud and clear. Over."

"This is Bravo One. Are you okay?"

"We're okay. We took a couple of pretty close rounds, but First Squad is okay. I have lost contact with the Second Squad team, so I'm not sure about them…Wait…stand by, One." Sandoval had seen movement below him.

"Bravo One, Alpha Team. The PNN are starting to move again. They are coming in squad rushes up the hill. They're still out of range for my shooters. Crank up those mortars again… Right five zero. Drop two hundred and wait for my command to fire. Over."

"Roger. Right five zero, drop two hundred…Standing by for your command. Over. By the way, the bastards are shooting at the church steeple here."

Sandoval and Mejia watched the enemy advance up the hill. First one squad-sized group, then another. They tried to pick up some sequence, but none was apparent. When their lead elements moved into the area he hoped the mortars were now laid on, he ordered them to fire.

The rounds struck to the left of where he expected. They hit among the right flank platoon. The left flank unit was pretty much out of the impact area.

"Right one hundred…and lay it on them."

"This is Bravo One. Right one hundred…Stand by. Four volleys on the way. Over."

This time twelve high explosive mortar rounds bracketed both platoons in a devastating pattern. They stopped, but within seconds of the end of the barrage, they resumed their advance by squad rushes. Sandoval observed with considerable satisfaction that the attacking units had taken casualties. Fewer of their number were participating in the advance. Their leading elements were approaching the area were the Recon Platoon Survivors were laying. He alerted his rifle teams and ordered them to fire at the rushers as they came in range. Then he sent Corporal Mejia to check Second Squad's Team Charley.

The action had been all-absorbing. He had lost all track of time. He checked his watch and was surprised to see it had been over two hours since he first saw the PNN units assembling on the stubble field below. He tried to relax and as he shifted his position to fire on the advancing enemy, he became aware of the ache in his right leg. He turned to look at it for the first time and noticed his trouser leg was soaked in blood. A few moments later, Mejia crawled back to report that the Second Squad people had lost their radio but were otherwise in position and ready to engage.

"That's good. That gives us a couple of more shooters. Thanks, Mejia. By the way, do me a favor and take a look at my leg."

Mejia twisted around. He saw Sandoval's trouser leg was soaked with coagulated blood. He turned farther to reach it and ripped the material to see a deep wound in the thigh just above the back of the knee. He also saw what looked like a piece of wood or maybe bone protruding from the wound. "My God, Sergeant. You've got a pretty big hole in the back of your leg. I think a bone is broken, too. There is a lot of dirt in it, but it's not bleeding. I'll try to bandage it." He reached for his first aid kit. "Doesn't it hurt?"

At that moment, they heard a large volume of automatic weapons fire emanating from their right. Sandoval raised his binoculars to check the advancing PNN unit. They were on the ground, and some of them were firing at something on their left. As he watched, he saw the tank which had been disabled by the mortar round explode in a ball of fire.

"By God, that is Charley Company finally hitting them. Mejia, we're getting some help!" Sandoval keyed his radio transmitter to call his teams. "Okay, that firing we hear is Charley Company at the PNN. Continue firing at any target you can hit...but be damn sure it is PNN. The first man to see our people, immediately order cease fire, and make yourself heard...and if I hear anyone taking a shot after that, I will personally shoot him. Acknowledge."

Sergeant Sandoval suddenly felt pain in his leg and felt very tired. He handed the radio to Mejia. "Mejia, take over...I don't feel so good." Then he fainted.

• • •

From his observation post on the back crest of the rocky knoll south of La Campana, Major Marco Johnson had a bird's eye view of the action across the highway to the west. He had watched his infantry company, reinforced by the Cascavel platoon, advance across the open ground toward its objective, the high ground to its front, with some satisfaction.

He liked the efficient manner in which Quiroz had deployed his unit and his promptness in moving it forward. He was pleased with the discipline evident in the way the platoon commanders were handling their men. *Not bad for a green unit in its first engagement,* he thought. Good training showed.

Then he heard the *tunk, tunk, tunk* of mortars firing from somewhere in the village. Seconds later the rounds began exploding among his troops. He saw them go to ground for cover. *Come on, Quiros, don't let them stop. Get them moving,* he silently urged. Then he saw them get to their feet and resume their advance as the Cascavels commenced firing at the far ridge. "Good man, that Quiroz," he said aloud to the commander of his recon company, who lay beside him watching the action.

The extent of the mortar barrage surprised and disturbed him. Colonel Davidson had assured him the ALIB had only a limited supply of mortar ammunition, but the intensity of the fire did not indicate any shortage. He estimated forty or fifty rounds had already been fired and the barrage was continuing, landing in patterns which kept a pace with his advancing troops. He could see the unit was taking casualties but the men kept moving forward, which increased his pride in them. He estimated they would be in position to assault the hill within minutes. He began to breathe easier when suddenly a high volume of small arms fire erupted from Quiroz's left flank. The advance faltered and stopped as his force prepared to defend against the new threat. His heart sank. They had been taking fire from their front and now from their flank.

Then he saw a rocket arch out of the scrub tree line beyond the beleaguered company and strike the center Cascavel. The vehicle exploded in flames. Moments later, another rocket struck a second Cascavel—no flames this time, but he could see its turret was now askew and obviously out of action.

Johnson acted to save his unit. He ordered his recon company to move his two uncommitted platoons, which were then screening the east and south side of the rocky knoll against possible enemy attack, to a location where they could support his trapped infantry by machine gun fire. At the same time, he ordered his two uncommitted Cacavels into action in support of the Recon Company units now moving. By radio he informed Quiroz of the actions being taken to support him.

For the first time since the battle began, it occurred to Johnson that he might not succeed in his mission at La Campana. Clearly the rebels had a larger force defending than his intelligence reports had estimated. *Had Davidson sent a boy to do a man's job?* he wondered. In any case, it was clear he would need reinforcements if he was to turn the situation around.

By radio he ordered his reserve, the Casador Company waiting on trucks two kilometers behind him, to advance at speed and to dismount and assemble under the cover of the south side of the rocky knoll, his location. They were to be prepared for immediate action.

Marco Johnson was a stubborn man. "This is one fight I'm not losing to you, my brother. Carlos, if that is you over there, I have a surprise for you."

• • •

At that moment, Carlos "Gin Pot" Johnson was not thinking about his brother. He was in his tractor shed command post, absorbed in tracking the developing actions of his now fully committed battalion. The place was crackling with activity. His executive officer was busy communicating with his company commanders by radio and cell phone, and an operations sergeant was struggling to depict the changing situation on a makeshift hand-drawn battle map. He felt that the situation was well in hand, although he had been surprised at the discipline, competence, and the courage displayed by the PNN units attacking his positions. They did not act like green troops. Obviosly they were led by competent men who knew their business.

He had been particularly concerned by the threat posed by the Cascavels with their powerful ninety millimeter guns, which had caused casualties among his Bravo Company's Tirador Teams on the hill defending his right flank. Now they had hit the steeple of the village church several times, apparrently believing he had observers up there. The big guns on the tanks were psychologically intimidating, and he knew his units had never faced anything like them and wondered how they might react. However, he breathed easier when Charley Company managed to destroy two of them with just two javelins, the first two ever fired in anger by an ALIB unit. It proved the Cascavels were vulnerable.

Gin Pot was trying to anticipate the PNN commander's next move. "By now he knows we have a stronger force arrayed against him than he expected. He must be wondering if he has the force to win this fight…so what is he thinking? What would I do in his place? I guess I would consider breaking off and pulling back to save as much of my force as I could. On the other hand, he still has not committed his reserve company waiting down the road, and he might believe he still has enough force to tip the battle his way. It is difficult to know what he will do…If it really is Marco out there, he is stubborn, and my guess is he will continue the fight."

He remembered the many boyhood scraps he had had with his younger brother. Marco had always been aggressive, even when he was losing. He was dogged and determined and often when it appeared he was beaten he became desperate, lost his focus, and made bad decisions, but he would never give up. *If it is you, little brother…be smart and pull back…because you are about to lose again.*

Gin Pot had reports from his recon platoon of activity on and around the rocky knoll south of La Campana. The speculation was that it was the PNN command post. It was the right place for it. From there one could see the entire battlefield, the village and all approaches to it, and it was out of mortar range. It also seemed to be a logical location from which the reserve unit could be deployed. From there it might be committed to the west in support of the attacking units. He concluded the PNN commander, whoever he was, would elect to commit his reserve in a counterattack to the west, probably in an effort to outflank Charley Company, now engaged there.

He studied the situation and made his decision. He ordered his Alpha Company to advance from its defensive position and move down the riverbed and seize and hold the high rocky knoll. Alpha One responded with considerable enthusiasm. *At last his unit could get into the fight.* "We're on our way, Jefe. My third and first platoons are moving now. We should be on that hill within the hour."

CHAPTER 18

The fight at Rocky Knoll was the last action of the battle of La Campana. It was mid-afternoon when Alpha Company left its defensive positions to advance on the knoll. Its third platoon led, moving carefully along the dry riverbed in a column of twos, taking advantage of the sparse cover the shallow willow-lined banks afforded.

Gin Pot Johnson walked beside his company commander immediately behind the point squad. A six-man Tirador squad accompanied them. The sounds of the battle taking place west of the highway to their right disturbed the afternoon. The incessant crackle of small arms fire occasionally interrupted by the boom of a Cascavel big gun, followed a split second later by the crack of the exploding shell, reverberated around the valley.

Although he appeared calm to his companions, inwardly Gin Pot was in turmoil, tormented by the thought that it could be his brother out there leading the forces against him. He prayed it would be someone else. The idea of fighting his own brother, although they had long been estranged, was abhorrent to him. It brought home the special cruelty of civil wars which pitted brother against brother. "God, forgive us," he prayed. "And if it is Marco, let him come through safely."

The squad ahead suddenly halted its advance, the men sinking to their knees against the river bank. Immediately word was passed for the company commander. Gin Pot went forward with him. They found the platoon leader and squad leader, with their point man, crouched down behind a willow clump, looking up at the knoll through binoculars.

"What do you see, Lieutenant?"

"On the knoll, sir. One recon vehicle mounting a fifty caliber machine gun. We can see three men up there…All looking west…Watching the fight over there, I guess. There may be more over the crest, though."

Gin Pot studied the hill. "Damn fools," he muttered. "They're supposed to be watching this flank. Get your Tiradores up here and prepare to mount a two platoon assault on that hill. Move as soon as those incompetent idiots have been knocked out."

It went without a hitch. The Tirador squad leader picked three shooters and designated a target for each. "Say when you're ready. Fire on my command."

"One is ready."

"Three's on."

"Two is on."

"Fire on my three count…One…Two…Three."

The three PNN recon men never knew what hit them. They were downed by three simultaneous shots. The shots were the signal for the assault. Alpha's two platoons raced up the hill in extended formation. There was no resistance. At the top they deployed around the crest and prepared to defend against a counter-attack from the south and west.

Gin Pot, panting mildly from the exertion of the climb, was right behind. He arrived in time to see six trucks on the highway approaching from the south. They stopped in a defiladed area about sixty meters below his position. PNN soldiers dismounted as each vehicle arrived and immediately deployed to positions along the highway facing to the west.

Then he saw him. Marco was below among the dismounting troops, directing their deployment. It was clear he was unaware

Alpha Company had taken the knoll behind him. Not leaving a greater force up there had been a fatal mistake.

The Alpha Company commander, without hesitation, ordered his units to attack the troops below with aimed rifle fire. The attack was a surprise and the men below were unprepared and vulnerable. Gin Pot saw a number of PNN fall, among them his brother. One moment Marco was standing erect, gesticulating and shouting orders, the next he was facedown on the highway. He studied his brother's prostrate body through his binoculars, hoping to see some movement, but there was only a spreading red stain on the ground where he lay. He put his head down and closed his eyes and remained in that position for a time, wrestling with his emotions.

The PNN troops tried to rally. The ones still mounted leaped from their trucks and sought cover behind them as the devastating fire poured down from the knoll. Some of the bolder ones tried to return fire but it was disorganized, sporadic, and ineffective, and after a few desultory rounds, they stopped trying to resist. Their position was untenable. They were exposed and in shock from the unexpected onslaught. Survival became paramount, and all they could do was hunker down behind their trucks or whatever cover was at hand.

Gin Pot, recovering control of himself, realized the PNN were no longer returning fire. He ordered his Alpha troops to cease firing. When the last shots had sounded and all become quiet, he arose, stood erect, fully exposed to the men below. In a booming voice, he shouted down to them, "PNN soldiers, I have ordered my troops to hold their fire. You are surrounded and cannot escape…I now offer you a chance to surrender…and thereby save your lives."

Nothing happened. There was no movement below, nor reply. He continued. "Why are you fighting us? Are you fighting for Figueroa? Why? The man has seized control of our country illegally. He was not elected by the people. Why are you defending him? Are you doing it for the money he pays you? Maybe you are if you're Cubano or Nicaraguense, but what about you

Naranjeros? Can you not see he has turned Naranjero against Naranjero? Brother against brother?"

He pointed down at them. "That is my own brother lying there with you. Why did he have to die? I'll tell you why… He died because he was offered a position of power…Because Figueroa craves power and wants to grow rich and could only do that by shooting his way into power. It is he who has turned Naranjero against Naranjero. He doesn't care how many of you have to die as long as he gets what he wants. Think about it. Do you think he cares about you? Does he even know who you are?"

He waited and, after a moment, resumed. "We care about you. We have nothing against you except that you are fighting for a tyrant. We don't want to kill you…But we will if you force us to. Surrender and we will protect you…But we will kill you if you do not. You must know I mean what I say. If I have just killed my own brother, why would I spare you? Surrender now, or I will give the order to resume firing, and I will not stop until every one of you is as dead as my brother. Now those of you who wish to live do as I now order. First, throw your weapons on the ground well in front of you…Then stand up and lock your hands behind your head and face away from me. I want to see only your backs. We will not shoot you, I give you my word."

He waited. After a long moment, which to him seemed an eternity, he saw movement. AK-47s and other weapons were being tossed forward. First a few. Then more and more. Then the men began to stand hands behind their heads, two or three at first. Then it became general. Gin Pot gave a long sigh of relief.

The battle was over. He gave the order to secure the prisoners and collect the weapons. Then he made his way down the slope to be with Marco.

• • •

General Portero had made a special effort to keep out of his battalion commander's way during the La Campana battle. He was well-pleased with the way Gin Pot had managed the action. Captain Jaime Hanson, General Carmody's aide, had arrived with the young captain commanding the special forces observer group, and the three of them had remained at the Tigre Battalion Command Post to monitor the action. Portero was exhilarated when the PNN resistance finally collapsed, and he showed it. He was now more than ever convinced the PNN High Command had miscalculated and, in doing so, had given him a great gift, the gift of opportunity. The decisive ALIB victory could dramatically alter the strategic situation and he was sure there was now an opportunity to end the war, perhaps in only weeks, instead of the long, expensive conflict contemplated in his carefully planned Northern Strategy.

Portero turned to Captain Hanson. "Jimmy, you can tell your boss I am taking his advice and am going to win this war quickly. I believe Figueroa and Davidson have made a fatal mistake. They sent too small a force against us, a force which has now ceased to exist. In doing that, they have weakened themselves to the point we have both the strategic and tactical advantage over their forces remaining on the mainland. We now can take them on and defeat them piecemeal. The key to victory is to keep them from bringing their brigade on Isla Grande to the mainland. If we can do that, we've won. But to do that we have to move fast…we have to take control of the landing point at La Boca, and we have to do that in the next couple of days. We're in a hurry. I will need your helicopters to ferry troops down there…only for a couple of days. And Jimmy, this is not a request."

"Well, General, I have my orders and I can't recall anything in them that would compel me to resist your…ah…non-request."

"Thank you," Portero said, smiling.

• • •

As anxious as he was to return to the base at Valle Escondido, Portero's first priority was to talk to Gin Pot Johnson. He, with Captain Hanson and the special forces officer, caught up with him on the high ground near the Bravo Company Tirador hide. The Charley Company commander had established a temporary CP there, from which he could supervise the cleanup of the battle field. A number of PNN prisoners under guard had been put to work carrying the wounded to a makeshift aid station in which both ALIB and PNN medics were attending to the wounded.

Portero found Gin Pot kneeling by a stretcher on which Sergeant Ramiro Sandoval lay. Sandoval saw the general approach and saluted him from the stretcher. Johnson turned and greeted his commander.

"General, this is Sergeant Sandoval, the NCO in charge of the Bravo Sharp Shooter Teams. They are the ones that held this hill five long hours for us against a vastly stronger force."

Portero knelt by Sandoval. He took the sergeant's hand. "It's an honor to know you, Sergeant. How are you doing?"

"I'm doing fine, thank you, sir. In fact, I feel pretty damn good. The medic gave me a shot of morphine a little while ago and it is kicking in. I'm feeling great. General, you ought to try it."

Portero laughed. "Maybe later. Right now we've got to get you to the medical facility where they can fix your leg. But first I want to thank you and your men for the gallant action you have just fought. We've just won a major victory, and you played a key role in it. Your courage and initiative have earned you special recognition. I will recommend you for promotion to Senior Sergeant as soon as I can talk to Colonel Johnson."

"The talk is over. Recommendation accepted and approved," Gin Pot said with a delighted grin. "Congratulations, Sergeant, and thank you for what you accomplished here today for our country."

"Thank you, sir...General...I didn't expect anything like this. Especially since I lost some good men up here. I'm not sure I deserve it."

"That was not your fault, son. You couldn't have prevented that. Those men are heroes, too. We are all proud of them...and we'll miss them...and we'll remember them...and we'll honor them always. War is a nasty business, as we all found out today. A lot of good people laid it on the line and some made the big sacrifice for our country. You laid it on the line, and your country will remember your leadership and courage. We can't win it without men like you and your tiradores up here. Now we have to be sure we win the rest of this war quickly and, Lord willing, without more such sacrifices."

"Well…thank you, General. And don't worry. We're going to win it for you." Sandoval reached again to shake his commander's hand. Then he smiled at them. "Where is that damn medic? I need another shot of that stuff!"

They all laughed. They watched as Sandoval's stretcher was loaded onto a pickup truck doing duty as an ambulance, and waved good-bye as it headed down the hill. Then Portero took Gin Pot aside. "Is it true about your brother?"

"Yes. I saw him go down. He was doing his duty, at least. That's something to remember…But I never expected anything like this would happen."

They talked quietly together. Portero felt an overwhelming sympathy for his grieving friend. He wanted to comfort him but was not sure how. Finally he said, "Well, Carlos, we have learned something about war. It is more than a military exercise. People get hurt. People you love get killed. We don't expect that. But why don't we? We should if we remember history. Why is it such a surprise when it happens to us? I guess if it wasn't, we would choose another profession."

"I don't know, Pancho. I think we'd go on doing what we are doing. We do it because we want to protect good people…God's people…from their enemies, those who would harm them, exploit them, enslave them. There is evil in the world, and I believe our job is to fight it. We are on the right side, and that is why we will win. That's why we won here today. That's why we have the Sandovals. Having men like him is why we are going to win this war. Figueroa hasn't got a chance as long as we oppose him for the right reasons."

• • •

The ATB and the battalion commanders met early the next morning in Valle Escondido. Captain Hanson and the Special Forces officer were also present, as was Lieutenant Hank Ruedas, commander of the brigade Reconnaissance Platoon.

They critiqued the action at La Campana. It had been a very successful operation and the Tigre Battalion had achieved a total victory. Its casualties had been low; eight killed and four-teen wounded. The PNN, on the other hand, had suffered heavy losses; thirty-six killed, sixty-four wounded, and the ALIB had taken one hundred and ninety demoralized PNN prisoners.

In addition, the Tigres had destroyed two Cascavels and cap-tured two more intact and a third which, though damaged, was probably reparable. They also captured a number of operable Recon vehicles. However, the greatest prize of all was the six trucks believed to be functional despite a number of bullet holes in some, captured at Rocky Knoll.

General Portero was elated by the victory, which he credited to Gin Pot's leadership, and the magnificent performance of the Tigre Battalion. "Gentlemen, we have handed the Figueroa forces a serious defeat. A defeat which has swung the balance of power, at least on the mainland, heavily to us. It will take them some time, weeks at best, to recover."

He paused, looking at each of them. "But, gentlemen, we're not going to allow them any time at all. As of today, the Northern Strategy is scrapped. As of today, we have a new strategy. Call it 'Operation End Game.'

"My commander's concept is as follows: I see it as a three-phase operation. Phase One, prevent the PNN from moving their new brigade from Isla Grande to the mainland. Phase Two, seize and hold the key pieces of geography Figueroa depends on for re-supply and outside assistance, namely Puerto Hondo and the International Airport. Phase Three of End Game, having isolated the government, we take control of La Capital and, with luck, arrest Figueroa and his thugs…and thus end the war.

"Now as to Phase One, it is absolutely crucial. We start today. Davidson will be moving fast to bring his brigade across. We must move faster. Start organizing now. Captain Hanson has agreed to lend us his two choppers to reinforce Hank's observers in La Boca. Hank, get the rest of your unit down there by noon today. Your job is to scout the town and keep an eye on the ferry landings and, if necessary, block any PNN effort to bring more troops across. Do it whatever the cost. You'll have help there as soon as we can get it there. At least one infantry company.

"Colonel Ochoa, prepare to airlift a company, reinforced with mortars, down there today. Use the Tigres because I want Gin Pot to command the containment operation at La Boca. What do you think, Gin Pot?"

"Take Bravo…they're ready with a full basic load of ammo, if you can pick them up in La Campana, it'll be faster. With only two Black Hawks, it will take all day and part of the night getting Bravo down there, but they are fresh and ready to go. I'll move a platoon from Alfa to the roadblock while Bravo is moving."

Plans were to move the remainder of the Tigres by truck and the four captured Suburbans directly from La Campana to La Boca the following day.

"Okay, gentlemen, Phase Two of Operation End Game. If we stop Davidson from moving the Isla Grande troops, he cannot muster a force large enough to stop us from occupying the airport and Puerto Hondo. We then cut him off from re-supply and reinforcement from outside the country. We also, and this is important, keep him and his supporters from leaving.

"Which brings us to Phase Three of End Game. Once he is isolated in the La Capital area, we can concentrate our force and move in there, and hopefully capture him and his government, which will end the war.

"I believe we have one week, no more, to get this done. Your job now, gentlemen, is to develop a plan to achieve these objectives. I want it ready by thirteen hundred today, approved and modified if necessary, and in the hands of the battalion commanders by fifteen hundred. Meantime, alert all battalions to prepare for extended combat operations, and be ready to move by zero five hundred tomorrow. Are there any questions?"

There were no questions, and Portero noted that his staff was smiling to a man. "Good, I am going to call General Carmody. Then I am going to get some breakfast. Call me when your plans are complete. Good day, gentlemen."

• • •

"What in the living hell happened, Davidson? I thought you were to reduce that goddamn roadblock. Instead, you tell me you have lost our goddamn armored battalion. What happened? And what do we do now?"

"I'm not sure what happened, Mr. President. We had the force to do the job. But I believe Major Johnson made some mistakes. He was too timid and fed his troops into the action piecemeal. He screwed up. We had the forces to win that action. I would try him by courts-martial if he hadn't been killed."

"How goddamn convenient for him. But what do we do now, goddammit?"

"We can still pull it out. We bring the Second Brigade back from Isla Grande. I have alerted Molina, and he will start moving them across starting the day after tomorrow. We have a little time. The ALIB will be recovering from the beating it took at La Campana. Portero won't be able to move very fast. Don't worry, Mr. President."

"Don't worry? You've told me that before…And as it turned out, I had reason to worry. So I'm damn well going to worry now. But Davidson, you'd better be right this time, or we are all in big trouble."

Davidson hid his anger. *If the SOB had listened to me and allowed me to bring the Isla Grande brigade across before he kicked off his war, we wouldn't be in this position.* Although he was seething inside, he said as calmly as he could, "If we can get Molina's Brigade across before Portero can stop us, we'll be okay. If we cannot, you are correct, Mr. President, we will be in big trouble. I can only assure you I will do my best not to lose this war. So let me do my job. Don't interfere, for a change."

CHAPTER 19

The ALIB battalions began carrying out their redeployment orders before dawn the next morning. The Alpha, Charlie, and Headquarters Companies of the Tigre Battalion departed La Campana by road at first light to join its Bravo Company, which had been airlifted to La Boca the day before. Gin Pot Johnson, his staff, and two of the US Special forces observers arrived ahead of the battalion by helicopter. His orders were to occupy and control the ferry landing facilities and prevent the repatriation of the PNN brigade from Isla Grande. He was prepared to take the port by force as intelligence information presented at the ATB briefing estimated the ferry docks were being secured by a company sized PNN unit.

The Oso Battalion, commanded by Major Mix, followed the Tigres to La Boca, moving directly from La Campana by civilian buses chartered in La Mesona and the operable, captured PNN trucks. The two battalions would then combine as Taskforce La Boca under the command of LTC Johnson.

The Lobo Battalion, which had in its blocking position at Tuxla captured several PNN vehicles and a number of stragglers retreating from the La Campana battle, moved toward Puerto Hondo with one company loaded on the vehicles and two operable captured Cascavels. The other Lobo units had moved out on foot earlier. LTC DaSilva's orders were to capture and control the port and prevent re-supply of the PNN forces. He was to allow all normal civilian commerce destined for the north to pass, but to bar all commerce, civilian or military, to or from La Capital, the international airport, or Puerto Hondo.

His captured Cascavels were driven by PNN soldier drivers who had indicated willingness to serve with the ALIB. They and their gunners had been disarmed and operated under the orders, and watchful eyes, of a senior sergeant and four soldiers detached from the Lobo weapons platoon, who had been charged with the task of learning to operate the vehicles and their weaponry.

The newly activated Toro Battalion, commanded by LTC Emilio Sanchez, had orders to capture and control the International Airport, situated eight kilometers north of La Capital. He was to suspend all flight operations in or out of the country. The battalion had been reinforced with a section of mortars and three teams of shoulder-fired Stinger anti-aircraft missiles. The battalion was quietly shuttled in relays to an assembly area in the wooded hills four kilometers north of the airport.

• • •

Portero established his command center in the ATB room at ALIB Headquarters in Valle Escondido. From there he and the staff could monitor the actions of his various battalions by radio and cell phone.

Securing the ALIB base was a major concern. Because all the line units had been deployed away from the base, a provisional security force had to be organized. The brigade headquarters Company commander was given command of it. The force was formed with personnel from the Combat Support Company who had not been deployed, members of the brigade band, off-duty cooks and clerks from the headquarters, and a contingent from the post engineers. It ran patrols outside the base perimeter led by NCOs with line unit experience at staggered intervals and maintained a platoon-sized mobile standby force reinforced by a single Javelin Team to address any incursions. It was unlikely the PNN had the forces to attack his base but Portero opted to play it safe.

• • •

In the afternoon of the battalion deployments, Portero, accompanied by Colonel Ochoa and Major Lacerica, met secretly with Ramon Sanchez Avila of *Vida Nacional*, and the editor of *La Prensa*. The newspapermen were given a detailed briefing on the action at La Campana and handed an advance copy of a press release embargoed until noon of the following day, which read:

> General Francisco Portero, Commanding General of the Autonomous Light Infantry Brigade, reported today that an ALIB unit was attacked by a battalion-seized PNN force near the village of La Campana. In the ensuing ten-hour battle, the PNN force was defeated by the veteran ALIB Tigre Battalion, commanded by LTC Carlos Johnson. ALIB casualties were light, but the PNN suffered heavy losses in killed and wounded. In addition the Tigres took several hundred PNN prisoners, and captured five PNN armored cars, a number of trucks, weapons, and other equipment. Portero declared the attack against ALIB unit at La Campana could only be understood as a declaration of war by the Figueroa government against the brigade, and that it signaled the end to any possibility of a negotiated settlement of our differences. We now have no alternative but to resist militarily. We will act in the name of the people of Naranjeras and actively oppose the dictaotor's government attempts to further subvert our constitution and destroy our democracy. Viva Naranjeras Libre.

The newspapermen were also briefed on the on the plans for the next phase of ALIB operations. Both men expressed some anxiety as to how the contemplated actions might affect civilian populations in the areas involved. Portero emphasized that it was his intention to strike in a manner which would allow little chance for resistance by the government forces, and if he was successful in that, there would be no bloodshed, and no collateral damage to civilians.

"What will you do with Figueroa, Davidson, and other junta members if you capture them?" asked Sanchez Avila.

"It is not a question of if, Don Ramon. We will capture them. When we do, I intend to try Figueroa and Davidson by military courts-martial. Both of them still hold commissions as PNN officers and therefore are still under military jurisdiction. They will be tried for treason, leading an insurrection, murder of Colonel Soto, six ALIB soldiers, and my wife, and whatever other charges may be appropriate. As for the other junta members, any who are indictable for crimes will be tried in the civilian courts.

"Let me add for the record, my objective is not personal revenge. My objective is to take whatever steps are necessary to re-establish constitutional law in Naranjeras. The people must once again have confidence in the power of law."

"You realize, General, that once you have defeated Figueroa, you will be expected to govern the country. Are you prepared to do that?"

"I am aware that will be expected. I am also aware that politics is not my strong suit. I will need help from you gentlemen and others who have experience and expertise in governance and public administration. Again, for the record, let me repeat, I do not intend to involve myself in government any longer than it takes to elect a new, constitutional administration to govern our country."

With abrazos all around, they wished him Godspeed and departed.

• • •

At dawn the Lobo and Toro battalions moved out of their jump-off positions to undertake the unique missions assigned to each.

The Toro Battalion quietly occupied the International Airport without resistance. It followed the plan which had been carefully developed by its battalion commander, LTC Emilio Sanchez, and his staff, which was carried off without a hitch. The PNN Airport Security detachment was taken completely by surprise.

Colonel Sanchez had entered the facility with the men of his recon platoon the previous evening dressed in civilian clothing. They arrived in small groups of two or three, as would airline passengers. Their weapons and uniforms were concealed in suitcases and duffle bags. Once inside the complex, they assembled at an appointed hour near the headquarters of the airport's PNN security detachment and quickly occupied that building. From there Sanchez and one squad quietly entered the quarters of the PNN commander and surprised him at dinner with his family. Sanchez announced to the bewildered officer that he was assuming control of the airport complex by order of General Francisco Portero, Commanding General of the Autonomous Light Infantry Brigade, and escorted the man and his family to the PNN Headquarters, where they were placed under guard.

Once the police headquarters had been secured and its men disarmed and locked in their own holding cages, Sanchez, accompanied by the now-compliant PNN officer and a small detail of recon men, proceeded to the airport superintendent's quarters and briefed him on what was to happen. Sanchez ordered the field closed and all flight operations be suspended as of midnight. The superintendent agreed to cooperate without questioning. The man seemed a bit too eager to cooperate. Sanchez did not trust him and guessed correctly he was a political appointee, a Figueroa loyalist, who would seek a way to inform the government of the seizure. Taking no chances, he ordered the man and his family be searched for cell phones and be sent to join the others in the PNN lockup. He then sent a staff member to the control tower to close down flight operations.

When he was satisfied the situation was under control, Sanchez used his cell phone to notify his executive officer who was waiting with the Toros in the nearby hills ready to execute the occupation of the airport complex. The battalion moved onto the airport during the early morning hours and quietly deployed its companies into their pre-assigned positions, where they greeted the early morning shift of airport employees as they arrived for work.

Shortly after 0800, Sanchez sent a message to Portero via the ALIB communications center. "International Airport secured, compliments of the Toros. Complete surprise. No resistance. No casualties."

One hour later he sent a second message. "I have in custody thirty-six airline passengers who were in the airport hotel awaiting a Lan Chile flight scheduled to depart this a.m. I am delighted to inform you that among them are the following persons of interest: Marco Menendez, Minister of Interior, Mario Fox, President of the Assemblea Nacional, and one Hortencia Malapropino, editor of *El Diario,* with one of her assistants. We also have in custody three individuals who were members of the TV crew accompanying our friend, la Senora Molly Moran. They have informed us the lady returned to the USA two days ago."

Portero immediately responded, congratulating Sanchez on his "brilliant operation" and instructed him to hold Menendez, Fox, and Malapropino for investigation of possible criminal activities. He also ordered that the US TV crew be restricted to their hotel, pending completion of an inspection of their equipment and a determination as to whether or not they have the proper custom clearance to leave Naranjeras.

• • •

While the Toros were occupying the airport complex, the Lobo Battalion was entering Puerto Hondo in three columns. The Cascavels and the captured PNN vehicles, loaded with DaSilva's soldiers, boldly entered from the highway and were waved through the police checkpoint entrance by the PNN agents on duty, who assumed it was a PNN column. They realized their mistake when they were unceremoniously disarmed and taken prisoner so quickly they had no chance to sound an alarm.

The column moved into the port area and stopped in front of the PNN security force barracks just as its men were turning out for morning calisthenics. Again the surprise was complete, and there was no resistance. The PNN were made prisoners and the facility was occupied by the ALIB personnel to become the Lobo Battalion Command post.

The two dismounted companies entered the port by secondary roads north of the highway. The lead company had orders to seize the dock area and any ships moored there. The second company, reinforced by a Javelin Section, established a defensive perimeter around the port city to block the highway and secondary roads. The battalion recon platoon had already deployed two kilometers west of Puerto Hondo on the highway to provide warning of a possible PNN counterstrike and to intercept and hold civilian traffic approaching the port area.

The occupation proceeded without incident until the lead company entered the dock area. The three man point of its leading platoon rounded a warehouse on a quay, where a vessel unloading cargo was moored. They were startled to see a sandbagged machine gun emplacement one hundred meters ahead manned by PNN. They halted to study the situation. It became clear the PNN had established a security cordon on the dock around the vessel. They stood there for a minute or two before a not-so-alert PNN soldier noticed their presence, yelled something, and pointed their way. His companions scrambled behind the sandbags and manned their gun. Finally someone shouted at them, demanding they identify themselves. The Lobo trio quickly retreated around the warehouse corner just as the PNN fired a couple of shots in their direction.

Their platoon leader, hearing the shots, ordered his men to halt and sprinted forward together with his squad leader. The corporal leading the point hastily described the situation as best he could, given the time he had to assess it. "All I know, Lieutenant, is we turned the corner and there is a ship tied up about a hundred meters down the dock. There were a bunch of PNN behind sandbags who yelled at us and began shooting, so we ducked back here. It looks like they are protecting that ship."

"What about the ship? What was it, a freighter?"

"No, sir, it was smaller. It looked like a big fishing boat or something."

"What is a fishing boat doing at a freight dock?"

"Beats me, Lieutenant."

The platoon leader pointed to the warehouse across the street from where they stood. "Sergeant, take your squad over there and set up a fire base behind those containers. Those jokers will probably send some people to see who we are. If they come around the corner, take them prisoner, or if they resist, shoot them. I am going to take the rest of the platoon around the backside of that warehouse and work our way around so we can back you from your left. I've got to find a place where I can get a clear view of that ship down the dock."

While the lieutenant jogged back to his platoon, he used his tactical radio to advise his company commander of the situation. The company commander came forward with his radio operator and joined the platoon while it circled the warehouse, using parked fork lifts and palletized freight as cover. When they reached a point along the quay side of the warehouse where they had a field of fire covering the vessel and the PNN manning the sandbag barriers, they took up defensive positions.

"That looks like a big purse seiner. Probably a tuna boat," the company commander said to those nearby. "What is it doing over here at the freight docks?'

He ordered his two uncommitted platoons to cordon off the warehouse by the dock where the ship was moored, "Detain anyone who tries to enter or leave the area but do not, repeat do not, engage those PNN unless they shoot first."

Then he called LTC DaSilva, his battalion commander, to advise him of the situation and request a Cascavel be sent forward to him. "That PNN force is small, no more than a platoon. They obviously are providing security for that vessel. Whatever it is discharging must be important stuff. So far I haven't seen anything happen there. But, Colonel, what is a tuna boat doing over here?"

"Who knows? But maybe it is not unloading cargo. Maybe it is loading something. We've got to prevent that boat from leaving. I'll send up two Cascavels and our Javelin team. If it tries to leave, we can sink it."

The two armored cars arrived twenty minutes later. The company commander briefed the sergeant in charge of the situation. When all was ready, the big vehicles and the point platoon turned the warehouse corner and advanced together down the quay toward the PNN position. All dockside activities ceased as they came in sight. No shots were fired by either side. When he was close enough to be clearly heard, the platoon commander shouted an order to the PNN officer in charge to come forward.

After a short delay, a PNN sergeant appeared at the sandbag parapet and demanded to know who they were and by what authority they were interfering with official government business.

"We are a unit of the Naranjeras Autonomous Light Infantry Brigade, and we have occupied Puerto Hondo. We are acting under the authority of General Francisco Portero, who at this moment is arresting President Figueroa and his cabinet. You are now under our orders, and I order you to surrender your unit to me. You are surrounded and cannot escape. Have your men throw their weapons out in front of the sandbags and stand facing away from us with their hands locked behind their heads. You have five minutes to comply. If you do not, I will order my men to fire on you, and we will kill you all."

It did not take five minutes. Almost before the lieutenant stopped speaking, the PNN were throwing out their weapons and standing with their hands in the air. They were taken into custody and marched away to join the rest of their unit in their barrack building, now serving as a prisoner stockade.

Another Lobo platoon boarded the vessel and took its crew into custody. They discovered that the vessel was the Guajira Moreno of Cuban registry. It was soon apparent its crew were not fishermen. They claimed they were members of the Cuban merchant marine, but suspicion soon arose among the Lobo officers who questioned them that they were, in reality, naval personnel. To a man they admitted that they had off-loaded twelve Russian-built 120mm mortars, and a quantity of ammunition. The mortars and ammunition were soon found in the warehouse, but the interrogators found it strange that the crew had been so forthcoming about them. Were they trying to conceal some other activity they were engaged in? Upon hearing their suspicions, DaSilva ordered the vessel be examined with a "fine tooth comb," and that crew members and the PNN soldiers be systematically re-questioned by his team of interrogators. The search resulted in the discovery of six large, steel-strong boxes double-locked and labeled "Barclay Bank S.A.", which were shipped to ALIB Headquarters.

The surrender of the PNN and the capture of the ship and its crew completed the occupation of Puerto Hondo. The Lobos then addressed themselves to defending the port city against any effort by the regime to recapture it.

There was one important dividend. After the action on the quay, a man was found hiding in an empty container in the warehouse. He surrendered without resistance. He had with him two duffle bags filled with personal clothing and other effects. He admitted he was to be a passenger on the Guajira Moreno when she departed. An examination of his papers revealed that he was Cuban, and held a major's commission in the PNN army. His name was Roberto Serra.

CHAPTER 20

There were smiles all around in the ALIB Command Center as the reports from the battalions trickled in. Portero was elated by the casualty-free ease with which the Toros and the Lobos had accomplished their respective missions and by the capture of the several regime leaders. However, his immediate concern was the La Boca Taskforce, which had the critical and more dangerous mission. He was well aware that success or failure in La Boca could be the difference between victory and defeat in the war against the Figueroa regime.

Portero prayed his timing in launching the operation had not been too late. He knew Davidson would be desperate to move his brigade back to the mainland from Isla Grande. The success of Gin Pot's La Boca Taskforce depended on how many units the PNN had brought across in the last few days. It would be a difficult operation if he had to contend with more than one or two companies. It would be very costly in terms of casualties if there were more.

His other concern was for the civilian population of La Boca. Estimates had about three hundred people living in the town. They were mostly fisherman, but a segment were employed by the three ferry operators. Portero had ordered as many civilians as possible be evacuated before the battle began. Johnson had informed him that there had been no hesitation in the general population, which had streamed out of town in a mass exodus as the word of the impending action was passed to them. He believed even most ferry employee families had left.

The latest communication from Johnson indicated his units were engaged and meeting resistance. That concerned Portero because it suggested the PNN had indeed reinforced its forces in La Boca beyond the levels indicated in recent intelligence estimates. His hope that they could walk in without serious opposition apparently was not to be.

He grew ever more anxious for hard news. Waiting in the command center was too painful. He decided to be where he could personally observe the action. He sent for Captain Hanson, General Carmody's aide and the officer in charge of the HJRAF observer group. When Hanson reported minutes later, he greeted him saying, "Jimmy, isn't it time you started earning your pay as an observer? I have two battalions committed in La Boca, and I am sure your boss would want you to see what we are doing down there. Do you agree?"

"I do, General. I absolutely agree. I have been thinking the very same thing. As a matter of fact, the chopper is winding up as we speak." Hanson laughed and added, "By the way, sir, as long as we are going that way, would you like to go along? We have plenty of room."

Portero grinned. "That's very thoughtful, Jimmy…I thought you would never ask. Colonel Gutierrez and my operations sergeant and I will meet you at the helicopter in thirty minutes."

• • •

Gin Pot Johnson had deployed his taskforce to enter the village of La Boca from all directions. His Tigre Battalion was on the northeast sector of the village, its Alpha Company anchoring the left flank with its own left flank platoon on the beach, its mission to bar any ex-filtration by the PNN along the shore line. His Charlie Company was on the right flank, straddling the main road leading to the ferry landing. Bravo Company filled the gap between Alpha and Charlie.

He had deployed the Oso Battalion in a similar manner to the south and west of the village with Bravo, its right flank company on the beach, and Alpha Company closing the gap between Bravo and Tigre Charlie. Oso Charlie had been held in reserve in the area of the truck park and Medical Aid Station to the west and inland. Thus La Boca was surrounded, cutting off escape of any PNN units.

Charlie Company of the Tigres had led the assault along the main road into the village and hadn't advanced two hundred meters when it met unexpectedly heavy resistance. It was immediately apparent the PNN security force had been reinforced. The volume of fire from the defenders was greater than a single reinforced platoon could muster, and Gin Pot now estimated that his units were facing at least a company, perhaps two. Charlie Company was stopped cold with a number of casualties, including its excellent young commander and his radio man, who were killed leading the advance into the village with the point platoon. Johnson was immediately aware of the urgency in taking La Boca quickly. He was convinced the PNN had ferried additional units across during the last three days, and his paramount concern was they would bring more units across to reinforce further. If he couldn't take the ferry landing quickly, the situation might spiral beyond his capability to contain the enemy. To allow the PNN to bring more troops was unthinkable. If that happened, it could end his force advantage, and he could be overpowered, in which event his alternatives would be to concede the battle and withdraw or allow the destruction of his command. Losing his command would significantly weaken the ALIB to the point of forfeiting its overall force advantage and thus prolong the war.

Gin Pot had no choice. The situation called for a maximum effort, no matter the cost. To meet the new situation, he changed his plan of attack. He ordered his Charlie Company to halt its advance, to dig in and consolidate its line, and prepare for a counter attack. He ordered a section of mortars forward from its support position to Charlie's new position, which would put them in range of the ferry landing. Once in place, they were to immediately commence interdictory fire on the landing area to discourage ferry operations.

His new concern then was that the enemy might, in desperation, try landing troops on the beaches north or south of the village. To avoid such a surprise, he ordered Hank Ruedas to split his Recon Platoon and maintain surveillance on likely landing areas north and south of La Boca.

He summoned Major Mix, the Oso Battalion commander, and they together formulated a plan to aggressively reduce the PNN beachhead. Tigre Charlie was, on signal, to feign resumption of its attack, kicking it off with a show of sustained automatic weapons fire and a mortar preparation, first with high explosive ammunition, then followed by smoke rounds. The smoke barrage would be the signal for all taskforce companies to advance into La Boca, their final objective being the ferry landing complex.

The main effort was assigned to Tigre Alpha on the shoreline to the north and Oso Bravo on the shoreline to the south. The plan provided that if the main effort companies were able to advance on schedule, the interior companies would halt their advance and hold their positions as they were pinched off by the main effort units. Should the main effort companies be stopped, the interior units would renew their advance. Thus the defending PNN units would be squeezed into an ever-decreasing perimeter.

The danger was that a determined PNN counter attack might affect a breakthrough of the taskforce lines. To counter that eventuality, Gin Pot ordered Oso Charlie, the reserve company, to a staging area immediately behind Tigre Charlie, from which it could be quickly deployed to close any breach to the north or to the south.

"This is going to be very tricky. It would probably get us flunked out of any tactics class. But we have no other choice," Gin Pot said to Mix. "To be successful, we must coordinate both our movements and fire support closely. I will be with my command group between my Alpha and Bravo Companies. You place yourself between your two companies in your sector. That way we can exercise direct personal control of our units. It is essential that we do not allow our interior companies to encroach on the main effort companies' line of advance as they move forward. We will have to be in constant contact with one another on the command channel while we monitor our companies . If we lose radio contact, we'll use cell phones as back up. Have you anything to add, or any questions, Major?"

"No, sir, you've covered it. I believe we can control it enough to make it work, given the few units involved. What time do we jump off?"

"I'll let you know exactly, but it will be as soon as the mortars and your reserve company are in position...It should be in about one hour. Set your watch. I have exactly 0928 now."

· · ·

Colonel Xavier Molina, the Cuban commanding officer of the PNN Second Light Infantry Brigade, had moved from Isla Grande to La Boca with two companies of his First Battalion, and a limited staff of three operations specialists, in preparation for moving the brigade to the mainland. He had anticipated the ALIB would make an attempt to prevent the operation, and he had moved his time schedule forward by a week in anticipation of such a move by Portero.

He had arrived the day before the ALIB Taskforce made its unexpected appearance in the port area. He was surprised at the early arrival but thankful that he had brought the force he now had on hand. His two companies had each been reinforced with two additional machine gun sections which with the original security platoon, which had been providing security at the La Boca ferry terminal, and had itself been reinforced by four pickup trucks carrying heavy pedestal, mounted fifty-caliber machine guns, gave him a formidable force, which he thought sufficient to secure the landing area until the entire Second Brigade could be brought across. He was confident he had the firepower to meet almost any situation.

His original plan had been to complete the move in six days, but he had accelerated his plans. He now believed he could do it in three-and-a-half days, with a little luck. He had directed his chief of staff to prepare to meet the new timeline.

Molina estimated the ALIB force in La Boca at a single company—no more than two at the most. His estimate was based upon what his scouts had reported seeing come in by helicopter and the few trucks they had seen arrive. His confidence was reinforced by Davidson's assurances that the ALIB did not have the capability of transporting larger formations at once. He believed time was on his side.

Now that the ALIB force had arrived in the area, his immediate task was to hold it far enough away from the ferry terminus to prevent it interfering with the transfer operations. Accordingly he deployed his available force to intercept and deny the ALIB any approach into the village toward the terminus.

Molina was confident, but he also was an experienced soldier and a careful planner. He subscribed to the rule of war: 'If something can go wrong, it will.' His worse case scenario would be that the enemy force was larger than he assumed it to be, in which case, he might not be able to hold it away from the landing site. In that case, he would be prevented from bringing the remainder of his brigade across. If it was stuck on Isla Grande, it would be useless. *However, on the mainland, it could well be the key to victory for the national forces over these goddamn rebels.*

In his mind La Boca had become the most important piece of real estate in this miserable country. Holding it could mean victory. Losing it could spell defeat and the end of the Figueroa regime, and a setback in the march of socialism in the Caribbean. The brigade had to be brought across. Molina decided to play it safe and asked Davidson for re-enforcement by forces available on the mainland, just in case. A battalion or even a reinforced company of PNN approaching La Boca from the north would drastically alter the tactical situation for the ALIB, and assure him the time he needed to land his brigade.

He picked up his cell phone and called his boss, Colonel Davidson. Davidson answered immediately. He explained the situation and asked to be reinforced by the Casador Battalion, which was only hours away in the La Capital, and still uncommitted, insofar as he knew.

"I thought you had the situation in hand. Aren't you bringing your brigade across now?"

"I am. I have two companies on this side and expect another today. I am just being cautious because an ALIB unit has just arrived in the La Boca area and more will certainly be coming."

"How strong a force from the ALIB?"

"At least a company—maybe two. I'm not sure yet, but you can bet more will be coming."

"You should be able to handle that with what you have…I mean, you should be able to keep them away from the landing while you get the rest across."

"I think so, too, but I want to be sure. We can't afford to have anything interfere with bringing the rest over. Lend me the Casadors. Doesn't have to be the battalion, only a company or two. Just as insurance, to divert the ALIB's attention until we're across. They probably won't even have to engage. I'll send them back up as soon as we are across."

Molina was troubled by Davidson's reaction. He expected immediate agreement. The man seemed to understand the need, but he was hesitating for some reason.

"It is just for a couple of days, Davidson. Should be a good practical exercise for them…Some added training."

"I understand, Xavier, and I'll see what we can do. We have a bit of a problem. I have to talk to the President. I'll get back to you this afternoon or tomorrow, at the latest."

"Tomorrow? You don't understand! Dammit, Davidson, the point is to get the help today! The units you send should be on the way within the hour if they are to do any good. I repeat. It's just until we are across. After that, we won't need them. But timing is important now. Once I have the brigade on the mainland, I'll win this goddamn war for you. Surely you understand that?"

"I do understand, Molina, but the President has been adamant about keeping the Casadors up here. He has another mission for them."

"Then send me a couple of units of the armored battalion instead."

Davidson paused, then in a quiet voice. "Look, Molina, I guess you haven't heard. It is not generally known, but…we lost the armored battalion and one Casador company at La Campana."

"You what? My God, when did that happen? How in hell did it happen?" Molina was shocked and speechless as he tried to digest this new information. "Listen, Davidson, I don't even want to know how we managed to screw up that operation. Taking out a roadblock doesn't seem a big deal to me. My God!

"Right now I am concerned about my situation here. Your news makes it all the more critical…and it should be obvious to you and Figueroa that our best hope…maybe our only hope now, to defeat the ALIB, is my Second Brigade. I've got to get it to the mainland. And I'm asking you to help me do that!"

"I'll do my best, Xavier, but the President is not listening to anyone these days. He believes we are going to get help from outside the country. I don't know how it is going to get here. Just this morning we learned that the ALIB has taken control of Puerto Hondo and the International Airport."

"Good God!"

"Figueroa has ordered me to form a taskforce to take back the airport. I only have two Casador companies, which we are beefing up with a couple of platoons of combat trained police, two platoons of Cascavels, and some odds and ends, engineers and truck company soldiers…And—"

Molina interrupted, yelling into the phone, "Listen to me, Davidson. Send those troops down here. Order them to attack the rear of the ALIB taskforce to divert their attention long enough for me to get the whole Second Brigade ashore. In light of what you just told me, that may well be our last chance to win this thing. Later we can take back the airport and Puerto Hondo one at a time, and tear up those ALIB units while we do it!"

"Okay, Molina, take it easy. I'll see Figueroa this morning. He is being pretty damn stubborn. But I'll work on him."

"Good. Make him understand. He must understand! It is our one chance, and it has got to happen today. If it doesn't, it may be too late. Advise me as soon as you know something. Now I've got to go keep these rebel bastards away from the ferry landing. I should be able to hold them today, but if I don't have help by tomorrow, it could all be over."

He hung up in a state of shock. *How in hell did he get involved with these damned incompetent Naranjeros in the first place?* But as the professional soldier he was, he quickly turned his mind to solving his immediate problem. If the situation at La Boca was to be saved, it appeared he and his staff would have to do it. He contacted his executive officer on Isla Grande, directed him to expedite sending the remainder of the First Battalion across, and to follow with as much of the Second Battalion as he could cram onto the ferries. Then he turned to the problem of defending La Boca.

Molina had anticipated the ALIB would attack down the main road leading into the village and the ferry docks. He had prepared for it. He placed a company in defensive positions straddling the road. It had had time to dig in and conceal its presence, and was waiting for the ALIB. The attacking unit, Charlie Company of the Tigres, had been surprised by the ambush and was easily stopped by its determined defense. Molina was inwardly gratified by the performance of his troops in their first action. Tough training had paid off.

The situation clearly called for an immediate counter attack. He had the second company ready but was reluctant to commit it. He had no hard intelligence on the size of the attacking force and decided to wait. A counter attack would have cost casualties, and he had no other reserves available in La Boca. He thought it prudent to husband his resources and hold the company in reserve until he could see how things developed. He opted for a holding action until reinforcements from the island arrived.

Molina suddenly felt tired. He'd been awake since 0400. It wasn't yet midday, so he decided to take advantage of the lull in the fighting and eat something. He sat with his feet on the desk in the ferry terminal office he was using for his command post. He had almost finished a can of black beans and rice when he heard the sounds of renewed fighting. First it was intense automatic weapons fire, followed shortly by exploding mortar rounds. It seemed obvious the ALIB unit they had stopped earlier was launching a new attack.

"The bastards are going to have another go at us. Alert the reserve company. Tell them to be prepared to move up, and await my orders," he spoke to his operations sergeant, who was standing by the tactical radio.

At that moment, mortar rounds began exploding within the ferry terminus complex. "What the hell? They've moved their mortars…forward to bring us in range. Get the reserve company moving now. We've got to knock out those goddamn mortars, or at least force them back out of range, or we are going to play hell getting any more of the brigade ashore. Order its commander to close in on the left rear of the defending company. Once in place, both companies are to make a limited attack with the objective of capturing those mortars if possible, or at least drive those damned rebels back to their lines of early this morning, where they will be out of range."

Suddenly the rain of high explosive shells stopped and soon were replaced by the hollow pops of smoke shells bursting in the area of the defending PNN company. Clouds of burning white phosphorus particles billowed upward and spread an acrid haze around the PNN positions, blinding the defenders.

"They'll come now, but we'll meet them," Molina said to himself. He waited for the sound of firing from his defending company to build. He heard nothing. Five minutes passed—then ten minutes—still nothing. Finally he heard the sound of small arms fire— but it was coming from the wrong direction. It was coming from his right and moments later from his left.

"They're hitting our flanks," he yelled out to his staff. "Cancel that attack order and pull the reserve company back. Order its commander to send one platoon here and move the rest to the south well past the ferry landings. He is to set up a defensive line where he can block whatever ALIB forces might be coming at us from that direction. It can't be more than a platoon.

"I will take one platoon and a machine gun vehicle from the security platoon and go to the north end to do the same. I'll have both the command net and the tactical radios with me. He is to keep me informed. Tell the defending company what we are doing…and to keep me informed of his situation. Also let the brigade exec know what is happening, and tell him to get as many units across as soon as he can today. They are to be prepared to come off those boats fighting."

Molina departed his command post on the run. That was the last his staff heard from him that day.

• • •

Gin Pot Johnson ordered the advance at 1030 when the mortar barrage began. He, with his radio man and an operations sergeant, moved forward with his Alpha Company. Its objective was the ferry terminal. Bravo Companies signaled it was moving and Major Mix confirmed his Oso Battalion units had entered the village from the south and were also moving toward the ferry terminal area.

Alpha company moved with two platoons abreast, spread out in assault formation, straddling a narrow dirt lane running parallel with the beach on the left, and passing between a number of small, wooden houses interspersed with boat sheds and fish net racks. The unit covered two hundred and fifty meters without resistance until it approached an intersection and a jog in the lane. There both units were surprised by heavy small arms fire emanating from a cluster of ramshackle buildings to their right front. The right flank platoon took cover and immediately answered with high volume suppressing fire, while the left flank platoon continued its advance uninterrupted, intent on enveloping the PNN ambushers.

It became evident the PNN unit had not had time to fortify its positions and the flimsy wooden structures offered them concealment, but little protection. Although they were courageous, they were no match for the advancing Tigres who threatened to encircle them. They soon began to ex-filtrate by twos in an orderly manner.

Gin Pot observed the action from the shelter of a boat shed. He noted with pride the professionalism of his soldiers, who had maintained discipline despite the several casualties they had taken. The volume of fire from the ambushers had dropped dramatically, and it became obvious they were falling back. When the right flank platoon resumed its advance moving forward in squad rushes, he and his radio man left the shed to follow them. Just as he stepped into the lane, he was knocked off his feet by a heavy blow to his left arm and shoulder. It felt as if someone had hit him with a baseball bat. Simultaneously he heard, *rrriiipp-rrriiipp,* the unmistakable sound of an AK on full automatic.

The fire seemed to come from somewhere to his right front. Expecting another burst, he rolled to his right and the thought came to him it might be the last action of his life. When it didn't come, he began to look for the shooter. His eye caught movement between buildings. It was the back of a PNN soldier retreating at a full run. *The idiot had me,* he thought. *If he had been one of ours, he would have finished the job. Thank God he wasn't.*

He rested for a moment. His arm and shoulder were numb. He could see his upper arm was badly mangled and bleeding. He tried to climb to his feet but couldn't. He heard his operations sergeant shouting for a medic, who seemed to materialize immediately. The man gently forced him to lie back, gave him a shot of morphine, and began to work on his wound.

"Get the radio and get me Major Mix," Gin Pot ordered. Then he fainted.

• • •

Mix was with his Bravo Company, which was working its way along the beach south of the ferry landing, when his radio man received a call from Colonel Johnson, Tigre One; he took the radio handset and found himself talking to Tigre Alpha One. He was informed Johnson had been wounded severely and was being evacuated, that they were waiting for the Tigre Battalion executive officer to join them. "You are now the taskforce commander, Major. I await your orders—unless you tell me differently, I will proceed to my objective—the ferry docks. Over."

"Right, Captain, proceed as planned. I'll meet you there. We are eight or ten blocks—maybe a kilometer south of there. My Bravo Company is working up along the shoreline. My Alpha is on its left, approaching the center of town, and should hook up with your Charlie shortly. Charlie is in reserve and is moving in behind your Charlie as we speak. So far resistance has been light, but we are starting to receive some fire in the village—mostly in your Charlie's sector. Advise your units we are moving their way. We don't want to shoot each other up. Over."

"Roger that, Major…Wait. Stand by, One." Mix waited. Four long minutes passed before Tigre Alpha One came back to him. "Good news, Major. My first platoon advises he has captured a PNN colonel. He believes he may be the PNN commander here."

CHAPTER 21

The Black Hawk carrying General Portero, Colonel Gutierrez, his operations sergeant, Captain Jaime Hanson, and his three-man observer party approached La Boca one hour and fifty minutes after lifting off from Valle Escondido. The forty-minute flight had been extended by a stop at International Airport, where Portero had directed Colonel Sanchez, Toro Battalion commander, to be prepared to send one of his companies to La Boca to reinforce the taskforce there.

As the helicopter approached the port area, its passengers could see signs of the battle below. A bluish haze enveloped the center of town, and from time to time, they saw an exchange of tracer fire and the occasional flash of an exploding mortar shell.

The pilot, Chris DaSilva, had begun her descent and prepared for landing west of La Boca at the Taskforce Rear Command Post, near the medical aid station and truck park, when Portero asked her to fly over the battle area. He wanted a closer look at the situation. She promptly added power to regain altitude and eased toward the area where the fighting seemed most intense. She bled off forward speed and went into a semi-hover over the area at eighteen hundred feet.

Portero studied the ferry terminal complex and the six miles of water between Isla Grande and the mainland with his binoculars. He was about to declare he could see no ferries operating when a string of tracers suddenly rose up at them from the ferry building complex. The Black Hawk was hit. The impacting bullets sounded like hammer blows as they struck its metallic skin. Chris made a violent turn to the left and nosed the machine over into a rapid descent, heading for her originally intended landing point.

Smoke began streaming from the bird's left engine. Leveling off at three hundred feet, she tried to add power but got no response. They continued to lose altitude as the powerless rotor wind-milled above them. She knew she could not make the landing area and quickly checked ahead for a suitable site for a power-off landing. She ordered her passengers to tighten their harnesses and to prepare for a hard landing. She recognized the ALIB position straddling the main road into town near a reasonably broad intersection, made her decision, and committed to landing there. Using all her skill, she fought to balance her rate of descent with her forward momentum to reach her fast-approaching chosen landing point. She almost made it, hitting the ground thirty meters short.

The big machine landed hard, blew the left main gear tire, skidded forward, creating sparks for fifteen or twenty meters, before coming to rest in the intersection between the ALIB and PNN positions, but closer to the ALIB. The tip of the main rotor hit a concrete power pole and disintegrated, launching a shower of deadly high speed splinters in a great circle throughout the area. Chris checked her switches, making sure all were off, and ordered her crew chief to grab the handheld fire extinguisher and use it on the burning engine compartment. She ordered the passengers to exit the aircraft from the right, the side toward the ALIB position.

The crew chief with the fire extinguisher was first out of the aircraft, and he was followed by Jaime Hanson and his observer team. Both the ALIB troops and their PNN adversaries had watched, fascinated by its dramatic decent, which caused a lull in the fighting. However, the sight of the crew chief emerging and climbing the side of the helicopter broke the spell. An over-eager

PNN soldier began shooting at him and triggered a renewal of the battle. The crew chief was the first to fall, shot in the head.

Colonel Gutierrez and his sergeant followed Portero out. Gutierrez was hit, a bullet in his left hip. He fell to the ground, screened by the wrecked fuselage. His sergeant began firing in the direction of the PNN with his handgun. Portero's radio man got out unscathed and he, with Jaime Hanson and his fellow observers, armed only with pistols, took cover behind the wreck with Gutierrez.

Portero looked around, expecting to see Chris DaSilva and her co-pilot exiting the wreck, but they were not there. He crawled over to the pilot's door and, crouching as bullets cracked around him, looked for Chris through her shattered Plexiglas window. She was still strapped in her seat, her head forward, chin against the restraining harness. He tore open the door and spoke to her. She lifted her head for a moment but did not answer. He reached in to release her harness and saw the blood staining the front of her flight suit. Then he saw her copilot dead, with part of his head blown away.

"I've got you, Chris. I'm going to get you out of here. Just relax. You're going to be okay." She groaned as he lifted her out. Her left shoe caught on the door, but he heaved and it came away. Then he made an instant decision. He ran, cradling her in his arms, dodging left and right toward the ALIB position some fifteen meters away. The moment he and his burden became visible beyond the wreckage, the PNN directed a fusillade of fire at his retreating back. Bullets cracked all around and kicked up dust around his heels. One grazed his head, split his right ear, and nicked his cheek. Another hit Chris's left hand, which was dangling away from his body. Somehow they made it to the cover of a Charlie Company machine gun emplacement, where eager hands gently relieved him of his burden. "Hey, it's the general," someone exclaimed, finally realizing who he was.

"Get a medic here now. Take care of Captain Lane…and tell him to bring a couple of stretchers. We have more wounded out there…And I want covering fire out there…keep those PNN bastards away from that helicopter. Do you have radio contact with your company commander? Get him for me, please."

"This is Charlie Exec General. Charlie One has been killed. Are you all right?"

"Don't worry about me, Lieutenant. Get your mortars going with smoke and HE on that PNN position. I've got Colonel Gutierrez out there wounded, and I want to bring him in."

While he waited, he tried to talk to Chris. She made an effort to answer. He saw her lips move but couldn't hear what she said. He put his good ear close to her lips and she whispered, "I want to see Tony."

"You'll see him…Don't worry."

The medic arrived and saw Portero bleeding profusely from his torn ear and gashed cheek, and made a move to treat his wounds. "Let that go, son. Take care of this great lady and get her to the doctor at the aid station as fast as you can."

Portero, still bleeding, then led a rescue party back to the wrecked helicopter for Colonel Gutierrez. Captain Hansen and his observers had stayed with the old warrior, while his operations sergeant tried to provide what first aid he could. They were prepared to fight off any attempt by the PNN to capture him, and they had suffered for it. Hansen received a shoulder wound, and one of his observers had been killed.

Now the concentrated fire from Charlie Company kept the enemies' heads down, and the occasional smoke round made it difficult for them to see what the rescue party, led by Portero, was doing. With help from three Charlie Company soldiers, they managed to bring the wounded and the three dead Americans back inside Charlie Company perimeter.

Portero, breathing hard from the effort, refused to be evacuated to the aid station. He moved to the Charlie Company command post, where he was informed Colonel Johnson had been wounded and that Major Mix had assumed command of the taskforce. He immediately contacted Mix by radio and learned that the operation was proceeding against some resistance—that the Osos were in sight of the ferry terminal and that Tigre Alfa had taken twelve prisoners, including a PNN Colonel, and was then in the process of outflanking the enemy unit opposing Charlie Company. He assured the general the battle was in hand, and that all should be over except for some mopping up in an hour or so.

Portero commended Mix for a job well done and told him of the casualties from the helicopter. Then, using his cell phone, he called Colonel DaSilva to inform him about Chris and that she was calling for him. He told him to find a way to La Boca fast, that the other Black Hawk was on its way down to evacuate Chris, GinPot, Gutierrez, Hanson, and the other wounded. He guessed it would be ready to go in about an hour or two, so there was no time to lose. He told DaSilva to call the Cattlemen's Association, as they had offered the use of their helicopters. "You'll be cutting it short, time-wise at best. So get on it, Tony!"

• • •

Portero was reassured by his conversation with Mix. All seemed to be going well, and there was nothing he could contribute by remaining forward with the embattled Charlie Company. He allowed himself to be escorted back to the taskforce medical aid station to have his wounds treated. In reality he was less concerned about his wounds than those of Chris DaSilva, Gutierrez, and Gin Pot Johnson. He was most concerned about Chris and Gin Pot, whose wounds seemed really serious, and he was anxious to learn how bad his Tigre Battalion commander was injured.

At the aid station, he began to shake as the tensions of the last hours left him. He covered it by complaining to the doctor who had stitched up his cheek and was struggling to bandage his split ear. "Come on, Doc, I've got to get going. You act like you never saw a wounded ear before."

"You are right, General. I never have, and if you don't hold still, I may accidentally amputate the damn thing."

"I can't hold still. I've got the damn shakes. Any decent doctor would be zigging when I zigg—so get in rhythm, can't you?"

"I'm a doctor, not a damn dancer. Don't expect too much from me." They both chuckled at the exchange.

Before leaving, Portero quizzed the doctor on the state of his wounded colleagues. Chris DaSilva was of the greatest concern. A bullet had passed through her from back to front. Her left lung had collapsed and there was considerable internal bleeding, but the doctor didn't think there had been any damage to her heart or aorta. She was being treated for severe shock with an IV drip, and she was breathing oxygen. The doctor said she needed surgery which he was not capable of providing in the field, that she had to be gotten to a hospital without delay. He added had she not been in excellent physical condition, she would have been dead already.

Colonel Johnson was also seriously injured, apparently struck by two bullets in his left upper arm and shoulder. There was bone damage, and he also needed considerable surgery. However, the doctor did not feel his wound was life-threatening, unless there were secondary complications with blood clots or infection.

Colonel Gutierrez had been shot in the hip. The bullet which had lodged against the pelvis had been removed, and the wound was now clean and ready to be closed.

Captain Hanson's shoulder wound was clean and without bone involvement, and he should be up and around in a matter of days.

The doctor briefed him on the condition of seven soldiers from the Tigres who had received treatment. Three of them had been wounded severely and needed to be evacuated. The remaining four would recover with the care available there, and at Valle Escondido.

• • •

Portero sat in the hospital tent with the wounded, waiting with them for the arrival of the helicopter which would carry them to Panama and Gorgas General Hospital. He spent time with each individual but lingered with his officers, who over the years had become personal friends.

Gutierrez's was apologetic. His hip was painful and immobilized. "I am sorry to have gotten myself shot, General. I should be up and around soon, so if you need me here I can work out of a bed or wheelchair."

"Thanks, Juan. We need you, but we need you back on your feet. You had better go with the others and get fixed up at a hospital, where they know how to do it."

Johnson's injuries were more serious. He had been hit twice, and there was bone involvement. He was in considerable pain and although he had been well-sedated, typical of the man, he made an effort to be cheerful. "How are we doing, Pancho? It looks like we didn't get to La Boca any too soon. Thank God we got here when we did."

"That's right, another day or so, and it would have been a different story. But we did get here in time, and you won an important victory. You did a great job, Gin Pot. I am pleased to inform you, the fighting is winding down. Mix is a good man, and he is mopping up, so it is pretty well over…"

Johnson struggled with his words. "Our casualties? I know… lost Jose Brons, my Charlie One…good man…reliable…first class commander."

"Yes. And we lost a few others. I don't know how many yet. But I believe it may be less than at La Campana."

"Good…What happened…your ear?"

"Someone tried to shoot it off, I guess."

"You're going t' look…funny."

"I guess it will have some entertainment value." He smiled and squeezed Johnson's hand. "I'll be seeing you, Gin Pot. Now I've got to check on Chris DaSilva. You hurry and get that shoulder fixed. We're going to need you here. There will be a lot of work to do."

Portero moved down the tent to Chris. He had a particularly soft spot in his heart for her, not only because she was Tony DaSilva's wife but also because of her enthusiasm for the ALIB. He and Betsy had grown fond of her and had come to regard as the daughter they never had. Chris was in critical condition. She was pale and struggling to breathe through her oxygen mask. He looked at the IV drip bag. It was working. Portero understood the doctor's concern. He willed the helicopter to hurry.

Chris drifted in and out of consciousness. He sat beside her stretcher and held her hand. Once she opened her eyes and recognized him. "Tony?" she managed to ask from behind the mask.

"He is on the way, Chris. Just relax, he'll be here." She managed a wan smile. Later she whispered something which he couldn't hear. She used her good hand to try to lift the breathing device. He helped her and placed his good ear close to her mouth.

"Tell Tony…I love him." She coughed weakly. "And…if I don't get to see him…I'll be waiting…later…not to worry about me."

The lump in his throat made it difficult to speak. "I'll tell him, Chris. Don't you worry. Now you should rest. Save your strength. They will take good care of you in Panama. You are a wonderful person and you'll have all our prayers. God bless you."

He sat holding her hand until the Black Hawk arrived. She and the others were gently loaded aboard. The pilot was not worried about weight but about space. Six stretchers and attendants would use all available space, so Captain Hanson volunteered to stay behind. He stood, arm in a sling, with Portero watching the big bird lift off and disappear to the south.

A feeling of loss and grinding anguish consumed Portero. These were his friends, his comrades, people who trusted him, and they all would be okay now had he not ordered Chris to fly over La Boca. Hanson sensed his distress. "They'll be in good hands, General. My boss will keep us posted."

Portero was suddenly tired. He returned to the hospital tent, lay down on the ground, and fell into a deep sleep, with Jimmy Hanson sitting nearby watching over him.

• • •

An hour and a half later, General Portero awakened. His cheek and ear were throbbing and his back was stiff, but he felt refreshed. He stretched and saw Hanson smiling at him. "General, do you know you snore?"

"Jimmy, what the hell are you doing here? You should be in bed somewhere, shouldn't you? What time is it? I've got to go to work. You go see what the doc wants to do with you…I'll call you if I need you. And thanks, Jimmy, for babysitting me."

Portero collected his gear and cell phones which had been left in the surgical tent, and set up a makeshift command post under a tree near the medical tent. Someone had found a table and two rickety chairs, and with his maps anchored to the table by a couple of stones, he was back in his role of ALIB commander.

He first called his chief of staff, Colonel Ochoa, in Valle Escondido. He informed him of the military situation in La Boca, and gave him the details about the helicopter crash. They agreed Major Vargas would assume the B3 responsibilities until Gutierrrez could return to duty. They decided to establish the forward headquarters at La Boca because of its proximity to La Capital and decided to move the ATB staff, minus the B4 and Lacerica, there. The legal officer and his staff were to move immediately with Colonel Banning, the B2. They would assist Mix and the Osos in processing, screening, and managing the transfer of the PNN prisoners on Isla Grande. They expected it would be an arduous and time-consuming operation. Portero emphasized the importance of careful screening, as he did not want Cubans, Naranjero criminals, or any individuals who might be witnesses to crimes committed by the PNN or officials of the Figueroa regime to slip through their screening.

Then Portero called the Toro Battalion CP at the airport and spoke with Colonel Sanchez. He countermanded his earlier order to send a company to La Boca. "We won't need it here, but prepare your battalion for a move to La Capital, leaving one company to secure the airport. You'll be a part of a taskforce with DaSilva's Tigres, which I will command. We're going to finish off whatever PNN forces are left and shut down Figueroa."

He then placed a call to Colonel DaSilva but was informed he was on his way to La Boca in a Cattlemen's Association helicopter.

Portero smelled coffee brewing in the medical station mess tent. He ordered a pot for himself and sat relishing the taste of the steaming brew as he began to plan how to move against La Capital. Where was Figueroa? And where was Davidson? They had to be there in La Capital, but where in the city? He considered trying to reach Figueroa by cell phone, but thought better of it. It was best not to let them know he was coming. People in the city would have a good idea where he was, so why don't we ask them? He sent a runner for Lieutenant Hank Rueda, commander of the brigade Reconnaissance Platoon.

Then he wondered if the PNN commander the Tigres had captured might have information about Figueroa and Davidson's whereabouts. Well, he needed to interrogate the man anyway, so he called Mix and asked him to send Molina back to his CP.

Forty minutes later, a freshly shaved Molina arrived under armed escort. Portero, who was seated at his table under the tree, did not stand to greet him. "Please sit down. You are Colonel Molina, I believe. We have not met. I am Francisco Portero. Would you care for a cup of coffee?"

"Thank you, sir. A cup of coffee would go well about now." He took a long sip, savoring the fragrant, hot liquid. Then he looked at his captor, smiling. "I cannot say I am glad to meet you under these circumstances, General. Nevertheless, I congratulate you your operation here. You moved faster than we expected you could. If you had given me a few more days, it would have been a different story. We underestimated your capability to move your forces as you have." Molina spoke in a quiet, friendly tone.

Portero did not return the smile. His voice was hard in his reply. "What counts is I did not allow you a few more days. You and Davidson and your tin horn boss, Figueroa, have made a habit of underestimating us. That is why you have lost this war. Your brigade was the last thing that stood in the way. You do realize it is over?"

"Yes. But I didn't until today when I talked to Davidson this morning. He told me about La Campana and that you control the airport and Puerto Hondo. I was surprised. I had been under the impression we still had the initiative. I had called him for some support here, and he admitted he had nothing left to send."

"That is not true, you know. He still has two companies from his Casador Battalion and two or three platoons of armored cars."

Molina looked surprised. "How do you know that?"

"As I said, you continue to underestimate us. Why did he refuse to send you help? Anything, even a couple of platoons, would have slowed us down."

"I tried…goddammit, I tried. But he said Figueroa wanted to use those units as a taskforce to take back the airport."

"When?"

"He didn't say."

"Where are Davidson and Figueroa now?"

"In La Capital, I suppose. Probably holed up in the presidential palace. There is no place they can go."

"What do you think of Figueroa?"

Molina thought it an odd question and considered his answer. "Well, I can say I was impressed with him at first. He seemed an astute political leader. He knew where he was going. He is a planner. He seemed tough-minded. And dedicated. In some way he reminded me of Fidel, without the charisma. But after I got to know him, I saw he had weaknesses. He is arrogant and overconfident. He thinks he is invincible. He thought he couldn't lose. However, when things don't go his way— when people disagree with him—he gets angry and doesn't think straight. Then he makes bad decisions and doesn't listen to advice. He is quick to blame others and is vindictive. He dominates Davidson, I think, but then I have never seen them together. I believe Davidson is loyal to him, although it sounded like they were not seeing eye to eye when we talked this morning."

"Thank you, Colonel. You have given me some new insight on Figueroa. More coffee?" Portero softened his tone of voice, deliberately trying to sound friendly.

"Yes please, General, and thank you. I am a fan of Naranjeras coffee."

"We have that in common. Now, to the reason I called you here. I will require your assistance and that of your staff. My Oso Battalion has been assigned the mission of disarming your troops on Isla Grande and bringing them across to be screened and demobilized here at La Boca. What is your head count? Two thousand, I believe."

"Twenty-two hundred-and-forty-five, counting the units here in La Boca."

"You will understand that we haven't the means to feed and house that many prisoners of war. I will expect you to assist us with your rations, your tentage, and the supplies necessary for their welfare during the processing period. They are your men, after all, and will be until they have been officially discharged. It should make it easier for them if they know you are cooperating in the matter." Portero waited for Molina's response.

"This not why I came to Naranjeras, you understand. But it seems I have no choice under the circumstances. Yes, I agree to help you in this process, and I assure you my staff will also agree. Having said that, General, may I ask something in return for my cooperation? Ah…I would like—"

Portero cut him short. "This is not the time to bargain, Colonel. Let us wait until the work is finished. We'll see how it goes. If there are no problems and all has gone smoothly, that will be the time to ask for favors. Not now."

"I was only going to ask—"

"Not now, Colonel. You may ask later. You may go."

Molina stood. Portero signaled the soldiers escorting him. Then he noticed his recon platoon commander waiting. "Oh, Ruedas, come on over. Glad to see you in one piece. I believe you and Colonel Molina have met."

"You are correct, sir. In La Rioja. He was there with Gallo, the Cuban hijo de puta that beat Campinas to death." He turned to Molina. "Hello, Colonel, I have looked forward to seeing you in this situation for a long time. And here you are."

"Yes, Lieutenant, here I am, I regret to say…But at least it pleases you."

Before Ruedas could respond, Portero intervened. "Thank you, Lieutenant. Please stand by. I should be finished with Colonel Molina shortly."

"Very well, General. But before I go, may I ask him a question?"

"You may."

"Colonel Molina, whatever happened to Captain Simoni?"

Molina was startled by the question. He looked at Portero, who nodded and directed him to answer. The name had jogged Portero's memory.

"Simoni is with my troops on Isla Grande. He is an assistant personnel officer. He is not good for anything else, I might add."

General Portero waved Ruedas away. He watched the young officer depart. When he was out of earshot, he turned back to Molina. "I take it you do not approve of Captain Simoni?"

"I do not, General. He has been a disappointment to me. He is hard-headed and tends to be insubordinate at times. Not the kind of staff officer a commander can rely on."

Portero looked hard at his prisoner. "I'm sure you are right, Colonel. Nevertheless, I wish to talk to Simoni. He may be a witness to a crime. You get word to your people that he is to come across on the first boat. And Colonel Molina, I am holding you personally responsible to see the man arrives here safely. Do I make myself clear?"

"Of course, General."

"Thank you. And by the way, speaking of crimes, tell me who was responsible for the bomb which killed my wife and my chief of staff and my six soldiers?"

Molina paled. Swallowed. His hand shook. He cleared his throat, then looked Portero in the eye. "I hope you believe me when I tell you that I had no part in that. They wanted to eliminate you, of course. I was never consulted, and I knew nothing of their plan until after the fact. General, I am a soldier, not an assassin. Had they asked me, I would have opposed the action… and, General, I tell you now…I am ashamed it happened."

Portero studied the man. He was not sure of what to believe. He finally said, "I believe you, Molina, but you must know who was involved. Who were they? I want names."

"I'm not sure who was involved…I would rather not say. I could be wrong."

Portero's expression hardened. "I insist, Molina. Tell me whom you think were involved. If you do not, I will have to assume you were one of them. Who killed my wife?"

"I am really not certain…but I can tell you it would never have happened had not Figueroa approved it…so Davidson had to know…and I really don't know who built the bomb. The only man I know who has the expertise would be Roberto Serra, my colleague…but I would be very surprised if it were him. I've known him for a long time. He is a friend, and that is not the type of thing he would do. In any case, I heard he has returned to Cuba."

Portero arose. "Well thank you, Molina, for your help. You may return to the prisoner holding area." He beckoned to the escort still waiting out of earshot, and Molina departed with them.

• • •

Lieutenant Rueda approached Portero as soon as Molina left. "Reporting as ordered, General. Sorry I interrupted your conversation, sir."

"That's okay. I'm glad you did. Seeing you here seems to have shaken him up a bit."

They discussed the Cuban mercenary for a few minutes. Portero believed the man was a Fidelista ideologue. Why else would he be here in Naranjeras, supporting the Figueroa regime? They agreed that while Molina could be useful in helping screen his troops, he was not to be trusted, and that he should be held in custody until he could be thoroughly investigated. Simoni would be helpful there.

Portero got down to business. "How is your unit, Hank? Any problems? Is it ready for a new mission?"

"We're in good shape, sir. All we did here was watch the beaches. We did not get any action. We're ready to go."

"Good. I've got a job for you."

• • •

Mid-afternoon. Portero heard the Cattlemen's Association helicopter arrive. He walked out to meet DaSilva. The men exchanged salutes.

"You okay, General?" DaSilva was looking at Portero's bandages.

"I'm fine, Tony. How are you doing?"

"Worried about Chris. I take it she's been evacuated."

"Yes. Three hours ago. She and Gin Pot and Guttierez. They should be in Panama by now, in the hospital."

"How was she?"

Portero stopped and looked into the eyes of his friend. "Not good, Tony. Her injuries were the most serious of all. The doctor here did all he could to stabilize her. She was on oxygen and an IV drip. I sat with her awhile. She was drifting in and out of consciousness. She was very weak, but I did manage to speak with her. She sent you a message …She loves you…And if she can't see you here, she'll see you later…That she'll be waiting for you… And that you are not to worry."

"What did she mean?"

"I don't know. She knew you were coming. Maybe that was it."

DaSilva was silent for several minutes. He turned away from Portero while he tried to control his emotions. Finally he said, "I don't think that was it. She thought she was going to die. Chris has strong faith. I think she meant the hereafter. That would be just like her."

"Why don't you talk to the doctor? He can tell you more about her condition than anyone."

"Yes…but I wish I'd been here for her…I love that woman. She is the best thing that ever happened to me."

"Maybe I can get you to Panama, Tony. When the Black Hawk gets back. It would have to be a fast turnaround, because I'm going to need you here."

"Thanks, General. I need to see her. If only to say…"

"She's strong and healthy, Tony. And she is a pretty determined person, from what I know. She has a fighting chance, according to the doctor."

DaSilva smiled through his grief. "She is a hard head…We've joked about that. Yes. I'd like to go down, if it's okay with you, sir."

"Okay. The helicopter should be back here this evening. Fly down tonight. And try to come back with it tomorrow if possible, or as soon you can. We'll need you here. While you are waiting, get a hold of your people in Puerto Hondo and tell them what you're doing, and alert them to be prepared to move into La Capital. Leave one company behind to occupy the port area and to keep it closed down. Okay, Tony? We've still got a war to finish. Now go see the doctor."

"Thank you, General."

Portero felt DaSilva's anguish. He gently placed a hand on the man's shoulder and looked him in the eye. "I know how you feel, Tony. I never had a chance to see Betsy. I wish to God I had."

CHAPTER 22

Ten days after the Battle for La Boca, the Osos had managed to screen about half the PNN on Isla Grande. Of that number, seven hundred and fifty Naranjeros had been cleared and given a certificate of discharge. They were allowed to keep their uniforms stripped of all insignia, given a canteen, a can of black beans and rice, fifty pesos from the PNN brigade's payroll fund, and a pass authorizing them to travel to their homes.

The screening process had been conducted under the supervision of Major Mix of the Osos, working with Colonel Banning, the intelligence officer, the brigade legal officer, and with the enthusiastic assistance of Captain Simoni. The PNN officer had made himself known to Major Mix immediately after landing on the mainland. He became instantly important, not only as a long sought eyewitness to the Campinas murder, but one who had a personal history with the Cuban, Molina, as well.

Aside from the large number of Naranjeros, of the PNN troops screened, over two hundred were identified as foreign mercenaries, mostly Cubans and Nicaraguans, a few Europeans and two disaffected American students from Columbia University. All had had some history of affiliations with leftist organizations, and many admitted to having fought on the side of the Sandinistas in Nicaragua, the FMLN in El Salvador, or as soldiers with the Cuban forces in Grenada. Many of them were serving as non-commissioned officers in the PNN Brigade. These men were kept in a well-secured section of the POW camp, under the watchful eyes of Bravo and Charlie Companies of the Osos.

A handful of those screened were discovered to have criminal records. These were held in a separate high-security camp away from the POW compound, guarded by the men of the Oso Reconnaissance Platoon.

While the Osos were screening and supervising prisoners, the Tigres had been transported to Isla Grande to control, disarm, and supervise the transportation of the PNN remaining on the island. The Tigres Recon Platoon had been left behind on the mainland, assigned as security for the ALIB Forward Headquarters, which had been established in tents near the medical station just outside La Boca.

• • •

Lieutenant Hank Ruedas and Chequelo Sepulvida, a sergeant section leader from his platoon, dressed in tattered jeans and dirty shirts, lay with their heads under a shabby pickup truck, pounding on something underneath. The truck was parked out of the way in a new Citgo Service Station near the government plaza in La Capital. They had been under there for thirty-five minutes, periodically pounding and uttering angry expletives. It appeared to all that they were trying to make some repair to their vehicle. In reality they were killing time, waiting there to make contact with Sergeant Emilio Carranza, former platoon sergeant of the ALIB Truck Company, now a platoon sergeant in the PNN Truck Company, and a agent of the ALIB.

The two men had begun to wonder if something had gone wrong. The place and time had been confirmed by Carranza, according to a coded radio message received from their ALIB control. Ruedas was beginning to think about what his next move would be if Carranza did not show. He was growing increasingly nervous about the possibility of some individual offering to help them with their mechanical problem when, in reality, there was no problem.

"If he doesn't show up in the next ten minutes, we'll go into the store and get something to eat and then get the hell out of here."

Even as he spoke, a PNN military truck pulled up to a pump, and its driver dismounted to commence fueling. The passenger door opened, and Ruedas saw Carranza climb down and stretch. The sergeant looked around and glanced their way. After a moment, he sauntered toward them. "Having a problem, amigos?" he asked cheerfully. He leaned down and whispered, "Welcome to enemy territory, Lieutenant. Glad to see you. Sorry to be late. We got held up in a traffic checkpoint."

"Let's get some place where we can talk." Ruedas responeded in a low voice.

"Okay. Are you hungry? I know a little quiosco which sells great empanadas. No one will bother us there. I'll go sign for our fuel, and you can follow us. It's not far."

"Good. We'll be right behind you. What about your driver?"

"He's okay. He was with me at Valle Escondido. He didn't like it much then, but he has since found out he had it made there with the ALIB. He hates working with this PNN outfit. He has no friends but me. He thinks I'm his father or something. He'll go along with whatever it is you want us to do."

The empanadas at Carranza's favorite food kiosk, Quiosco Naranjense, turned out to be as good as advertised. Ruedas, Sepulveda, and Caranza sat under an umbrella at a table farthest from the kiosk, enjoying their meals and beers, talking quietly.

"The armored cars and two companies from the Casador Battalion and a bunch of PNN police types are all at the military base in the woods just south of La Capital. They are training for something. I am not sure what it is, but the rumors indicate it is something to do with recapturing the airport, or Puerto Hondo. Nobody knows for sure."

"How many police types?" Ruedas asked.

"I would guess two or three platoons…Maybe sixty or seventy. They're not a trained combat unit. Looks like a bunch of security types put together for the mission, whatever it turns out to be.

"How do you know all this?"

"Hell,Lieutenant, I go by them every day. Our company head-quarters is right there near them."

"Who's training them?"

"I'm not sure. There is a captain in charge of the armored cars who seems to have a lot of say. But Davidson is there every day too. Maybe he is the guy."

"Davidson? You mean Colonel Davidson, the top PNN commander?"

"The very same. He might as well be there. That is all the troops he has left, around here anyway."

"That's all?"

"That's it except for the three PNN Security Companies which guard Figueroa and the Estado Mayor complex. They're sandbagged in everywhere and are loaded with machine guns and automatic weapons. They mean business too. No one gets close without a PNN escort. They have already fired at a couple of civilians who wandered beyond a certain point."

"How about you guys? Can you get in there?"

"Yea, but we're about the only ones. We have a couple of trucks go in there everyday delivering food and supplies and carrying out trash and other crap."

"Every day?"

"Every day."

"And you say Figueroa is in there?"

"Yea. He hardly ever leaves these days…and when he comes out it is only with an armed escort."

"Interesting…but let's talk some more about the military base. Can you get us inside? We should take a look around … See what they are doing."

Carranza took a pull from his beer bottle, thinking. "I could get some PNN uniforms for you and take you in with us. But that could be dangerous. There are a couple of sergeants in my company who watch me pretty close. I don't know for sure but I think they are informants. There are still people who don't trust me … they suspect I am a plant for the ALIB. If I suddenly show up with a couple of new strange soldiers they will wonder and do some checking. That could give us away. I think it will be safer if you let me do the snooping on my own. They are used to seeing me around. Just tell me exactly what you want to know."

"We need to know more about the PNN intentions. Are they preparing to leave the base? Are they preparing to defend it? What about their morale? Do they not know the war is all but over, or do they think they are still in it? What about their leadership? Who will they follow? Davidson or someone else? If not Davidson, then who? How do they feel about Figueroa? If you can get a feel for that stuff it will help."

"That's a big order, Lieutenant. I can't talk to too many people or they'll think something is screwy. But I'll see what I can do. Give me a couple of days. Meet me here for a beer Thursday around noon."

• • •

The Naranjeras Autonomous Light Infantry Brigade was moving into position to initiate what Portero believed would be the last batttle of the war. The Toro Battalion was approaching La Capital from the west, while the Lobos were moving in from the north, and two companies of the Tigre Battalion, which had been pulled back from Isla Grande, were closing from the south. The plan was to surround and isolate the city from the rest of the country, to overcome any resistance by destroying or capturing whatever PNN forces remained.

The Brigade Reconnaissance Platoon under Lieutenant Ruedas, having carefully scouted the area around the Estado Mayor, had been assigned the special mission of capturing President Figueroa and his personal staff, alive if possible. It was to enter the city with the Lobos.

General Portero standing at the side of the road by his parked Tracker, watched his Toro Battalion advance in full battle gear, toward the city. The men acknowledged his presence with, "Hey, there's Pancho," when they noticed him, and with, smiles, salutes and waves and an occasional verbal greeting as they passed. He returned their salutes, wished them God speed, and sent them on with words of encouragement.

The Toros had been assigned the mission of capturing the PNN forces in the redoubt area. According to the intelligence provided by Ruedas and his contacts within the city, the enemy was dug in in a strong defensive position within the wooded area of the PNN base. Their defense promised to be formidable. It was built around the ninety millimeter guns of the Cascavel armored cars which were reported to be half buried underground with only their turrets showing above sand-bagged revetments. The Toros had been reinforced with all the Brigade's Javelin missile teams. In addition all available mortar teams were in position prepared to provide fire support.

At Portero's side stood LTC Emilio Sanchez, Toro Battalion Commander. The two had been engaged in conversation, mostly small talk about the troops passing by, the weather and speculation as the whether or not the PNN would actually offer resistance when finally confronted. Sanchez wondered how they could be induced to fight.

"They must know they have lost the war. I can't believe they are willing to defend Figueroa any longer." The words were barely out of Sanchez's mouth when Portero's cell phone buzzed. He answered. A voice announced, "President Figueroa calling for General Francisco Portero."

Portero glanced at Sanchez, a puzzled look on his face, "Portero speaking," he said into the phone.

"Ah, General, I am glad to have reached you. This is Antonio Figueroa."

"Oh ...this is quite a surprise. I had not expected to hear from you. What can I do for you?" He almost added 'Senor Presidente' but caught himself in time.

"I would like to arrange a meeting with you to discuss cessation of hostilities."

"Frankly, Figueroa, I don't see that there is much to discuss. All you have to do is to order your forces to stand down. That will end hostilities."

"Yes, I know that, but there are matters which we should agree upon before I do."

"Oh … What might they be?"

"The matter of transition between my government and yours, for one thing. And the disposition of my people, for another."

"You are talking like someone who has a bargaining position. I can't think of anything you might have to offer, which would cause me to alter my plans."

"Look, Pancho, I am offering my cooperation. I want to save the country more bloodshed. Furthermore, I can help you as you assume the reins of power. I made mistakes when I assumed the presidency. I learned from those mistakes. You can benefit from my experience … General, I assure you I can make it very much worth your while."

Portero did not answer immediately. His mind suddenly flashed back to his meeting with Figueroa in the school at Tuxla where the man offered him a bribe. He wondered if the sonofabitch was trying to do it again. He thought for a moment and finally said, "Okay, Figueroa, I'll meet with you. You order your units to lay down their arms and surrender to my forces and we will meet."

"Not so fast, Pancho. I am not stupid. We meet first and if we come to an agreement my units will stand down. If not, you will have a major battle on your hands … And it will not be easy. We have the fire power and are well prepared for what may come, I assure you."

Portero made a quick decision. "Okay, Figueroa where and when do we meet?"

• • •

Brigade units entered the city without resistance. The Lobos established road blocks on all roads to the north and west and took up positions within hundred meters of the Estado Mayor, the Presidential Palace and other government buildings.

The Toros and the two Tigre Companies established road blocks to the south and encircled the PNN redoubt positions but halted leaving a sufficient distance between the forces not to initiate combat, although a PNN Cascavel did fire a couple of rounds into a Toro Company area inflicting no damage.

By agreement made by telephone, both sides ordered its units to withhold their fire unless attacked. White flags were raised by the units of both sides to signal the cease fire was in effect.

. . .

The meeting between Portero and Figueroa took place two days after the cease fire became effective. The delay was caused by the negotiation as to the location of the meeting site. Figueroa wanted it to take place in the Presidential Palace or the Estado Mayor building but the ALIB staff advised that it should be on neutral ground both for security and psychological reasons. His staff settled on the site of the Quiosco Naranjense which was suggested by Lieutenant Ruedas, but Figueroa would not agree. Finally Portero grew impatient and wanting to get the meeting behind him, agreed to meet Figueroa in the Estado Mayor building.

After discussion between representatives from both sides it was finally decided the meeting would take place in the large vestibule of the building. A table with two chairs was set up in the middle of the space and was surrounded by screens so that no one could watch the participants through the large windows surrounding the room. It was agreed that all doors entering the room would be blocked and guarded by four sentries armed only with billy clubs, two from the PNN, and two from the ALIB.

Portero, dressed in his combat fatigues, arrived at noon, escorted to the site by the fully armed Brigade Recon Platoon. He left them at the steps to the building's entrance and entered the building alone. Figueroa, splendidly attired and wearing the blue-and-white presidential sash of Naranjeros, stood by the table waiting for him.

The men nodded to each other. Figueroa offered his hand, which Portero ignored, saying, "Let's get started. Take a seat, please."

Before he sat down, Figueroa removed the presidential sash and carefully folded it and laid it on the table between them. He took his seat and smiled at Portero, but said nothing.

Portero wondered what the *dramatic posturing by this son of a bitch* was leading to. He broke the silence after a full minute. "You called this meeting. What do you want to talk about?"

"First let me say that I recognize that this war is at an end and that I will be on the losing side. I do believe, however, that I still have some ability to influence how it will end. My hope is that we can come to an agreement which ends it without further bloodshed. There has been far too much of that already. Do you agree?"

"I do agree. I, too, would like to see it end without more bloodshed. But we are prepared to continue the fight as long as it may take. How it ends is up to you. You have the power to stop it today…Now, if you wish to."

"I do so wish…very much. And I am ready to end it now if we can reach agreement on a few matters which I believe are in the best interests of the country."

Portero tried to recall any time Figueroa had put the best interests of the country ahead of his own. He could think of none. He was sure the man, true to form, was now trying to negotiate something for himself. He guessed it was safe passage out of country. "What agreements are you talking about?"

"You will understand, General. I wish to leave Naranjeras with dignity. I realize that history may treat me harshly but it is important to me and to my family, now in Spain, that I salvage some of the honor due a man that served as president of the country we both love. I believe that while I have made mistakes, I also have brought some good things to our people. You do understand, don't you, Pancho?"

Portero marveled at the man's unabashed effrontery. *Does he think I am buying this crap? The man is living in a different world.*

He thought for a moment and then spoke quietly, "I understand you want a way out of the box you have put yourself into. I do not understand why you think I will help you get out of it. I am not exactly a friend."

"Friend or not, I am hoping you will help me in return for the help I can offer you."

Portero thought, *Here it comes.* "What help are you offering me?"

"Well first, I can help you smooth the transition between my administration and yours. Symbolically, I would like to present you now with this emblem of office, the presidential sash of Naranjeras. He pushed the folded cloth toward Portero, who said nothing and made no move to take it.

Figueroa sat back. After a moment he continued. "You will find, General, that governing is not an easy task, as I have found. One has personalities to deal with. One has to learn who he can trust. Who can make things happen and who can't. I can tell you who is who in the bureaucracy. Some are good and some are worthless. My experience can help you."

"You'll have to do a lot better than that. First, I do not intend to establish what you refer to as 'my administration.' I do not intend to be president. I will be acting as military governor only until we can organize an election. Besides that, what makes you think I would respect, even believe, any recommendation coming from you? In a very short time, you have managed to completely disrupt, I might say ruin, the country. You have bankrupted us. You have alienated most of the population. You have almost killed a once humming business climate. You couldn't even win a war—even when you outgunned us.

"In my view, you are an incompetent. In my view, you are a self-serving, egotistical son of a bitch who thought you could grow rich as a result of your illegal coup. What can you possibly tell me that I could believe?"

Figueroa stiffened and hesitated. Finally he said, "You have me at a disadvantage, Portero. You are free with your insults, and I am in no position to respond to them. But the fact is I do have information I am sure you would like to have, even if you don't become the president."

"For example?"

"For example, I am sure you would like to know the source of the financing and the support for our coup—how it came about."

"I have a good idea about that: Lybia and Cuba. We're not without intelligence resources. I also know that your motivation, aside from expecting to enrich yourself, was to embarrass the North Americans in the international arena. You don't have much to offer there."

He continued. "What I do want to know is who was responsible for the murder of my wife, my chief of staff, and six fine young soldiers. I want to know that. I also want to know who organized the propaganda campaign against the ALIB in the U.S., and how you connected with the anti-American activists up there. I want to know how you thought you had the legal authority to close down the newspaper in La Mesona and arrest its editors. These are the things I want to know…and you can add, what part you played in the murder of my Sergeant Campinas in La Rioja."

Figueroa sat studying Portero, wide eyed, then spread his hands, palms up in a conciliatory gesture. Then spoke quietly, earnestly." Please believe I knew nothing about the La Rioja affair until it was over. Also I had no part in the bombing incident which killed your wife. I regret that. It was a mistake. Clearly you were to be the target. Some overzealous people, Davidson included, thought we were close to war and believed by eliminating you, a war could be averted. As to the campaign in the USA, as I recall, Tercio Ortega worked on that. And as to the La Mesona newspaper, I believe Marco Menendez organized that."

Portero remained silent.

Figueroa continued. "I am guessing why you want to know the details about the things you have mentioned and I believe it is because you would like to take legal actions against those involved. Am I correct?"

Portero still said nothing.

"Okay, General, if I am correct, I can help you there. I am willing to provide you with my depositions on whatever I am aware of in these matters. I will provide you with any information I have: names of those involved, dates, everything insofar as I know them. You appoint the lawyers. I will do this in a spirit of cooperation with you. In return, will you give me your word I will be allowed to leave the country without problems?"

Finally, Portero responded. "That is a start, Figueroa. A small step in the right direction. What else can you do for me? And, don't even think of holding me hostage for an order from you directing your troops to stand down. I will tell you now, if only one Naranjero on either side is killed or injured because your units resisted, I will hold you personally responsible. You will give the order for them to surrender…that is not negotiable. Do you understand?"

Figueroa fidgeted. He stood up and walked around the room, agitated, for a long minute. When he returned to the table and resumed his seat, he declared in a quiet voice, "You have me over a barrel, General…ah, I am coming to you now as a supplicant. I really have nothing more to offer you except…I hesitate to bring it up, because you once turned me down when I offered you money. But now it seems it is all I have left to offer. What else can I do?"

"How much money?"

Figueroa raised his head and sat forward in his chair. Portero studied him closely and saw a hint of the slyness he remembered from their Tuxla meeting creep into back into the man's expression.

"I don't have a lot of money…but I can manage two million in US dollars?"

"Where would that money come from?"

"I have a Swiss account. It is my personal account. Don't worry, it is not tax payer money. It came from sources outside the country." He waited.

"Five million." Portero said quietly.

"Good God! I don't have that much."

"Get it…you do want to be with your family in Spain?"

"Yes. But I must have something to live on. My God, Portero. Be reasonable."

"Think of what is at stake." Portero arose, as if to leave.

"If I can get the money, will I be able to leave the country?"

"First, you make the depositions. Then hand me an irrevocable bank draft for five million US dollars, payable to the account of Naranjeras Veterans Family Education Foundation at the Banco Central de La Republica. When these things have been accomplished and the money has been deposited, I will use what authority I may have to see you safely out of the country…as soon as it may be possible. You have my word on that."

CHAPTER 23

On the fifth day following his meeting with Figueroa, Portero received notification from the president of the bank that five million dollars had been transferred and deposited to the just-established trust fund for Naranjeras Soldiers Family Education Foundation. At the time, Figueroa was under house arrest in the presidential palace and was being deposed by three lawyers of impeccable reputation, recommended by Ramon Sanchez Avila and the ALIB legal officer. Word that the money had arrived was delivered to Figueroa along with instructions to the Lobo company commander responsible for the security of the building that Figueroa was to continue under arrest until otherwise ordered.

In addition, Figueroa's, key military and civilian staff and junta members were being held incommunicado in separate locations, pending interrogation. Included among them were Davidson, the Cubans Molina and Serra, the former ministers of interior and foreign affairs, Menendez and Ortega, Mario Fox, former president of the Asemblea Nacional, and Figueroa's personal secretary.

Colonel Banning's staff, assisted by PNN Captain Simoni, were charged with identifying and contacting witnesses to possible illegal activities involving Figueroa and members of his administration. That became an exceedingly time-consuming undertaking as accusations proliferated when it was publicly known investigations were underway. Banning predicted it would be months before the process could be completed, which was frustrating to Portero, who had hoped for a speedy resolution.

• • •

The ALIB Headquarters had been moved into offices in the Estado Mayor, which also housed the PNN Headquarters Staff. Portero had named LTC Sanchez of the Toro Battalion "Acting Commandant" of the national police forces, pending the return of Gin Pot Johnson. Sanchez was spending long days interviewing and evaluating the PNN Chiefs of all police posts in the country, most of whom he reappointed.

The three PNN security companies that had provided security for the Estado Mayor complex had been disarmed, except for batons, and kept on duty, one on one with Lobo Battalion personnel assigned to security duties in the area.

The PNN combat formations in the defensive redoubt area adjacent to the PNN main base, when confronted by the Toros, offered no resistance and surrendered en masse. Their personnel were being screened in a process parallel to that established in La Boca for the PNN troops captured on Isla Grande.

• • •

General Portero's days had grown longer and much busier since the cease-fire. His time was occupied not only with his duties as brigade commander, but now also as Military Governor, trying to deal with a whole new set of problems associated with re-starting the government which had collapsed with the ouster of Figueroa—problems outside Portero's experience.

Bureaucrats from the various departments had remained in place but were without direction, and the affairs of state were grinding to a halt. Portero was spending much of his time trying to learn how the machinery of government was meant to work, and trying to get it restarted. There was a seemingly never-ending stream of department heads coming to him for direction on issues he knew little about. For the most part, he had no solutions to offer, but his advice to them was consistent. "Conduct your business as usual, but keep your expenditures to the minimum. You will be informed of changes to be made in your operations when the time comes. Meantime I trust you to make the right decisions. Remember, your duty is to serve the people—and not yourself or your department. As long as you do that, we'll get along fine. You are the leader in your department, and as such, you have a sacred trust to serve Naranjeras. If I find that you or any one of your subordinates violates that trust to even the slightest degree, you will wish you were in hell. I am not a forgiving man. Do you understand?"

After a week of dealing with the bureaucratic establishment, the general began to receive feedback. The phrase, "El Oreja is not a forgiving man," had apparently gained considerable currency around capitol offices. He was puzzled at first by being called "El Oreja," until he remembered the notch in his ear caused by a PNN bullet in La Boca. He resigned himself to the fact that he had suddenly acquired a nickname—he thought it could have been worse, and he was both amused and pleased that his oft-repeated admonition had made an impression.

• • •

The process of screening the captured PNN troops in the capital area was well underway, assisted by Major Mix of the Osos, who had had the experience screening the PNN from Isla Grande. As was the case with Isla Grande Brigade, about half of the captured PNN were foreigners, and tensions between them and the ALIB men persisted. The Naranjeros deeply resented the fact that Cubans, Nicaraguans, and others had come to fight them in their own country.

However, the situation was different with the two Lobo companies on security duty at the capitol complex. They had settled in on their new assignment and were working smoothly with the three PNN companies, which were all Naranjeros. Any suspicion or rancor between the sides quickly disappeared and was replaced by respect and budding friendships. The same thing was occurring between the Lobo units occupying Puerto Hondo and their PNN counterparts there. The willingness of the troops from either side to accept one another as equals did not go unnoticed by the ALIB staff, which began to consider the possibility of integrating some PNN formations into the ALIB.

• • •

With the fighting ended, tensions among the people in La Capital and in the country began to relax. It was as if the nation breathed a great corporate sigh of relief, and the people began to resume their lives, which had been disrupted by the fighting.

The newspapers and radio and television broadcasters were occupied with the breaking news mostly centered on General Portero's activities. He was the man of the hour. The media had taken to referring to him simply as "Pancho." He was lauded everywhere as their national hero and savior of the country. Mothers were naming their babies after him. Musicians were singing songs about him. His picture materialized on billboards and on the sides of buildings throughout the country. He had become the focus of the nation's attention.

The adulation embarrassed Portero and made him uncomfortable. He was not used to it, and he considered it all distracting, unwarranted, and emotional nonsense. He was particularly irritated by the fact that it forced him to act a part which he not only did not deserve, but more importantly, it took time he needed to learn his new responsibilities.

Portero also worried about his soldiers getting spoiled. After the victory, they too were treated as heroes, eliciting smiles, *abrazos*, and applause wherever they went. Needless to say, they took full advantage of their new celebrity. The problem was that some of them were inclined to exploit it, and step over the line in their conduct. This was a matter of concern to their commanders, who were under orders to come down hard on any excesses. The new theme to be hammered into the consciousness of the men was "Remember, you are liberators and not conquerors. Your job is to serve the people and not to be served by them."

Portero subscribed to the age-old military axiom that soldiers occupied in useful pursuits are less apt to get themselves into trouble. His biggest challenge in that regard was finding the useful pursuits. For those units not occupied in demanding security and screening missions or civil rebuilding projects, he ordered rigorous new training regimens. Military spit and polish was back in vogue with a vengeance three weeks after cessation of combat operations.

· · ·

The general also drove himself, putting long, tiring days at tasks he did not enjoy. Among the complications in his new life was the unanticipated demand for interviews by the foreign media, particularly by US newspapers. He was surprised at the sudden unprecedented interest in Naranjeras affairs. There had been five or six requests per week. Many of them he handed off to Major Lacerica, but he felt obliged to meet the reporters of the most influential publications.

He had given personal interviews to the *Washington Post*, the *Miami Harold*, the *New York Times*, and later the *Wall Street Journal*, and was fascinated by the differences in the interests of each publication. Some were fairly straightforward seekers of facts, while others were confrontational and approached the interview with obvious biases.

He was particularly annoyed by the meeting with the *Times* reporter. She had brought an interpreter with her and was surprised to discover he spoke English. "Oh General," she gushed, "Where ever did you learn your English—it's so good? You even have an American accent."

He thought, *What a stupid woman,* but smiled and said, "In school. Now how can I help you?"

It soon became obvious that her interest was more about possible US involvement in the war than about Naranjeras affairs. After cursory questions about himself, the ALIB, and his quarrel with the Figueroa government, she surprised him with, "Do you think, General, you could have won the war without the support of the US Army?"

Again he smiled and quietly asked, "What support?"

"Any support it might have given you?"

"We received no support from the US Army."

"Oh? But General, it is a fact isn't it, that the Army sent you two helicopters when you attacked Figueroa troops at La Campana?"

"My dear young lady, first, please understand, we did not attack the PNN at La Campana. They attacked us."

"But didn't you start it? Our information indicates you first blocked traffic on the main highway between the capital and La Mesona? That you paralyzed commerce between the two cities?"

"Your information is wrong. It is true that we established a roadblock in La Campana, but we did not stop traffic on the highway. We allowed all north-south civilian traffic to pass, and we allowed all southbound government traffic to pass. We only blocked travel by government vehicles going north."

"Why?"

"That action was taken to protect the rights of the press in La Mesona. Our national constitution guarantees a free press, as does yours. Were you aware the Figueroa government had illegally arrested the publisher, the editor, and senior executives of *La Prensa,* after that newspaper criticized certain actions taken by the regime, which it believed were unlawful?"

"No, I wasn't but—"

"Well the Figueroa government did make those arrests, which were clearly illegal under our law. I had a choice, either to do nothing or to act in consonance with my oath as a commissioned officer of the Republic, namely to 'defend the constitution against all enemies foreign and domestic.' I believe members of your own armed forces take a similar oath. To make a long story short, we liberated those journalists and returned them to La Mesona. The purpose of our roadblock was to prevent the PNN from going back to re-arrest them. Would you not have done the same?"

"Ah...well...But we are getting off the subject, General. What about those US helicopters that arrived during the battle?"

"It is true that two US Army helicopters did arrive then. However, they were not sent to support us. Quite the opposite. They were sent to observe our actions...to monitor us. Those choppers brought observers sent by the commander of HJRAF to track the situation on behalf of the United States and the HDO—to monitor us. In other words, they came to observe and report what we were doing...Presumably to insure we acted in accordance with the rules of war—whatever they might be. They certainly did not come to support us."

When the reporter finally filled up her recorder, she thanked him for the interview and departed. He later learned that the article, when published, declared that the "ALIB commander had been evasive and not completely forthright in answering the question about the US Army involvement in the war."

A week after the *New York Times* interview, he met with an editorial writer from the *Wall Street Journal*. He assumed it would be more of the same but was pleasantly surprised to find that she was fluent in Spanish, despite her Irish name, and was exceedingly well-informed about Latin American affairs and the history of Naranjeras. She had background information on Figueroa, which he was able to confirm and expand upon.

She also quizzed him at length on his thoughts about the Hemispheric Defense Organization and its Rapid Action Force. He was frank to say he had first believed the HJRAF had been an effective and necessary means of meeting regional defense needs. However, he added that its organizers clearly had not solved the problem of keeping the military units contributed by the member nations from becoming embroiled in local politics. His conclusion was that in the end, the concept of the HJRAF would have to be abandoned. But he declared a great positive resulting from the initiative had been the standardization of the various national forces, resulting from the training they had received from the US military. He thought that training had created a new closeness, a better understanding, and built mutual respect between the participating nations and the United States.

• • •

Portero's immediate personal focus was planning for an event he dreaded but knew had to be done and done well. It was his address to the nation in which he would pronounce himself "Military Governor, acting for the President yet to be elected". A group of his advisors, led by Ramon Sanchez Avila, had urged him to call himself "Acting President," which he stubbornly resisted on the basis that the constitution provided the President be elected by the people. They also had recommended the address be a comprehensive recitation of his plans for the nation. He rejected that advice also, declaring that he was not a Fidel Castro who could talk on for hours. Aside from that, his plans for the nation were still in development. He insisted the speech be limited to two themes—a declaration that there would be elections for the presidency and the national assembly within six months, and that it be a simple overview of the actions to be taken to initiate the national recovery.

His event planning committee was chaired by the mayor of La Mesona and included Ramon Sanchez Avila, the publisher of *La Prensa,* the chairmen of the Cattlemen's Association, the presiding bishop of the church, the chairman of the National Bankers Association, and five mayors from the most populace municipalities in Naranjeras. The members wrangled internally about what its recommendations were to be on the content of the speech.

Portero was willing to look at the committee's recommendations as a matter of courtesy, but he had made up his mind that if the speech was to be his own, he had to be its author.

The address was planned as the central feature, the climax of an elaborate victory ceremony in the capital square before several thousand attendees. During the week before the ceremony, there would be parades and band concerts in the residential districts of La Capital. The day before there would be a soccer game in the national stadium, featuring the ALIB team, ill-prepared and out of practice due to the war, challenging the Naranjeras national team. All of the events were to be broadcast on national radio and television, and would require guest appearances by Portero or his battalion commanders.

· · ·

General Portero was in joint conference with his staff and the ceremony planning committee when he was handed a message that LTC Antonio DaSilva, the Lobo Battalion commander, had just arrived from Panama, where he had been for some time at the side of his critically wounded wife. They interrupted the meeting and invited him in. He was grinning broadly, greeting his colleagues and shaking hands with the civilians, most of whom he had not met. His joy was evident, irrepressible, and contagious. Everyone present was smiling and laughing with him.

"Welcome back, Colonel. It seems you bring good news for us." Portero was first to speak.

"Yes, General, Chris is going to be fine. She is still in pretty tough shape, but the doctors believe she will make a full recovery—more importantly, she says she will. She kicked me out and sent me home. She sends her love to all, and especially you, General. She insists you saved her life...For which I also thank you." He gave his commander an enthusiastic abrazo.

The group cheered, and everyone congratulated DaSilva with abrazos all around.

He brought additional good news. Gin Pot Johnson was also recovering from his wounds, and he expected to return to duty within weeks. He sent saludos to all.

That was particularly good news to Portero. He needed Johnson to assume command of the PNN as its interim commandant, Sanchez was anxious to return to his Toros and get started with his additional assignment of reactivating the ALIB Recruit Training Center in Valle Escondido. Both Gin Pot and Sanchez were in line for promotion to Colonel, a rank commensurate with their time in grade and their new responsibilities. Portero took advantage of the festive situation to announce their promotions. He also announced that Major Mix would be promoted to Lieutenant Colonel and Lieutenant Rueda to Captain. Mix and Rueda were invited to join the group and refreshments were brought in, and the group enjoyed a brief but happy promotion party.

• • •

That night in his quarters, Portero, exhausted by another long day, lay down on his cot and waited for sleep. He remembered DaSilva's joy over his wife's prognosis, and his own sense of relief at the news that Chris would recover, having been convinced in his own mind that she could not survive her wounds. He took a moment for a prayer of thanksgiving and felt a rush of the same joy Tony had so obviously felt that morning.

Suddenly his thoughts jumped to his own wife, and a sense of guilt overtook him. It was a shock to realize that he hadn't thought of Betsy for a number of days. He had been so busy that she had been completely out of his mind. "Forgive me, Betsy, for neglecting you. Things are happening pretty fast here. And, I find myself in another one of those situations I don't know how to handle. You always knew how to straighten me out when that happened…I really miss you. I wish you could be here. I have won this damn war, and now I have to figure out how to run the country. What do I know about doing that? I could sure use your help now."

He got up and put one of her favorite CDs into his player. Her music concentrated his memories of her. He remembered her loving nature, the fun they had together, her kindness and patience with him when he was preoccupied with something, the support and wise counsel she had offered him when he needed it most. Suddenly, a vivid memory of her quoting him quoting General Patton came into his head. He could hear her sweet, impatient voice admonishing him. "Pancho, dammit, do not take counsel of your fears. Go do what you must do."

With that thought, Brigadier General Portero, commander of the victorious Autonomous Light Infantry Brigade and now acting as Military Governor of the Republic of Naranjeras, fell into a deep, restful sleep, his first in many nights.

• • •

At six o'clock the next morning, Portero, feeling refreshed, was lingering over his breakfast coffee, reading the newspapers when his cell phone began to chirp. He answered to hear a familiar voice. "Good morning, Pancho. I hoped to reach you before you got to work. Do you know who this is?" A surprising question which immediately alerted Portero, and he was cautious with his answer.

"Ah...Yes, I do."

"Good. I am on my way north and want to stop and see you briefly. Our estimated ETA there is zero nine forty-five your time. Can you meet me at International?"

"Certainly...I'll be there."

"Good. Come alone and keep this under your hat...Ah, Pancho...way under. Understand?"

"Yes, and will do."

"Thanks...See you there. Out."

Portero left his coffee and newspapers and headed for his office. There he called for Major Lacerica, who arrived promptly.

"Good morning, Guillermo. I've got to go down to Puerto Hondo to see DaSilva on a confidential matter. Order a tracker from the motor pool and drive me yourself. We should leave here at eight thirty, no later. This is pretty sensitive. I'll explain it to you later, so don't talk about it."

"I understand, sir. I'll be waiting out front with the car at eight fifteen."

Portero then called DaSilva and advised him he expected to arrive in Puerto Hondo around eleven or eleven thirty, and that Lacerica would be with him. The Lobo commander indicated he would be pleased to see them and invited them to lunch.

Lacerica and the general drove away from the Estado Mayor at eight twenty-five, headed for the national highway. Once underway, Portero, informed his aide that they were to make a stop at the Aeropuerto Internacional before proceeding to Puerto Hondo, and that he was to meet General Carmody, who was stopping briefly on his way north. "You know nothing about this, Guillermo. All you know is that we stopped off at the airport to do some business on the way to Puerto Hondo. Understood?"

"Understood, General. And, General," Lacerica said, smiling, "for the record, I asked to drive you myself this morning in order to have some time to discuss several matters I had pending. You have been so busy lately. Thanks for giving me the opportunity, sir."

Portero chuckled. "You're welcome, Major."

They reached the airport at eight fifteen. Lacerica went inside to discuss some public relations matters with the Toro Company commander in charge at the airport, while General Portero waited on the tarmac in the arrivals area.

A sleek business jet, sporting the Panamanian flag on its tail and the name "Transportes General de Panama" on its fuselage, pulled up and parked fifty meters west of the main arrival gate.

The passenger door opened and a steward, a package in hand, descended and waited at the foot of the extended aircraft steps. Portero strolled toward the jet and was greeted by the crewman who handed him the package. They appeared to engage in conversation, during which the general seemed to point at the aircraft, whereupon the man stepped aside and motioned him to climb aboard.

Portero entered to see General Carmody sitting with his aide Captain Jaime Hanson at a table in the well-appointed cabin. He greeted them smiling, happy to see them. "Hello, General. Jimmy, how is your arm?"

"Welcome aboard, Pancho. Sorry about all this cloak and dagger stuff. The fact is I am not here. You never saw me. This is only a currier flight, and that package you have contains some sensitive material ostensibly from me to you. I must emphasize…it is important that you play this little game.

"Now please sit down for a moment. When you get back to your headquarters, you'll find in that package are some official documents, full of legalese, declaring the US Army is severing all ties with ALIB. You are no longer part of the HJRAF. Officially that was the decision of the Secretary General of the Hemispheric Defense Organization. But between you and me, he was reluctant to sign it and only did so because of pressure brought on by US government. I might add it was pushed by certain left-wingers in the senate. You can guess who."

"El Raton Blanco, for one. The Sandinista lover, I'd guess."

"You'd be right, my boy. It seems he was a Figueroa lover as well."

"I admire your country, General, as you well know. But I cannot understand why assholes like that guy have so much influence. He must have backing from the people somewhere."

"He does—from the left wing, the hate-America crowd who manipulate the thinking of a substantial number of know-nothings who are, shall we say, economically dependent on government subsidies. They are a minority, but they are easily led and their voices are loud, and the press loves them because they make for lively news stories. Look at the stir that silly woman from Minnesota created down here when she went after you."

Portero was puzzled. "I can't understand why the people up there did not react when Figueroa illegally took control of our government here…Or why they are not cheering that we took it back."

"Because, Pancho, most of them never heard of Naranjeras until the war started. They don't know a thing about the country except that you and the ALIB overthrew the government. You have become quite a villain up there among some people. Now they are adding the HJRAF to their hitlist. They are saying the HJRAF has manipulated the United States Army…and that I permitted it to happen. I'll be lucky if I am allowed to retire with my rank."

"That is ridiculous! I am sorry that I put you in that position."

"Don't be, Pancho. You did the right thing. You did what you had to do for your country. And that brings me to the reason I wanted to talk to you face-to-face. First, I want you to know that I am proud of the way you have handled your little war. It was masterful! And I am not the only one who thinks that. The Chief has told me that among your admirers is the Secretary of Defense himself, and there are plenty of others around the Pentagon. I can also tell you that your counterparts in the HJRAF, including the Secretary General of HDO, are all rooting for you."

"That surprises me. I can't tell you how gratifying it is to hear it. Thank you for telling me, General."

"What I really want to say is that in your new role as the country's leader, do not allow the changed status between Naranjeras and the United States to create new animosities, to become something other than what it is. Don't let your spokespeople get bellicose about new tensions. In Washington, it is what it is. It is CYA politics as usual, and it will pass. Meantime there will be people in Defense in your corner—and even some at State,

I'm sure—probably plenty at Commerce as well. They all will be working quietly to rehabilitate your reputation. It is in both countries' best long-range interests to do so, and the conscientious people know that. So don't let anything happen here that will dampen that reservoir of goodwill toward Naranjeras up there. Do you understand. Pancho?"

"Yes, sir. I most certainly do. To be honest, I haven't had time to think about what our relations with the U.S. should be. Now you have given me something to build on. It is heartening to know there are some bridges left unburned up there. Thank you, sir."

"Come on, Pancho, quit 'sir'-ing me. Hell, it should be the other way around. You are a head of state now. I should be 'sir'-ing you...And I am proud of you and what you have accomplished. Congratulations, Mr. President...sir."

"I am not President. Only a temporary military governor. We'll have elections within a year, I hope."

"Well, I'm betting you will be President someday."

Carmody stood up and offered his hand, then turned it into a hearty abrazo. There were tears in his eyes. "Good-bye, son. If I can help you, you know where I am. Now get the hell off of my airplane. I'll be late getting to Washington, and don't forget that package."

Portero turned to Hanson. "Thanks for all your help, Jimmy. If you ever need a job, I'll have one for you." They also exchanged abrazos. Portero saluted them and stepped out of the aircraft, a lump in his throat.

• • •

Colonel Banning, Captain Simoni, and the ALIB legal officer, after several days of research, compiled names of likely witnesses of alleged crimes committed by individuals connected with the Figueroa regime. They focused mainly upon two signal events. The first was the assault on Carlos Campinas in La Rioja by the Cuban, Gallo, which resulted in the death of both Sergeant Campinas and Gallo. The witness list for that event included Siomoni himself, Lieutenant Rueda, Molina, Serra, the La Rioja Hotel manager, the bar waitress, the bartender's girlfriend, and Sanchez Avila, who supplied witness names.

The second focus was on the assassination attempt on Portero, which resulted in the deaths of his wife, Colonel Soto, and six ALIB soldiers. That witness list included Figueroa, Davidson, Molina, Corporal Rubio, Angelita, the barber, and Sergeant Carranza.

Both crimes fell within military jurisdiction, so the decision was the trials would be by courts-martial, and the convening authority would be the Commanding General of the ALIB.

• • •

By coincidence, Portero was informed that Figueroa was anxious to meet with him just as he was reading Banning's witness lists. He noted with interest that Figueroa had been listed as a possible witness in the assassination attempt.

He directed that Figueroa be brought to his office that afternoon and ordered a secretary be present to record the minutes of the meeting. He also asked that both Banning and the legal officer to be present.

Portero and the others were waiting in his office when Figueroa was escorted in by two Lobo Battalion soldiers. The man showed some surprise at seeing others present. Turning to Portero, he said, "I had thought, General, this was to be a private meeting."

"Do you know Colonel Banning, my B-2? And this is my legal officer. The corporal here is my secretary. He is here to take notes. What did you wished to see me about?"

"Well…if you are sure you do not want this to be a private discussion between us. I personally would prefer it be private… ah…I expected to discuss our agreement."

"What agreement is that?"

"We agreed that if I deposited the money in the Banco Nacional account, you would allow me to join my family in Spain."

"Apparently you misunderstood me. I made no such agreement. What I did was give you my word that I would do everything within my authority to see that you were given safe passage out of the country as early as possible, once you had provided certain depositions and those funds were received."

"Well, General…I have provided the depositions and the funds have been deposited, so why am I still here?"

"You are still here because under established Naranjeras law, I do not have the authority to permit your departure. You may recall that under our law, persons under indictment for crimes, or under investigation for crimes, shall not be permitted exit visas until the matters have been resolved. Since you are under investigation, I have no authority to permit you to leave."

Figueroa's jaw dropped and he stammered, "But under the law, the President has the authority to pardon or commute sentences."

"You are correct. But you forget I am not the President."

"But you are acting in that capacity, aren't you? For God's sake, General. You're splitting hairs. An agreement is an agreement!"

"I am not Acting President. I am temporarily the military governor of Naranjeras, nothing more. Presidents must be elected under our constitution. That is a fact you overlooked when you engineered your golpe."

"If you are military governor, the country must be under martial law…In which case, the civil law does not apply. Isn't that correct, Major?" A visibly desperate Figueroa turned to the legal officer.

"In a country under martial law, the law is established by the governing authority. In this case, General Portero."

Portero looked at Figueroa, who was visibly agitated and was glaring at him in disbelief. "You mean…?"

"That is correct, Figueroa. As military governor, I have chosen to reinstate civil law as enunciated by our constitution. Part of my oath of office as an officer commissioned in the military forces of Naranjeras is to uphold the laws of the nation. That is what I intend to do. By the way, you took the same oath when you were commissioned in the PNN. Had you forgotten? I don't have to remind you that you violated that oath...or do I?"

"But you made a commitment...a man-to-man commitment...I kept my part, and I expect you to honor your part."

"And so I will. If you are found to be without guilt in any crime in which it is alleged you have been involved, I will keep my word. I will see that you leave the country without delay. Is there anything more you wish to say?"

Figueroa was suddenly angry. "And if some kangaroo court... produces some trumped up charges against me and declares I was implicated in some alleged crime, what then?"

"Clearly you understand how kangaroo courts work, having used them yourself after seizing power. I tell you now, those days are over. Naranjeras will no longer tolerate such courts. But to answer your question, if you are found to be implicated in any crime, you will be charged and tried in a real court, and if you are found guilty, you will be punished according to law. Is there anything further?"

Figueroa was escorted out, sputtering in protest.

• • •

Despite his busy schedule and the pressure of preparing for his address to the nation, at the back of Portero's mind was the memory of his meeting with General Carmody, and particularly the general's advice on what the relationship between Naranjeras and the United States should be. He had given some thought to foreign policy and to the relationship with the colossus of the north. Personally, he greatly admired his wife's country, which had played such an important part in his life and career. He liked North Americans, by and large, but had been disappointed by their lack of interest and knowledge of Central America in general, and in Naranjeras, in particular.

He had entertained an idea that his country's relationship with the U.S. should be cordial but neutral. But now that the military alliance under the HJRAF Treaty had been ended, he assumed the close ties and spirit of cooperation between the countries would fade away. However, Carmody's assurance that key leaders in the Pentagon and in other Washington bureaucracies held a certain regard for him and Naranjeras had caused him to rethink what the relationship might be.

He addressed the question as a military man, asking himself, *If the objective is to build a continuing close relationship with the United States, what must I do to bring it about?* Two actions came immediately to mind. First he had to signal in his coming address to the nation that Naranjeras would continue to be open to cooperation with Washington and with American business. He recognized that any such statement had to be carefully crafted not to alarm the nationalist element in his own population, influential men like Sanchez Avila. Also he was aware of other groups which were angered by the notion that the U.S. had not supported them in their time of need during the struggle against Figueroa.

The second action, and an extremely important one, was to make sure that proper channels of communication be established between the two governments. That meant that his selection of the foreign minister and the ambassador to the United States had to be right. Of equal importance would be the selection of the military and commercial attaches to be posted in Washington.

He understood the foreign minister must play the key role in building solid international relationships. It had to be someone experienced and knowledgeable in international affairs, who would be respected within that community. However, he knew of no one who passed his simple screening matrix. His candidates had to be patriots, intelligent, educated people, interested in world affairs, fluent in English, and experienced in working with North Americans. He had good candidates for the subordinate foreign policy posts, ambassador and attaches, but no one for the top job. He knew little of the career people in the Foreign Ministry, but he tended to distrust them as entrenched bureaucrats and was determined to look elsewhere for his foreign minister. He decided to ask the advice of his advisory committee in the matter.

However, he thought he had excellent candidates for the ambassadorial post in two of his senior ALIB staff officers. Both Colonels Roth and Banning fit his matrix and seemed equally qualified. Both had developed close relationships up north as a function of their ALIB responsibilities; Roth with the logistics community, and Banning with the intelligence people. Both men were level-headed, clear thinkers, and well-educated. Both had proved to be adept problem solvers, and both spoke English with almost no accent. It was a toss-up between them, but in the end, he picked Banning as his first choice on the basis that the intelligence community in Washington might have greater political influence than the logistical people.

He thought DaSilva, Mix, and Rueda would all be good candidates for the Military Attaché post, and that the President of The Cattleman's Association would make a strong Commercial Attaché. At least he would be able to recommend someone capable for the job.

Aside from the foreign minister, he supposed the ambassador designate should have some say in the selection of the attachés who would be part of his team. His first task then became persuading Banning to accept the assignment. He suspected it would be a tough sell. Banning, despite his Dutch descent, was the most enthusiastic Naranjero on the staff, and Portero was sure he would be loath to exchange his comfortable home in Valle Escondido for the high pressure lifestyle in Washington, D.C. It would mean moving his family and finding schools for his seven children. But Banning was a patriot and would rise to the challenge, or so Portero hoped.

CHAPTER 24

The day the national media had labeled "Restoration Day" finally arrived. It was the day General Portero was to announce the restoration of democracy in Naranjeras. The weather was perfect, bright and clear. Rain showers the previous night had washed the capitol plaza clean and left freshness in the air as the morning sun warmed the scene.

The perimeter of the great plaza in front of the Estado Mayor was decorated with national flags and bouquets of blue and white bunting. A large, raised stage also draped in blue and white had been erected on the steps leading up to the Estado Mayor building. At its front, the speakers' rostrum was already festooned with a battery of microphones. Technicians were testing and adjusting the sound system over which the speeches would be delivered to the assembly via loud speakers strategically place throughout the square.

Teams of Lobo Battalion soldiers and PNN policemen in crisp parade uniforms were taking their positions around the perimeter and at the several entrances to the square.

Hawkers' stands, offering commemorative souvenirs, small flags, balloons, cushions, and pictures of General Portero, were being manned as were booths selling empanadas, elotes, fruit, coffee, and soft drinks.

Excited people, mostly dressed in their Sunday best filtered into the plaza carrying blankets and folding chairs to stake out a place in the square. There they were entertained by the folkloric musicians of the ALIB band, who traded the stage periodically with a variety of popular local musical groups.

By noon, the square was full, a sea of people laughing, singing, and dancing to the music, eagerly anticipating the ceremonies to come. Roving TV cameras from national stations worked through the crowds, doing "man-in-the-street" interviews and recording the antics of the happy people.

At the stroke of twelve, the ALIB band, which had taken seats by the stage, struck up familiar military marches interspersed with traditional Naranjeras dances and festival music. The crowd erupted in delighted roars of recognition as the first familiar chords of each piece of music sounded.

While the music boomed forth, the invited dignitaries and guests began to occupy their assigned seats. The ALIB Battalion commanders and key staff officers took seats in the back row. The two front rows were reserved for ambassadors and their wives from neighboring nations, and city mayors and their families, except those functionaries who had been appointed by Figueroa were conspicuously absent. The presidents of various banks and larger private businesses, who had not cooperated with the Figueroa administration, were also given seats of honor along with the bishops of the church, and the editors of all newspapers except *El Diario*. Conspicuous in the first row seated at both sides of the podium were the Archbishop of Naranjeras, the Mayor of La Mesona, the editors of *La Prensa* and *Vida Nacional*, the President of the Cattlemens Association, Ramon Sanchez Avila, and General Francisco Portero.

Portero arrived to a standing ovation by the dignitaries which spread to the crowded square. He took his seat as the band concluded its rendition of the ever-popular Mexican march, "Zacatecas." Trumpeters blew flourishes to a drum roll, and all stood once again as the band struck up, "Patria Nuestra," the national anthem of Naranjeras. The voices of the entire assembly joined in, lustily singing the familiar words. It was a magic moment which stirred powerful emotions in Portero, who smiled broadly as he sang. The end of the anthem was greeted with another roar and loud applause from the packed square, which was finally quieted by the familiar voice of a local radio announcer.

"Fellow Naranjeros, welcome to restoration day—the day we celebrate liberty regained!" Another roar [arose] from the crowd, louder than ever.

When it quieted, the voice introduced the Archbishop of Nranajeras who blessed the throng and gave the invocation, thanking "Almighty God for delivering the country from the dark days of oppression and returning it into the sunlight of freedom." He lauded General Francisco Portero and the brave soldiers of the Light Infantry Brigade as "instruments of God's delivering angels."

The voice then introduced each dignitary seated in the front row of the dais, who stood in turn to wave to the crowd. The procedure required ten minutes to complete, interrupted as it was with the cheers of the regional constituents of each mayor. The loudest and most universal applause followed the introduction of the Mayor of La Mesona. The venerable old gentleman was helped to his feet by an aide, once standing, he threw two-handed kisses at the cheering throng, then he walked to Portero to embrace him, to the further delight of all.

Finally, the announcer introduced Ramon Sanchez Avilla, the respected senior reporter and columnist of *Vida Nacional*. He received a warm reception from the assembly. Somewhat embarrassed by the applause, Sanchez Avila finally managed to wave them silent.

"*Mis hermanos Naranjeros.* Thank you for your welcome. It is probably more than I deserve, for reasons I will explain. First let me say thank you for being here. The fact that you are here in such numbers, and with so much enthusiasm, is clearly an endorsement of what His Excellency, the Reverend Father, called our beloved nation's 'delivery from dark days of oppression.' I agree. It is certainly that—and I also agree that we owe our liberation to our magnificent infantry brigade and its commander, the man of the hour, General Francisco 'Pancho' Portero." A deafening roar of applause.

"I agree…Viva! Don Pancho!"

When the applause finally subsided, he continued in a quieter tone. "Now my confession to you. As some of you may remember, I have not always been a fan of Pancho Portero, nor of his brigade, nor, for that matter, the HJRAF. I believed then it was all a contrivance to strengthen North America's hegemonic hold in our part of the world. I thought the brigade's presence in Naranjeras demonstrated disrespect for our sovereignty as a nation—and I confess to you, I thought Pancho Portero was an opportunist who was more gringo than Naranjero. In fact, I wrote a column or two saying as much. May God forgive me for that."

Some laughter from the crowd.

"I was wrong, and I apologize to you and to General Portero now. That was before I understood who Antonio Figueroa really was, and what his intentions were for our country. I naïvely believed his coup against the Juan Moreno administration was meant to rescue us from an inept and unpopular government, the actions of which was causing unnecessary economic disruption. I believed what Figueroa proclaimed when he took power—that the country was in danger and that a change was necessary to save it. Well, I was wrong…very wrong, and I now admit it to you and to the world.

"The man that knew Figueroa…The man who sounded the alarm…The man who warned us, was Pancho Portero." More applause.

"I first met him at a press conference he held at Valle Escondido. I attended that conference expecting to confirm my suspicion that he was no more than a military puppet of the HJRAF and, by extension, of the United States. But as I listened to him that day,

I changed my opinion—or I should say he changed my opinion. He clearly was no puppet. I saw an intelligent, educated, and very articulate man, and I discovered in him a passionate Naranjero. While I still believed he was somehow an instrument of the U.S. in Latin America, I also recognized he was a man worthy of my attention, and that of my employer, *Vida Nacional.*

"Well, what happened after that day is now history. Tensions grew between the ALIB and the regime. The people began to take sides, and the situation finally erupted into war. In the end, Figueroa was defeated and Naranjeras escaped, having a statist system of government imposed upon it. And it was Pancho Portero and his great Autonomous Light Infantry Brigade which saved us from that."

The crowd exploded with cheers and the waving of hundreds of flags, hats, scarves, and babies. The old reporter waited patiently, and as the demonstration subsided, he continued, "But, my friends, it was not only Pancho and the ALIB we have to thank for our liberation! I confess to you now that it could not have happened without the Hemispheric Defense Organization, or the HJRAF, or the United States of America. I was once wary of US hegemony, but I tell you now, I would rather live free in Naranjeras under the protective eye of the United States than under the sort of oppression our brothers in Cuba suffer still today. So I say to you now…Viva los Estados Unidos! Viva the ALIB! Viva Pancho Portero! And viva Naranjeras libre!"

Again the assembled mass of people erupted with *vivas* and shouts of joy in another demonstration, which continued for a number of minutes. Finally the band played a few bars of "Patria Nuestra" and ended it with a fanfare which returned the crowd's attention to the podium.

There stood General Portero. The crowd saw him, and after a number of shouts for quiet, it stood silent, waiting for him to speak. He paused, looking over the crowd. He was impressed and thought that he had never seen such a great assembly of people in his lifetime. He felt an overwhelming sense of gratitude. Finally he spoke.

"My beloved countrymen, on behalf of your own Naranjeras First Autonomous Light Infantry Brigade, I thank you. I thank you for being here today. I thank you for the support you gave us in the fight against the dictator. You have given us credit for the victory, but I tell you it could not have been achieved without the faithful support of a vast majority of Naranjeros. God has blessed our nation with strong, capable, and dedicated people. I thank God for you—and I thank Him for the opportunity He has given us to together build our future as free men and women in a free country.

"It is that future I came to speak to you about here today. I know you are waiting to learn what is to happen next, and since there is no government yet in place, I know you expect to hear it from me, as interim governor.

"The first thing I want to say to you is I am not the Acting President, as I have been labeled by some. Nor am I the Interim President. I am not any sort of president.

"I am no more than what I am—a Naranjero military officer trying to do his duty in holding our government together until our new president can be elected by the people."

An aide approached Portero and handed him a bundle which he took, and raised for all to see. "I hold in my hand the Naranjeras presidential sash, the symbol of that high office. I will not wear it. It is to be worn only be the individual elected by you, the people. To wear it would violate and dishonor our Constitution, I will not dishonor it as did Figueroa."

The crowd was silent for a moment, and then a few shouts grew into a chorus. "Ponga la! Put it on! Wear it! Take it, it's yours! You've earned it! We elect you!"

Portero held up his hands, demanding quiet. "Thank you for your kindness to me, but...no! I will not wear it! As I have said, that honor and privilege is reserved only for the person we elect to the office of president. Only he can wear it. I have not been elected, so I cannot wear it—but I will keep it in trust for our next president, who I hope will be elected in six months! I have directed the proper authorities to prepare for and schedule a national election six months from today. That is what I came here to say to you and to the world."

New applause swelled into an enthusiastic demonstration. Again Portero signaled for quiet. After several minutes he could continue. "Six months is a short time and presidential campaigns take time to organize, so I am urging all who would be candidates to start tomorrow! Prepare your campaigns. Take your message to the people. Build your constituencies. Because it is my aim to return constitutional civil government to Naranjeras six months from today."

There was more applause. "The second thing I have to tell you is I have given orders to disband the National Marketing Board, which was created by Figueroa against the will of the people. The government is now out of the export business. You bankers out there can relax. There will be no more pressure from the government to force our banks to work for the state rather than for their clients."

Here the applause was spotty. Many present were not aware of the National Marketing Board; however, the dignitaries from La Mesona seated on the dais leaped to their feet and cheered. They were joined by happy vaquero yells from the ranchers and cattlemen in the crowd. Portero smiled and waved in acknowledgement.

"Now…as to the disposition of Figueroa and his co-conspirators who tried to steal our country, many have asked about them…where they are and what will be their fate. Rumors are flying about them, as you know.

"I am pleased to announce that they are in custody. They are being held in undisclosed locations. Investigations of their activities are being conducted with the purpose of determining what crimes they may have committed during their illegal seizure of our government. These investigations are expected to produce indictments for a number of crimes, ranging from malfeasance to even possibly murder.

"If indicted, Figueroa, Davidson, and others, who are still members of the military, are subject to trial by courts-martial. The Cuban mercenaries involved with Figueroa will have to be tried in the civil courts because they are foreign nationals. Former ministers, Menendez, Ortega, and other civilians will also be tried in civil court if indicted. There may be indictments of some who are no longer in the country. If that is the case, the government will seek their extradition to Naranjeras. If we are not successful in that, they will be tried in absentia.

"The world must understand that Naranjeras will not allow crimes committed on its soil to go unpunished—that our laws are to be respected."

More applause and a few shouts of "Viva Naranjeras" and "Viva la patria." "I also want you and the all the world, for that matter, to know what the Naranjeras foreign policy is to be during the interim period until the government has been restored. It is not something that can languish for six or eight months awaiting the new president and national assembly. We cannot allow uncertainty to grow about how we see our place on the hemisphere and the world. This applies particularly in those foreign markets for Naranjeras export products which are important to our domestic economy. We must declare our course immediately, lest we lose the confidence of our trading partners.

"Accordingly, I now declare the following. First, Naranjeras will withdraw from the Hemispheric Defense Organization. That means we will no longer be an active participant in the Hemispheric Joint Rapid Action Force. We will accept no further subsidies for support of the ALIB. In other words, Naranjeras will be independent of any military commitment to any organization outside its borders.

"Second, we will make it clear that Naranjeras will continue to avoid isolationism. What does that mean? For one thing, it means we will continue to honor all existing treaty obligations, excepting any promulgated during the Figueroa regime—those will be evaluated to determine whether or not they are in our national interest. It also means our markets will remain open to foreign products with origins in countries whose markets are open to Naranjeras products.

"Third, we stand prepared to enter into free-trade common-market negotiations with any democratic country in the western hemisphere.

"And finally, we also commit ourselves to the common defense of the hemisphere, should the necessity ever arise. We recognize the concept of Pan Americanism as a brotherhood of nations with shared history and common interests.

"It is important that these positions be made absolutely clear anew, because they may have become somewhat clouded during our recent internal conflict. So let them be known. You who are engaged in foreign trade, you bankers and others who have maintained foreign contacts, please carry that message to your contacts."

There was polite applause from the great assembly but another standing ovation from the people on the dais. Portero paused to take a sip of water. He continued in a less serious tone. "And now, my friends, it is with great pride in our nation and its reunited people that I make the following announcement.

"A trust fund has been established to be known as 'N.S.F.E.F.,' which stands for Naranjeras Soldiers Family Education Foundation. Its purpose is to provide scholarship assistance to Naranjeras families who have lost someone, or who have a loved one who has received a disabling injury in the war. These scholarships will support a family member who seeks a secondary education in professional or technical institutions in Naranjeras... or abroad.

"I emphasize it does not matter on which side the soldier served, ALB or PNN. These scholarships will be available to any qualifying family—the one requirement being Naranjeras citizenship, and of course, that they served during the war.

"The war is over. We no longer have enemies among us. We are all Naranjeros together, and for the good of our country, we must reunite. These scholarships will help in that process."

New applause and cheering erupted. As it faded, a smiling Portero re-approached the microphone. "And now, my dear friends...It has been a long day, and you have been very patient. It is time we called an end to this celebration. I understand there will be continuing festivities tonight around the capital and elsewhere in the country. I would like to attend them all, but that will not be possible. I will try to attend some and hope to see you there.

"Again, I thank you for making our victory possible, and for being here today. I now ask the archbishop to send us home with his benediction."

• • •

The happy crowd began to depart the square. The ALIB Band struck up favorite Naranjeras tunes while the still celebrating people dispersed. Conversations were about the day, about the information they had received, but they focused mostly on Pancho Portero. The General had clearly added luster to his status as national hero. He had become the idol of his people—the man who would lead them back to national recovery. More than a few were already declaring him their candidate for President, and discussing how to draft him for the job.

While most in the crowd were happy and content, there was one individual, a swarthy, bearded, man who was not smiling. Portero to him was an object of hate, a danger to the great cause, a man to be dealt with, a man who would not live to become president if he could prevent it

• • •

Portero entered the Casa Mayor to the cheers of invited guests, dignitaries from all areas of the country. He made his way smiling through the well-wishers, pausing only to exchange short pleasantries with people he knew, and with some he did not who pushed up to shake his hand.

He was tired. The tensions of the day had sapped his strength, and it took extra effort to play the part expected of him. Ordinarily he was not a drinking man, but he had accepted several drinks to exchanged toasts with friends and began to feel the liquor. After an hour or so, he went to a podium and picked up a microphone and asked for attention.

"My dear friends. This has been a great day, the day we have long dreamed about. There were times when I thought it might never happen. But here it is. I thank God for all of you who did so much to bring it about. I thank God, as we all should, for the wonderful people of our country, and for those abroad who helped us in our hour of need. Most of all, I thank the Lord for His support in this war. I have no doubt His hand was with us all the way. There is no other way to explain the mistakes made by our opposition, Figueroa and Davidson, and for that matter, Molina. They are not stupid men, nor are they without experience, but they made some very stupid, amateurish decisions. If they had not, we would still be at war, and by now our supplies would have been all but exhausted, and the tide would be turning against us. They could not beat us on the battlefield, but we could well have lost the war as a result of our limited reserves. It can have only been the Lord's intervention which brought us victory.

"I believe that sincerely, and I am humbled by that knowledge. Now a new chapter is opening for Naranjeras, and let us all pray that what we do from this point on is also with God's supporting hand.

"That is what I wanted to say to you—other than good night. Get some rest because starting tomorrow, we have work to do.

I would like to stay and enjoy your company, but a hot shower and a good bed beckons…So I now bid you good night with my heartfelt thanks. Viva Naranjeras libre!"

• • •

Portero welcomed the quiet of his quarters on the third floor of the Casa Mayor building, an unpretentious, carpeted two-room suite with bath, closets, and a kitchenette. He had replaced the cot in the bedroom with a more comfortable bed, and his staff had insisted on replacing the card table in the office/living room with a solid, wooden antique table and a comfortable set of matching chairs. He used the room as his private office and for private conferences. He also took some of his meals there when not in the field. After several weeks his suite felt like home, and he was happy to be home after the high pressure day. He felt secure there as two ALIB soldiers stood twenty-four hour security duty on each end of the hall outside his suite.

Photographs of Betsy Portero and some of her paintings decorated his rooms, reminding him he had had another life outside the military. He silently greeted her and wanted to feel close to her. He put some of her favorite music on the CD player. After a shower he dressed for bed, poured himself a glass of port, and relaxed in his one armchair, listening to her music and remembering her.

He had a renewed feeling of guilt at not having kept her in his mind during the last hectic month, so he focused on her and talked to her in his mind. "Well, Betsy, here I am again, needing you. We won the damned war, and now I am facing a new, major challenge. I find it scarier than the war. I need you now more than ever. I remember you told me back in Valle Escondido, the night after you…left. You said you would always be with me. Was it in a dream? But I keep remembering that…and I try to believe it is true. Sometimes that is easy to believe, sometimes not so easy. But I sure wish you were here.

"Dammit, Betsy, now I've got another job I don't know how to do…and I know damn well what you would tell me to do if you were here. So maybe you are here. As always, I will follow your advice." He finished his wine and went to bed and fell asleep, listening to the sweet sound of an *arpa* playing one of her favorite *Recuerdos de Ipacaraiyi.*

• • •

The next morning he informed his staff he had decided to take some time off in Valle Escondido—that he needed time to finish his After Action Report and to plan for the future. In reality he felt a great need to complete mourning the loss of Betsy—a process which had been interrupted by the demands of the war.

The staff understood his need but insisted he not drive himself to Valle Escondido without a security detail, which would remain with him there. After all, he was now the national leader and as such had become a target for whatever crazies might be hidden in Naranjeras society. When he expressed surprise at the thought that he might have become a target, Banning agreed it was unlikely, but why take the chance? Who knows who may be out there? For example, one of the Lybians who came with the Cascavels had informed PNN authorities that five of the twenty-six technicians had secretly remained in the country with false identity papers.

The informant himself was not one of them. He insisted he had stayed because of a girlfriend, and besides, he liked Naranjeras better than Lybia and now felt some loyalty to it. However, he believed the others who remained in the country were militant Muslims who stayed deliberately for the purpose of carrying out some sort of undercover mission. Banning had the PNN searching for the others with the informant's help.

Portero agreed to the armed escort, and Captain Rueda's Reconnaissance Platoon was assigned the duty. He departed the next morning for Valle Escondido, looking forward to his first vacation in two years—a time to be alone and to rejuvenate.

Epilogue

One week after his return from Valle Escondido, General Portero, Military Governor of the Republic of Naranjeras, met with his friend and supporter, Ramon Sanchez Avila, the popular dean of Naranjeras journalists. The men relaxed in the presidential office, enjoying fresh brewed coffee and each other's company.

Sanchez Avila armed with a large notebook and several sharpened pencils had come to interview the country's acting chief executive for a series of feature articles to be published by his newspaper, *Vida Nacional*. The old reporter initiated the conversation with a smile.

"Well, Pancho, a new chapter has begun for you and for all of us. How do you feel?"

"How do you think I feel? I feel like a fish out of water. Better yet, like I am holding a jaguar by the tail and don't exactly know what to do with it. In short, I am not sure of what I am doing. I am a soldier trying to become a politician and haven't figured out how to do it yet. It is a different world for me, and I am trying to learn how it is all supposed to work."

The older man chuckled. "You know, my friend, I don't see much difference between the military and politics. In both one has to determine what his objective is to be. Then he has to plan how to get there. And then he has to conduct a campaign which achieves it. You have been doing that all your life. Just do what comes naturally. Or is it that you haven't identified the objectives yet?"

"That may be part of it. I do have ideas as to where I'd like to see our country go. My problem is where to start. I have done a lot of thinking about some general objectives, though."

"Good, Can we begin?" Sanchez Avila turned on his recorder to begin the interview.

"Thank you, General, for granting this interview. I understand you have recently returned from two weeks in Valle Escondido. What was the purpose of your visit there?"

"Primarily to rest and relax, I suppose. I have been working pretty hard during the last few months, and I wanted time to myself. I also needed time to finish my After Action Report on the war, and to think more about the needs of our country."

"Okay, let's talk about the war first. In your comments made at the Estado Mayor reception following the Restoration Day speech, you indicated the Figueroa leadership had made some mistakes which helped account for your victory. What were those mistakes?"

"For one thing, they were too much in a hurry to take us on. We were in no position to start the hostilities because world opinion would have condemned us. Figueroa's bunch could have waited several months before they acted, but they didn't. By being in a hurry, they surrendered the great advantage they held, namely the balance of power advantage. On paper they out-manned us and out-gunned us. They had that brigade training on Isla Grande, which in itself equaled our ALIB strength. In addition they had formed and trained that armored battalion built around a company of fifteen Brazilian armored cars, mounting ninety-millimeter guns—that's serious firepower. And then they had organized a light infantry *Casador* Battalion, mostly manned by foreigners with combat experience in places like Nicaragua and El Salvador. Had they waited until they had consolidated those forces on the mainland, they might well have won the war. We had limited resources. Especially ammunition. And they could have outlasted us logistically."

"Why do you think they were in such a hurry?"

"I have no idea. Perhaps it was Figueroa's ego which made him overconfident. He seems to have believed that being president brought power – and maybe invincibility. He always has had a big ego. The type who believes he can achieve what he can conceive, and doesn't accept contrary advice well. Also he is a bit of a bully, and Davidson is not the kind of man who will stand up to men like Figueroa. He should have known better than to allow the piecemeal commitment of his forces

"But perhaps Figueroa was being pressured by his financial backers from outside the country. And perhaps he was frustrated by the fact that the public had begun to side with us. Clearly he wanted to end it while he still had some support. But I really don't know why they were in such a hurry. Perhaps it was because the Lord was on our side. "

"What do you mean by 'outside financial backers'?"

"The Lybians...and obviously the Cubans were involved. Maybe even some F.A.R.C. money was there. You know, the anti-US crowd who are always ready to support leftist movements in Latin America."

"Do you know for sure the Lybians were involved as financial backers?"

"I do. Yes. But I am not at liberty to say how I know...so please do not quote me on that. But it is no secret that the Cascavels came from Libya, so you can use that."

"Okay, that is enough. You have told me about the mistakes made by the Figueroa people. But you didn't win only because of their mistakes. Their mistakes aside, you conducted a very efficient operation which clearly truncated the fighting. Do you care to discuss how you managed to achieve the victory so quickly?"

"When it became apparent that that Figueroa was willing to commit his forces piecemeal, it became easy for us. The fact is that we never engaged them in any action without having the ratio of forces in our favor. Not once—from the liberation of the *La Prensa* people in La Colina, or our capture of the PNN Post in La Mesona, or the battles of La Campana and La Boca, or the bloodless occupations of the International Airport, Puerto Hondo, and La Capital. In all those actions, we had the force advantage. At La Campana, we were close to parity, but there we had the advantage of a strong defensive position—a commander's dream."

"Had you anticipated the way it worked out?"

"Are you referring to La Campana or the war in general?"

"The war in general."

"No. Not at all. We had planned for a longer war, which we were prepared to fight from bases in the La Mesona area. We called it our Northern Strategy. But the decisive victory at La Campana, in which we were able to destroy or capture Figueroa's entire force including five *Cascavels* changed all that. That was his entire armored battalion except for ten Cascavels, which were not committed. That engagement changed everything, because defeating them there swung the balance of power to us which made a major change in our plans feasible. We abandoned the Northern Strategy and directed all our resources to blocking their bringing their Isla Grande brigade back to the mainland and to, cutting off their access to re-supply.

"The decisive event was preventing Davidson from bringing the Isla Grande Brigade across. That was a close thing, timing-wise. We got our forces into La Boca just in time. A day or two later would have resulted in a very different outcome. The Lord certainly helped there too."

"I agree, the Lord was with you. But so were our people."

"Yes. That was important. The way it all worked out saved hundreds of lives on both sides and many months of fighting which would have cost our country dearly.

"Speaking of cost—the big question mark we had about the Northern Strategy was cost. The ALIB would have run out of money within a few months of the kick-off of hostilities. We would have been financially broke before we ran out of supplies. Payroll being the biggest cost. As a matter of fact, we are facing a payroll crunch now, even with the shortened war. We will no longer have the equalizing supplement aid we used to receive from the HDO."

"What will you do about that?"

"We will have to reduce our forces. We will not need to maintain our current strength because we no longer have a commitment to hemispheric defense. But we have to phase down slowly, if for no other reason, we don't want to shock the economy by turning hundreds of people without jobs loose in a short period of time. That means for the near future, the government will have to pick up the tab.

"Now, Don Ramon, how about some lunch? Turn off your machine for a while."

The friends sat together and enjoyed a Portero favorite, a generous serving of *Ceviche Naranjero* over freshly baked *bolillos*, and more coffee. When they had finished and the dishes had been removed, Sanchez Avila resumed recording.

"Now, General, can we talk about the needs of our country? What did you think about while in Valle Escondido?"

"I thought about changes I would like to see happen to improve our economy and the lives of our people. And I thought about our foreign policy and how it might help affect the changes we need."

"I can see that foreign policy can affect economic policy, but can you be more explicit?"

"I cannot, other than to say that what I want for Naranjeras cannot be achieved unless our markets are open to those democratic countries whose markets are open to us. Common interests open doors to cooperation and to mutual benefit. One does not have to be a genius to understand that opening those doors does not happen through goodwill alone. It has to be the result of building understanding, two-way understanding, I hasten to add—and trust, which in the end becomes allegiances. It seems to me building that kind of relationship can only result from an effective foreign policy, which I see as a high priority for us."

"Makes sense, and it sounds like you have been doing a great deal of thinking. But aside from an effective foreign policy, what exactly is it you want for Naranjeras?"

"I would like to see a major change in our social and economic culture, which I believe will bring a new...ah...a new, never before dreamed of prosperity to our people. I am not sure you will approve. You once questioned my credentials as a Naranjero. You suggested I had been overly influenced by my experiences living in the United States. Remember?"

"Yes, when we first met...at your press conference in Valle Escondido over the *transito* flap. Incidentally, you did a good job that day."

"Thanks. I had to make a point."

"You did...And very well, too. And I have apologized for doubting your motives then, and I want to say for the record that I have no doubt about your motives now. You are an honorable man, and I know you only want what is best for our country. Now tell me what it is you want for us."

Portero thought about the many conversations he had had with Betsy over their years together, about his country and how they had tried to identify its strengths and weaknesses in relation to what they knew about her country, the United States. He carefully chose the words of his response to his friend, knowing him to be a heart and soul Naranjero nationalist. He spoke slowly.

"I want to see Naranjeras emulate the United States in one single respect. I want us to empower all our people, economically, as it has been done up there."

"Please explain."

"I mean, we are too much like most Latin American countries…particularly Central American countries. Our societies are by and large structured into two classes of people. There is the minority, consisting of relatively well-educated and consequently relatively wealthy people. They own our ranches and our established businesses, and they operate the few industries we have. Then there is the majority—the rest of our population, which is employed for the most part by the minority.

"In our country, the minority is the major job creator, and the jobs they create are predominately labor jobs which offer limited opportunity for advancement and only very rare opportunities for the individual to escape from the majority into the minority.

"How many people, Don Ramon, can you name who have moved up in class? Moved from the majority into the minority? Very few, if any. The fact is we have created a permanent majority, which is trapped in the underclass with little chance to escape. It is a fact of life and a system we all, people of both classes, have come to accept. We take it for granted. People think, 'That's just the way it is, so what else can we do?' We are locked into a tradition, a social structure, which we have lived with so long that we are inured to it. We can't think outside of that box. What is worse, we feel comfortable in that tradition. It is a sort of stagnation. I believe we must change that if the country is to compete in the world."

"Okay, General, I might argue that our system is not so bad the way it is—that our people are reasonably healthy and happy—that we have been reasonably successful for a small country. Some people might construe your idea as dangerously revolutionary. I would not agree with them, because I know you. But I might argue that with all the problems we are facing today, why should we set about fixing something that seems not to be broken?"

"But our system is broken. We just don't recognized the fact. Our economy is okay, but it is far from vibrant. It is not growing apace with the U.S. or Canada, or Chile, or Panama for that matter, insofar as job creation is concerned.

"Do you realize, Don Ramon, that in the Unites States, there are hundreds of thousands, maybe millions, of small businesses which employ from one or two to hundreds of people? Do you realize those small businesses provide far more jobs than do all their great industries combined? Those small employers are the engines that power their great economy...and those small businessmen are the majority there. Think of it. Up there the employers are a part of the majority...not of the minority, as they are here.

"You will say the U.S. is a large country with a population of hundreds of millions, while by comparison, Naranjeras is small with a relatively tiny population of only several millions—that what works for them cannot work for us. I will answer that is not a valid argument. Population is not the difference. Attitude, perspective, the way we think, is.

"And I would add parenthetically that it should be easier to change the way we think in our country precisely because it has a smaller population. Here we have fewer minds to change... fewer people to convince. We are fortunate to be blessed with an intelligent and hardworking population. As people hear how a change can benefit them, they will listen. I believe with time we can change the paradigm of thinking which has made us perpetual captives of our system.

"Look how Naranjeros took to democracy. If they could make that change in a few short years, why can't they make the change I propose?"

Sanchez Avila chuckled. "You are very persuasive, General. You have me almost believing it can be done. But what you are proposing it is a huge undertaking. My next question is how do you do it? Where do you start?"

"I am not exactly sure, but I know we must start with the way we educate our children. We must find a way to plant an entrepreneurial spirit in our working class people, our majority. We must make them believe they can change their lives—that they need not be forever dependent on low wage jobs to live. That change in thinking can best be generated in our schools. It is a major change which I see as a first step in changing our national economy. If we can make it a mission of our schools, we will transform Naranjeras—make our country a player in the modern world.

"The second thing is, we must seek ways of making capital available to the entrepreneurs that are discovered—uncovered—as a result of the new school effort. I am speaking of people who have been stimulated to dream and come forth with ideas and have the ambition, the courage, the energy, to test their ideas by putting them to work. If we can achieve that, we have job creation at the grass roots.

"Making capital available to those people must become a mission for our banks. It will require a big change in the way bankers think about their business. We think of ourselves as being a capitalist society, but we do not have 'democratic capitalism,' as Michael Novak defines it in his book of that name, because capital is not available to all. Our bankers must be brought to an understanding of the difference and the importance of the change to our nation's future—and incidentally to their own success."

Sanchez Avila sat silent for a long moment. He was pondering what he had just heard from his friend, wondering and admiring the thought process which he found so creative, so unusual among even his most intellectual colleagues. He thought they were brilliant ideas but wondered if they were achievable. He finally spoke.

"I am impressed with your objectives, Pancho. They are certainly different, and I can see that they would change the way our society works—improve it—if, and there is a very big if here, if they could be made a reality. That brings me to a question.

Where do you start? How do you start with education, for example? Our schools are and always have been the responsibility of the local community. Are you proposing the government take control of education?"

"No, I am not. I don't believe any government can manage any enterprise as well as people who are personally dedicated to it and depend upon its success. Naranjeras has a few excellent schools, some good schools, and probably more than a few marginal to poor schools. If we tried to centralize their management, we would have to create standards for them to meet. That would probably result in some uniformity, but it would most likely reduce the effectiveness of our best schools while only slightly improving the marginal ones.

"The correct approach, in my judgment, would be to study our best schools to determine why they are successful and then translate their practices to the marginal operations. Some agency has to coordinate that effort. It could be a government operation, but it could also be some sort of non-government entity headed by the best educators we can identify. Obviously such an organization would have to operate with some government oversight and financial support. I think I would lean toward the non-government option. We already have too many overpaid, marginally effective career bureaucrats without adding a new layer."

"Okay, Pancho, I am turning off my recorder. We are about to discuss matters which should not appear in the news. I am now talking to you as a friend. Do you realize how sophisticated your education and your banking reform ideas are? They are going to cause controversy, and it is not going to be easy to make them happen. To succeed in that will require time and strong and persistent leadership. It will not happen unless you find the people who understand what you want to do and buy into the reasons you want to do it. They have to become true believers, absolutely dedicated to the project. Getting them to that point alone is going to take time and salesmanship. How will you do that in the five-plus months you have before the election?"

"I know it will take years to finally get it done, but I can get it started. Then I can work on it as a citizen volunteer with the new administration."

"What if the new president has other priorities or if he thinks it is a bad idea? What if the assembly doesn't support the project?"

"In that case, I'll have to use my powers of persuasion. I expect there will still be some residual goodwill remaining."

"There will always be that for you, my friend. You will continue to be a national hero and honored for what you have done for the country. You will always be an important historical figure. For a time, you will continue to be an important political figure. But that will last only as long as you dominate the scene as you do now as military governor. But please understand your influence will fade as the new administration takes office. Because people then will remember you as a great general and the savior of the country does not mean they will also continue to see you as a statesman or national leader, especially if you are without some kind of government portfolio which keeps you in their focus."

"What the hell are you saying?"

"I am saying that your objectives for changing our economy, as noble as they are, will be no more than dreams unless you lead the country into accepting them."

"I thought that is what I would do before the goodwill fades... Do you think I am loco? You evidently have some doubts."

"I don't think you're loco. But I think you are a little naïve about politics."

"How so?"

The old reporter took a moment to frame his answer. "First, let me say that you have identified some clear, and I believe, worthy objectives for changing Naranjeras. You are a visionary of the kind our country badly needs. I believe the objectives you have outlined, if achieved, would be very good for us. However, they represent a radical departure from what we are accustomed to. Making them a reality will be much more difficult than you seem to believe.

"You are not facing a military campaign. You are diving into a political campaign. Because the changes you are seeking are so foreign to the way we think, they will certainly be resisted, and I expect the resistance will come immediately, even before you have a chance to make your case. Because you are in a hurry, you will be pushing hard for them, and because they represent a major change in the way things have been done, they will scare people. It is human nature to resist change.

"Your proposal it is likely to create a new set of enemies— even among men and women who are among your supporters today. Why? Because, some will see the changes as inimical to their personal interests. Some will see them as good ideas but something for the future, and of a low priority. Some will think you have lost your mind.

"To be sure, some will understand and want to help you implement your dream, but experience tells me that they will be outnumbered by those who will give the projects lip service, because they respect you, but will work against them behind the scene. I believe in the end more people will be in opposition than in support. The bottom line being people are more comfortable with the status quo—they stick with what they know in preference to gambling on the unknown."

"You sound like you don't think these goals are achievable."

"On the contrary. I think they are achievable but only with time and great leadership. You don't want to hear this, but I firmly believe you are the one man who can make it all happen. But you can't do it in six months or maybe even in six years. To get it done, there must be a comprehensive, long-term, and gentle education campaign to plant your vision in the minds of the people. And you are the only one who has the stature to lead it. And you can't lead as an honored national hero or elder statesman. To do it, you must have real political clout. You must be down in the trenches. You can only do it as President."

"My God!"